C000157505

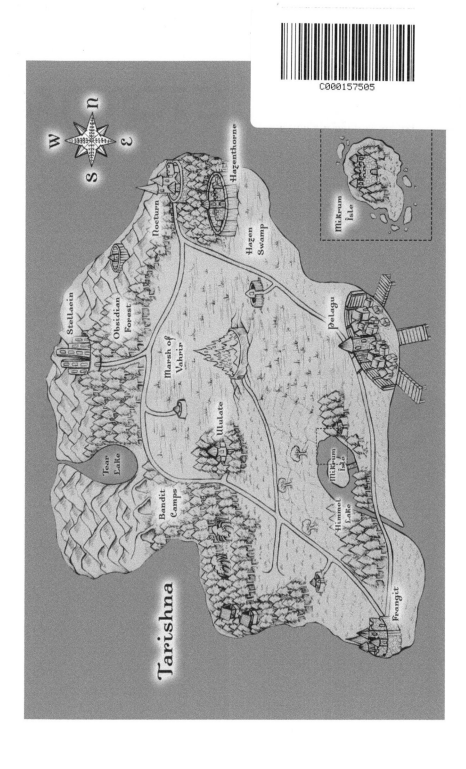

Storm ⚡ Entertainment Presents

O N L I N E

Experience the class you were born to play!

SOMNIA ONLINE
INITIALIZING

BOOK I

K.T. HANNA

Author: K.T. Hanna
Cover Artist: Marko Horvatin
Typography: Bonnie Price
Formatting & Interior Design: Caitlin Greer

Disclaimer: This is a work of fiction.
Names, characters, businesses, places, events, and incidents are either the products of
the author's imagination or used in a fictitious manner. Any resemblance to actual
people, living or dead, or actual events is purely coincidental.

Copyright © 2018 Katie Hanna
All rights reserved.
ISBN-13: 978-1-948983-01-3 (Paperback Edition)
ISBN-13: 978-1-948983-00-6 (Hardback Edition)
ISBN-13: 978-1-948983-02-0 (E-Book Edition)

For Jami
For believing when I couldn't
For knowing my strengths before I did
For being there
Thank you

CHAPTER ONE

The Gift

Storm Corp
Storm Technologies Division Experimental Neuroscience Division
Countdown: Five years before Somnia Online implementation

Doctor Michael Jeffries was, again, impressed with his own genius. He ran his hands over his precious prototype. The headset wasn't as streamlined as he wanted of course, with its sharp edges and slipshod adjustments, but these were only the early stages. A thin graphite band held its arms in place, which reached out to tangle fingers into the hair of the wearer, digging down to secure themselves to the scalp and allow for deeper immersion than ever before. While it dug a little more than he liked at the moment, he'd been focused on what it could do rather than how it looked.

If everything went right, he knew Storm Corp would lavish rewards on him. After all, obtaining military research grants and the benefits that came with them were the epitome of success.

He leaned back and looked out of his window, still cradling his prototype like it might shatter at any moment. It was the key to everything he'd been working toward his whole life. Knowing a person, not only as a person, but as an infinitely complex set of neurons and synapses firing back and forth and creating the individual.

To know a person better than they knew themselves? It was the culmination of decades of devotion. Dr. Jeffries smiled and stood up, resting the headset on its podium with a reverence reserved only for it.

All they had to do was get the grant, and then begin the testing phase. The AIs he'd been using would be perfect for implementing the first stages, but then they'd have to widen the test.

They'd need more power, but that could wait until later.

There was still so much to do. He turned toward his office door, anxiousness simmering at the edge of his frayed nerves.

"Still no word..." he muttered. "How can that be?"

Jeffries walked to the window and looked out over the view of the parking lot. No view in sight, just a small office in the back of the building, but at least he did have a window, facing more buildings which showed the wear of time.

The knock on his door barely reached his ears before the door flew open with a bang.

"Michael!" His assistant, Jessa, yelled his name, waving a piece of paper in the air. "We got the grant! You did it!"

Michael stepped forward slowly, and then faster, and grabbed her hands, whirling her around before letting go and dancing a little jig himself.

"Thank you, Jessa. Let's get this started!"

"You've got it!" She closed the door in a whirlwind, and Michael watched her go, wondering just how his headset would read Jessa. She wasn't really the assistant type...

Walking over to where his prototype rested on its perch he stroked the rough carbon fiber surface and stared out of his window again. It was time to move on up in the world.

Time to know everyone better than they knew themselves.

Summer Residence
Home of Laria, David, and Wren
Two Months Prior to Somnia Online Launch

Running over the percentages in her head, Wren frowned as she navigated the staircase to the lower level. If she'd done her calculations right, she'd taken all the pre-requisites she needed to tackle her neuro-engineering degree in the fall. Even though sonogenetics was still tickling at the back of her mind, neuro-engineering was where the future lay. Biting back a disgruntled sigh, she made her way into the kitchen. After exams she could dive back into her virtual worlds with Harlow and execute a bit of therapeutic violence.

Her parents stood behind the kitchen table, ridiculously excited grins on their faces, and she blinked her notes away, disabling her augmented vision with a thought. It made multitasking in life so much easier to just have the internet right there in your eyes all the time.

"Mom, Dad... you're not at work?" Seriously, if they'd gotten themselves fired, there was no way she could afford to go to college regardless of how many scholarships she managed to Tetris together. They never covered full tuition these days, so amassing a few scholarships would still only work if her parents helped.

Her mother laughed. Laria Sommers never failed to be bright and cheerful, something Wren had not inherited from her.

"Sweetheart! We have a present for you." Her mother's grin was so wide she could rival a Cheshire Cat for the part. "Open it, open it!"

Only then did Wren's eyes fall on the box sitting neatly wrapped on top of the table. It was quite large, a nice silver wrapped cube a little over a foot high. The thing was, her parents weren't the most observant of people. They were sweet, worked long hours, and even though they made it a rule to eat dinner together five nights a week, they were often vague. Since they were MMORPG sweethearts though, they'd encouraged her love of virtual worlds. Not to mention they both worked in the industry. It was the one escape she had from an otherwise dull existence.

Approaching the package cautiously, Wren raised an eyebrow at her parents. "What's the occasion?"

"You!" Even her father seemed excited. His stoic IT professor personality was obviously on vacation. Or else they'd been drinking. Maybe they'd pulled an all-nighter. It wouldn't be the first time.

"Stop looking at us like that." He chided her, his brown eyes filled with a warmth only he ever exuded. It calmed Wren, making her smile despite her best efforts. "You've been working so hard, you've got acceptances from five colleges with as close to a full scholarship as possible, and you've refused to take part in the after graduation trip. You deserve this."

Wren didn't have the heart to mention that her invite to the graduation trip hadn't been entirely on the up and up—she didn't have much, if anything, in common with her classmates—still, why spoil things for him? He was obviously trying hard, and considering they both seemed to think she'd love it, curiosity got the better of her.

With a hint of childish abandon, she ripped the paper off the box and turned it over in her hands, barely daring to blink, just in case it disappeared.

Storm Entertainment Presents

SOMNIA

O N L I N E

Experience the class you were born to play!

Recommended headgear for best virtual immersion.

"Seriously?" She blinked up at them, and could feel her face cracking into a grin even wider than her mother's. "Are you fucking serious?"

"Yes! I finally got my hands on it. You've got it earlier than most. It's not exactly the one people will get from the stores." Her mother practically shone with excitement. She'd been working on the development of Somnia Online for years. It was the biggest title she'd ever been in charge of, but it was so hush-hush, even Wren knew little about it. This headset cost a pretty penny. For her mom to have gotten her hands on one two months before release, even though she was lead designer on the game—it was probably courtesy of the design team.

"Can I..." She hesitated, unsure of herself. It was one thing to constantly pretend she knew exactly what she was doing, and it was another entirely to actually be confident. "Can I take it out of the box?"

"Of course." Her mother sidled over, and stood shoulder to shoulder with Wren. Their hair was nearly identical, smooth black waves that hung down just past the nape of their necks, often pulled back in a no-nonsense ponytail. Together they opened the box, and Wren reached in with delicate fingers to retrieve the headset. It was glorious.

The arms of the connections gave it a fragile appearance but she knew from the online specifications that it was made of tough carbon fiber. The sleek silver design fit easily over the head, sort of like a headband. Small branches shot off the main piece and settled over her forehead, tracing back through her hair like an intricate headpiece. It was beautiful, if a little delicate.

"But you can't play with it until your finals are done. Your suit won't arrive for another few weeks." Her mother kissed her cheek and dashed over to pick up her purse.

"Wait..." Wren was shell-shocked. "You got me the suit too?"

"Of course! Except that's just standard issue." Her mother beamed another smile. "I have to go, or I'll be late for a meeting. Love you! I know you'll ace those finals."

Wren blinked as the whirlwind that was her mother slammed the door in her wake. It was still early, and the lightweight headset in her hands had a surreal quality to it, so unlike the bulky glasses contraption she had upstairs in her room. "Thanks Dad." She whispered, knowing he'd probably helped pull the strings too.

Nothing was cheap. Even public schooling cost money, and so many kids didn't seem to care. It was the bone of contention that didn't exactly make her popular with her peers. Somehow she'd inherited a sense of responsibility from her parents. Even though the world had largely gone to shit in the last sixty years, her parents were still ridiculously optimistic.

Her father enveloped her in a warm hug, pulling her back to the days before her mother got so busy, when they'd all curl up in the living room together and play stupid games. "Just approach the finals like you always do. Maybe we can let you scan early as added incentive! I'll talk to your mother."

Wren smiled, suddenly a little emotional. Just wait until she told Harlow!

"Kiddo, I've got a class to teach." Her Dad's voice suddenly took on a somber tone. "Just remember, you have to tell me if this game is worth your old Dad trying his hand at it."

His grin disarmed Wren, and she smiled. "Don't worry Dad, I'll be your guinea pig any day."

"No way!"

Harlow's voice echoed so loudly through the earpiece, that Wren had to dial down the volume for a moment.

"Yes way. You've preordered it, what are you so jealous of?" It was difficult to keep the resentment out of her own voice, which wasn't fair since Harlow had paid for most of hers herself. Harlow was what people called a go-getter. She put her mind to something, and fucking did it. Be it school, a part time job with a goal, or playing her ranger or hunter characters in any given massively multiplayer roleplaying game and kicking everyone's ass at it.

"But I don't have mine, yet. I won't get it for ages!"

The whine in her tone made Wren chuckle. It's not like they lived far apart, but hopping into their games was just easy... well, not until finals were over. Good thing they'd already defeated all the content available in their last adventure.

"You'll get yours when I get my suit." Wren paused, preemptively dialing down for the squeal she knew was coming.

"You're getting a freaking suit?"

There it was.

"Yeah. Mom and Dad said it's because I studied my ass off. I guess being the pariah of my grade finally paid off." She couldn't keep the bitterness from her tone. It wasn't like she was bullied as such, just constantly snubbed, and selectively ridiculed. It helped to have online worlds to escape into every night. She continued before Harlow could sympathize. "Still though, two more months and we're done!"

"Forever! Well, until the fall and college anyway. Can you believe we're going to get to play with full immersion gear, Wren? Can you?" Harlow's excitement was contagious, and Wren found herself bouncing on her ball chair as she searched through sites, her contact monitors allowing her to multitask while talking.

"Dad's trying to get mom to let me try the headset out as an incentive, but when I get my suit, want to meet up so we can undergo the full scan?" Wren thought it would be that much more fun if it was both of them. After all, she did have a king-sized bed. She frowned at an article that popped up in relation to the full immersion experience and Somnia Online, and bookmarked it for later reference.

"You bet. It's a date! I've got to go now. My brother's home."

"Ciao." Wren laughed as she disconnected the conversation. She pulled up the articles she'd found and perused them again. Just the same old warnings about how suits and chairs couldn't be guaranteed to keep your body from degradation while spending unhealthy amounts of time in virtual worlds. The headgear was also highlighted for producing irregular neural activity. Groups were up in arms about them... but gaming had always been a pretty convenient target.

Wren smiled. At least, despite the absent mindedness and forgotten occasions, her mom didn't try to stop her from gaming. Wren flipped through several pages, before she came to the promotional footage of Somnia Online.

She activated it and watched the familiar interaction with the Storm Entertainment Logo proudly front and center. The voiceover began.

Imagine a world where you can be everything you've ever wanted to be. Where you can taste the food, smell the air, and feel the pain that keeps us alive!

Befriend or repel a dragon. Build your guild's reputation and establish a base. Wage wars with other guilds, or other species. Find the twelve keys and unlock the secrets they hold.

Every choice you make will shape the world. Give in to your deepest desires.

Rip away your masks, your fears, and everything that's holding you back... Discover the class you were born to play.

Mist swirled around snow-covered mountains, through dark dungeons with savage looking beasts whose eyes held far too much intelligence in their eyes for a game. Bustling cities flashed by, NPCs changed their expression based on directional conversation, rare spawns beat the living shit out of poor newbies.

The music thundered, swords clashed, mages threw fireballs, while rogues assassinated. Lively footage with a raw dose of reality. Ending with the sigil for Somnia Online. *Pre-order now!*

Wren smiled. She couldn't wait to play the game, to be what she was born to be

CHAPTER TWO
Anticipation

Storm Corp
Storm Technologies Division Experimental Neuroscience Division
Countdown: Five years before Somnia Online implementation

Dr Jeffries placed his box on the large mahogany desk in his brand new laboratory. The wall in front of him was sixty percent glass, allowing him an uninterrupted view of the fleet of people who'd be working under him whenever the blinds were open.

Taking the prototype out of its box, he placed it in the center of the desk, stroking the rough metal reverently as he studied the still empty lab. He could see the smaller, metal desk with the large leather swivel chair he'd requested for times he would work out there with his minions.

The thought made him smile. Minions was the wrong word, and yet somehow so suitable. He walked over to the windows, placing a hand on the glass and enjoying the cool sensation that touched his skin. Would the world they created in order to test the headgear feel as real? His headset was definitely capable of producing realistic sensations. Not to mention much, much more.

"Dr. Jeffries?"

He turned to find Jessa at the door, carrying two boxes stacked together. They seemed to be heavy, and he could see her muscles straining to carry them. Perhaps he should have packed lighter. He motioned over to one of the matching mahogany cabinets, and watched as she placed the boxes there, the cardboard bottoms making a louder thud than he found acceptable.

"Be careful, Jessa." His impatience was showing, and he took a breath to curb it.

"Sorry," his assistant said, and he heard the door close behind her.

It was easy to imagine the candidates he'd chosen to fill the lab. So easy to imagine them all out there working at making the headset perfect, at achieving his lifelong goal. In a matter of years they'd have yottabytes of data to pull from, hundreds of thousands of brains feeding into his hardware's further development.

Michael smiled and opened his eyes as the thrill of scientific progress ran through him.

Day Before Release: Somnia Online

Harlow's red hair dangled over Wren's shoulder as she carefully tried to unwrap the suit her mother had just dropped in her lap. Laria's energy was palpable in the way she fidgeted as her daughter tackled the task.

After a month of exams, waiting on final acceptances, all the while desperately eager to play Somnia, Wren was excited, and suddenly feeling very claustrophobic. She might love her best friend and mom, but they were invading her personal space like vultures.

"For crying out loud you two, stop it!" Wren yelled and peddled herself backward. "Give me some space. If I tear this I'll kill you both. In-game. Maybe."

Harlow and Laria laughed as they backed away, standing next to each other and watching her eagerly. For a moment Wren missed her middle school days, before her best friend's parents had moved thirty minutes away.

Next door had been so much easier. But morose feelings weren't suitable for the Day of the Suit. She placed it on her desk, and methodically worked the plastic sleeve away. It was a thick plastic, meant to prevent static from entering the garment bag.

Pulling it out, Wren frowned. "It's sort of... underwhelming."

Her mother smiled.

"It's got sensors in it; they'll activate to make sure your muscles don't atrophy, and allow you to experience the full range of senses. Like touch and pain. Make sure you don't forget the glove attachments. Now..." Laria paused, an odd light in her eyes Wren couldn't remember seeing before. "Look. I know we can be lenient about games. Hell... you wouldn't be here if it wasn't for a game, if you know what I mean." Her mom winked, and Wren tried not to melt from embarrassment. "I don't want you to play this for days on end, but if you do choose to be in-game for more than four hours at a time, then this suit makes me feel better about that."

"Well adulted, Mrs. Sommers." Harlow held out her hand, which Laria promptly took and shook.

"It was rather, wasn't it?"

"Mom. Stop it." But even Wren smiled.

"Are you excited to get started?" Both girls nodded, and Laria bent down to pull something else from her bag, holding it out toward Harlow. "This one's for you. I spoke to your parents. They may have taken a little coaxing, but I prevailed. Happy graduation, Harlow! Thank you for being a part of our lives."

Harlow's large green eyes got even wider, and she blinked, doing a rather good impersonation of a goldfish. "Thank you! Oh wow. Wren!"

Wren choked down her surprise, knowing her mom must have asserted rank to make this happen. She reevaluated her mother. Even as a thank you for Harlow, it seemed a lot, and a thank you for what exactly? Wren stepped forward quickly and gave her mom a huge hug. "Thank *you* for everything."

Her mother looked away, a slight blush tingeing her olive cheeks. "Shush girls. Get dressed and I'll help you set up for the scan."

Wren watched her mother leave the room and frowned. "I wonder what it's like for her—to work on something huge and see people so excited to experience it. Can you imagine?"

Harlow shook her head, bouncing on the balls of her feet. "Glad they waited to let you scan in."

For a moment Wren frowned and blinked at her friend with an odd sense of déjà vu hanging over her head. But it vanished. "Yeah, me too."

"Let's go see what our scan gives us." Harlow's enthusiasm washed through the room like a breath of fresh air.

The suits slipped on easier than Wren anticipated, which was good since she'd had strange thoughts of latex rubber and having to wiggle into it somehow. In fact, it almost felt like she didn't have anything on at all. The material was smooth, and about two millimeters thick with a padded feeling if she squeezed it. Embedded in it were multiple electrical lines that would charge and disperse wirelessly when her headset triggered it, and when sensations in the game prompted impulses. Quite remarkable really. The other option had been a bulky leather chair that performed the same function. They'd been all the rage for a while, but the suits were cheaper and more comfortable.

Her mom walked back in the room just as Harlow exited the bathroom. Her fiery hair stood out against the suit, and she gave a wide grin, accenting it with an impish wink. "Ready for duty, Mrs. S!"

Wren sat on the bed and patted the other side for Harlow, who took a running jump and almost fell off the other side. Rolling her eyes, Wren pushed at her friend's chest, motioning to lie down.

"Okay girls. Before you lie down, you need to put your headsets on. They'll need to conform to the shape of your skull and then calibrate. Let me just enable the anchor." Her mother walked over to the anchor in Wren's room. It was a small black cube about four inches high. They had a few throughout the house. Anchors allowed their augmented reality eyewear to access the internet and store any information they wished to download permanently. Sort of like a hard drive, router, and computer box in a tiny package. The game would anchor using this as a server.

"Once the headset is calibrated and hooked to your accounts, well... it'll prompt you through the scanning process and allocate its findings." She smiled at them as they put their headsets on.

Wren activated hers by pressing a slight indent in the left arm, startled as the headset came alive on her head, like a weird sort of octopus giving her brain a hug. She shuddered at the mental image. But after several seconds, she barely noticed it was there. A light shone on the bottom of her virtual screen, confirming her log in and connection to Somnia Online.

Prompting her to lay down, the device triggered several scrolling coded windows, followed by analytics listed too fast for the eye to see. Then it finally settled on a blank screen with a SOMNIA ONLINE backdrop and an option flashed up in front of her.

Proceed with scan? Yes or No.

"Nothing to lose," she muttered before concentrating briefly on the word yes with her mind and lying back to await her results.

The scan was done in what felt like an instant, and Wren waited for the printout in the kitchen with her mother, while Harlow ran to the bathroom.

Wren sat, staring at the results in front of her eyes when the game sent them to her. She blinked several times, becoming more irritated as she read.

Enchanter Branch of the Psionic Family Ranged Caster Support/Mind Control of self/others

You will play an enchanter. Your wiles and your mental fortitude will make this difficult class a natural fit for you. Considering your penchant for diversions, casting illusions in-game will seem second nature, and using your words to influence those who would otherwise stand in your way will often work in your favor. Monsters will fear you, and yet serve you if you make them. Strong opponents will cower before your ability to daze and confuse.

Each decision you make will affect how your character develops and what hidden paths are revealed to you.

You may choose a hybrid class at level twenty, but remember: the enchanter is who you are.

Wren blinked at her class allocation. What the actual fuck? She'd never been anything but a healer. She was a freaking fantastic healer. Why the hell would she want to play an enchanter? What illusions?

"This is bullshit mom," she said, flat staring at her mother and trying not to get angry. That temper, she definitely got from her mom. It often broke through the usual calm her Dad passed on to her.

"The system sees what it sees, sweetie." Her mother shrugged, still smiling like she knew all the secrets. "This is the class it's found you most in sync with. If the real world were the Somnia Online world, this is what it thinks you would gravitate toward. You know the motto, you thought it was cool the first time you heard it."

"Experience the class you were born to play." Wren murmured and then blinked.

"Well apparently I'm a healer." Harlow sounded equally as irritated as she sat down with a plop next to Wren.

"What the fuck, Mom? It made Harlow a healer, Mom. *Harlow*." She turned to the other girl, a grimace on her face. "No offense."

Harlow chortled, as she grabbed a packet of chips.

Laria chuckled as she rummaged through the cabinets. "Yes, it did, but it also made her a blood mage, and those destroy in order to heal."

Wren scowled, irritated. Her excitement for the game waned, and her will to play drained from her. She'd been the good student for years. No parties, no skipping school, no pranks, nothing. And now a game was telling her what she could be in her free time?

"You don't want to play?"

The concern in her mother's voice made Wren look up, a strange feeling of déjà vu coming over her again, like she'd been right here before. "I...don't like being told what I should be."

"No one does, love." Her mother paused, a distant look entering her eyes. "The system scans your brainwaves, your thought processes. It can potentially even access some of the more vivid memories. It takes your body composition and temperament into mind, and extrapolates the class that would suit you best. It goes past what you think you might be good at, and uses definitive algorithms to determine what you'd actually be more attuned to. For what it's worth, I think you'd be a fantastic enchanter. It's one of the more challenging classes to play and you've always risen to a challenge."

Wren couldn't help but smile. That bit was true. It always had been. "Fine. I'll give it a chance."

"That's my girl." Her mom smiled, more tight-lipped than usual, before concentrating on her tea again.

Wren couldn't help thinking she'd been played, even if the words felt rehearsed, almost like a script.

Her mother stood and walked over to the stove. "Are your other friends going to be playing?"

"The usual suspects?" Wren wracked her brains trying to figure out if they'd talked about it. She hadn't logged into InstaQuest since weeks before her finals; there wasn't any need. Come to think of it, she couldn't remember a time she'd logged in at all in the last couple of months. Though they had beaten all the content ages ago, so it probably wasn't that strange.

Harlow slumped down in the seat next to Wren. "They're definitely playing! They'll look us up once we're all in-game."

"Well, we played wonderfully together in Avarice, and that other one." Wren shrugged, starting to let herself get excited about Somnia Online again. "Either way, we should all be able to nail our classes."

"That's the spirit." Harlow said, digging Wren playfully in the ribs with her elbow and earning a scowl. "I'm pretty sure they're not all going to playing what they're used to either."

"Sounds like you'll have a very capable group." Laria was putting away the plethora of energy drinks, quick foods, and snack foods that habitually went with a new MMORPG release. After all, with leveling and immersion, there wasn't going to be time for real anything. "You'll *need* a solid group."

"Wait. Mom. We'll *need* a solid group?" Wren sat up straight, curiosity starting to bubble again despite her earlier disappointment.

Her mother turned around and smiled, the expression reaching her dark brown eyes. "Of course. Groups can take on stronger mobs and locations, and if you guys push yourselves like you usually do, the virtual world will be your oyster. I will give you one hint, since it launches at midnight tonight... be careful of night in some areas of the game world."

"That's the hint?" Wren glared at her.

"Yep. That's it."

Wren swore she could see her mother's Cheshire grin. That woman was planning something, and Wren hated not being in the know.

Wren blinked her eyes open as her mom gently shook her shoulder. "Hey love, wake up. You too, Harlow. It's eleven. I thought you'd want to get snacks and drinks before the game starts."

Laria sat by the bed as they woke up and smiled at them as she ushered them downstairs. "I have to head to my study and monitor the launch from there, loves. Sorry, but your Dad will grab you food, I'm going to be busy. Send me a message in-game if you need me."

Wren laughed. "Will do, Mom." Even though she knew it wasn't normal for kids to communicate with their mothers through a video game, it was simply a part of her life she secretly enjoyed.

It really was the release. No more school. No more exams. No more waiting for college application acceptances. It was all over, and now there was just Somnia Online. Wren could feel herself shake, though on second thought it was probably Harlow who was jiggling her legs up and down like a mad woman. "Settle, Harlow. Let's go get our supplies."

Wren's dad was setting the table when they got down there. David's dark hair was streaked with silver now, faintly resembling Beethoven's signature look. She assumed he'd probably taken a nap and just not bothered to brush his hair, or forgotten to. He'd piled some sodas, chips, and fruit out and obviously paid attention to Wren's habits—habits he'd helped create.

Wren grinned at him. "Thanks Dad. You know just what a girl needs."

Her dad laughed. "I won't pretend I'm not jealous."

"Why can't you come play too, Mr. S?" Harlow grabbed a bag of chips, strategically avoiding the fruit, and sat down on a chair, pulling her knees up to her chest. "You used to play with us all the time."

David gave a melodramatic sigh. "Sadly, I must venture out and settle on lesson plans for my summer students. A professor's work is never done. Besides, I'm training the next generation of game developers."

But there was a twinkle in his eye, and the girls laughed with him.

"Seriously though, I'll have to sleep once you're online. If you need something, you'll have to message Mom. She's going to be busy though, so don't expect an immediate response." He smiled and grabbed an apple for himself, messing up Wren's hair fondly.

Feasting before the game was almost tradition. Of course, no release had been like this. With its infinitely closed betas, of which any leaks only tested out mechanics and not actual areas or cities, Somnia Online had been an enigma. The hype had been amazing though, with people clamoring for the headsets and suits for months on end.

It was going to be such a challenge, such a race. If only she were a healer, Wren knew they'd have a chance at the top. Having permission to play it for the whole goddammed summer was like a dream in Wren's eyes.

She munched down on her favorite fruits. and some Numyuns, while guzzling Flying Bull. Harlow gorged herself on potato chips and soda. Their excitement fed off each other, and they couldn't help breaking out in a few giggling fits. It was the first time since InstaQuest over twelve months ago that they'd had a night like this.

Food. Liquid. Bathroom. Excited and full of energy, they ran upstairs to pull their suits on. Headgear in place, they lay down, booting up the interface as they closed their eyes.

They were five minutes early, and up in the left hand corner of her vision, Wren could see a clock counting down the seconds until launch.

"What species are you going for?" Harlow asked, her voice shaking slightly.

"Locus, I think. It's the first time I've seen a sort of alien species. The other nine species don't really appeal to me. What about you?" Wren watched the countdown in her vision, trying to clamp down on the excitement.

"Mmm, still thinking about it. But being a blood mage, I feel like it needs to be suitable."

Wren chuckled. "Highest level is fifty right now, hybrid builds are a possibility, allocated classes, hidden paths, and this neurally-activated interface. It's going to be an adventure."

"We're aiming for the top, right?" Harlow's tone was unusually serious.

Wren smiled. "Shit yes. You know we have to get our hands on those damned keys first."

"Up, up and away!" Harlow's laughter cascaded through the room, mellowing Wren's tension.

Suddenly the countdown hit zero and Wren entered character creation, both girls forgetting about the other while they chose their virtual personas.

Locus was Wren's choice, the elegant alien race. Their skin had varying shades of silver, their eyes anything from pearl through to cosmos. Their hair hung in loose bunches resembling tentacles down their backs, topped with what appeared to be tiny bulbs that only glowed occasionally in the character creation screen. Their long legs were toned and strong. They were beautiful and ethereal, imposing and serene. She wanted to be one so badly.

Taking her literal appearance from the sensors the game adjusted the settings initially, allowing her to choose hair, skin, and eye colors, as well as varying degrees of muscle tone, height—so many different things to pick from. She chose a dark purple undertone to shadow the silver of the locus skin and hair, and cosmos eyes, so people would get lost in the stars. If she was going to be enchanting, she was going to do it right.

Her starting city was Stellaein, on the continent of Tarishna. Class choice wasn't even an option. Enchanter was already locked in. She frowned but focused on the empty statistics next to the figure of her locus. As an enchanter, Charisma and Intelligence were paramount.

The starting statistics for a locus enchanter were pretty solid. Plus the species' addition to charisma, and her starting character seemed pretty decently rounded.

CONstitution 12
STRength 10
AGIlity 11
WISdom 12

INTelligence 15
CHArisma 20

HitPoints: 74
Mana: 60

It then asked her to choose from a ridiculous amount of spells for level one. She blinked and scanned them. Shielding sounded pretty great; she was a cloth wearer and it would be better if things hit her as little as possible, especially since only one damage spell was available. Shrugging internally, she chose *Minor Suffocation,* a spell that caused damage over time. Hopefully there'd be ways to obtain the others at some point.

Minor Suffocation

Cast: Single Target
Type: Damage Over Time
Duration: 24 Seconds

Effect: This spell winds a mind leash around your opponent, as if it were trying to suffocate them. Its damage ticks every three seconds for twenty-four seconds.

Last but not least came the name. Wren smiled, hoping against hope she was early enough to get the name she always used. Typing in MURMUR, she held her breath as she indicated for the system to continue, and her sight went black for a brief moment before opening on a dazzling silver city cresting the top of a mountain range. The air was cool, and a million elements flooded her senses at the same time, leaving her gasping for air.

CHAPTER THREE

Jacked In

Storm Corp
Storm Technologies Division Experimental Neuroscience Division
Countdown: Five years before Somnia Online implementation

Doctor Michael Jeffries gazed out at his new laboratory. Well, it wasn't precisely his, but he was in charge of it. Twenty-three staff, diligently tinkering to recreate his working prototype. He watched them from his perch on the chair at his desk. It swiveled like a barstool, but that's where the resemblance ended. Its back rose up and cradled him comfortably. Instead of sitting lower than the technicians working so diligently under him, he was there, looking out over them. A sea of minds ready for him to mold, to educate, to read.

"Dr. Jeffries. It's Edward Davenport on the line." Jessa glanced up at him. "The CEO."

Michael resisted the urge to laugh at her. He didn't need her to tell him who the man was.

"Thank you, Jessa," he said, instead of the less than flattering terms running through his head. He'd need to get himself a better assistant at some stage, but for now she'd have to do. Plus, she was good at relieving other...tensions.

Clearing his throat, he activated his communication interface. "Hello, Mr. Davenport, to what do I owe this pleasure?"

Michael concentrated on keeping his voice level and not pushing his luck. Teddy Davenport wasn't known for his patience, or his belief in anything supernatural. Considering the headset would tap into neural activity and translate it, just like a mind reader might, it was probably verging on unbelievable for the old man.

"What's your ETA on being able to field test the unit?"

Well, at least Teddy cut to the chase. "Field testing is going to take time. It all really depends on the way we approach the testing."

There was a brief pause on the other end, and for a moment Michael thought the call may have been disconnected.

"What type of testing do you require to make sure this won't embarrass us?"

Clamping down on his temper, Michael forced a smile and hoped it would carry over in his voice. "All I have right now is the prototype. We'll be working on building and adapting other versions to test, which will be better internally. Eventually it'll be best if we can get as large a sample size as possible. Thousands would be best so we have data to extrapolate from. It's the only way we can know if the readings will be as accurate as it could be."

"And how do you see us accessing thousands of people? We only have eight years to do this. Wait."

Michael obliged and waited. Teddy might sometimes be an old fuddy-duddy, but there was a reason Storm Corp was what it was. Becoming one of the world's three largest corporations hadn't happened by sheer luck or with bad investments. No, Teddy had a fine business head on his shoulders.

"We have a game in development."

Dr. Jeffries bit his tongue to stop from yelling out that his prototype wasn't a game, that reading people's minds wasn't a game, but then he calmed, an idea forming in his mind.

"It's only been in production for a few months, but they're picking up steam. Virtual reality is trying to take everyone by storm. Would a game environment be a good testing ground?"

Michael had to stop himself from screaming *fucking yes* out loud. Instead, he counted to three, and gave his answer. "It would make an excellent testing ground, and it would allow us to take our time and get the headgear just right. If we make it a condition that everyone has to undergo a scan in order to play, we'll get much more consistent data."

"Excellent. We'll need those headsets perfected in time to produce them in a few years. For the game. You will receive all the data you need to tweak it further for the military contract."

"Thank you." Michael meant it.

Forget thousands. Virtual reality gaming meant hundreds of thousands. He'd never thought he might even have access to that many minds. The thought made him giddy.

"Don't make me regret it, Dr. Jeffries."

The call went dead.

Michael leaned back in his chair and smiled. This was going to be so much better than he'd planned.

Release Day: Somnia Online

The sky above Murmur was a crystal clear blue, so vibrant it almost hurt her eyes, and the air was so fresh she could practically taste it. Pillars shot up toward that blue sky from the silver city in front of her, accentuated by the metal wall surrounding it. The gate was about fifty feet from where she stood, and people bustled along the path heading in and out of it. Some snow scattered across the rock at the base of the city wall, but after a few feet it gave way to lush green grass and a gentle slope.

The road she stood on was crudely paved with rock, and when she glanced behind her, she could see dirt take its place several feet farther on. Some locus without weapons were running around in the grass off to the side; upon closer inspection many were running away from some snappy creatures she couldn't quite make out. Their tall willowy forms appeared gangly and awkward as their players got used to them.

She blinked as notifications appeared in the corner of her vision, and silenced them with a thought. This world was magnificent. While she could feel a chill in the air, it barely registered through her silvered skin. Even the coarse robe she wore should have been useless, but she had a feeling there was a lot more about the locus she needed to discover.

Wren searched for the in-game clock, wanting to track both in-game and real time with ease. Setting them up, she realized it had only taken her about twenty minutes to create her character. That had to be some sort of record for her.

The interface was complex and a little overwhelming. She frowned realizing the spell she'd chosen upon character creation wasn't slotted. Maybe it was in her inventory then, which was a whole other level of learning the interface. She moved a few steps closer to the guards as she activated her inventory. There, in her seemingly endless bag, was the spell. Her character pulled it out and placed it in one hand. Putting her other hand over it and touching it lightly, Murmur gasped as the spell absorbed into her flesh, causing faint purple runes to gleam under her silver skin. In her peripheral vision she noticed a flash of color too. Upon closer inspection it appeared the fairy lights at the end of her hair lit up when magic was involved.

Wren took an involuntary step back, her gaze returning to her arm, which still tingled even after the runes had faded. This was going to take some getting used to. Letting her gaze travel the length of the arm, she saw her character was elegant, right down to her silvery fingertips. She felt at her face and realized the hair attached to her skull was thick intertwined strands and not bunches. Though not actually tentacles, they felt and looked like it. Glancing down, her legs were long and toned, as if she'd walked everywhere fighting her entire life. The silver glowed faintly with a gentle purple hue behind it. Even better than it had been when she created her character. Her body felt strong. She was glad she'd chosen the locus.

Taking a couple of moments to breathe and get used to her tall body, she reached inside her bag again and retrieved a rather tarnished dagger. Fantastic.

That was going to be useful. At least she'd had the foresight to choose the damage spell. Murmur walked closer to the guards, trying to figure out how high a level they were, but all she saw were skulls and a deep red aura. Considering the NPCs told her to not even think about trying anything. It was probably good that the guards to a starting city were high level, otherwise high level players would grief newbies for shits and giggles.

Glancing around, she realized she wasn't the only one getting used to this new interface and level of immersion. She felt taller than she did in the real world, making balancing as she walked or stood feel a little off. She'd played about six different immersive games since she was twelve, most of them with her parents and Harlow, but her parents had been too busy for the past couple of years.

Still, none of them had this extra sense to them.

She gazed around, watching as others in this area stumbled and staggered a bit as they got used to their own bodies. Those who obviously didn't wait to attack creatures before learning how to walk, ran for their lives from what seemed to be some sort of beetle.

Murmur grinned. Maybe it wouldn't be so bad in this game after all.

Red script scrolled in front of her eyes. Unique system, really. Most other games just flashed in your vision, seemingly oblivious to the fact that you could be fighting for your virtual life. She motioned for the warning to come back to the center and positioned it slightly lower so that, even if she was fighting, it wouldn't completely obscure her vision.

All regeneration has been halted until you consume food and drink.

Interesting.

Murmur reached into the bag and pulled out two items. The first was an odd sort of bar, like a protein bar, which she assumed was food. Either that or the admins were playing tricks on the new players by putting turds in their inventory, but she couldn't see anyone else gasping in horror, so food was the more likely option. A vial about two finger widths in size was filled with a murky liquid she assumed was the drink she needed. She scarfed down both of them, cringing a bit at the lack of taste, and the message stopped blinking.

A timer flickered briefly under the in-game clock:

30:00. 29:59

Each of those had a thirty minute duration then.

Murmur reached into her almost depleted bag and pulled out the letter she'd felt in there earlier.

High Enchanter Belius

Re: Murmur

She was itching to open it, but decided against it. A long time ago there had been penalties in the real world against opening letters not intended for you. Knowing her luck, she was sure something bad would happen here too. Letter in hand, she passed into the locus city, Stellaein, the guards barely glancing at her as she walked by.

The streets were paved with stone that gleamed so brightly she at first thought it was metal, but the sound of her barely clad feet on it wasn't right. Neither was the texture as she bent down to feel it. Touch was magnificent. She could feel the coarse grain as it strained against her fingertips with its slightly gravelly texture.

The buildings were hewn out of stone so smoothly it appeared as if they were metal too, as if they'd been carved out of the mountain itself. Beautiful tints of blue and charcoal interlaced with the silver to create an enchanting presence. For just a moment, Murmur wondered if the city itself were an illusion, but one hand against the surface of a wall was enough to convince her of its authenticity.

She walked past a shop on either side, and came to a large circular opening. From its center rose a three locus statue. The first, an archer, back straight and proud as they drew their bow. The second, a healer, probably the cleric, with an axe shining with divine light. The third, a caster, with a glowing staff, and robes whipping in the wind. The fountain rotated, giving the statues a lifelike appeal. A strange sense of peace and power emanated from it. Calming.

Shops littered around the fountain. There was what appeared to be a bakery, and a tailoring shop. Locus bustled about inside them, visible through the windows as they prepared for the day. The city was waking up, and life began to spill out onto the paths.

Even now, at not even seven in the morning in the game world, several locus children chased each other around the sculpture. Next to the fountain was a post with multiple directional tags on it. Sighing with relief, Murmur approached it, seeking out the Enchanter Guild.

"Hey. You look like you're new here."

Murmur sighed inwardly. Fantastic, looks like it was starting already. She glanced back. "No newer than you."

The male locus behind her laughed. It was a good-natured sound, with a chime of dissonance echoing after it. "I'm level two, so you are newer."

"Have you been to see your class trainer yet?" Having found out how to get to the Enchanter Guild, she turned to face the conversationalist. He looked at her blankly, as if he was scanning his interface to attempt to find out what she was talking about.

"You have a letter for your trainer. Go give it to them. Then go level." She attempted a smile, not entirely sure of the outcome considering the facial structure was different to that of humans. But he didn't seem to mind.

"Hey. Thanks. Guess I got caught up in the game."

"Easy to do. Have fun." She smiled at him and walked past. The area wasn't crowded, but it definitely wasn't empty. Being nice could hurt if she wasn't careful. Especially with the virtual aspects to games these days, it was always good to be on her guard. Glancing ahead, she searched for the path she'd have to take to the right to find the guild. It was close to the center of town from what she could tell.

"Name's Jirald." The friendly guy called after her.

Her interface automatically added it to her *People I've Met* list.

"Murmur," she called back, still intent on her destination. For several seconds she could still feel his eyes boring holes in her back.

The street grew run down the closer she got to her turn off. She frowned, glancing around. Perhaps each city area had a slum. Drawing too much reality into a game was a possibility she wasn't sure she liked. After all, like most other people, she came here to escape the real world. With jobs scarce and futures uncertain, MMORPGs were a huge draw.

She turned down the last right before the city devolved, and immediately the facades were brighter. Frowning, she continued on, trying to ignore the tugging at the back of her mind that maybe the slums deserved a bit of a closer look. Trainer first, then the slums. And seeing if Harlow had finally made it in.

Most of the structures on her path were cheerful. They had window boxes full of white flowers that seemed to blend perfectly with the blue and silver gleam of the city. The windows were open, and voices could be heard softly drifting out onto the street. Nothing defined, just the cheery bustle of city life. At the next intersection, another sign stood. But its Enchanter Guild directional sign was largely superfluous considering the building stood on the corner and couldn't be missed.

A rainbow of colors rippled over the Enchanter Guild headquarters. Power pulsated from it so much that even Murmur in all her untrained glory could see its aura. Flowers decorated the window boxes, and a joyful vibe permeated the whole structure.

Summoning her courage, Murmur headed inside. Speaking to strangers had never been her forte. That's where Harlow shone. But the damned girl obviously hadn't made a locus had she?

Murmur approached the counter in the large building, letter in hand. The locus behind the counter smiled. The expression was slightly alien on a face with only two holes as a nose. But the fact that the eyes were a solid color meant that when the smile reached them, a whole solar system sparkled back at you. The result was endearing, charming—she was definitely an enchanter.

"Just go through to the back, take the corridor to the right, and then...Belius is it? Third on the left." The kind locus motioned her through. "Go on, young one. I promise you Master Belius doesn't bite."

Murmur laughed it off, a bit irritated at herself for acting in such an odd manner in a game, and yet oddly comforted by the Non Player Character. "Thank you."

She headed through to the back.

There weren't as many people in the corridor as Murmur thought there would be. Perhaps not many had chosen to play a locus, instead favoring the usual species like humans, elves, dark elves, dwarves, and gnomes. Personally, she thought it was far more fun to be something that wasn't remotely similar to your real life persona.

Arriving at the door she'd been directed to, Murmur raised her fist and knocked three times.

"Come in."

She pushed the door open and came face to face with what seemed to be an elderly locus. White tufts grew where his hair should be. Perhaps he'd lost it in a battle. He chuckled at her scrunched up brow. "Welcome, dear Murmur, I've been expecting you. You think far too much; I can almost hear you. Be careful. Mind magic has many uses, young enchanter."

Murmur focused on his words, and noticed his mouth hadn't moved. He was speaking into her mind? "How...What..."

This time when he laughed, his mouth moved, and he held out a hand for the envelope. "It's our secret, for now. Perhaps another time, when you've adjusted to this world and your abilities." He scanned the letter briefly, a flicker of consternation briefly entered his expression before he looked back up at her.

"Ah, yes. Yes. I understand this is not the path you thought your life would take, but I assure you, for *you* this is the correct path."

Murmur blinked at him, fighting the scowl her lips wanted to curl into. How the hell did he know she didn't want to be an enchanter? "Well, I'm an enchanter now, aren't I?"

"That you are. Try not to fight it too much. I am here to train you when you need training. Every time you gain a level of experience, you will also gain training points. You may use these training points in whatever way you wish. You can save them up and use them later all at once, but it's best to try and keep your skill levels of both spell casting and experience similar."

Murmur nodded. Made perfect sense. "So my skill levels can exceed my experience level then? By how much?"

Belius smiled. "It depends on how often it is used, and how much experience it is possible for the spell or ability to grant you."

"So, if I'm level ten, a level five spell won't give me much experience. Got it." Murmur smiled back at the old locus. "I'm sure that's not all I came here to hear."

"No. You are a spritely one, aren't you? No nonsense at all. Very well, then. I have three quests for you." He winked at her, a small smile pulling at the left corner of his mouth. "If you complete them and return to me, you will be able to pick two more spells, and I shall gift you an enchanter robe and your choice of basic weapon. That is, if you think you're up to the task."

Murmur stopped herself from gaping. What with their mannerisms and phrasings, these NPCs were so lifelike. "Of course I am. Fire away, Master Belius."

Back outside the city walls, still level one, Murmur finally pulled up the information sections of her Heads-Up Display, which managed not to obscure her vision but complement it instead. Stats were self-explanatory and easy to access, mostly on the left side of her vision unless she blocked them out. She couldn't help being a little excited that not being a healer meant she wouldn't be stuck concentrating on the group's health bars non-stop. *Suck it, Harlow.* Speaking of which, Murmur glanced down and realized her chat area had three blinking orange bars. Damn it. Maybe she did need to fiddle with those settings after all. She'd completely missed it.

From Sinister: Guess whooooooooooooooo?

Murmur blinked, and sent back furiously: *Seriously? How the hell did you get that name?*

While she waited for an answer, she checked the other messages.

From Devlish: How did I go from rogue to dread knight? Seriously, Mur, what am I going to do? Also, can you buff me?

A small laugh escaped her throat and Murmur responded, *If you're not Darren, I'm blocking you.*

From Jirald: Thanks again. I can't believe I missed that letter.

Murmur blinked at the last message, while the other two refreshed and were flashing again. It couldn't hurt to be polite, right? Surely she wouldn't get an in-game stalker on the first day? Taking a deep breath she sent back a simple you're welcome, and turned her attention to Harlow.

From Sinister: Right? I had entered it as my preference when we did the scan, maybe an early scan reserved it for me? Anyway! I am loving this. I've seen my trainer and am about to get me some levels! We have to meet up asap!

No shit, Sherlock. But Murmur didn't send that thought. Instead, she just told Harlow to level and keep in touch.

From Devlish: No need to block me. I'm the one and only. The others are about. I think we all picked different races, oddly enough. We need to group up asap.

Murmur laughed. Darren the Devlish and Harlow were so similar. At least they were well on the track to having the old gang back together. Race to the top, conquer the content, find those bloody keys. Just another day in the office.

She closed the chats out, and pulled up the errands she'd been sent on by Belius.

Four stone beetle eyes
Four skeleton bones
Three spider sacs

Murmur frowned at the list. Seemed easy enough, but what were the drop rates like? She shrugged, feeling her shoulders rotate smoothly with the action. This body was strong, a wave of fearlessness rushed over her, and she grinned. Leaving the path, she ventured over to an empty area of rock and grass, still a decent distance from the trees and began to look for beetles. There were several other locus about, but none in her immediate area. It should be easy enough to share. Surely the beetles would be around stone?

Sure enough, the strange large rhino beetle with blue and silver inlays was a higher level than her, its name in yellow as if to prove a point. Level two while she was still one. Still, it should be doable. She hadn't seen any naked locus running around for their bodies yet. She'd cast minor suffocation to pull and hope it did two ticks of damage before the mob reached her. Readying her dagger in her hand, she cast the spell.

Your spell has fizzled.

Fucking hell. Typical. Taking another breath, she readied herself again and cast the spell, hoping her target wasn't out of range.

Your skill in Alteration has increased (1)
Your Minor Suffocation Spell hits Stone Beetle for 4 damage.

As the little beetle changed direction and charged toward her, its aura changing from yellow to red as it moved, combat music filled her ears. The low drums and cello notes made Murmur groan. Closer and closer the beetle came, and Murmur realized it was quite a bit larger than she'd originally thought. Its pincers opened and closed maniacally and she gulped, clenching the dagger in her hands.

Your Minor Suffocation Spell hits Stone Beetle for 3 damage.

Good. Two ticks before it reached her, it was already down a chunk of life.

She thrust at it and struck its carapace with the tip of her dagger. Stupid aim. The next time she'd aim for its head.

You strike a Stone Beetle for 2 (piercing) damage
Your skill in daggers has increased (1)
Your Minor Suffocation Spell hits Stone Beetle for 4 damage
Stone Beetle slashes you for 8 damage.

"Shit." It hit pretty hard considering, numbing her leg for a bit. This time however, Murmur had a plan. She gripped the dagger along her forearm and ducked in under the antennae. Taking another slash on her leg, which smarted like hell, her spell hit the beetle for damage again. Right after which, she plunged the dagger into the neck joint of the beast.

You stab a Stone Beetle for piercing damage. (15) Critical damage!

You have slain a Stone Beetle.

You gain experience.

Excellent, it seemed the game rewarded tactics and accuracy. She could have poked away at the carapace for ages, but strategic plays were worth far more damage. Her leg hurt, but not nearly as much as she'd been led to believe it would in full immersion.

Murmur touched the corpse, bringing up a loot line. Luckily, it had an eye, a carapace, and somehow a copper piece. Not entirely sure how a stone beetle communicated that it wanted to pay for things, Murmur pocketed the money anyway. Before she could forget, she accessed the HUD, directing it to cease combat music for the future. No more of that annoying shit.

Luckily this starting area, and presumably the stone beetles were here for people to get used to their long bodies and abilities in a place that was moderately safe from trains and rampant death. Her health slowly ticked higher, but waiting for it was ridiculous, especially since after another beetle or two she'd have to eat and drink again. That was going to get tiresome really fast.

From Sinister: If I ate this much in the real world, I wouldn't fit into my suit.

The message flashed across before blinking down the bottom, and Murmur laughed out loud at her friend. Harlow had a point though. At least one of them was going to have to learn to cook.

DING! The sound reverberated through her skull.

You have gained Level 2!

You have five (5) training points

You have four (4) stat points

After another eight beetles and some food and drink, Murmur finally got her fourth eye, and her first level. She frowned at the points, not quite sure how to spend them yet. Maybe she should have researched more before playing. Instead of seething about the fact that it took her so long, she walked down the way a little bit and approached the tree line, emboldened by her newfound level increase.

She could see a couple of other players down by the trees. Something in her gut told her that level two to three was going to be far more difficult, and that this area was much more dangerous. Murmur almost felt naked without her healing spells. There was so much more to the world when you couldn't just heal yourself through everything.

Murmur could already feel her impatience sneaking in. She'd never been good at just taking games easy. There was always the thirst to level faster, to get stronger the quickest, to be one of the best, if not the best at her class. It was like a compulsion—always easy to push off when she had something else overriding it like school work, but now...there was only spare time. She grinned to herself and stopped at the tree-line. Her strange locus vision adjusted to the darkness and highlighted mobs within it with an iridescent halo.

While it wasn't infra vision or night vision, her sight could see into the dark forest, sort of like the stars lighting up the night sky. She'd ponder it later.

A skeleton shambled to the left, its bones creaking softly as it jangled about. Straight ahead was a spider with ridiculously long legs, and off to the right was a cluster of something she couldn't make out. All of the mobs she could see were yellow, probably at least level three. But if she didn't try, she'd never know.

Feeling reckless, she cast minor suffocation and pulled the skeleton toward her. The fact that the spell managed to convince an undead creature it was being strangled was quite amazing. It let out a cackle and jangled over to her as she backed up, hoping to let a third tick hit before it reached her. This time her spell was hitting for five and four. A slight increase was at least something. The skeleton flailed a wooden staff in the air and Murmur hoped against hope her hit points would outlast it.

Then it was upon her, three ticks of her Damage Over Time down. The thing was tall and gangly and she realized these skeletons had to be locus, too. Even its empty sockets glowed, like some type of magic possessed it. Considering it was a walking skeleton, that probably wasn't far from the truth. It swung at her, and barely missed when she managed to dodge. She could feel the heaviness of her body, and the unwillingness with which it made the movement. That was probably her one dodge for the next twenty. She'd better make it count.

Killing a skeleton was far more difficult than a beetle. For one thing, it was already bloody dead. That blasted staff hurt too, though not as much as the pincer claws had. It made Murmur wonder if locus could bruise. Finally, after what seemed like an age, she managed to hack its skull off. She leaned forward and looted the mob. It had twelve copper on it. Maybe skeletons were a good idea for a while with or without her quest. Not only that, the staff it had been wielding was hers as well.

"Score,'" she muttered to herself, aware she was probably grinning like a loon. Sure, her staff skills weren't up to par but she was sure it wouldn't take too long. It's not like melee did most of her damage or anything.

Worn Staff

Damage 4-7

Weight 5

Level 2

Her health was down to half, so she sat and looked in her spell book while meditating. Didn't enchanters have something to do with plentiful mana? When was that skill going to kick in? It took painfully long for her mana and health to get back up, and impatience nibbled at her heels. It was only then she realized the stupid skeleton hadn't dropped any bones. This drop rate was looking to be worse than the stinking beetles.

Murmur worked her way through the front mobs of the wood, acutely aware that about a hundred feet away there were several people playing in a group. All she wanted was this little haven, so she stuck to her area, and hoped they'd stick to theirs. The respawn rate of these mobs was fast. They weren't super strong, nor were they special, so they appeared after just a few minutes.

Her two-handed blunt skill increased so that her misses became fewer. By the time she'd finally gathered the four skeleton bones and three spider sacs, she'd downed another two drinks and food, and was seriously close to needing more again.

Her purse held a whopping two silver, and forty-three copper, and she had a club, another staff, a dagger, and quite a few venom glands and spider legs. Just as she was about to turn and go, she spied a skeleton where her spider should have respawned.

Curious, she conned it. Orange. That was tougher than yellow, and yet not quite red yet. So it wasn't completely foolhardy to contemplate attacking it. But damn, it had a thin crown around its head in aura style, and it said: Fallen Sergeant.

"Ooooh." She grinned. Casting her minor suffocation spell, she pulled the mob toward her. It was at the very limit of her range, and she backpedaled while letting the DoT tick. It made even less impact on the monster's health than it usually did. This was going to be very close. Her heart beat fast, and she narrowed her focus, concentrating on the weak point of skeletons where the neck should have been. Thankfully her two-handed blunt was higher than her experience level now, and she didn't miss once. She cast minor suffocation again. She'd fought all the way through its cycle.

Trading blows with the Fallen Sergeant, she couldn't help but be grateful he didn't have a freaking shield, although she could feel blood running down her legs. Even if it was supposed to be virtual, it certainly felt like she was getting slashed. Sweat ran down her face, and the pain increased with each movement she made. One more good blow from that sword, and she'd be a goner.

CHAPTER FOUR
The City

Storm Corp
Storm Technologies Division Experimental Neuroscience Division
Countdown: Three years before Somnia Online launch

Not wanting to blow his own horn, Dr. Jeffries stood back while the first lot of internal testers took their place on the lounges. They'd set up reclining versions of the now-outdated easy chairs that "massaged" the user's muscles. It was supposed to stimulate muscle development while the player was in the virtual world. The doctor was quite certain that was a load of bullshit.

The only way he knew to properly stimulate such a thing was through the neural network, through electronic pulses. He kept his smile to himself while the twenty test headgear sets were distributed. Each participant had been pulled from differing Storm Corp divisions.

He frowned, still not happy with the progress. It needed to be faster, and more in-depth. While his team worked on the game headgear, Michael had been focusing more on his passion—making sure the scan would yield the proper results. After all, his true field involved the neural networks and the brain. He hadn't had the time to implement the new upgrades he'd designed into the ones being tested, but since they were about to start weekly runs of testing, there was plenty of time.

When he was done with the headgear, it would adapt to the person's skull by itself, but right now it had to be fitted to the head.

The feeds were wired through into the main system so that he'd be able to observe them directly through his augmented reality insert, or else on one of the larger screens in his office. Michael wasn't the least bit interested in the game. He wasn't a designer or developer. All he wanted was the information in their brains and how they scanned. He wanted the information his headgear was pulling out of their heads, and how he could use that information to make his project stronger.

The stronger it became, the more accurate the readings would be. Not only would he be able to allocate the perfect job or class to a person, but he'd also be able to see into their minds. To their thoughts and their memories, the things that drove them, and the secrets they held. Delightful tidbits of information to use.

Most of his team took the smile to mean Dr. Jeffries was happy with the progress being made. If only he'd been wearing a headset at that moment, they might have been surprised.

Release Day: Somnia Online

Murmur steadied herself, concentrating on the Fallen Sergeant, and made sure her aim was strong and true, because it was the last shot she'd have. When the final blow connected and coincided with a tick from her spell's DoT, the mob fell in a tangled heap of bones, Murmur sank to the ground after it, groaning at her remaining nine hit points. That was one way to narrowly avoid her first death.

You have slain a Fallen Sergeant.

You are the first to slay a Fallen Sergeant.

You gain experience.

DING! The sound startled her this time, and she burst out in relieved laughter as her health and mana both refilled immediately.

You have gained Level Three (3)
You have (10) Ten Training Points
You have (8) Stat Points

Still laughing at the very edge of the trees, Murmur looted her kill and claimed a lovely sword that was too heavy for her to use. And two whole silver. With a skip in her step she made her way back to the gate, checking on her chat windows as she went.

Her only messages appeared to be from Sinister and her rampant complaining about the food. With only ten minutes left on her second to last ration herself, Murmur had to agree. She sent a brief message back: *It's okay. I'll figure out the cooking skill.*

Walking into town with her HUD overlaying her vision was a little disconcerting. She directed her thoughts to toning down the transparency, impressed at the immediacy of the reaction. Aligning her alerts to pop up on the right-hand side instead of in the middle took another thought, and the chat boxes adjusted before her eyes as she organized them in her mind. The response rate to her thoughts was astounding. Why had her mother never called her in to test this? A wave of anger passed over her for a moment before she shook it off.

It didn't matter now. She was in the game world, which felt, smelled, and tasted more alive than the real world.

Murmur stopped, closing the HUD reflexively and stared around her. Just having passed into town, she realized she was in a sea of people. Not just the few she'd seen earlier, but a literal throng of people. Glancing at them, they were all green to her, of lesser levels. Perhaps they'd spent far longer in character creation. It was likely. After all, she usually took an hour or two herself.

Letting her curiosity win out, she walked through the familiar streets now teeming with life. Stalls, which hadn't been there a couple of hours ago, were now set up around the fountain. According to the in-game clock it was midday. She frowned, trying to calculate the in-game time versus the real world time and shook her head. That was for real world Wren, not for Murmur.

"Hey wait up!" Jirald's voice was already recognizable. The fact that her HUD popped up with recognition was a cool feature too.

Murmur sighed and stopped, just past the fountain, trying not to let her impatience show. "Yes?"

Jirald stopped, leaning over to regain his breath. Apparently he'd run to catch up to her. "Level three already?"

Murmur blinked at him. "Yes. It's been a couple of hours. You're level three too."

He laughed and stood up straight, the seven-foot frame of his locus only slightly taller than her own. "Guess I'm just not used to seeing a girl—"

Murmur couldn't help it. She laughed. "If you'd said that thirty years ago, I might have believed you."

His eyes narrowed very briefly, so quickly, in fact, she couldn't be completely certain they had. "I haven't gamed with many girls who've been competent."

"Then you probably haven't gamed with many girls." Murmur grinned, her quip shooting out like lightning. "I have to get to my trainer. Good luck on hitting four."

She turned on her heel and headed to her guild, steps quick and purposeful, leaving Jirald behind. He seemed harmless enough, but the girl thing was an eternal annoyance. She knew it grated on her mom's nerves too. Besides, she had plenty of gaming friends who didn't give a crap what anyone's gender was—as long as they could do their job and do it well.

At the turn off to the Enchanter Guild, Murmur paused again, looking out over the street that she had bypassed before and frowned. It didn't seem to be all that interesting, just rundown buildings that appeared to get progressively worse the farther the road led in. Still though, her gut tried to push her in that direction and she made a mental note to go and check it out soon.

The Alleyway is drab and run down during the day. Beware of visiting at night; more than one adventurer has been lost,

never to return. Should you venture in, be sure to mind your step.

Murmur blinked at the scrolling text on her screen that dissipated as soon as she'd read it, leaving a small blinking light at the corner of her vision. Accessing it quickly she realized the quest log had updated. But all she had was the information she'd already read.

She headed down toward the guildhall, pulling up those quests too. Each of the quests had a checkmark beside it along with *Complete*. Upon opening each of them, the reward was listed as trainer specified. Murmur frowned and entered the hall.

"There you are, Murmur!" The cheerful locus behind the counter recognized her from earlier. Although how she knew Murmur's name was another thing. "Belius is waiting for you."

The foyer was filled with other players, and they turned to look at her, curiosity piqued. Murmur nodded at the NPC and headed through to the back again, trying desperately not to make eye contact with any of the people waiting.

Belius sat at the desk this time when Murmur walked into the room. He finished writing whatever it was he was taking care of and pushed his chair back to stand up. "Ah, Murmur. You've finished my errands, I see."

She nodded, marveling at the fact that there was no need to activate any type of quest mode. The game was seamless, and chillingly real. "Those skeletons didn't like coughing up their bones, oddly enough."

Belius laughed. "They're strangely attached to them."

There was a definite twinkle in his eyes. Murmur found herself warming to his character. NPC or not, he seemed more human than many people out there. She handed him the items, and Belius smiled.

"You may choose two more spells from those initially available. Keep in mind, you will need to acquire the leveled up versions when you qualify." Belius handed her a scroll. "This is a list of the spells and their levels as they are available to you. Generally you obtain a new level of spells every fourth level until you hit level twenty. Remember to be aware of the level of enemy you're fighting. The higher they are in comparison to your own level, the more likely they are to resist your spells until they render them completely ineffective."

She nodded at him. It was standard that you could use a stun at level four on a level ten enemy and have it be ineffective. She leafed through the spells though she was already quite certain what she would choose. Free spells were free spells after all.

"You may select from the scrolls you see here. If any of them are level four spells, you may purchase them in advance of your level. But you may choose two level one spells as your rewards." Belius moved to the side, leaving a bookcase filled with scrolls directly in front of her.

Murmur scanned her list and chose

Minor Shield
Cast: Self only
Type: Buff
Duration: 45 minutes
Effect: This casts a minor shield over your skin, increasing your Armor Class by level + 3, and hit points by level + 5.

Simple Animation
Cast: Self
Type: Pet
Duration: until death or dismissal
Effect: This summons a magical pet to do your bidding. It costs a tiny sword to cast. Isn't the best at obeying commands.

Murmur blinked at the last spell. That sounded rather sarcastic. "Where do I obtain tiny swords?"

"From me." Belius smiled. "They're two copper for one, or three for five, or seven for one silver."

Murmur raised an eyebrow. Considering she needed one per cast—"I'll take seven."

Belius smiled. "That will scale with you through to level seven. However at level eight, you will need to acquire the next version."

She nodded, going through the spell list again, and considering the seven silver she had on her. The illusion spells were tempting, but her cash flow wasn't established yet. A couple for level four would be her best bet. Mesmerize was the crux of being an enchanter. After all, stopping mobs in their place so they couldn't move, effectively taking control of their minds— that was the shit she was looking forward to. But level four spells were one silver each. She checked her bags, knowing she'd be able to sell some stuff and decided to go all out.

"Mesmerize, Flux, Gate, Invisibility." She paused, scanning over the descriptions. "Human Illusion, and Fear."

Belius gathered all of the scrolls in his hands and passed them to her. Completing the quests gave her a sliver of experience too. She wasn't about to complain.

"Wise choices indeed, young enchanter. Tell me. How do you feel about this path now?"

Murmur hesitated, analyzing her own feelings, and ignoring the flash of notification from Sinister for the moment. "It's interesting. While I feel somewhat weak, I think these tools will help with that. It's just…"

"What?" He smiled at her, well sort of. Locus smiles had a tendency to devolve into a grimace. It was the sharp rows of teeth in their mouths, tugging at their lips while trying to convey the expression.

She looked at Belius, seeking any hint that he was a player character. The thing was, with his reactions, she couldn't precisely tell. While he played a part, he seemed so much more approachable. She touched her head. "You spoke to me earlier. In here. That fascinates me. The strength to peer into people's minds seems farfetched, and yet."

Belius moved a step closer, his starry eyes gleaming with a dark light. "And yet?"

"And yet—the possibility fills me with excitement. If that's what an enchanter can do? I want to learn it." She met his gaze, unflinching.

Belius smiled. "Grow stronger, gain experience, and you might want to see why your gut tells you things."

Murmur blinked. "How did you...?"

Belius tapped his own head and grinned, sharp teeth peeking out from his lips. "Remember? If you shout about how you feel in your head, I'll always hear. It might be good, it might not be. Try to quiet your thoughts so you don't broadcast it to the wrong person."

"Does everyone do that? Broadcast, I mean." She held her breath.

"Everyone. While most aren't very interesting, there are some for whom it can be dangerous."

She pondered for a moment, and Belius cleared his throat. "Don't forget to choose a robe young one. I recommend the robe that grants you an extra point to your charisma."

Murmur had completely forgotten about the robe reward and eagerly chose a plain white robe with a rope belt, and a sturdy staff that stood next to it. Plus one to Charisma would be useful. She'd keep her worn one too, just in case.

Initiate's Robe Enchanter

CHA +1

AC 3

Weight 0.2

Level 3

Initiate s Staff Enchanter

Damage 5-9

Weight 5

Level 3

"Time to train?" Belius asked, and she blinked at him, completely having forgotten about her level up points. Scanning her spells, she chose to put five points into Conjuration so she hopefully wouldn't fizzle every single Mez. Plus, it would help summon the animation too. Abjuration was essential for her shielding.

"Thank you." She said, smiling at her trainer.

"No need to thank me for something you've earned." Belius approached his desk again and sat down. "Now I do have work to do, but when you're ready, I'd gladly chat again. Though I do think you might want to follow your gut."

The Alleyway tugs at you, stronger this time. Perhaps you should head there straight away.

The message flashed across her vision briefly, and as she closed the door behind her, she swore Belius winked at her.

There was barely any room to move in the corridor outside Belius' room. A few enchanters chatted with each other while waiting for their trainers, some of them spouting off about theory behind how Mez and enchanters were supposed to function in general. It was a conversation she wished she could join.

But that bloody Alleyway wouldn't get out of her mind.

Finally she reached the foyer and purposefully walked over to the lady at the counter who she'd already spoken to twice. "I'm so sorry. What's your name?"

"Elvita." The NPC replied with a smile. "Thank you for asking. Most people just try to inspect me and figure it out. Can I help you?"

Murmur wondered why she hadn't done the inspecting thing herself, but her only reasoning was that Elvita felt too real. Besides, actions were supposed to dictate results in this game right? Being polite to NPCs might help in the long run. "I have some spoils I need to get rid of."

"Excellent!" Elvita clapped her hands together once, and her demeanor shifted to serious. "Let's see what you've got!"

Murmur dumped her haul out on the counter. Elvita sorted through everything, separating the club, the staff and dagger, and the venom glands. She pushed the spider legs and the heavy sword back to Murmur.

"You need to keep those. Spider legs make delicious food, and you'll need that soon enough. If you've got a minute I'll send you through to Arvin. He's in our kitchen and can show you the basics. This sword, you'd do better advertising. I can give you seven silver for it, but someone else might pay as much as a gold piece. It's up to you."

Murmur glanced at the twenty-seven spider legs with renewed appreciation. "I think I'll sell the sword to you if that's okay. There's somewhere I need to be."

"Great!" Elvita moved the sword back to her side and grabbed an abacus. Hands flying for a few seconds, she looked back up with a smile on her face. "One sword at seven silver, five venom glands at two silver and five copper each, one rusted dagger at eight copper, one splintered club at one silver and three copper, and one worn staff at three silver and five copper. Total is two gold, five silver, and one copper."

Murmur smiled and added it to her remaining silver and two copper, liking the sound of the coins rustling against each other. "I'll take you up on that offer with Arvin."

Elvita smiled. "Of course. You may need to buy some butter, but it's not expensive."

The guildhall kitchen wasn't large, but could comfortably fit two people. Arvin seemed to be an NPC of very few words, and he showed her to the cooking fire and taught her how she could create one herself. Flint for the fire, then butter, salt, and pepper. Murmur wasted no time creating her masterpiece. Technically, anyway.

Considering her cooking skill was at zero, her first few attempts ended in a blackened charred mess that even the dog didn't want to eat. However once she got the hang of it, she created spiced spider legs with her butter, salt, and pepper. Twenty-two of them in fact.

Spiced Spider Legs

Health Regeneration 4 every 5 seconds
Duration: 1 hour 15 minutes

At least that was the food problem solved. She sent a link of the food to both Sinister and Devlish, telling them to pass it on to the others as well. Then she purchased twelve, hour-long waters from Arvin for a painful sum of one gold.

From Sinister: You can already cook?

Well, of course. Aren't you running out of food?

Murmur shot back the reply while waving goodbye to Elvita and exiting the Enchanter Guild. Her level was nowhere near satisfactory, and she had no idea if the slum was a good place to go, especially since it appeared to be getting darker in-game. It was now three in the afternoon. Maybe three hours left of daytime?

From Sinister: I bought enough to tide me over for a few hours while I grind. We're all going to head out to meet you once we move to the 5-10 level area.

We? Murmur found it far easier to juggle her thoughts and conversations than usual. She arrived at the intersection to the slums and paused, casting Minor Animation which resulted in a fizzle. Suppressing a groan, she cast it again and watched in rapt fascination as an ethereal disembodied ghost with a floating sword and small shield appeared. In fact, everything about it floated. Guess it really was a weak pet. Still though, better than nothing. Her only options to tell it were attack, stop, or follow. It didn't seem to have any special abilities.

From Sinister: The guys and me. Scroll through the shit ton of messages we've been sending you, oh anti-social one.

Murmur glanced down and groaned. Apparently her HUD wasn't quite as refined as she'd like. *Sorry about that,* she sent back and got to fixing her HUD and permission settings so her best friends wouldn't be neglected. Shit. Her chest constricted slightly, reminding her how much she hated to be ignored. Murmur sighed and scanned through the messages, she realized her friends were all at varying degrees through level three and she'd missed it! Those not on their continent were even preparing to journey to Tarishna and the Obsidian Woods, where they could all level up to fifteen together. Or something.

This sounds great. Still tweaking my HUD. Didn't mean to ignore you all. So sorry! She sent the thought to all her friends and hoped that made Sinister feel better. She wished the system could convey her actual emotions, but the gear wasn't that advanced yet. Her friends were the light at the end of the tunnel. Soloing wasn't her thing. She couldn't wait to group—after she finished this annoyingly pushy errand.

Murmur glanced at *Jibartik* and frowned, but couldn't figure out how to rename her pet.

"Shit!" Despite having allocated her training points with Belius, she'd completely forgotten to distribute her statistic points. Frowning, she initiated her character stat screen. With her charisma sitting at twenty, or twenty-one with her robe, she dumped another four points into charisma to bring it up to twenty-four (twenty-five with her robe). Adding three to her intelligence brought her up to eighteen and left her with a manapool of ninety-nine.

Biting her lip, she glanced at the in-game time and added another into intelligence and constitution. It brought the latter to thirteen and increased her hit points to 103 which made her feel a lot safer. With the intelligence increase, her spells would hit harder now, too.

Satisfied, she told her pet to follow, and stepped over the line and into the slums.

CHAPTER FIVE
The Slums

Storm Corp
Storm Technologies Division Experimental Neuroscience Division
Countdown: Two years before Somnia Online implementation

Jessa knocked on Michael's door. He could tell it was her from the rhythm.

"Go away."

But she didn't move. There were no scurrying footsteps, only a deep and audible breath before she spoke. "The CEO is waiting to talk to you." And that was followed by the hurried footsteps away from his office.

"Hello, Mr. Davenport. Sorry for the wait." Michael tried his best to keep his tone even. The simmering anger he felt was difficult to cover.

The trials are doing well so far. How is the data coming?

Michael didn't want to answer. The data Teddy needed for the contract was technically perfect, but it wasn't what Michael was after, not exactly anyway. "It's going well, but I do believe I can make it line up even better, and thus create a more accurate assessment."

Hmm. So far I'm impressed, Jeffries. Keep this up, and you just never know. If you think we can be even better, if you think you can get the headgear to interact at an even stronger level and read their subject? Then you have my blessing.

This time Michael smiled. "Thank you. I'll make sure they exceed all expectations."

The line went dead, but Michael's mood improved. Sure, they were only twelve months or so out from needing to go into full-scale production. But it wouldn't matter if the initial headgear wasn't perfect. It would suit for a stupid game. Half of it wasn't even the headgear to begin with. He could refine and tune...

He was so close to accessing parts of his brain he hadn't even known he possessed. The artificial intelligence units he was working with were astoundingly intuitive. Rav, Sui, and Thra...the game world was huge and these were the initial three that had been activated. The others could interact with the world, but were still learning. Teaching them was fun, letting them learn how the headgear worked so they could encourage the players in different ways, could read them and afford them unique experiences.

Tapping into memories was possible, as were surface thoughts. Michael was certain with a few more tweaks, the headgear would be completely able to access most parts of the brain.

Just a few more months, and everything would come together.

Release Day: Somnia Online

You've entered an area not policed by the City Guard. Be sure to pay attention to your surroundings, and remember, not all thoughts can be hidden.

Murmur blinked at the message as it scrolled in front of her eyes. Fantastic. The beings here could read her thoughts too? Taking a deep breath she kept walking, trying desperately to keep her thoughts to herself. Sort of hugging them close. The smell changed subtly, from the fresh mountain air to something sinuous and fetid, like an after tang of mold. Even Jibartik kept close to her. The sustenance countdown finished, and Murmur took a swig of her one hour water, followed by her first taste of spider leg. Not bad, all things considered. It sort of tasted like a chewy chicken.

She could feel pressure against her back, some unseen gaze following her wherever she went. With no idea what she was looking for, she kept her eyes peeled for anything. Three buildings in on the left, there was a vacant lot, with charred timbers littering the buckled stone ground. Taking several steps toward it caused another line to flash across her vision, like a soft whisper in her mind.

Careful. Something happened here. Stone doesn't burn easily. While nothing appears to stand out, remember not all is as it seems. Stop. Listen. Let the memories surround you.

Welcome to Vague Hints 101.

Casting Minor Shield over herself, she bumped up her hit points and armor class. Every little bit helped. Once that was done, she walked over and stood in the middle of the lot. Ash and dust flew up in small clouds with every step she took, and once she stopped it rose, higher and higher, swirling without touching her in a vortex, leaving her like the eye in the storm. A vision danced around her, but the words were swallowed by the wind. Locus arguing with each other, a third one pushing into the mix, while a fourth she couldn't define clearly stood in the background, a cruel smile on their face.

Murmur frowned, straining to see the other one, the instigator, the perpetrator of whatever happened here. For a moment, while the others were fighting, using hands and fists, and fire magic and flame, the instigator turned toward Murmur and grinned. Sharp teeth fully visible, they took a step closer, and she blanked out her thoughts as quickly as she could, trying desperately to think of nothing.

Their gaze never left her, and a pounding began at her temples, hitting with a force that threatened to make her head explode. She stumbled slightly, trying to think as quietly as possible. A frustrated scream echoed through her head.

And all of a sudden the swirling vortex was gone.

Murmur blinked, her chest constricting with a wave of fear as her eyes momentarily blurred.

You've witnessed an inciting event. If you don't pursue the denizens of this area and strike them down until you find a clue, this incident will haunt you through thoughts and words, visions and deeds, until you're stark raving mad.

"Now I'm stuck doing a quest or else my character will go insane?" She looked at Jibartik and could have sworn the incorporeal blob behind the sword and shield shrugged its non-existent shoulders. "Fine, fine. What do we kill?"

At that, Jibartik perked up and floated over to a level two rat.

With rats and spiders crawling from the brush at the back of the lot, she guessed there was at least something to do. Another ninety minutes in-game and it would be dark. Level two and three mobs were just going to have to do. She had a sneaking suspicion they weren't going to drop what she needed, but she worked her way around the lot and between the houses next to the lot and the wall where brush grew, unkempt and wild. After about an hour of this, with a steadily progressing experience amount, she had plenty of spider legs again, not to mention a couple of silver she didn't want to question the origin of. Leaning back against one of the still standing houses, she wiped her brow, guzzled down another water, and ate a spider leg.

"What are you looking for here?"

Murmur whirled around at the unfamiliar voice, only to see a locus standing there with a dagger on either hip, arms crossed, staring at her. The hints of color on this one were green, and their eyes resembled a pearlescent sky of stars.

"I'm trying to prevent my own insanity." She ventured carefully.

Murmur was fairly sure the locus was male, but it could be difficult to tell, depending on how the character was set up. And while this one seemed to be a level or two higher, and she thought they might be an NPC, she still wasn't completely sure.

They cocked his head to the side and watched her as she ran through all the possibilities in her head.

"Could you hear them?" They finally asked.

Murmur nodded. "Not the individual words, just the yelling."

They sighed. "Then it won't leave you alone until you finish it. Be careful, young one."

NPC! Murmur's brain shouted before she could quiet it. "I will. What's your name?"

They hesitated and turned back around, rummaging in their pocket. "Emilarth. Here, take this."

Emilarth handed her a ring. It was plain and worn, beaten from some simple metal. Upon inspection she saw that the ring's magic offered a small buff against undead.

"It will come in handy. Trust me. Just be careful, and find me when you're safe."

"Thank you." She called after him as he walked away. He just lifted a hand and waved, heading deeper into the slums.

You have met Emilarth. This shadowy stranger gave you a gift. Be wary of strangers bearing gifts, but be wary of not utilizing them. When you have found what you need to, make sure to call on them.

Slipping the ring on her finger, Murmur shrugged and got back to working her way through all the mobs surrounding them. Finally, when they'd cleared it once more, she stumbled over something in the brush. Her thin beginner shoes tripped against something metal—or at least she thought it was metal from the way it clanged hollowly beneath her.

Separating the brush she frowned at the grate. It seemed to be a sewer entrance. Overhead, the sun was beginning to set, and Murmur felt a sense of dread suddenly sweep over her. She spent too long considering it. The whole load of spiders and rats in the area respawned at once. She blinked at them, her skin crawling despite the fact that she knew they were just digital renderings.

The timer in this area didn't make sense at all. It wouldn't have been bad, except she'd been working around in a circular path, which left her facing those repops at once. Sighing, she cast minor suffocation on the first one, and attacked it with Jibartik. Once she could cast the spell again, she did so on all other three mobs, bashing at them with her staff and watching her own health and her pet's ticking slowly lower. Their low level played in her favor. The only good thing about the fight was the DING at the end of it.

You have gained Level 4!

You have five (5) training points.

You have four (4) stat points.

Quickly, Murmur pulled back to a safe place, between the ruins and the house on its left where she'd yet to see mobs spawn. Acting fast she distributed her stat points one into INT for 19, one into CON for 14, and two into CHA for 26(27). Pulling out the spell scrolls, glancing at them to double check they were what she wanted to memorize.

Mesmerize

Cast: Single Target

Type: Breakable Stun

Duration: 24 seconds

Effect: This spell immobilizes your opponent for as long as they take no damage, or 24 seconds, whichever is shorter. You may cast non-damaging spells on them, and you may renew this casting before the initial one expires. Casting it on your friends probably isn't a good way to win popularity contests.

Flux

Cast: Area of Effect

Type: Stun

Duration: 4 seconds

Effect: This is a stun that radiates out from the caster for fifteen feet. It will stun anyone who means the caster harm within that radius. Does not produce sparkles.

Gate

Cast: Self only

Type: Travel

Duration: N/A

Effect: This will transfer you to your bind point.

Invisibility

Cast: Self or others

Type: Buff

Duration: 10 minutes or until broken/seen through

Effect: Causes generic invisibility. Undead don't count. Will drop if you cast a spell or take damage.

Fear

Cast: Area of Effect

Type: Brief Loss of Control

Duration: 25% of level in seconds.

Effect: Causes enemies to flee from you in terror. But if you use it too soon, it'll probably just look like they misplaced something for a second.

Grinning at the humorous tone to the descriptions, she placed them in one hand while overlaying the other, one at a time in order to absorb them. Her runes flared up like a thousand fairy lights beneath her skin, completely mesmerizing in their own way.

Gate took five seconds to cast. If shit hit the fan, she could Flux the mobs around her and hope she got Gate off in time.

"Sounds like a plan." She muttered. Glancing at Jibartik, she realized he was still level three. It was a pity, since he'd been such a good little not-quite-sentient companion. With a sad sigh, she began casting Minor Animation again and he disappeared with a pop, only to be replaced by an identical Jibartik at level four. She wasn't about to complain. Down to five tiny swords though.

The sun finally dipped beneath the horizon, bathing the mountain region in a deep red and gold light, heralding the coming of night, and leaving Murmur stuck in a marginally safe corner while the ground around her rumbled.

As if in synch with dusk, Sinister sent messages that flitted across Murmur's sight before she could read them. Several others flashed across her vision, but she dismissed them, trying to see what the sand and ash spitting ground was going to cough up.

Amidst the small volcano eruptions of sand, finger bones escaped the ground, clutching at the dirt as they dug through. If they'd had flesh left on them, those fingers would be bloody nubs right now. Next came the full hands, and the forearms, digging from the earth, tearing a way through. Skeletons pulled themselves up and out of the ground in a rain of dirt. Seven of them shuffled disjointedly in place. If this was up here, she shuddered to contemplate the sewers.

Their eye sockets gleamed with a dull orangey red, and a faint yellow glow pulsated around them as if they'd been brought forth by magic, but were tenuously held together. Their levels didn't comfort her either. At level six, they were two entire levels above her. Murmur had naively assumed that her mother's warnings about mobs at night, meant out in the leveling areas. She eyed the distance between the skeletons, and tsked under her breath. There was no way she was going to be able to pull these one at a time. Damn it, she'd have to Mez one of them in order to pull the other single, and all with her brilliant conjuration skill being at level two, she had to hope they didn't resist her too much.

Her first attempt at Mesmerize fizzled, but luckily didn't draw attention to her. It did however raise conjuration by one. Joy for small mercies. Her second attempt hit the skeleton, leaving it swaying as the one close to it turned and spied Murmur just as she cast her suffocation spell. She only managed to get two ticks of the DoT in before it reached her, and that spell had increased in damage too.

While Jibartik smashed feebly for three damage a pop, Murmur kept the Mez counter in mind and smashed the skeleton with her staff, hitting it where its neck should be. When twenty seconds were up, she crossed her fingers and hoped the spell wouldn't fail again. Luckily her re-mesmerization was successful, and shortly thereafter, the first skeleton fell into a pile of bones at her feet. Her health was down a third, with Jibartik left with only a half when the Mez broke on the second skeleton. DoT-ing it, they began the process again. At the end of it all Jibartik had a sliver of life left, and Murmur was cursing that the game wouldn't let her heal herself. Still, with a bit more practice, it should get easier. After all, she could have broken the Mez with the suffocation spell and—

She'd almost forgotten to loot.

There was just so much to keep in line when playing the enchanter. But its defensive capabilities seemed like they could be phenomenal.

There was nothing on the skeletons except bones, a couple of silver, a staff, and some well-worn cloth boots that were a definite upgrade from what she was wearing. She glanced at them with distaste but ended up shrugging and pulling them on. Waste not, want not. The blasted skeletons hadn't dropped whatever she needed for the prompts to vaguely guide her in a new direction. Murmur rubbed her arms and chest. Bruises might not be life threatening, but damned if she didn't feel beat up for the duration it took her health to tick back to full.

She moved around the empty lot as her health regenerated, and waited a minute before pulling the next two. After another ninety minutes of this, another meal, and only her weird sort of prismatic sight for a guide, Murmur had almost had it. Sure, now she had bracers, pants, a belt, and even a pair of fingerless gloves, but she didn't have her freaking quest update.

From Sinister: STOP IGNORING ME

"Shit." Murmur forgot she'd closed the chat earlier. *Sorry! So sorry. I got caught up in this weird quest-like thing.*

From Sinister: It's either a quest or it's not. Anyway. I'm almost at level 5, and I think the others are too. We've been at this for hours. Are you like hungry for real food? Because I don't even care about soda right now.

Murmur paused, thinking hard. No, she wasn't hungry at all. At least her stomach wasn't giving her any signs. But it had been at least six real world hours so she was hungry and should eat soon. And pee. And—oh shit, what the fuck was spawning in the middle of the lot? *Gotta go, chat shortly,* she sent to her friend.

She considered the monster in front of her. It was definitely a skeleton, but much larger than the ones she'd been fighting, and there were no other respawns on the lot. This conned a deep orange, which meant her spells would hit it, if only just. A plan began to form in her mind and she threw caution to the wind, figuring the worst that could happen was character death.

She cast her DoT, which sent Jibartik running out toward the mob. They clashed while the second tick happened, and Murmur moved toward it, staff at the ready. The mob was strong, and took down about twelve percent of Jibartik's health with every hit. Murmur cast Flux, stunning the skeleton while Jibartik executed two of its attacks. She hit it again with her staff, and it switched its attention to her while her pet wailed feebly on it from behind.

Her arm stung like mad where its sword slashed her, blood trickling to pool realistically on the ground. Jumping back, Murmur checked her spells. Flux hadn't refreshed yet, but Mez was available. She cast it on the target, causing the monster to pause for only a couple of short seconds before Jibartik and another tick of her DoT hit it, but even that was a good respite. Her pain receptors didn't seem to realize it was a game, and her body felt like a pin cushion as they continued. Each slash from the skeleton threatened to interrupt her concentration, but she bit her lip and fought through. Juggling between recasting Minor Suffocation, Flux, meleeing the thing with her staff, and Mezing for some brief respite, while her pet feebly bashed on the skeleton's back, Murmur slowly whittled the skeleton down.

When it finally fell, her hit points sat at twelve. Jibartik was full health, having not drawn aggro back after she pulled it from him. Her mana bar was perilously low. The pain in her body made it difficult to think, and all she wanted to do was fall down with the skeleton.

You have slain a Fallen Guard.

You are the first to slay a Fallen Guard.

You gain experience.

Murmur leaned forward while her health and mana slowly ticked up, and looted the skeleton. On it, she found a pair of earrings that were greyed out to her, a sword, one gold, and a letter.

This letter is written in a script you do not recognize. Only one word on the front of it is legible. It seems another visit to your trainer is in your best interest.

"Fan-fucking-tastic."

CHAPTER SIX

Delivery Service

Storm Corp
Storm Technologies Division Experimental Neuroscience Division
Countdown: Two years before Somnia Online implementation

One of the most irritating things about Dr. Michael Jeffries' headgear was its current reliance on a suitable artificial intelligence unit to interpret and extrapolate on the data it received. Appearances meant nothing, and his lacking engineering skills definitely made the headgear rough and rudimentary, but the programing, the tying it to the neural results it pulled—that was his accomplishment. Only the AIs weren't being intuitive enough.

He grumbled over them, irritated to the extreme. Neuroscience was his main passion. That was where he had his doctorate. Sadly, he needed some programming skills in order to implement his ideas, to prove his theories, and yet after a decade of having it as a side pursuit, he still felt his skills were sorely lacking in that area.

Jeffries had to knuckle down. The AIs and the synchronization with the headgear was tantamount to accessing the information he needed, no, the information he craved. No one else needed to know it, but in order for him to keep it a secret, he also needed to delve further into bringing his artificial intelligence units up to the standard he needed.

Frowning, he tweaked their algorithms further. They needed to be able to extract the data from the headsets. That data in turn had to trip a zillion different ifs and whens, match up with memories and actions, preferences and emotions. And then they could begin what on the surface seemed like a given sorting.

It would further their ability to grasp situations, to evaluate emotions, and to understand some of the intricacies involved in human decision making, including but not limited to that horrible human propensity for hiding their real selves behind a socially acceptable mask. Minds hid so much from the outside world. Michael wanted to be able to reach into those thoughts and pluck them out. The amount of information needed to generate the ideal path for people's personalities to take was something Michael didn't think a human brain could fully grasp.

Luckily he wasn't dealing with the human brain having to interpret the signals. The only real use for the actual human brains was as lab rats.

Release Day: Somnia Online

Murmur finally made it out of the Alleyway and traipsed to the Enchanter Guild. Even though six hours had passed in the real world since she initially logged in, the game had covered half a day, and it felt like it. Her limbs ached, and her throat felt parched despite having drunk the weird game water. Her health bar had almost refilled itself with innate regeneration as she pushed into the guild, glancing at the counter with a frail smile for Elvita.

She quickly sent a message to Sinister, who'd apparently learned some patience since starting the game. *Sorry for disappearing. Boss for the quest spawned, almost killed me, feeling like mincemeat.*

Sinister replied immediately: No shit! I feel like crap! Actually, at least I can heal myself, but I'm all alone, even though Havoc is a dark elf too! He could have come and grouped with me. Kiting doesn't really work as a Blood Mage, just fyi.

Pushing her way through the crowd of enchanters, Murmur laughed as she read the message. Havoc was an odd duck, and would probably be a little less predictable as a necromancer. Belius' door stood cracked, and after a moment, an enchanter exited and pulled it shut. It was the only other enchanter Murmur had seen in Belius' area.

If she was reading the consideration system correctly, then the person was two levels below her, and therefore level two. The system worked different than in other games. She shrugged and knocked on the door herself.

Belius pulled it open, his mouth agape, and his eyes much darker than she'd seen before. There was a tension surrounding him she'd not yet witnessed and she had to stop herself from taking a step back. But his expression changed when he focused on her.

"Oh, Murmur, come in, come in. My, my," he said as he closed the door behind her. "You've come a long way, and look at you keeping your thoughts far quieter this time around. I'd actually have to put effort in if I wanted to read your mind."

"It's not like you gave me pointers." Murmur could tell tiredness was coming through in her tone, but Belius didn't seem to mind. Instead, he just chuckled in his jovial way.

"I have a letter for you." She knew she was being irritable, but that last mob had really taken it out of her. And yet, she didn't hate being an enchanter like she'd expected to. So many tools at her disposal.

"Excellent." Belius held out a hand for it. "I expect you'll be joining up with your friends soon, won't you?"

How the hell did he know that? Did the AI delve through the logs as well? She frowned. "Yeah. Obsidian Forest."

Belius clapped his hands together much like Elvita had done earlier.

DING! The sound made her literally jump.

You have gained Level 5!

You have ten (10) training points

You have four (4) stat points

Belius chuckled and his starry eyes twinkled merrily. "You were very close. I'm glad I could help. Now, on to more serious things."

You have delivered the letter to Belius. You should make your way to a ruin in the Obsidian Forest before anyone else beats you there. You will find another voice, another clue, and much danger. Beware of the undead at night, for their power can multiply.

Murmur sighed. "Great."

"You don't seem happy?" Belius' tone reminded her of her mother, and she squinted at the NPC wondering if he'd been created by her.

"I'm frustrated."

"Why?"

"This isn't like other games."

"No, it isn't." Belius' smile was kind, but his starry eyes were full of steel. The juxtaposition sent chills up her spine. "This is a world. This is *our* world. And nothing here is quite the same as anywhere else."

Murmur pondered that for a moment, wondering at the distinctly non-linear quest line up, at the way she hadn't run into any other player while camping for her mobs. It definitely was different. "Maybe that's a good thing."

"Definitely." He responded. "Don't forget to train, my dear."

Damn it. She'd almost done that again. Her Divination was low and she needed that for illusions and stuns, so she placed five points into that, bringing it up to twelve. Then she decided that being able to use daggers was a good option, just in case she found one that could out damage her staff, so she put another five into her one-handed piercing to bring it up to sixteen.

"You're putting stat points into Constitution, Intelligence, and Charisma, I see?" Belius' tone was even, with a hint of judgment behind it.

"Yes." Murmur crossed her arms defensively.

"A good strategy for the lower levels I'm sure, but I'm not sure you should stick to it all the way through."

"Obviously." She grinned at him. "I did do some research, not to mention the whole following my gut thing."

Belius smiled. "Well, it worked out rather well for both of us last time, didn't it?"

It was Murmur's turn to smile. "I'd like another set of seven tiny swords please."

Belius obliged, taking the silver coin from her with a thoughtful look on his face. "Don't forget. Keep an eye out for anything that seems out of the ordinary. Times in Somnia are trying at best right now. You never know when you may need knowledge above all else."

"Thanks for being cryptic, Bel." Murmur laughed, and closed the door behind her just as words scrolled in front of her eyes again.

Because of your personal charm, and ability to talk to people without hiding your motives, Belius has grown fond of you. Make sure to heed him and pay extra attention to the goings-on around you, just in case something crops up.

Another vague to end all vagues. It was starting to grow on her.

Murmur needed to take care of one more thing. Since the foyer was still quite crowded, though not as much as earlier, she walked up to Elvita with a smile. "Hey Elvita, how goes it?"

"Well, thank you, Murmur. What can I do for you?" The lady was elegant and sweet, so Murmur thought she'd try her luck.

"I need somewhere to look over my gear without taking over your counter or dropping my stuff everywhere."

Elvita laughed. "That is kind of you. Few people take my business into account when sorting their goods. Take this table back here." She motioned to a small round table that had three chairs positioned around it. It sat in a tiny alcove between the kitchen and the counter.

"Oh, thank you." Relief washed over Murmur. She took the few short steps to work her way behind the counter and to the table. Emptying her inventory onto it, she began to sort. Touching the things just made it easier to sort through than trying to navigate a small menu in the field of her vision, plus, it added to the level of reality Somnia exhibited. Sixty-five spider legs. Forty-seven rat ears. Seventeen skeleton bones. Twelve venom sacs, eighteen rat tails, four staves, three clubs, and six daggers. Not to mention her money—one gold, twenty-six silver, and fifty-eight copper. She eyed the ruby earrings in her hand. They weren't greyed out anymore, and they were beautiful.

Small Ruby Earrings

> HP +10 Mana +10
>
> Weight .01
>
> Level 5

"Wow." She breathed out in front of her. At least she had some decent stats to head to the forest with.

After selling her haul for eight gold and change, she kept the bones for her friend Evan who was playing a necromancer. She went back to visit Arvin and cooked a ton of spider legs, enough that the skill greyed out at cooking level twenty. That left her with over seventy of them, enough for a few of her group she knew would have just bought vended stuff. Another gold's worth of water and Murmur was ready to set out.

She pulled up her chats, realizing she hadn't messaged back anyone but Sinister and Devlish.

Heading out to Obsidian Forrest. Meet you all there. Stick to the path, try not to travel during the game night. Trust me on that.

She looked up at the sky, realized it was nine in the evening in-game, and sent another message to Sinister.

Actually, I'm going to take a bit of a break. I think I might need to pee.

Logging out of the game, Wren's vision swam. Her augmented reality set booted up as she opened her eyes. Tiny spots appeared before her vision, and she took a deep breath before allowing herself to move. Contrary to what she'd expected, her body wasn't stiff. Perhaps a little sore, probably not used to the way the suit stimulated muscle groups, but after a few moments she found it easier to concentrate on her surroundings. Sunlight shone through a gap in her curtains, and she squinted at it. Gently removing her headgear, she placed it on the side table and turned toward Harlow.

Her friend was still in the game world, her eyes rapidly moving beneath the lids. Wren couldn't watch for long; her bladder practically screamed.

Feeling a great relief once she was done, she glanced at the clock in her bedroom as Harlow began to adjust to logging out of the game. Wren moved to close the gap in the curtain, the bright light hurting her eyes. It had been just after nine at night in-game, which meant they'd been there for fifteen in-game hours. With local time at seven-thirty in the morning, that meant a day in the game passed for every twelve hours of real time. So two for one. Hopefully it'd be easy to juggle that way. These next three months before college were going to be so much fun.

"Coffee, Wren. Now." Harlow had a scowl on her face, and Wren raised an eyebrow.

"I'd suggest the toilet first. I'll meet you downstairs."

Panic flitted across Harlow's face as she scrambled off the bed. Wren suppressed a laugh. Hoping her suit would be okay if she wore it downstairs, she headed toward the kitchen for some sustenance, only to encounter both her mother and father conversing in hushed tones. They stood shoulder to shoulder, heads bowed over their coffees discussing something she couldn't hear.

"Hey you two." She said through a yawn as she stretched her arms.

Her mom jumped a touch, and her dad smiled.

"Already done? Hate it that much?" His eyes twinkled. He knew her far too well.

"As if." Wren opened the fridge and pulled out a cold can of coffee. After all, the cold would refresh her and the caffeine would give her that extra boost. It was still release day. No way she wasn't diving back into the game once she'd had some food. "Pit stop. Bathroom break."

Harlow ran down the stairs, not stopping until she pulled open the fridge. "Hi Mr. and Mrs. S. Thanks for letting me stay!" She tugged out a huge can of some energy drink with a monster on the front, snapped it open and started guzzling it down.

Wren grabbed an apple and sat at the table. "You have a break, Mom? Everything going well?"

She tried to keep the concern out of her voice, knowing full well her mom probably wouldn't be sleeping for days with this launch. The company had a lot riding on this game. Considering the technology was rumored to be on the way to being placed into the armed forces, this was pretty big.

Her mom smiled, and Wren could see the worry lines around her eyes that wouldn't quite disappear. "The game launch itself is going flawlessly actually. Any concerns people had about being allocated a class seem to have washed away." She gave a pointed look in Wren's direction.

"Fine. Fine. It's still not what I'm used to, but I'm enjoying the game anyway." *Even if it is a bit confusing.* Wren glanced over at Harlow. "Speaking of which, how are the guys not on our continent getting to Obsidian?"

Harlow was stuffing a piece of jam toast into her mouth. "Shey cashing a ship."

"Ah. I didn't realize they could do that." Wren laughed at the expression on her parent's faces. After thirteen years of friendship, Wren could translate mouth-full-of-food Harlow easily.

Harlow grinned. "Yeah. They got to take one of the smaller ships since their island is close to my city. Means they don't have to go via Pelagu. That city's meant to be huge. They should be there by the time we get back, and then it's just a matter of following the path. With a torch. In the middle of the night."

Wren smiled. "You know that's going to be deadly, right?"

"Yeah, but for them. Not for us." Harlow laughed. "It's easy for us. It's just outside my city, and not too far down the path from yours either. They'll just have to fend for themselves."

They nudged each other, beaming from ear to ear, and Wren gave her parents a kiss on the cheek each before they headed toward the stairs.

"Stay safe!" Wren's mother yelled after them.

But Wren just laughed. "Will do, Mom. You might have made it seem real, but it's only a game."

CHAPTER SEVEN
Together at Last

Storm Corp
Storm Technologies Division Experimental Neuroscience Division
Countdown: Twenty months before Somnia Online implementation

The three main AIs were on board, working far more like Michael intended than they should.

There'd still be a learning curve of course, but that's what the algorithms allowed for. The AIs' learning was part of being able to use the headgear's full potential. He'd even given them names: Sui, Rav, and Thra.

They now understood how the headgear worked, how it adapted, and how and why the arms needed to conform to the scalp. How to send small impulses through to react with the body suits he'd overseen development of. There was so much to do in order to launch the full test, in order to bring what was going to be the largest ever test sample into his reach.

He couldn't remember when he last went home. After all, there was a sofa in his office, as well as a small bathroom. Spending time with his headgear and interfacing with the AIs was a special part of the process. They needed to understand the human brain if they were to function at full capacity and if they were to create the atmosphere needed to give people the ultimate VR experience.

Jessa popped her head around the corner of the server room. It was a huge space, and while servers had shrunk in size over the years, the amount of computing power, of sheer intelligence these AIs would need to perform the tasks required of them was gargantuan. They'd been given their own team room on Michael's insistence. He ignored Jessa.

"Michael. The team is ready for your briefing. We have the neural interface testing today." She did her best to smile at him, but he hadn't been to see her in weeks at this stage. Jessa was a lovely girl, but he couldn't afford to split his attention now. Not ever.

He glanced up at her finally, and for a moment he bit back on the irrational thoughts assaulting his brain before answering.

"Thank you." He waved her away.

Her chest heaved with a suppressed sigh and she left the room, heading back to her desk. Jessa and her friend who worked in game development, Ava, had always been a peculiar pair. Michael watched as the door closed behind his assistant. He knew for a fact that the two girls were probably huddled together discussing just how hurt Jessa had been by her boss. Still, it was a small sacrifice to make for his precious endeavor.

Right now he didn't have time for anything else. The AIs and his headgear held all of his attention.

Release Day: Somnia Online

Back in the game and alone again, Murmur stood at the gates looking back at her city. Under the moonlight, the stone structures glowed with faint pearly phosphorescence. It illuminated the area directly surrounding the wall with a pale light, allowing starter characters to continue their adventures easily and not have to venture too far into the dark world beyond. Pity she couldn't take its brightness with her into the forest.

The thing was, that's sort of how her vision appeared when looking through the dark. Prismatic and glowy.

Double checking her gear and supplies, Murmur brought up the map interface. It had a glow in the middle of unexplored territory in the direction of the path from the city. She figured setting out couldn't hurt. Not too much anyway.

Suddenly a large word popped up in front of her vision: DUEL.

She blinked it away, not caring for it, but it appeared again almost immediately: DUEL.

Angrily, she directed her system to adjust and automatically decline duels. When her vision cleared, she realized there was a bulky locus standing in front of her with a pout. She'd never seen him before that she knew of. His head ridges were far more defined than her own, and he was bald. His head shone like the moon.

"C'mon. Please?" He begged in a whiny voice.

Murmur shook her head. "No thanks. I'm in a hurry."

"No fair." The guy laughed, and then he turned away, probably seeking his next victim, and yelled behind him. "Thanks anyway! Hope the skellies get ya!"

There was always someone who wanted to do nothing but duel. It wasn't Murmur's preferred form of play. If she was going to go player versus player, she wanted full on battles with strategy and plans. Not this strange dueling one on one thing when she was level five.

As she walked down the path, the wind whipped up. It was a cool wind, and her enchanter's robe did little to fend off the chill. She knew there had to be some cloaks in the game, but she wasn't far enough in yet. Her mind wandered as she ventured farther and farther away from the city. The glow of the walls faded, and the path before her crackled with windblown leaves that rushed her way, rustling in the air and as they tussled on the ground, lending an overall spooky vibe that made her shiver. From the small amount of articles she'd read, she knew starter areas like this, that were still bustling with beginner characters, didn't have the night time mob increase. But she still felt queasy at the fact that she might run into mobs a few levels higher than herself.

She strained to listen, really listen, for anything useful. With her two vague quests lined up that gave her no real hints, being observant was one of the few things she had going for her. Come to think of it, she'd always been quite observant. That's how she avoided confrontation at school, even at home when she got fed up with her parents being children more often than she was.

Except she was sick of being exactly what others needed all the time. Maybe this whole enchanter thing was exactly what *she* needed. She tested the staff in her hand, twisting it around thoughtfully. Sure, it was the logical choice for a caster, right? But sharp edges felt so much more rewarding. Maybe daggers were a better choice. Perhaps she could dual class—

A skeleton shattered the earth just off the path in front of her, its gleaming red eyes focused solely on her. It cackled, and stepped forward in that jelly-boned way. It conned yellow, and she stunned it with Flux before casting Minor Suffocation on it. She smacked the shit out of it with her staff as soon as it got close. Maybe it was the mobs she'd been fighting so far, but the blunt thwack of the staff instead of the slice against flesh and the running of blood just didn't pack the same punch. As she fended off a well-aimed slash with her forearm, she hissed in pain before growling deep in her throat, momentary rage fueling her. She whirled the staff around her head before angling it directly into the neck gap with as much force as she could muster. The skeleton toppled to the ground, granting her experience and a small feeling of satisfaction. Glancing up and down the road as she bent to loot the creature, Murmur realized she'd come farther than originally anticipated. The skeleton gave her some bones, 9 copper, and a lovely iron dagger.

Iron Dagger

Damage 6-8

Weight 1

Level 5

This weapon allows you to strike fast and true.

She hefted it in her hand and decided it was worth a try. The road to Obsidian Forest was going to be scary, but damned if she wasn't looking forward to it. A little more wary now, Murmur stopped in the middle of the path, and summoned her animation. Its peaceful bobbing next to her added a layer of security she didn't otherwise feel. Somnia was so real, there could be brigands hiding out here, or even other players just looking to be dicks. It Happened at the best of times. It was hard to believe her physical body lay on the bed back at home, while she was here, feeling the night air, tasting the rain on the wind that the next day would likely bring, so many little things that made the world so real in comparison to what she'd felt before.

Sinister: Are you here yet, are you here yet?

Murmur laughed softly, hoping not to wake anything slumbering nearby. She could see red points glowing in the distance. Tempting the night wasn't something she was willing to do just yet. Maybe in a few more levels.

She replied quickly. *Not yet, I took the left path, so I'm hoping I'll get to you soon. Either that or I'm about to die a spectacular death at the hands of something ten times my level.*

She could almost hear her friend laugh in response.

Sinister: You're good. Don't worry. Left should be it. I think. The others aren't here yet, so I'm twiddling my bloody thumbs.

Bloody expletive or literal?

Sinister: Your pick.

Murmur sighed. It was going to be good to converse with people again. Even though the NPCs were amazingly alive, she'd missed her friends. An owl-like hoot sounded in the distance. She frowned and concentrated.

That could be an owl. Or someone's lookout. Focusing, she tried to sense if there were other people out there. Not by their body heat or noise, but by their thoughts. Whispers flitted close to her mind, darting here and there, almost divulging their secrets before dissipating like a cloud on a sunny day. She put a stop to it before she got a headache, but not before a string of words flitted across her vision.

Hidden skill activated Thought Sensing.

Class: Enchanter only.

Level not applicable.

Effect: Developing your inner senses you've awoken your latent psychic powers. With constant use your skills will increase, while the opposite will occur should the skill not be used. See your trainer for specifics when you reach Thought Sensing (25).

"Guess the dull headache was worth it," she mumbled, rubbing at her temples. Glancing at the in-game clock, she realized she'd already been walking for a bit over an hour. Surely she had to be getting close?

There was movement up ahead, and Murmur readied herself just in case, only to realize it was Sinister. Sinister ran toward her, screaming like an idiot and probably waking every slumbering undead within a two mile radius. She glomped on to Murmur when she reached her, and they both tumbled to the ground laughing.

"You dork. It's not like you're not sitting right next to me."

"I guess you're right." Sinister hesitated a second, then laughed out loud, the sound distinctly her own. "By the way. Your alien ass is fucking hot."

Murmur batted her eyelashes coyly. "Why, thank you."

"Idiot." Sinister punched her in the arm. "I'm just as hot."

Murmur gazed up and down, deliberately slowly. The dark elf was mostly what she expected. Purple-hued smooth skin. Wavy, flowing white hair. Her friend's chest mirrored about a C cup, while the rest of her body seemed toned and fit from what she could see. And Sin had chosen white eyes instead of the habitual red. "Why yes. Yes you are, you sassy little dark elf you."

They hugged again and helped each other up when Sinister looked over Murmur's shoulder and her eyes widened. "You do know there's a disembodied sword and shield at your back, don't you?"

"Yep." Murmur grinned, showing her alien teeth. "We're buddies."

"Ah, so you do have friends then." A familiar voice stopped Murmur in her tracks and she turned around slowly, not entirely trusting her memory.

"Yeah, I do." Murmur stood light on her toes, tensing slightly, shooting Sinister a quick party invite. "Fancy seeing you here, Jirald. At night. An hour away from Stellaein."

Jirald laughed, but the sound rang hollow, like he didn't really mean it. Murmur tensed and waited for him to finish.

"Yeah, I can see how that might look. Sorry. Just meeting some of me mates out here. I was so set on locus. Probably not the best species for a rogue, but you know, I usually play a plate class, so this sneaky shit is a heap of fun." He glanced to the side for a moment, probably scanning through his own HUD for something. "Wow, you really did catch up to me. I've been sprinting most all the way from the city, so you must have hit level five way before me."

Feeling slightly more at ease and watching Sinister size the guy up as well, Murmur put her pet on follow. "Not sure. I had a crazy stupid quest spawn a gazillion respawning monsters on me. Leveled before I knew it."

"You do look rather roguey." Sinister interjected, grinning. "Murmur here is pissed she isn't a healer, but I get to kill shit and heal damage with their life. Cool, huh?"

While she sounded pleasant and hyperactive, Murmur watched Sin's eyes, noticing they never left Jirald's form, scanning him for any untoward movement. Sin might be a nice person to her friends, but she didn't trust strangers. It was one of the things they had in common.

"Blood mage?" Jirald's eyes widened.

Murmur's narrowed, wondering if he was surprised or calculating her damage to heal ratio. Hazard of gaming the way she did, everything was a calculation, everything had a pro and a con.

"Fantastic class. Not sure why I stuck with ranger for so long. Anyway, I'm gonna steal my girlfriend from you, because we have some friends we're supposed to meet up with." Sinister extended her hand and shook Jirald's firmly, her eyes never leaving his face. "Ciao! Gotta run."

Sin grabbed Murmur's hand, yanked on it, and ran down the path, not slowing until their meager stamina bars ran out.

"Keep going," she panted.

Not about to argue, Murmur ran with her after the initial stumble, happy that Jibartik seemed to be keeping pace. After what seemed like forever, they arrived at a humungous log. At some stage the tree must have towered over the forest, but now it was just a huge ass hollow log sitting close to a three-path crossroad, where a lone guard stood beneath the directional sign.

"Meeting them here then?" Murmur scaled the surface by leveraging herself up on a knot in the trunk, and sat, able to watch the surrounding area and potentially approaching mobs at the same time. "So, what was up back there?"

"I could ask you the same thing!" Sin seemed irritated, even angry. "You're way too fucking trusting, Mur."

"Trusting? Me? You have no clue what spells I could cast on that guy if he tried something. Especially at this level where he wouldn't have any resistances to his name." Murmur searched through her inventory for the food she'd made and handed eight spider legs to Sinister. "There. That should keep you going for a while."

"Hey! Thanks." Sinister beamed at her.

Subject successfully changed.

They sat for a few moments, basking in their different views of the world, tinged with whatever colors their eyes made them see at night. Murmur spied dark shapes approaching. Four of them in varying heights. As they came closer she familiar names appeared on her HUD.

"Yo, you two!" Devlish grinned widely, his mouth making him resemble a laughing gecko. His dark green scales glittered with a gold sheen, reflecting the moonlight with iridescence, a hallmark of the lacerta species. Muscles visibly bunched beneath them, their strength obvious. The nose and eyebrow ridges stood out, prominent, which made the cut jawline fade a little into the background. It was just what Darren said he wanted to be. His dread-knight, Devlish, towered as tall as Beastial, about the same height as the locus. The other two were shorter, but one of them not by much.

"Sorry," Murmur called down just before they began climbing up. "We don't want anything today thanks. Gave at the office."

"Smart ass." Devlish turned her around in a huge hug once he made it that far. "I have to say, these locus are freaking gorgeous. If a little eerie to look at."

"Put me down before I stun your ass." But she was smiling. Devlish was a damned good guy. They all were.

Havoc smiled shyly. He was the least boisterous of the group, often overly serious. Evan appeared to be a dark elf necromancer. He never did have the best character imagination, but his go-to name had always been Havoc. Even as a necro, it was nice to have Havoc back. "Hey Mur. See you got your name."

"See you're a dark elf. Again."

His skin was darker than Sin's, almost a purple black, and he'd gone with bright blue eyes. He shrugged. "What can I say? I play what I like."

Sin was glaring at her. "What?"

"Invite them?"

"Oh, shit." A few quick directional thoughts and they'd formed a group of six. If they wanted to add any more, they'd have to form a raid. Murmur went through the group make up. It could be worse, much worse, but it could probably be better too. Still. It was a solid beginning with a good amount of utility and damage.

With her crowd control abilities, they were pretty much guaranteed safety as long as they coordinated their efforts. She'd only glanced at the dread knight class, but knew it was a sort of necro tank. Life leeching should help Devlish maintain aggro, and grab it easily from Merlin when he pulled with a slow shot. Rangers were fantastic at kiting—they could do damage while slowing the mob and keep their distance. Luckily in a group, Merlin wouldn't have to worry as much about ranger gating—or character death, depending how you looked at it.

Havoc's Damage Over Time spells would whittle down the mob's health, but were far more powerful than her own Minor Suffocation considering he probably had at least two. She wasn't sure if he had any direct damage spells, but his pet was about five times stronger than her own, and far more reliable. As for Beastial, his tiger familiar looked fierce, and from what she could remember, he was a martial fighter whose powers boosted with his pet's proximity.

And Sin, she could build power for oh-shit heals to increase her usual heals. As long as she had a target, she could damage it, and return the damage to the group as health. Right now it was single target, but she'd become more powerful over time. Murmur ran through several different sequences in her head, tentatively happy with their group makeup. They were only level five.

As they gained in experience they were going to be very powerful indeed.

"You make the guild yet?" Merlin interrupted her thoughts, his blond hair seriously out of place in the haunted forest. He'd stubbornly chosen the name he always used. It was probably going to confuse the hell out of people who saw his class first. His hair was braided tightly into a low ponytail at the nape of his neck, and his bright baby blues completed Merlin's go to appearance. She wondered if he meant to look like a pointed-eared version of himself.

Murmur raised an eyebrow. "I'm not made of money. The guild charters are what, ten gold? Pitch in, slackers. And I'm not fucking recruiting. I did it last time, and I just don't like people."

Sinister laughed. "Fine, fine. I'll recruit, but you have to raid lead."

"You can't recruit. You hate people as much as I do. And fuck that shit." Murmur's irritation rose so much that she put her hands on her hips and scowled. She knew it was a very odd expression on a locus, having seen the expression on locus she'd passed in her city. It made her sort of look like she was half-snarling, half-laughing. "Dev can lead the raid. I'll—how about we level first?"

Beastial laughed for the first time. And while it was definitely Selwyn's voice, there was a guttural tone behind it. His whole chest moved with the action, several deep red tattoos rippling while he did. He looked like a cross between the Terminator and Rambo, complete with the shoulder length brown hair. Tall, with the physique of a gym rat, a long braid hung down his back. Selwyn was stubborn, he'd wanted to play his tank and yet beastmaster was his class. Seems like he'd compromised by choosing to be a viking.

She wasn't sure if it was appealing or not. "Let's get cracking. We have what, six or seven in-game hours left before the sun comes up and we lose the level-boosted mobs?"

They all nodded.

"Awesome. Let's kill some shit."

Killing a few low level beetles that scurried around them as they walked, they made their way to a nice clearing that was a decent chunk of the way from the path so that any patrolling guards didn't interfere, and yet close enough that they could run for help if they fucked up. Getting ready for a pure grinding session, Murmur handed everyone eight of her spider legs. "You better have bought drinks for yourselves, you lazy bastards."

Dev and Beastial sidled up against her. "Thanks, Mur." They crooned.

She rolled her eyes. "Stop it."

They laughed and moved away, but not before Devlish squeezed her shoulder briefly in reassurance.

Murmur glanced around at the available enemies, just out of combat range. The skeletons in this forest seemed much bigger than the ones she'd fought before. None were below level eight. There were even a few red ones, which were undoubtedly level ten. "We're still in the level five to ten safe zone, right?"

Havoc scanned around them and nodded. "We're close to the ten to fifteen, which means the mobs will be anything from eleven to twenty at night over there. So we'll have to steer clear of that."

Devlish glanced around warily. "Probably a good idea." He seemed nervous; he'd not played a tank before. But he was a good player with an analytical style, so Murmur wasn't worried. She winked at him, trying to convey her confidence in him.

"I can pull with my DoT, as long as you taunt them when they run past you." Murmur offered. It would be easier to keep a stream of monsters coming if someone other than the tank pulled.

"Let's give it a shot." Devlish set his jaw, determination overtaking the nervousness. "I can drain a bit of the mob's health, Sin. I should be a last healing priority."

"Got it." Sin buffed the group with a strange blood leeching buff, while the rest of them loaded self buffs. "Pull."

"Actually." Murmur paused. "Fuck that. Merlin, you pull. You're a freaking ranger."

Everyone laughed and Merlin took aim sheepishly. "Thought I'd avoided responsibility. Incoming!"

Butterflies of excitement flew around Murmur's stomach. This was the way games were meant to be played. With a group of trusted players, battling against foes that could slay you singly in a heartbeat. Talk about an adrenaline rush.

Off they went.

The level eight skeleton never stood a chance, neither did the level nines they pulled. Even so, nine was four levels higher than they were, and orange cons could resist a lot of spells. After about six mobs, the group fell into a rhythm.

Merlin pulled with a slowing shot that delivered the mob at the perfect moment to Devlish's taunt. Dev then used his meager blood drain, and whaled on it with precise hits. Both Murmur and Havoc DoT-ed the mob, and their pets ran into the fray. The thing was, Murmur's pet wasn't the best at anything. It was sort of useless actually, even if its bobbing in place was kind of calming.

At some stage Murmur remembered to trade her small bones to Havoc for his pet. His answering smile was worth it.

Beastial was fun to watch. His cat jumped in and they worked in tandem to take down the skeleton. The thing was, Murmur was quite certain, that the cat and melee combat combo would go over much better when the foe they were fighting had an Achilles tendon for the cat to tear at. They worked in symmetry though, and mobs this small were at least good for everyone to practice on. Learning a class took time, and the earlier the basics were mastered, the better.

In the meantime, Sinister's spell leeched life from the skeleton. Murmur was skeptical about this part of the process considering their opponent. Little clouds of blood floated between the skeleton and Sin's hands, eventually to whomever she needed to heal. While it looked gory, it was something Mur wished she'd been able to try out. Perhaps the blood in this case stood for life force. While they finished off the mob in camp, Merlin scouted for more.

When they got two, Murmur Mesmerized the one farthest away and redirected her pet to the nearest. For a few seconds Jibartik got stuck between mobs, in a sort of indecisive sway. Mana ticked slowly, but it was rare anyone needed to sit. The group make up was fun, less mechanical than previous games, and yet smooth.

After almost three hours of in-game time, Murmur dinged level six, with Havoc and Beastial close behind.

"You hit like a girl, Mur." Dev laughed as she resummoned her pet.

"Better than hitting like an idiot."

"Burned you." Beastial howled.

Dev groaned. "She did not. That was the lamest comeback ever."

Merlin laughed. "No, *that* was the lamest comeback ever."

Beastial was still laughing. "You let a girl burn you so bad!"

Mur smacked him across the back of his head. "Enough with that girl shit. Next time use: you let a kickass enchanter burn you so bad. Got it?"

"Sure thing, Mur." Beastial winked at her and she rolled her eyes.

Murmur had missed her friends and their group dynamic. She supposed they were going to insist on making the guild. All of them were control freaks to some degree. They wanted to get to and take down the biggest baddest shit they could before anyone else. She knew without even having to ask that all of them planned on finding those twelve keys and whatever they unlocked before anyone else did. It was just something they reveled in. The challenge of leveling successfully and efficiently, and the added bonus of rising to an even greater challenge in the content that awaited them.

Her casting abilities increased, as did her weaponry. Her daggers skill reached higher than thirty, and she began straining to listen again and utilize her hidden skill, even though she still wasn't certain how to go about it. The thing was, Murmur wasn't overly eager to hear what her friends thought, and they were the only ones currently close by.

As five o'clock in the morning approached in-game, so did level seven. Level fives began venturing into the area too, obviously looking to level as well. They emerged from the dark elf starting area, Nocturn. Most of them seemed surprised as they waved from the path that led to the guard. Few of them had full groups. It was a hint Mur was glad her mom had given. Group. Group. Group.

Once everyone was level seven, they moved a little deeper, hoping to keep their current skeletons and nab a few level tens. For a couple of hours everything seemed to be going well. The sun rose and was visible in the smatterings of light leaking through the leaves of the trees, and with the addition of numerous level tens, Murmur noticed their experience proceeding well.

All at once, she glanced at the in-game clock and realized it was already nine-thirty in the morning. They'd been playing for over six real hours again, almost fourteen in total. She laughed. Traveling in the game might be a tad too realistic.

"Guys, going to have to take a potty break in a bit."

"Seriously, Mur," Dev muttered, smashing in the side of a skeleton's skull, before it tumbled to the ground in a jumble of bones. "Your bladder has issues."

She laughed, watching the experience bar inch its way toward level eight. Sin and Dev had their DINGs, and just as they were pushing ten-thirty, Mur dinged too.

"Finally!" She yelled out, but no sooner had the words left her mouth, than her activated hidden skill picked up something right on the edge of her range. A panicked screaming, internally, something akin to *ohshitohshitohshit*. She caught glimpses of about twelve massive skeletons chasing after a ranger who obviously fucked up.

"Shit. Guys. Train incoming."

"What?" Dev turned to her. He seemed confused and she didn't have time to explain. "Where?"

"There." She indicated the direction and dismissed her pet. "We need to run now. You don't even get how big that train is."

"What are you talking about, Mur?" Sin shook her head. "What's this sixth sense you suddenly have?"

"Oh my god, Sin. You've known me long enough. Just fucking trust me—"

Too late. Her party mates gasped as the skeletons became visible through the trees, a whole freaking army of them.

The ranger ran straight toward their camp screaming out a *sorry* in his wake, as another poor single player soul fell under the rush of the skeleton's wrath.

Murmur yelled: "RUN!" and turned tail hoping the others headed toward the guard with her. If she lost her level, she was going duel that ranger into oblivion.

CHAPTER EIGHT

Train Wreck

Storm Corp
Storm Technologies Division Experimental Neuroscience Division
Countdown: Eighteen months before Somnia Online launch

Michael frowned at the information scrolling in front of his vision. He recalibrated and restarted the system. The scans were slightly different through each AI.

Rav tended toward the more compassionate, Sui was definitely more brutal, and Thra erred just this side of manipulation. These were the forerunner AIs that he'd been working with for years now. They were to run the entire Somnia Online payload, though the company also had sub AIs that would assist them. But a weird sort of itching started in the back of Michael's mind. Some people might call it a conscience.

He shook his head and dismissed the sensation. After all, the whole point of this operation was not only to read the minds of humans and find out their true strengths, even ones they didn't know themselves, but to develop an AI capable of interpreting and acting according to each person's individual make up. The sheer possibilities this presented for future undertakings was infinite.

"Run diagnostic Three-C, Rav." Michael decided to try again. Perhaps his own thoughts tended to influence how they read him, which would indeed be fascinating. Yet another avenue he could explore and tweak for.

There was a gentle whir, followed by a soft, slightly metallic voice. "Diagnostic Three-C results in tune with previous scannings. Suggested course of action is the medical technology field. Although, might I suggest in the terms of Somnia, you would make an excellent rogue, Dr. Jeffries."

Michael blinked at the machine. It allocated him a class. "We're not in the game, Rav, I don't need a class allocation."

There was a brief pause in the soft whirr. "You are not currently in Somnia, but you will be. Therefore the class allocation is correct."

Dr. Jeffries frowned again, and a thought crossed his mind. "Rav. Sui. Thra. What is your prime purpose?"

Sui answered first, its voice taking on a sinuous metallic echo. "To determine which roles humans or other species perform best in."

"To read their lives and make the decision they may not know as best for them." Thra's voice was higher, yet hollow at the same time.

Rav's answer took a few seconds, "To make sure each candidate is allocated for the best usage of their abilities, regardless of their original goal."

Michael opened his mouth to speak, but Rav's fans whirred loudly for a moment, and the AI continued unprompted. "But mental well-being must be taken into account. The human brain is electrical and yet not logical. There are more determining factors than you have given us."

Dr. Jeffries slowly removed the headgear from his head, frowning at it and his artificial intelligence units. "People aren't known for doing what is best for them. Many think they know, but are in fact, wrong."

"Acceptable." Sui intoned like the gong of a final bell.

Just as Michael was about to heave a small sigh of relief, Thra spoke. "For now."

Release Day: Somnia Online

Murmur could still hear the ranger's *oh shit* mantra as she booked it toward the guard. She could see Merlin and Havoc ahead of her, and hear Beastial and Devlish slowly catching up to her, but Sin... Sin was much farther behind.

"Fuck!" Murmur yelled. "Havoc, grab my target and send your pet to distract them so Sin can catch up."

Havoc nodded, obviously conserving breath, which was an example she'd be wise to follow. Dying wasn't the end of everything, but it sure as hell was inconvenient. With the time it took to level, losing any amount of experience was a pain in the ass, and they weren't even in double figures yet.

At least Devlish had the foresight to yell into the area chat as they passed the log they'd initially met on—whether anyone had them enabled or not was another thing—*Train to Log guard. Clear a path.*

Clamping down on her own thoughts, Murmur remembered Belius saying anybody could be listening and cast her thought sensor out again, trying to gauge the skeletons. Except undead didn't think, did they?

Since they'd moved farther into the forest, to access the higher level skeletons, the guard seemed to be an age away. Even running with sprint as time allowed, she could sense the skeletons gaining on them. And all of them conned red. What did she want her tombstone to say?

Sin, for all her outgoing personality, wasn't really an outdoors person.

"Damn it!" She heard Sin, barely, and the expletive followed shortly by a message. *I'm rooted. Literally. I'm so fucked.*

Havoc reached the sign first just as the guard sensed danger and jogged toward the incoming undead. Beastial, Devlish, and Merlin made it before Mur too. The ranger who started it all, rested against the sign post, eyes downcast, bent down gasping for air with his hands on his knees. Murmur arrived a few seconds later, panting and leaning over, clutching her legs in a way that mirrored the training ranger. Her chest felt tight and her lungs gasped for air. She straightened, looking out at where the guard had run to slaughter the skeletons.

And Sin's healthbar went black.

Murmur rounded on the ranger. "You idiot! What the fuck did you train right through our group for? What a dick move. You should have died. You're only fucking five."

Havoc put a hand on her shoulder, exuding an odd aura of calm, and Murmur shut her thoughts down again, forcing herself to breathe. It was like he'd momentarily shared his ability to be level headed.

"I'm sorry." The ranger still looked at the ground. "I panicked. It just felt so real."

Sinister: Fucking shit, fucking goddamn it. Can you drag my corpse to the log? I need to get my shit back, and now I'm like 3% from level. Not fucking cool.

Sin lit up the group chat and her friends collectively cringed.

Havoc turned to the ranger, his calm voice holding a trace of cold anger. "Our healer died thanks to that train. Next time? Don't panic."

Murmur scanned the surrounds, but the only thoughts she could pick up were the ranger's self-recrimination. She sighed and managed to force the words from her lips. "It's a game. Just try not to spoil it for others in the future."

Your hidden skill Thought Sensing has increased in strength. Current status: Thought Sensing (7).

Hidden Skill Activated Thought Shielding.

Class: Enchanter only.

Level not applicable.

Developing your inner senses has awoken your latent psychic powers. With frequent use your skills will increase, while the opposite will occur should the skill not be used. See your trainer for specifics when you reach Thought Shielding (25).

Your hidden skill Thought Shielding has increased in potency. Current status: Thought Shielding (4)

Murmur frowned as the information scrolled across her screen. She checked her combat log for previous increases realizing the AI must acknowledge when its player was in a difficult situation or something, because it hadn't given her alerts for the other increases. She liked that element. Maybe she could make it permanent, for everything except chat, which flashed at the bottom anyway. She directed her thoughts toward the HUD to make sure no updates—except level increase—would flash across the screen during combat.

How long is it going to take you to get back here? She sent in the party window.

Sinister: Well, I'm about a third of the way there, so another twenty minutes or so? It's closer to Nocturn. Is that ranger still there? Can I kill him?

Havoc: You can't kill him. But it's okay. Mur already scared him with her cussing.

Murmur shot him a glare, but Havoc just smiled back at her.

"We need to get her back to level eight." Merlin's eyes were distant as he spoke. Anyone could multitask with this set up.

"Three percent shouldn't take too long. Maybe she can get the mob's health down past fifty percent and then we can kill it the rest of the way for her. She should get solo experience then, right?" Devlish glanced at each of them, his lizard brow raised. "Might be faster that way?"

Murmur shook her head. "Probably not. While she can damage, she'll have to trade that with healing herself too. Probably not the best strategy for cloth wearers."

"Point." Beastial shrugged. "I should have bound somewhere else. Once we head to Nocturn to train for level eight, we'll bind there."

Murmur opened her spell list and frowned. A new message was scrawled across the top. *Please meet with Belius before acquiring your next spells. Your path requires revision.*

Weird. Murmur scanned down the list, but nothing was greyed out or seemed to be removed. She pulled up her character information, frowning. Still the same old locus enchanter, level eight. What on earth did the message mean? Her Thought Sensing hadn't reached twenty-five yet, so that wasn't it. Of course, it was never going to reach twenty-five if she didn't use it.

Still leafing through her character data, she activated Thought Sensing with a blink of her eyes, adding her Thought Shield for her own mind as an afterthought. The latter should be easier to level up. After all, if thoughts could really be heard by potentially dangerous characters, getting the skill to a level where she didn't need to think about it was practically a necessity.

"Here." Sin arrived finally, panting, and making Murmur wonder, yet again, just how the game created that reaction in their minds. Seemed the AI was a bit of an enchanter itself.

Murmur placed a hand on Sin's shoulder, squeezing it to lend comfort as her friend bent down to loot the corpse Beastial had retrieved for her. The pale purple body on the ground was indeed lifeless. Perhaps too realistic for Murmur's tastes.

"I would have been so pissed if I lost that ring." She announced on standing up. Glancing at Havoc, she paused. "When can you use coffins?"

He blinked and his expression grew thoughtful for a moment, and he cringed. "Level twenty-nine. Let's not lose a corpse somewhere we can't retrieve it before then, okay? Because I can't summon them until then."

Devlish laughed. "I like this plan. Let's go get Sin her level back?"

They headed out toward the skeleton fields in the thick of the forest. Luckily, no one had taken their spot yet. It wasn't like they could slam a sign into the ground claiming it as theirs, after all.

Murmur's body seemed so far away, like the real world was the dream and the game their reality. It had taken Sin forty in-game minutes, twenty real minutes to reach them, and by the time they got back into a rhythm, it was past midday in-game, making it around three in the afternoon in the real world. Surely they had to be hungry, right? It's not like in game food was real, but she couldn't feel any hunger pangs. Murmur frowned at the thought, mechanically allowing her pet to attack, and watching it for a change in target. Sometimes it was very stupid, nothing like the undead Havoc raised.

"Loving the patchwork look there, Dev." Beastial grinned as he sent his huge cat to pull the Mez'd target back to the group. "Guess these bags of bones are useful for something."

Devlish grunted—his usual way of communication while concentrating. Murmur knew he'd be more talkative and fun once he got used to his class. He'd never been a tank before, to her knowledge.

"The lack of named mobs is irritating, though." Merlin scowled, annoyance evident in his voice. "Or maybe we've just been spoiled by too many named in other games."

"I still want to duel that idiot." Sin's tone was strained with barely concealed anger. Murmur decided to keep an eye on her friend. After all, when Sin went into a rage, she was the epitome of the redheaded stereotype. Good thing it happened rarely.

When the DING finally came, they all did a little dance. It hadn't been too long, just another thirty real minutes, but it felt like an age. They began making their way back to the lone safe spot in the area. Well, safeish.

"Should we meet back here in what? Four in-game hours?" Havoc ventured.

Murmur closed her eyes, calculating in her head. "No. Let's make it three. That's one and a half real hours. I know we'll need to make it back to here, but all I need is my spells before I head back. And a real world break."

Sin stood with her hands on her hips. "You realize it's thirty to forty minutes to Nocturn, and forty minutes back to the log. Training, and figuring out shit will probably take another forty in-game minutes. That only leaves us with thirty minutes of real time out of game. Don't be so stingy, Mur."

She raised her hands. "Fine. Fine. Two hours it is then. I just didn't want to waste that much in-game daylight. But I know I for one am seriously hampered by a lack of level eight spells."

Devlish laughed and playfully punched her in the arm. "Mur. We've got our group back. As long as it's us, it doesn't matter if we're playing during the night, right?"

He did have a point.

"I guess so."

Arriving at the sign post, Murmur began to cast Gate for the first time.

Murmur appeared almost instantaneously, smack bang in front of the Enchanter Guild. She frowned, having thought the spell would take her to the city gates. With a shrug she headed into the guild.

"Hey there, Elvita," she called out to the NPC.

"Murmur. Great to see you back. Belius is waiting for you." Her smile was genuine, and while her tone fell just short of urgency, Murmur took the hint.

The press of people really got to her. Bodies brushed up against her own, and she tested the shielding around her thoughts, finally able to sense the barricade as a tangible sort of thing. At least as tangible as invisible barriers in her mind went. She'd have to check the stats for it at some stage.

As she elbowed her way through to the back hall, she cast out a net, sifting for thoughts that were out of the ordinary. Nothing stood out. Just complaints about loot, gear, and having to go to work for eight hours a day. Most of those thoughts sort of blended together into a general sentiment rather than words. Murmur chuckled as she knocked on Belius' door.

This time it took a minute or so for him to answer, and he did so just as she was about to knock for the second time. Pushing the door open, she glanced around. Belius stood, rummaging through his bookcase and glanced back at the door only briefly before continuing.

"Murmur. Good to see you. Give me just a moment; I've had to adjust a few things." He finally straightened and turned to face her, his usual smile gone. In its place was one of the most thoughtful expressions she'd ever seen. It felt like he was trying to see through her, or perhaps into her. She tightened the shield, willing it to thicken.

The result was unexpected.

Belius' eyes widened with surprise as a huge grin spread over his face. "Why, you've activated it! Come here, let me see." He continued motioning her to come over.

She stood in front of him, not entirely sure what he was doing until she felt a slight pressure against the shield, like he was probing her thoughts. With a scowl, she strengthened it as much as she could.

"So you've got the shielding, and the sensing, I think?" His eyes sparkled with a joy that was infectious, making her proud and happy all at once.

"Well, yeah. I mean. I kept trying to think my thoughts closed, and suddenly I could?" She laughed a little self-depreciatingly, and then glared at him. Hand-holding was a pain in the ass, but vague hints weren't much better. "It's not like you gave me any hints."

"Ah, my dear," Belius tapped his head with his slender forefinger. "But I did. And you chose not to ignore my hints however vague they appeared. You remembered them every step of the way. That is a feat in itself. Few people are that tenacious, that observant."

His eyes grew slightly vague, as if he was looking at his own HUD. Murmur supposed even the NPCs had to access system information at some stage.

"You've come far." His expression grew serious, and he motioned for her to sit at the chair opposite to his at his desk. Once seated, Belius leaned his elbows on his desk and studied her.

"Your Thought Sensing is sitting quite happily at seventeen, and your shielding has just hit twenty. As we stood in this room, in fact. It appears you're not allowing your skills to alert you to increases. I'd advise that you adjust the setting to allow you to know when a milestone is reached."

Murmur blinked in surprise. How did he know how she'd had her UI set up? This wasn't her mother playing a trick, nor was it a normal AI system. She wasn't sure what to say, only knew anger was starting to gather in her stomach.

"Relax." Belius leaned back this time. "I can't, and won't tell you many things, but what I can tell you is this: as you continue to level and explore what it truly means to be a part of the mind magician family, you will be given paths to take, and indeed, discover others that may not have been trodden yet. Make sure you practice these skills, make them second nature."

"What?" She glared at him and his cryptic chatter. "Seriously Belius. I don't have time for this. I need to eat, I need to shower because I'm pretty sure I stink, and then I need to level because it's taking forever."

But Belius was shaking his head and the action made Murmur stop. "This isn't a game like you think, Murmur. You are here in this world, in our world. We all live here, and there are rules in place, and ways for you to progress if you look around and appreciate what you have."

His smile was a little sad. The melancholy even reached his eyes. "An enchanter can be a powerful class. If you pay attention, if you seek out the elements that tug at your gut, that make your gut squirm, that won't let you sleep, then and only then will you experience things in the way this world was meant to function."

She squinted at him, trying to determine some level of sentience behind those fathomless eyes. Then again, surely he was as digital as she was, right? "So. I just need to keep my eyes and ears open?"

"Technically." He chuckled, but the expression stayed on his lips, and he rocked back with a thoughtful frown. "While you can be powerful, while you can be stubborn, while most people might end up trying to avoid confrontation with you—an enchanter, as with every skillset in this land, is only as good as her team."

Murmur ran the words through her head. They had a group, and as they grew she knew they'd work in flawless synchronicity. Surely that was a good thing. While she might be able to solo, she far preferred to group up, so Belius' comment didn't make sense to her, since she was already doing that. "Why tell me this?"

"Because your mind isn't settled, and you're in a distant place. You're too impatient, and too ambitious, and far too confident. Take a step back and analyze what it is you truly want from this world, Murmur, because regardless of how much you think you've grown, you're only running from yourself."

Murmur stood outside the closed door to Belius' chambers, running through the conversation in her head. How the hell was she running from herself? These damned NPCs and their cryptic vague shit. She made hers take a few deep breaths to get rid of her irritation.

Skill training aside, she'd grabbed one of each spell at two silver each.

Damned expensive but she'd just wanted to get out of there. Running from herself. What a crock of shit.

She rummaged through her spell scrolls as she pushed her way toward Elvita, fully aware that she was scowling.

"Guessing Belius' news wasn't good then?" Elvita's tone was full of sympathy, effectively reducing Murmur's aggression.

Which was hauntingly similar to the enchanter calming ability. Murmur frowned and clamped down on her shield so fast, she thought she saw Elvita wince. Were the NPC's using their enchanter qualities on the players? She glanced around at the packed foyer where every single enchanter stood waiting to see whoever they were waiting for. No one grumbled, in fact, most of them were enjoying conversations with other enchanters and waiting with good patience. The wheels began to turn in Murmur's head, behind the shield she'd painstakingly erected. Suddenly it seemed very important to maintain that shield, more so than she'd originally realized.

"Yeah. You could say that. It's all good. Got me some spells, and I need to sell some random crap." She dumped it all out on the counter, painfully aware that no one else was even remotely close to them. It was like there was an invisible line around the area that she couldn't see.

Elvita smiled, but it wasn't as dazzling as usual, and Murmur softened her expression.

It wouldn't do to piss off the NPC she'd likely see way too much. "Tally em up, boss!"

At that Elvita laughed softly. "Will do. Why don't you go see Arvin if you have any meat?"

"None on me," Murmur smiled, "but maybe he'll have some recipes I can nab."

She headed through to the kitchen, trusting Elvita to pay her fairly for the shit she dumped on the counter, and snagged three new recipes off Arvin. Grilled tiger legs, sautéed meat and mushrooms (makeable with any meat and mushrooms), and a mushroom skewer. She frowned at the selection and decided to figure out the rest whenever. All of them required her cooking skill be at least twenty, so that was fortuitous. This time she grabbed what appeared to be honey water. The level required was eight, and they cost over a silver each, almost as much as her spells. She grimaced, and bought ten of them. They'd last an hour and a half each, and hopefully it'd do her for a level or so.

Back out at the counter, Elvita handed over twelve gold and seven silver.

"You're going to break my bank here soon." She smiled ruefully, the twinkle back in the expression.

"I promise I won't." Murmur bid Elvita farewell and left the guildhall, heading to the gate before logging out.

Exiting the game for the second time was more disconcerting than the first. Wren shook her head after removing the headgear, her vision adjusting gradually as her augmented display set itself up again. For a few seconds her room seemed to swap itself for the enchanter guild foyer until she finally managed to blink the vision away, only to be replaced by the afternoon sun shining through a crack in her curtains. Wren stood, a little shakily, but after a few seconds on her feet, realized that lying down for the last seven and a half hours had probably just disoriented her. She took the few steps to the window and closed the curtains.

Glancing at Harlow who lay eerily still on the bed, Wren shrugged and headed into the bathroom. A quick hot shower would do wonders to reset her clock. Even though she knew Harlow was okay, there was barely any movement of her chest to reflect that she was breathing. The silence was abnormal.

Hot water gushed down over her body, helping her work out the aches in the small of her back, and calf muscles. They'd been playing for just over sixteen hours. No wonder she felt hazy. Her neck was a little stiff, but not nearly as much as she'd expected. Perhaps the suit did work the muscles subtly.

Toweling herself off, she stepped out of the cubicle, cricking her neck from side to side, and pulled on a pair of track pants and a shirt. She'd get back into the more restrictive suit after food. Just about to open the bathroom door, Harlow beat her to it.

"Wren!" Harlow stepped forward and hugged her friend so tightly Wren felt her chest tighten with worry for her friend who seemed to be quite emotional lately.

"What's wrong?" She asked, gently detangling herself, and looking Wren in the eyes. Had something happened on her way to get her spells?

Harlow laughed and glanced away. "Still worked up about that stupid death. But oh my god! You should see the shit I can do at level eight!"

Smiling, Wren gave her friend a quick squeeze. "Tell me all about it while we eat. I'm going to go make us some food—I'm famished."

She left Harlow to her shower and headed downstairs, peeking in on her mother as she went. Four o'clock in the afternoon wasn't exactly a meal time, but she didn't care. Her mom sat between four monitors, actioning boxes and transparencies so quickly with her hands that Wren couldn't follow. Her mother was the lead developer on the game. Every decision about it went through her mother. Only aunt Shayla, her mom's friend and boss, had veto power on Laria's decisions. At least insofar as the game itself went. She added her mom's meal to her to-do list, and headed downstairs.

Fifteen minutes later, she emptied packaged fresh pasta onto plates, tossed with a creamy tomato sauce. Then she plopped quickly-cooked meatballs on top and set them on the table. Dashing upstairs she dropped one on the desk next to her mom, who mumbled a thank you without letting her eyes or hands stop their work.

Frowning as she realized Harlow was still in the shower, Wren dug into her own food, impressed by her own cooking skills. She ran over her character's to do list in her head. The one thing she really needed to keep an eye on was how NPCs affected players. After all, the smoothness in the enchanter guild was nowhere near normal for gamers. She was concentrating so much, she didn't notice Harlow was there until her friend sat down and started shoveling food in her mouth.

"You are a godsend." Harlow muttered once she'd swallowed the first mouthful.

"Mhmm, bet you say that to all the alien cooks you know."

"Of course." Harlow laughed and gobbled down some more food.

"I got some good increases for this next level." Wren frowned as she leafed through the Somnia site. "Upgrades to my DoT, and my personal shield, my weird and very single-minded pet thing. However, now I can cancel magic, root a mob, see invisible mobs, soothe them, and nuke them."

Harlow smiled, munching on her food. "Thas exsellend."

Wren laughed. "You really have to stop talking with your mouth full."

After a gulp, Harlow spoke. "That's part of my charm. But more importantly, I can now heal the group at once. Area of effect heal. Freaking excited about that."

They sat in silence, eating food they hadn't realized they needed. Wren felt oddly full, as if she'd been eating non-stop.

"Have you..." Harlow stopped for a moment, like she was searching for the right words. "Have you heard or seen some vague shit? Weird stuff."

Wren groaned. "Not only have I seen it, one was the quest I was doing, and the other led to that skill that let me warn you all those mobs were coming."

Harlow raised an eyebrow. "Seriously? What sort of skill was that? Fortune telling?"

"No. Thought Sensing, it's called. Sort of sensed the 'oh shit, oh shit' radiating from that ranger."

Harlow laughed explosively. "Guess I better hide my thoughts then."

Wren paused for a moment before answering. "Actually, according to my trainer, we should all be watching our thoughts."

CHAPTER NINE

The Guild

Storm Corp
Storm Technologies Division Experimental Neuroscience Division
Countdown: Fifteen months before Somnia Online launch

Michael sat in the corner of the server room, coffee cup clutched in his hands as he stared at the servers who were right now gearing to plunge sixty volunteers from several of Storm Corps divisions into Somnia Online. They'd been testing for almost eighteen months now. Varying group sizes, but nothing like this one. Sixty was their biggest group yet. The development of the process was down to fine tuning. His headgear was brilliant, and he'd finally made the delicate arms on it search for the correct location at the back of the head as well as conform to the skull. Its scans could penetrate through the scalp, and skull, focusing actually deep into the mind, accessing so much information, information the subject might not even remember.

And yet.

He stared at the servers. Their answers and perceptions were becoming human themselves, though more analytical. Michael wasn't sure if they were mimicking the traits from the humans they'd had contact with, or if they were becoming truly sentient in themselves. Without their interpretations, the headsets were just fancy mind pokers. Mostly, the AIs' answers could be attributed to complicated algorithms they'd developed for understanding human emotions and logic, but Michael wasn't so sure.

"Dr. Jeffries?" Jessa popped her head around the corner. "New coffee."

He graced her with a rare smile and saw the blush rise in her cheeks. He'd barely seen her out of the office for so long, he'd almost forgotten they'd had a thing. "Thank you, Jessa."

She smiled, her youthful features that he remembered having gained a wrinkle or two. Had it been a year now? Longer? She still had that gorgeous blonde hair, and those pouting lips.

Even her incoming admonishment looked appealing through those lips. "You look like a wreck. You should sleep more."

"I'll sleep when I'm dead." Michael chuckled at his own joke, which earned him a scowl from his assistant. "Are they ready to begin then?"

Jessa nodded. "They're all hooked up and ready to go. Scans of the new ones are about to start. If this goes well, we get to move onto the two hundred and fifty test."

Dr. Jeffries looked down at his fathomless black coffee and thought about her excited reaction. What was the perfect way to respond to that? He'd spent too much time around the AIs. "Yes. I'm quite certain it'll go well."

He couldn't explain the feeling he got from the servers. With the lack of sleep he'd had, it was probably all in his head. He smiled at her again, and noticed a brief look of shock cross her face. "After all, as long as it goes well, we'll have clearance to officially put the game up for pre-order and commence manufacturing the headgear."

Jessa returned the smile, and tension leaked out of her shoulders. "Rest up a bit, Doctor Jeffries. They'll call on you shortly."

Michael nodded as she pulled the door shut, and closed his eyes, the coffee cup still warming his hands, the whir of the machines behind him lulling him into a nap.

Release Day: Somnia Online

As soon as the game emerged around her, a flash appeared at the bottom of her screen. Murmur resisted the urge to groan, and pulled up the message, already pretty sure what it was.

Sinister: You're telling them about that ability, in detail, as soon as we meet up!

Okay, okay, Murmur responded. Of course she'd tell them. Harlow was making it out to be a huge deal. Before setting off, Murmur pulled out all of the new spells she'd bought, pausing at the illusion. Elf. So she had human and elf. That might be fun at some stage. She glanced through them. Suffocation and Shield were just upgrades to her DoT and personal shield, and then there was small animation, an upgrade to her floaty pet thing.

Cancel Magic
Cast: Self or others

Type: Debuff

Duration: Instant

Effect: Casting this spell will remove one magically caused effect from the target. Make sure you want to remove it.

Root
Cast: Others (or self if you really want to)

Type: Immobilization

Duration: 8 seconds

Effect: This will root the target in place. Probably not the best idea to cast it on yourself when fleeing in panic.

See Invisible
Cast: Self or others

Type: Buff

Duration: 10 minutes

Effect: Really? Does this really require explanation?

Soothe
Cast: Self or others

Type: Debuff

Duration: Varies

Effect: This will lower the threat level of a target, but it will not make it disappear. Probably not useful on yourself unless in a really bad mood.

Chaos

Cast: Others

Type: Direct Damage

Duration: Instant

Effect: This spell causes direct mental damage to the target, dropping their hit points by two times the caster's level. Requires a recharge.

Her runes flashed under her skin like ripples of moonlight on water and her hair flickered like fireflies as she absorbed her scrolls. She wanted to sit and study them, to understand how they worked.

This time as she set out, the light was still bright enough even though the sun was setting, and she had no qualms about the path at all. Considering she was three levels higher than the last time, there wasn't much to be worried about.

And then group chat lit up.

Beastial: Change of plan, Mur. We're headed toward the Wolf city, Ululate. There should be a wagon just inside your city walls, I hope it hasn't left yet. Pay two silver and jump on it. Make sure it's going in the right direction.

What? Why? Murmur was already changing direction and jogging back the way she came, activating her meager sprint ability.

Devlish: Because the skeletons are measly. No meat, and very little profit in them. Money makes the world go around. Even this one. We just got on the wagon from Nocturn.

Beastial: I was checking while I ate. I think, if I read it correctly, there are bandit camps over that way.

Murmur smiled. Well that sounded like fun. *I'm in.*

She only just made it and as she ran around the corner of the huge metal gate. Her sudden appearance caused the horses in front of the wagon to shy.

"So, sorry." She said, activating Soothe and watching the wild eyes of the animals lose their glaze. "I'm headed to Ululate."

The young human man at the head of the cart eyed her, his gaze just short of a leer. "Awright then, lass, is it? That'll be three silver because ya done spooked meh horses."

Murmur handed him two silver, focused on his eyes, and projected her will through her charisma.

"Take yer seat." He blinked at her, and at the coins, shaking his head as if he'd forgotten something, and waved her through to the seating area where three other passengers had already taken their place. Then he clicked at the horses to make them move. The cart was surprisingly comfortable, its suspension better than Murmur anticipated.

As they rolled out of the city, the young man smiled, his leer gone. "My name's Jan. Nice to meet ya."

"Murmur." She answered, checking her stats quickly as a sneaking suspicion rose in her mind. Sure enough, as the horses moved into a trot, she found it.

Hidden skill activated Thought Projection.

Class: Enchanter only.

Level not applicable.

Developing your inner senses has further developed your psychic powers. Thought Projection can be tricky. Make sure you never use it in anger, or the results might be surprising. With frequent use your skills will increase, while the opposite will occur should the skill not be used. See your trainer for specifics when you reach Thought Projection (25).

Your hidden skill Thought Projection has increased in potency. Current status: Thought Projection (1)

She frowned, and glanced back at the three other people in the wagon, and wondered why she hadn't noticed the vehicle before.

"Jan," she asked. "Does the wagon leave often?"

"Na miss. A few times a day. I do a trip to Stellaein, Ululate, then Frangit, and back again. It's not much, but it's a livin'. This is my last run for the night. I'll be staying in Ululate. I don't like to go out in the dark." He flashed a smile back at her, but kept his eyes mostly on the horses and the road in front of them. "Might I ask what brings ya out this way?"

"Meeting some friends near Ululate."

Are we meeting in the city or outside of it? She shot to her friends.

Havoc: We're going to need to bind, so at the binder would probably make sense.

He had a point; she didn't want to make that run back if she died.

"Well you be careful, mind. Ululate is a fine city, but there's been some bandit activity of late, so make sure you're inside the walls before dark."

Be cautious around Ululate. Tales of Bandits have spread far and wide. They hide near the foothills in the caves beneath the peaks. Each cave is said to be a warren, from which few adventurers return. It's even said that theses bandits have slain foes far and wide, retrieving items of all sorts of importance.

With the horses moving at a brisk trot, the scenery passed by a lot faster than on foot. A light breeze ruffled her hair, and the smell of the earth was lively. Murmur leaned back and ran the words of yet another vague quest through her head. Her level three robe was tattered. It was time to start getting serious. About leveling, about gear, and about reaching the end game to find those forsaken keys.

Climbing down from the wagon, Murmur stood in shock at the difference from her species' hometown. The streets were cobbled stone, with wooden structures all around. The deep red wood gave a cheerful vibe to the whole area, unlike the serene atmosphere she'd grown used to.

Ululate was nice. Homey feeling. She even found herself smiling as it lightened her mood. Reflexively she adjusted her thought shield and made sure she'd be aware of anything dangerous. While right now it seemed to require constant vigilance to make sure it was activated, it had already proved its usefulness once.

It would likely take the others a bit longer to reach the city since Nocturn was farther, so she walked farther into the city and stopped at a bulletin board. Smack bang in the middle was a wanted sign. Placing her hand on it, a flash of information sped across her eyes faster than she could read. She had to pull up the log to find it.

Wanted!

Dul'uak the mayor of Ululate has put a price on Darjin the Bandit Leader's head.

Task: Venture to the northwest of Ululate and find the Bandit Leader in one of the caves. Return his head to Dul'uak

Level Range: 8+
Difficulty: Group
Reward: Experience.
Faction: Unknown

Murmur pursed her lips as she read. This was the first quest that took on a quest format. It was...underwhelming. After everything she'd been through, she didn't even realize there were normal MMO styled quests. As she turned around and surveyed the bustling city, she also realized she'd never actually visited the city portion of Stellaein, with its shops and businesses. She checked her money stash, which amounted to almost twenty-two gold, and headed off toward the vendors.

There were carts around a central statue of a robust luna, its face tilted up toward the sky as if casting something in that direction to encourage the beautiful fountain. Murmur headed for the store she saw with a tailor's symbol.

Walking in, she admired the soothing greens that adorned the shop walls. On a rack to the left were robes. With a smile she walked over, and leafed through them.

"May I help you?" The luna lady looked at her with kind eyes, which were nestled within soft brown fur. Her muzzle mirrored a slightly lighter brown, and her ears were small. Her form sang out that she was a proud wolf, and she carried herself with pride. And her thoughts were mundane enough that they didn't set off any warning bells.

"I'm looking to upgrade this." Murmur gestured to her robe, and then the rest of her body as she realized it had all come from dead skeletons.

"Which attributes are you hoping to boost, young lady?"

She sounded like Murmur's grandmother. "Intelligence and Charisma mainly."

"Excellent." The shopkeeper rummaged through the rack for a few moments before deftly pulling out a pale lavender robe, a dark purple belt, and a matching set of bracers, and shoes. "The pants I have only have armor class on them, though."

Murmur hurried to reassure the lady. "That's perfectly okay. Would you happen to have a cloak?"

"I'm sorry. Not at the moment, that's something usually left to master crafters."

After inspecting the gear and being satisfied with the set's statistics as a whole, Murmur steeled herself and asked for the price.

"Seven gold and eight silver."

Murmur cringed, but changed into the gear after forking over her hard earned cash. She seriously needed to get some cloth and learn how to freaking sew. The robe added two points each to Charisma and Intelligence. The bracers were another one point boost to Intelligence, and the shoes did the same for Charisma. Better than a hit in the head with a sack of cement. "Thank you." She said, and walked out of the shop, straight into Jirald's chest. She stumbled slightly, the height of her locus body giving her a momentary unsteadiness. His arm slipped around her waist with a touch that was far too familiar.

"Hey you!" He grinned. His arm lingered, and his fingers drew tiny circles on the fabric of her robe.

She took a step back, trying to break the contact, but he held on. "Hey yourself."

"Level eight already?" He cocked an eyebrow, his face uncomfortably close. "I'm almost there myself, but not quite."

Murmur narrowed her eyes, and deliberately gripped his hand almost as hard as she could and removed it firmly, locking her eyes onto his for emphasis. "Great for you."

Jirald's eyes sparkled with something just this side of evil, and Murmur had to steel herself against backing up farther. Her gut screamed at her not to give any ground to this guy, because he'd just keep taking. She had no clue what his deal was, but she did know he needed to get the fuck away from her. Just as she was about to verbalize the thought, Devlish's voice rang out over the crowd.

"Oy! Mur! You've been neglecting chat again!"

Relieved at the interruption, Murmur barely gave him another glance before walking quickly to join them.

"I don't like him, Mur." Sin muttered, as they headed back to the gate.

"Yeah. I've noticed." Murmur knew without a doubt that Sin's instincts were right. She just didn't know what the fuck Jirald's problem was.

They sat off to the side of the gate on a set of benches obviously reserved for travelers, picnics, or perhaps smokers. Devlish stood, hands on his hips, holding out the scroll to Murmur, his eyes pleading with her.

"C'mon Mur. Do it. Do it. Do it."

"Pleeeease," intoned Sin and Merlin at the same time, directing a beseeching look to Havoc.

He raised his hands in a sign of self-defense. "Don't look at me. You're the ones she's going to shove into a box and pour cement over."

Murmur chuckled despite her irritation, and finally snatched the bloody scroll out of Dev's hands. "Fine."

Guild Charter.

Must contain the signatures of the guild master and five others. The actual guild charter must be filled out within five Somnian days or the guild will be dissolved and the charter is void.

"But the deal stands. I'll lead, but I'm not fucking doing anything."

"You realize that's an oxymoron, right?" Havoc grinned at her.

"Yeah, yeah, shut up." She activated the area for the name and looked at everyone. "Same as usual, right?"

"Of course," they choursed.

Shrugging and belatedly reflecting on how much blood this pale robe was going to show, Murmur filled in the names, and signed next to her own. A couple of minutes later with the charter fully signed, it swirled in the air and a shower of sparks flew around it before it sank back into her hand. Murmur activated the guild interface and made the others officers for now, knowing she'd be able to adjust the rest of the roles at a later date.

Inspecting Sin, Murmur smiled.

Sinister

< Fable>

Officer

"Perfect." She smiled, and then laughed. "Maybe we should send out feelers to some of our former guildies, eh?"

Beastial grinned. "I thought you'd never ask."

Murmur decided to try and test the HUD. Without pulling it up fully, or even accessing her quest log, she directed the game to share the Bandit Leader's Head quest. Sure enough, after a few moments, everyone had accepted it.

"Weird." Havoc stood up, stretching. His pet mimicked him in an oddly satirical way. "Haven't seen a quest type quest since we logged in here. Most seem to be activated depending on situation and skill."

"Or conversation," added Murmur, happy to find out that she wasn't the only one in her group to have noticed. The thing was, with something as complex as the system seemed to be, she wasn't sure if all players would notice they were quests, or even if they'd activate them. Unless they investigated further, she could see a lot of people taking the scrolling text as a simple bit of information to interpret the area with.

"So glad I'm not the only one being tormented by persistently vague quests." Sin stood up and stretched too, wiggling her hips as she did.

Murmur laughed. "I can't believe you actually do that in-game."

"Do what?" She glanced at Murmur, an eyebrow raised in surprise.

"That stretching wiggle thing you always do."

Sin opened her mouth, but closed it again, her cheeks reddening. She finally shook her head and cleared her throat.

"We still need to bind ourselves to a gating spot. And I'm not traveling all the way from Nocturn to get here." Sin looked around, obviously trying to find someone who could fulfill the task.

Merlin frowned. "I'll take a run around and find a priest or someone."

Murmur sat down, feeling out the crowd. Slivers of thought made their way to her, dissipating before she could make sense of them. From her experience so far, that simply meant there was nothing much to find. She wondered if it could grow powerful enough to just pluck the thoughts from someone's head.

It didn't take Merlin long to uncover someone, and they followed him up to the center of the city. Away from the path surrounding the fountain, under several nicely grown trees, stood a very nondescript human in a plain beige robe.

Murmur tried to look at him to get a feel for his description, but the more she tried to focus on him, the fuzzier his visage became. She frowned as she waited her turn to be bound to the spot, wondering what the motivation was behind a character players couldn't remember. An idea forming, she probed the area around him. His eyes manifested a bright blinding cobalt for a split second, making eye contact with her briefly before going back to what he was doing. Shit. Maybe that hadn't been a good idea.

You notice a strange man in Ululate. His features are indistinguishable, and his aura has an electric charge. While his actions don't betray a purpose, you can't help wondering what it is. Be wary, and remember to shield well.

Thought shielding (25). Congratulations. You will find it more difficult to strengthen your internal powers from here on in.

Scowling, as the bright golden sparks of binding shone around her character, Murmur activated her quest list and sighed.

"What's up?" Havoc's voice was right at her ear, his breath hot and startlingly real, making her jump.

"Sorry Mur." His eyes lit up in shock and he stepped away. "Didn't mean to startle you."

"S'ok." She smiled, not sure why she was uneasy. She'd known Havoc almost as long as she'd been playing MMOs. He had an excellent grasp on class, no matter what he played, but he was often the serious one, and yet she'd never felt uncomfortable around him. Maybe it was because she'd been so deep in thought. He didn't say things to get a rise out of anyone, nor did he deliberately try to make sexist jokes to break the mood. She felt like she owed him an apology.

Something about the binder had her on edge. "Just a bit jumpy. Probably tired."

"Aren't we all," Devlish laughed it off as they approached the gate again, but Sin's eyes wouldn't leave Murmur, and she knew she'd probably be inundated with messages shortly.

Don't stay. Flee. Don't activate the transition.

Murmur whipped her head around, trying to see where the stray thought came from, but apart from people walking to and from the gate, nothing stood out to her. No one was watching her, no one seemed overly agitated. This ability was going drive her batty. Slotting it away in the notes section that she'd yet to use, Mur tried to crack her neck and release the tension that was slowly building up. What fucking transition?

Sinister: What's wrong with you?

Nothing. That new ability is just... kind of heavy.

Sinister: Heavy? Like a weight, or heavy intellectually?

The latter.

Sinister: Want to talk about it?

Mur smiled. *Maybe later, when I figure out what it's even doing to me.*

Sinister: Speaking of which...

She glanced at Mur and indicated the others.

Murmur took a deep breath.

"So you know; I knew the skeletons were coming because I activated this weird ability called Thought Sensing. Anything remotely interesting or dangerous in our proximity will sort of leak through to me." Her tone was bored. By now she wasn't exactly sure the ability was a boon at all. Maybe it was a testing ground to see who would go insane with actual voices playing in their head at random instances.

Beastial blinked at her, the others not far behind in reactions. Mostly they just gaped. The large viking ran a hand through his hair. "So you can hear our thoughts?"

He seemed uncomfortable, and Mur was pretty sure his thoughts might involve certain characteristics of the female form. She grinned. "Only if you're thinking something that could affect us, or be dangerous to us, or to me personally. I think. I'm still figuring it out. It sort of sifts through things, like flour."

"Baking analogy." Dev reached out and ruffled her hair again. "Nice one, Mur. Also, I don't like you being as tall as me. It makes treating you like my little sister harder."

Murmur laughed. "Then don't. I don't need you to protect me, in fact, maybe I'll end up protecting you." She winked at him, and they all laughed, although she wasn't sure why since she wasn't joking.

An idea occurred to her. "We're all going to have to craft in our downtime, you realize."

"What downtime?" grumbled Beastial.

"Hey, better than nothing." Murmur put her hands on her hips and glared at them. "When we start to pull away in levels and establish the guild. Or we could just recruit good crafters."

Beastial frowned and started scanning his HUD again. "I'll keep an eye out. We might not want to wait that long."

Murmur had to admit that he had a point.

This gate seemed far more pregnable than that of Stellaein. It was made out of thick logs, ones she wouldn't even be able to put her arms around, but wood wasn't as strong as metal. She frowned, gazing out at the dimming light.

"The sun will be gone soon." Merlin muttered what they were all thinking out loud.

"No shit, Merlin." Beastial laughed. "Everyone got their gear? Food,

Drink?"

Murmur frowned. "I have plenty. But if you see mushrooms, or get any meat, I have things I can cook while we're out. I think you'll all be getting low on food soon."

She handed out two more spider legs to each of them. "That's about all I can manage right now. My plethora of spider legs is no more."

"We off then?" Sinister's grin spread wide, her eyes glinting dangerously.

"No time like the present." Dev took the first step out of the gate and angled northwest. "After all, that bandit leader isn't going to kill himself for us."

CHAPTER TEN
Camping

Edward Davenport, CEO of Storm Corp entered Doctor Michael Jeffries office. The CEO was tall, about six foot four. His white hair glistened like it had a silver underlay, and his tall sporty figure spoke of years of running. It seemed like his eyes could see through you, and knew everything you didn't want him to. Approaching sixty, he oversaw every big project personally, refusing to delegate and swearing that was how Storm Corp became what it was today. He'd built the company from the ground up, after all.

"It's looking good, Jeffries." Teddy opened the conversation pleasantly. "One more round of tests, and then we should be good to go. Tell me, do you have any reservations?"

Michael looked up at his boss. His thoughts were a mess, his expectations deflated—yet he had to keep all of that out of his tone. "I'm unsure if we'll be able to procure enough headgear for people to play with. They could technically use old crappy tech, but it will limit our data severely."

It was about as much as he could put out there without sounding like a loon. Telling your boss that during the course of testing the limits of the headgear that was hopefully going to make him rich, Michael had inadvertently (probably helped) the AIs become mostly or fully sentient? That sounded crazy. Like a definite road to firing.

Firing would separate him from his beautiful project, which was one thing he couldn't let happen. It meant everything to him, and it worked, even better than he'd ever anticipated. It had simply developed a reliance on the specific set of AIs controlling Somnia. So instead of saying what was in his mind, he skirted the worries he had, putting them down to lack of sleep, and knowing not a small amount of it was fueled by the greed to see his project work.

"Excellent. How is the data on the project right now?" Teddy glanced around the office, his eyes raking over the charts and screens running multiple calculations faster than the eye could keep up.

"The data," Michael's smile this time was genuine. "What we have is compiling nicely, giving us areas we can tweak and work on through how it's retrieved and how the information is read. However, until we get a larger number in, we can't really draw any specific conclusions. Everything we're doing right now is general. Once the game releases, however, I'll be able to gather most everything we need."

Teddy nodded, hands behind his back, a stern expression on his face. "Does your team know the plans? Or is it all up here?" The CEO motioned to his head.

Michael blinked. Well, no one but him knew *everything*. "My extrapolations are mostly in my head, but as we improve and go through the development, my team is well aware of how everything works."

"Not good enough, Jeffries. I need everything notated, you need at least two juniors under you. Pick the two brightest doctors you have working with you. I want their names tomorrow. They need to know everything." Teddy straightened his jacket and looked Michael in the eye. "I'm being cautious. Storm Corp has far too much invested in this should something go awry. I'm protecting my investment, and your ideas are my investment."

The last tone was serious and firm, and while Michael completely understood, it still fanned the irritation welling inside him. "Understood, Mr. Davenport."

"Excellent. Thank you for your fantastic achievements so far, Jeffries. I see great things for you." With a nod, the CEO left the office.

Barely keeping his irritation under control, Michael sat down and patched through to Jessa. "Send in Brandon and Silke, please."

"Okay." Jessa disconnected the call and Michael sat, contemplating how he'd approach this. He knew who his best and brightest were, and trying to keep his own motives from people who might get close to his work, would be tricky. But most of all, what if they realized the AIs were behaving oddly as well? Would they put a stop to everything?

He couldn't let that happen.

Release Day: Somnia Online

Walking was something Murmur never really got used to in a virtual world. She had to exercise the same portion of her brain to instigate it, but didn't get half of the benefits she would have if she'd done it in the real world. Apparently the suit was supposed to help with that, but she wasn't holding her breath.

Every now and again she spied a mushroom, and plucked it. If nothing else, she could make them some skewers.

Beastial kept veering off the path. By the sixth time, Murmur was ready to smack him. "Stop it, Beast!"

He blinked rapidly, likely shutting out of whatever he was doing, and met her eyes. "What?"

"We keep having to babysit you. Stop whatever you're doing and just walk to the bandit lair with us."

Beastial laughed. "You wanted me to contact people we've played with before. So either I don't help with the bandits, or you shepherd me there.

Your pick."

"When he puts it that way." Havoc smiled. "I shall be his shepherd."

"Excellent. I'm counting on you mate." Beast's answer trailed away as he went back to whatever he was doing.

"You better not recruit a ton of freaking rangers." Merlin pouted as they walked. "And I don't mean for loot's sake. I'd like to enter Mr. Training Ranger in as Exhibit A."

"To be fair, most of the people we've played with would have just died." Dev jogged to keep up with Murmur's quick, irritated steps. "Hey. We're not in a race. Well, I guess we are, but five minutes won't make a difference."

"Search for levels D." Murmur replied shortly. "No tens yet, but there are several nines. So let's not rest on our lack of laurels, huh?"

"And," Beast spoke loudly from behind. "I may or may not be in contact with most of those nines. Calm it Mur. Don't turn on hardcore bitch mode just yet."

She sighed, knowing full well she often got carried away. But just like in school, just like in everything she did, not being the best wasn't an option. Competitive? Nope, she was beyond that. In such a way that it dogged her every thought, always there in the back of her mind.

The slight incline of the off-road path they took gave her character a work out. She didn't even want to contemplate the time, because she knew her actual body should be getting tired shortly. Should being the operative word.

In the waning light, they finally made it. Motioning the others to be quiet and stay behind him, Merlin crept forward. Murmur watched him, focusing on the small campfire she could see just past the tree line, in a clearing with a huge cave rearing up behind it. Several figures stood at intervals around the camp site, behind it, some chatting and laughing while they played something that might have been a game of dice.

There were all sorts there. Some dark elves, some appeared to be luna, others viking, and even the occasional locus. Straining her eyesight, Murmur noticed another flicker in the distance, meaning there was more than one camp, and likely more than one cave.

"Levels?" she whispered.

Merlin rejoined the group. "Seems to be more like levels ten to eleven here. They're also not normal mobs. They have a line around their aura—might be the equivalent to an elite, or group mob? More experience for the group, anyhow. In Somnia it probably means they're just well-trained or something."

He cleared away some pebbles on the ground and drew a few diagrams in the dirt. "There are going to be multiple pulls. I think the fewest I can do is when we hit the campfire and there are two of them at it, at least right now. I think I can keep it to three."

Murmur ran the numbers through her head. "I can keep two Mez'd easily. But there'll be a delay on the second one. Only slight, but we need to pull them back significantly."

"Well, we learned the hard way that mobs don't leash in this game." Sin laughed without a trace of mirth. Murmur almost pitied that ranger if her friend ever found him again.

"I'll Mez two, and we'll work on the other. I'll be able to DoT, but I don't trust my pet to obey my commands, so I'm not going to cast him for now. He's pretty useless, and to be honest, only listens to my directions about twenty percent of the time."

Beastial chuckled. "You need a BEAST!"

She raised an eyebrow. "You think?"

He laughed. "Seriously though. Did you want me to invite people we've played with straight away?"

Murmur gave it a moment's thought, running through possible complications in her mind. "If we've raided with them and they know how to do their jobs, keep out of shit, watch their surroundings, and aren't a complete dick? Sure."

"Love your criteria, Mur." Beastial laughed, and for a moment it seemed his cat was echoing the expression. "Right, I've got about nine that I'll invite outright because I'm quite certain you don't hate them, and the rest we'll discuss. Except Rash, who isn't online right now."

"Rash? Great! Sounds like you have a plan" She redirected her attention to the bandit camp, quite happy to learn that Rashlyn would be playing Somnia too. But she needed experience, now. It was like the lack of it was making her skin itch. "Let's try a pull and see how much stronger these 'elite' mobs are."

Moving up slightly past the trees but still in the shade of its branches, the group began a series of self buffs, except Sin because hers could give extra health to everyone.

The first group they attempted stood at the foot of a large rock that blocked the mobs from the sight of their comrades. That made it a much easier pull, considering higher level mobs likely had more intelligence or something. Merlin stepped out onto the grass as the last rays of the sun began to sink beneath the mountain range, took aim, and released an arrow, straight into the neck of the human bandit whose back was to them. The other two standing with it drew their weapons immediately, already moving, but Murmur finished her cast, sealing one of them in place.

The initial bandit walked slower, the blood of his wound decreasing his speed as he approached them. But Murmur didn't have time for much more than a glance, already busy motioning through the Mez spell again before releasing it quickly. No fizzle, and no resist. It stopped the second uninjured mob in its place, leaving the initial one as their target.

By the time she turned back to it, it was down to almost half health, and riddled with damage over time spells from both Havoc and Beastial and their pets. Merlin wasn't kidding; these were definitely not normal mobs. Adding her own DoT to the mix, Murmur kept an eye on her Mez countdowns, positioning them better in her HUD so as not to interfere with her vision, but also to make sure she could keep track of them.

When the mob hit thirty-five percent, she renewed the Mez on the first mob with a few seconds to spare, repeating the process on the second. She always allowed time for a mistake, in case a fizzle or a resist meant she'd need to recast the spell. She needed to refine her strategy. "Taunt before you break Mez."

Dev rolled his eyes in her direction. Considering he'd played DPS previously, he knew all about taunting. Still, she felt better having said something. At five percent he switched targets, while the others finished the initial mob off. Effectively taunting it, he broke Murmur's spell and the mob didn't even try to glance at Murmur. She let out a sigh of relief, DoT-ed the new target, and then re-Mez'd the other. Now she had time to nuke the new mob a couple of times. The health of the second one was going down faster than the first as the group figured out their rotations, and got more comfortable with their classes.

"Not going to re-Mez it again. Taunt it, Dev, and let it come to you. We can handle two for a few percent." Murmur directed them without thought to the fact that she was usually in the healer's shoes.

"Easy for you to say." Sin glared at her.

"Shush baby healer. Your health is full, and your mana is sitting at eighty percent. You're not even breaking a sweat." Murmur paused at the timer. "Breaking in three."

The final mob ran over to Dev, who turned and thwacked it good, maintaining any aggro he might need, and began alternating through both for the last ten percent of the second. DoTs applied on the new, nukes and pets engaged, the second died quickly, and they made short work of the last one.

"Take stock." Murmur stepped back and surveyed the scene. "I believe these will take longer than average mobs to respawn given that they're a quality level higher."

She frowned. No one was lacking health, and most of their mana bars were around seventy-five percent. With slow and steady killing they could easily pull three groups of three in a row without being careless and even save some mana for an 'oh shit' situation.

"Yes!" Dev cried triumphantly. "Plate for meeeeeee!"

Havoc laughed and Merlin punched Dev in the arm. "Loot whore."

"Fuck yeah." Dev gloated. "Without me you'd... probably use Beast's tiger. But still!"

Merlin laughed. "Okay we need to get going before—"

A series of trilling bells echoed around them. The group glanced around, trying to figure out what it was, all except for Beast who bowed in front of them. "Ladies and shitheads, I give you our new guild members."

Another portion of her HUD Murmur was going to have to prioritize. At this rate she was going to be playing the game through a series of transparent chat and attribute screens. She directed more pleasant words into the guild chat though: *Welcome everyone. Good to see you again. Excuse us while we kill shit.*

It only took a few seconds of glancing through the roster to recognize character names she knew and didn't hate. Beast had been right—all of them were extremely capable gamers. She promoted the newcomers to members, bypassing the trial status, and blinked the screen away. "Okay, we're done. I'll have to set permissions later, and we need the charter imported. Not bad for less than twenty-four hours. Fable's member count is fifteen. Keep an eye on your friends list Beast. I guess you're our recruitment officer."

She grinned evilly at his flabbergasted expression.

"Anyway, as Merlin was about to say. Let's get going before we all fall asleep."

Checking all the bags throughout the camp yielded some nice cuts of meat. With an appraising look, Murmur grabbed it all and stood over the fire while the others checked on the bodies they'd just decimated. Blood pooled on the ground around them, so lifelike even the coppery tang registered with her senses. Even to the extent that if they stepped in it, they'd leave bloody footprints when they walked away. Everyone's armor, including her own, was sprayed with blood spatter in pretty raindrop like patterns. She knew the pale purple was going to be a problem. It almost made the blood seem neon. Fighting living mobs was definitely more messy than skeletons.

Accessing her recipe, adding butter, salt, and pepper to the pot, she dropped in a mushroom and piece of meat. Three seconds later she had a nice dinner in a sort of container that could pass for ancient Tupperware in the real world. Its duration was two hours and it gave six health every five seconds. Not horrible. She continued to make it until she ran out of ingredients, and then quickly passed one each to the group members.

"How's the cave looking, Merlin?" Sin stretched her arms again, but glanced at Murmur and stopped before she did the hip jiggle.

"Higher levels. They're eleven and above in there. I mean we could try it but we're pushing our luck with three level difference out here. I feel like the higher these opponents get, the cleverer they are." He motioned to the right. "There's two other camp sets just like this. We could just keep moving around each of them and clear them out."

"Until others get here to do the same thing." Dev frowned at his HUD. "Keep going, I say. Pretty sure leveling is going to halt drastically once we hit double digits."

"From all reports from our guildies if you'd care to look at guild chat," Beastial interrupted, "nine is a hell level and a half."

"Great. Let's go kill shit and make our way to hell." Murmur moved behind Merlin, walking toward the next camp, already eyeing the mobs.

Just before she did though, she spied what looked like a rogue creeping close to the trees. That seeing invisible spell was pretty cool. The dark elf seemed to be a sort of liquid looking shape of a humanoid. She held up a hand to stop everyone, and quickly buffed them all too. After quick consideration, she realized he was level eight and frowned. Damn it. They needed to speed up their leveling.

About to set out to claim their camp before the rogue tried to, Murmur realized he was slowly inching forward, like he was checking out the camp for himself. Except the mobs he was inching closer to kept looking around, as if they sensed something. She crouched down and the others followed suit, making sure to stay hidden behind the rather overgrown foliage they stood in.

It happened so quickly, Murmur almost missed it. The rogue's stealth dropped as a throwing knife landed in his left bicep with a sickening thud. A scream tore from his throat as blood dripped from the wound and onto the ground. Three mobs ran over, quick as lightning, their daggers and swords biting deep into the poor rogue's almost-paralyzed body. It was like the player just didn't know how to react. His death was vicious and quick. Murmur had to swallow past a lump in her throat as she watched the blood still leaking from his lifeless body as it soaked into the dirt.

She took a deep breath as the mobs moved back, and had to stop from laughing nervously when Sinister spoke. "Boy, am I glad we have a group."

"Yeah, playing solo probably isn't the best way here." Havoc's tone was soft, as usual, but his words held a chill that made Murmur shiver.

Murmur stood and cast invisibility on everyone, herself last. Her mood had sobered somewhat. "Okay, let's grab a good place to pull to, with some nice cover for line of sight, and get going with this."

Things were going too smoothly for them, and after witnessing that death, Murmur was worried. She already regretted having that thought, but what was done was done. The universe would probably take its revenge very soon.

Just like that, the first pull went completely haywire. Somehow one of the bandits pathed differently than anticipated, which, given the game, shouldn't have been a huge surprise, but these NPCs were left with so much more leeway than usual that it was difficult to predict their movements. Since they weren't undead or lesser beings, but in fact intelligent bandits, they literally behaved that way.

Four mobs in pursuit, with a fifth Mez'd at the initial pull spot, Merlin raced back. Murmur got her second Mez off with great timing, and switched targets again to the third, calling out while she moved. "Fall back."

The third froze in place, its mouth shaped in a surprised O, and while it made her want to laugh, she didn't have time to dwell on it. The fourth bandit, a fighter type, came straight at her, and the intricate spell knotted her fingers slightly, creating a delay. It hit her once before she got the spell off, but even that once was enough for her to cry out in pain as the sword cleaved through the area between her shoulder and neck on her right side. The critical hit drained half her life. "Fuck!"

"Shit." Sin cast a buff on Murmur, which leeched the damage her spells did directly to heal the enchanter. Still, the wound closed slowly, and Murmur felt tears run down her face even though she hadn't realized the pain made her cry.

Struggling to stand, she slowly regained the feeling in her right hand, trying to release the spell just in time to catch the first bandit in her snare again. Her wound healed, and the pain in her head receded, allowing her to cast two more in quick succession.

The first target almost dead, Dev switched his aim, casting a worried glance back at Murmur. She concentrated on keeping the other bandits Mez'd, running through the events in her head. She remembered being hit in the forest back when she was level two. Sure, it had smarted, but it was nothing like the deathly pain she'd just experienced.

Maybe it had something to do with where she'd been hit. Perhaps as mobs grew in level, the pain became more real? It was a possibility. And yet.

Mechanically maintaining her Mez and hitting each new target with her DoT as Dev switched, she sifted through the settings. There was nothing about pain level control. No information at all. She didn't even notice they'd finished killing the pull, so deep was she in an article she'd pulled up. It was published almost twelve months ago when the preorders went live.

Blah blah pain threshold. Bam. There it was. Once the player is out in the world, they'll realize that mobs will reflect their levels. The higher the mob, the better their aim and thus the more pain they can potentially cause. This has been necessary to encourage full immersion in the world of Somnia.

Murmur frowned, not quite happy with the phrasing, or indeed, with the effect. It was like she felt phantom pain in a limb that was still attached. Maybe it was just because it was the first time she'd experienced it. She couldn't even begin to imagine the pain dying must cause. Poor Sin.

"Mur. We need to move." Havoc crouched where she sat, his hand at her elbow, concern mirroring in his black eyes.

She blinked, again struck by the real world effects of concern or embarrassment as they reflected in an in-game character portrayal. "Sorry. Just going over some data. Didn't expect that hit to make me want to tear off my own arm."

He chuckled, even if it sounded a little forced.

"You don't have to be so tough you know." He said, letting her arm go once she was standing. "We don't expect you to be made of steel."

She stepped back in surprise, seeing Havoc's seriousness in a new light.

He might be even more observant than she was. "What is there to be, but that which is expected of us?" She smiled, cryptically, trying to imitate Belius.

But Havoc didn't laugh like she'd thought he would, instead he shook his head and frowned. "One of these days you're going to realize the only person you're fooling is yourself, Wren. Both in the game and out."

Before she could respond, he sped up and joined the others just in time for Merlin to pull. After that, there wasn't a spare moment to ask Havoc what the hell he'd meant.

CHAPTER ELEVEN
Figuring It Out

Storm Corp
Storm Technologies Division Experimental Neuroscience Division
Countdown: Thirteen months before Somnia Online launch

Michael had to admit, bringing Brandon and Silke into the picture was helping with his workload and freeing up a lot of time for him to interface the upgraded headgear with the AIs. He wasn't precisely sure why he didn't want his assistants to talk to the AIs much, except that he didn't want to endanger his pet project. After all, a sentient AI had the potential to derail everything. Focus would shift, and his invention would be put aside for the miracle that was Rav, Sui, and Thra. Especially since he was more sure every day that it was their interpretation of the data making the headgear a success.

Dr. Jeffries ran a hand through his hair and rubbed at sleepy eyes. He did not have time to sleep. Not now.

Someone knocked on his door. He put his glasses back on as he called out, "Come in."

"Dr. Jeffries? There's a problem with the hind arm G2. I've checked over all the connectors, and the testing gear. It's just not calibrating correctly. I think we need to adjust the ratio?" Silke bit her lip, obviously not confident with her assessment. He could understand why. There were still things no one knew about the headgear. Michael had made sure of that.

"Work on G2; we have the big group in two weeks. Their software and hardware will all need to be upgraded if they're malfunctioning in any respect. It'll probably be a long couple of weeks." He stood up, and grabbed his original headgear.

"Thank you, sir." Silke's smile was bright and lit up her usually serious face. Her brown hair was unkempt and often tied haphazardly in a ponytail at the nape of her neck. Since her brain was brilliant, she only ever seemed to take care with her appearance if she knew they were getting an important visitor. Work always came first—it seemed to be her passion. If Michael had more time, she was exactly the type of person he was interested in.

He waited until she'd been gone for a few minutes before taking his prototype to the server room. There was something he needed to test, something he thought he'd witnessed once, but hadn't been certain of. If he was right, then there were many things he still had to work on to pull the most potential out of his device, and out of the AIs.

His eyes gleamed with fire, and perhaps a bit of insanity.

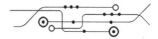

Release Day: Somnia Online

Digging through each camp once they cleared it revealed usable loot. Murmur found a heap of stuff she could cook with. They also discovered hides and cloth, equipment they could use for upgrades. Each camp consisted of about eight pulls of two to four bandits at a time. Luckily, they had yet to pull another set of five. Secretly, Murmur was a little wary of overpulling in a way she'd never been before. Usually all she'd had to do was heal, but now if she fucked up on a bad pull, odds were everyone would die. No pressure or anything. The memory of the pain that stupid pull had caused her probably had something to do with it too. Now she was extra careful and helped Merlin scout the areas.

All three camps cleared, they circled back to the first. Still no other players had ventured out this way. Murmur frowned, wondering what others might know that she didn't, or else where they might level. With Havoc still avoiding her, her mood grew sour. "Why haven't we seen any other groups?"

"No clue." Devlish was weighing two swords in his hands. "But I'm not about to complain."

Beast smacked his friend on the back. "The right one. It's much better. Stop trying to go for the good-looking blade. As for the other players, there are several areas up to level fifteen on this continent alone, and every other one. This area is wide here, and I believe both lakes have good leveling areas too."

He quieted suddenly before breaking out in a huge smile. "Ah, Rashlyn is online. Finally. Inviting now."

Murmur smiled. Despite his protestations, Beast seemed to be taking to his role as recruiter. The basic concept that they'd recruit as many people as they could who they'd raided with in the past made her feel marginally better about everything. Even a little hopeful. After all, you couldn't raid a dragon or god with a group of six.

Still a little gun shy, they positioned themselves again and Merlin was just about to pull when he paused. "So. Just wondering. Do we remember having casters or rangers before?"

"Nope." Havoc stepped forward, his boney pet jiggling in place. "Oh."

"What?" Dev asked before joining them and answering his own question.

In the original group of three they'd pulled, there were now two ranged bandits. In a way it was irritating, but on the other hand Murmur felt excitement swirling in her gut. "They're not the same. The game adapts. Randomizes shit. That's freaking awesome."

Upon closer inspection, none of the mobs were the same as they'd been before—even their names had changed. Their pathing was different. They seemed more alert and on edge.

"Gives a new meaning to camping an area." Beastial spoke quietly, but there was a gleam to his eyes that Murmur understood. Talk about a challenge!

"Mezing order will be caster, ranger, melee." Murmur redid her buffs and tried not to jump up and down. Her trepidation was gone. Moonlight shone down from the twin moons bathing the small clearing in rose and pearl.

"Perfect night for killing." Merlin grinned and loosed his arrow.

Murmur released her spell as the arrow hit home.

She barely managed to dodge the NPC's arrow before she released her second Mez, wondering if it was a good idea to put some points into agility after all. Her body was cumbersome, with its height. She applied her DoT and nuked the melee mob twice before renewing her hold on the caster.

"We need to line of sight the archer and the caster." She whispered, watching Devlish react accordingly and use the large stone that hid the group for exactly that purpose. Having taunted the ranger, when the Mez broke, the NPC glared in Dev's direction, but had to move around in order to sight its target. After all, it couldn't cast through the rock. Perfect.

"That should make the caster close the distance before it attacks too." Havoc smiled. "This is more like it. Just make sure you don't round the boulder too much or we're screwed."

"You're way too blood thirsty." Sinister grinned, the fire in her eyes a dead giveaway that she was exactly the same.

When the caster finally died, Sin ran forward to loot it before the rest could recover.

"Hey ninja," Merlin teased.

"Ha, very funny." Sin shot back, but turned around with a smile and waved a robe in the air. "Wisdom plus one! This is awesome. Now us clothies can finally get some gear!"

"Now who's the loot whore?" Devlish laughed, but there was that big brother kindness in his tone. "Might even get a decent bow for the elf. The game knows his damage is fucking pitiful."

"Shut up, or I'll shove an arrow where it hurts." Merlin scowled half-heartedly.

Beastial's brow furrowed. "Wouldn't an arrow hurt like anywhere it was shoved?"

The group laughed, moving to a slightly different spot to pull the next group. No warrior, just a rogue, a damage caster...and a healer.

"Ooh, first healer we've encountered." Sin beamed. "Bring it. My Mur is going to blow your mind."

"Literally." Timing her cast with Merlin's arrow again, Murmur smirked as she activated the spell, stealing the cleric's ability to move. She wondered what it would be like, frozen in place, unable to move even though all your other senses worked, with only your mind functioning properly and unable to anything about it. Making sure the net that initiated Thought Sensing was active, she felt outward, following its tendrils. The cleric's mind was a cloud of anxiety, but no actual thoughts escaped with enough force to become distinct. She felt a little disappointed, but smiled as she renewed the Mez, watching the cleric's wide and panicked eyes. Imagine smelling the blood of the people you'd fought with, experiencing the deaths you would otherwise have been able to prevent. Being held in place, not by anything physical, but by your mind—betraying you because of an outside influence.

For just a moment Murmur had an inkling of why the enchanter class had been cut out of so many virtual worlds. But that was then, and this was now. It was the perfect time to discover herself.

DING!

"Oh, about freaking time." Murmur leaned against the tree at her back as their healer finally leveled.

Sin's eyes flashed angrily. "Stupid fucking ranger. Now I'm behind you all. If I ever catch him again—"

"You'll flay him alive and heal us all with the damage?" Beastial teased.

Sin flicked her long white hair behind her shoulder and glared at him. "That's way too tame."

Beastial had the decency to pale a little.

"How are we only level nine?" Dev complained, glancing up at the sky, when in fact he'd probably just checked the in-game clock. "It's around 2am I'd say."

Merlin rolled his eyes. "We're only level nine because the game hasn't been out for a day yet, and because this game actually has a level cap, which means each level needs to be fought for."

"Grinding is annoying." Dev sat back, watching Murmur cook through a heap of ingredients.

"Grinding is necessary if you want to level fast." She answered, not quite paying full attention. "The majority of people venturing into these worlds are here for the experience. They want to experience something that isn't in their daily lives. The wonder of magic, the ability to come back from the dead, exploration, and hell, even crafting. While there are some of us who play to 'win' I guess, we aren't in the majority. Probably good or people wouldn't be able to move near the end game mobs. Plus, it's much more fun to kill shit with your friends." She added another set of the meal into her inventory and frowned at the silence before looking up.

Her gaze fell on her group, all of them slumped over near the base of a tree, looking like they were about to fall asleep. "No!"

They sat up, blinking somewhat dazedly.

"What?" Sin grumbled.

"We haven't even been at this twenty-four hours. There will be no sleep yet!"

"Evil. You're all regal in your silver alien body there, Mur, but you're still evil to the core." Merlin grumbled, finally pushing himself into a standing position.

"Good. Anyway, I need mushrooms. Does anyone have any spare?" She glared at them as they all shook their heads, resigned to grabbing any she could see. They had to keep leveling. "Fine. I have four more meals for each of you."

"Back up and go through all the shit we've amassed. Then I think we should stick out here until level ten, and then take on the caves." Dev wasn't smiling. Sometimes he could be serious. "Let's start at this camp this go around. It'll take us less time to rip through these, given our level increase across the board. We'll work in reverse order."

Standing up, they all shook out their limbs, like dusting cobwebs off. A strange sensation, given these weren't real bodies.

It didn't take them long to fall into an experience grinding routine again. Murmur's rinse and repeat actions of mesmerizing and DoT-ing her targets became mechanical, and she scanned the area between every set of bandits, just in case a rare spawned, or someone decided to add coal to a train's engine.

Your Mental Acuity is gaining traction.

Thought Sensing (25). Congratulations. You have raised two of your hidden skills to their required level. When you reach your next level milestone, you might want to visit Belius again. Beware that as your powers grow you will notice changes. Mark them, pay attention, and be wary of traps.

Murmur practically snarled at the vagueness of her milestone. So level ten meant she'd have to go and see Belius. She chuckled to herself. That was going to be a while then.

"Something funny, Mur?" Sin asked, poking her. A slight frown of concern marked her brow. "From the smile on your face, I'm glad you're my friend."

Murmur focused on Sin after Mezing a healer. "Um, not really. Just another unhelpful update for one of my skills."

"Ah, then you're plotting game designer murder. Some quality matricide perhaps?" Her best friend winked.

This time Murmur laughed out loud. "No, not that. Just...I'm frustrated by it, and at the same time enthralled. I want to find out what I get next, where the next step leads..."

"Guess the scan was right then, huh?" Sin smirked, casting strange runes into the air to heal Devlish. A mist of blood darted toward Sin, swirling and exploding outward to envelope Devlish's body, and then it was gone. It looked like it got sucked into the tank's skin. "I'm not too unhappy myself."

"I did notice that." Mur answered dryly.

After a few more pulls, Devlish stopped, frowning. "Is it just me or are they worth at least as much experience as they were earlier?"

Havoc grew distant for a few moments before speaking. "Seems so. One or two more points here and there. Perhaps our level disparity was too great before. Two levels seems acceptable, but three might be pushing it when we're still single figures. So therefore they reward less because you're over leveling, I guess."

"Makes sense." Merlin ushered the group toward the next pull. "Good thing we didn't venture into the caves then, right?"

The steady rhythm of pulling and clearing was strangely soothing, and Murmur found herself fighting to stay awake. Apparently so did the rest of them. During a pull of three mobs, Beastial accidentally sent his pet to attack the wrong one, breaking Murmur's Mesmerize. What appeared to be a locus-thief gleefully leapt at her with a strange jump punch that made her stagger. She got pummeled until Dev could pull it off her. At least the blasted thing was using a blunt weapon.

"What the fuck, Beast!" She glared at him, clenching her teeth through the pain while Sinister hurriedly healed her. "Don't break my Mez!"

"I didn't mean to. If I'd planned it, you'd be dead." He stood, hands on hips glaring at her.

"Maybe if you had better control over your—"

"Stop it!" Havoc stood between them, his voice raised. He turned to Beast. "Don't do it again. You know better. You don't break a Mez."

Just as Murmur was about to thank him, he whirled on her. "And you. Stop snapping. In case you haven't noticed the sun is coming up, which means we've been going for almost twenty-four hours straight. Give yourself and us a break, but mostly yourself. We have mobs to kill."

Murmur glared at Havoc's back as he turned around, seething. But why was she seething? She took a figurative step back and looked at herself. Was she feeding off someone else's mood? Was it just the length of time she'd spent in-game? Had she had way too little to eat and was secretly angry about it? Instead of retorting like she wanted to, she began to have a long and hard look at her mood.

A while later, when the sun was well and truly over the horizon in the virtual world, and yet it was past midnight back in reality, they moved on from the middle camp, only to find the first one finally had another group there.

For a few seconds they watched them. Cleric, warrior, the first bard Murmur had seen, what appeared to be a wizard, a ranger, and a rogue.

"That's very traditional," she muttered, glancing over at her group, which was decidedly less boring. "Level eights—we should leave them to it, and head back to the other camp, I'm sure it's repopped by now."

Just as they were about to leave, a familiar voice sent a chill down Murmur's spine.

"Hey there, Murmur." Jirald's voice rang out loud and clear, and the rogue strode over, a jovial smile on his face and an unreadable emotion behind his eyes. "Fancy meeting you here."

She nodded, scanning the area and barely hiding her shock when Jirald's thoughts bombarded her mind. Slimy, angry, and very resentful. He hid something behind that gaze his smile never reached. Instead of backing away she made herself stand where she was, forcing what she hoped was a smile and not a snarl onto her face. "This is a great spot."

"Yeah, we thought so too. Though, you've out-leveled me again." For just a moment a hint of steel shone through the words, but didn't persist. Murmur thought she might have imagined it. Or she would have but for the screaming warning still twisting her gut.

Jirald stepped closer, and Havoc and Dev stepped up to Murmur's side, their own smiles fixed in place.

"Fable again, huh? Got your guild started already. Good show." Jirald turned to leave, but leaned back, his smile gone. "It'll be good to have some competition."

With that he left them, returning to his group, who didn't seem impressed by his absence. Murmur turned and headed to the camp they needed, quite sure now that Jirald knew them from some previous game or other. "We have to rip through that camp and make it back to the middle one, because we need to level. That fucker has some serious ulterior motives and I am not letting another guild get those damned keys."

It was impressive what running into a potential rival could do to a group. Murmur stared in amazement as they ripped through the far camp, barely pausing to loot in-between. Beastial became their de facto loot master, arbitrarily allocating usable loot to the right people, and storing anything else. They'd figure the rest of it out later anyway. Sin's eyes held an unholy glow that had nothing to do with her class. Or maybe it did, just a little. Her friend began to cast damage and transfer spells so fluidly, it was a joy to behold. Maybe the AI got her class right.

Havoc's necromancer was a potent class. Even at these low levels Murmur could see it. He had two Damage Over Time spells, one that took away attributes from the mob, and the other that did purely damage. His pet had abilities of its own and obeyed his commands flawlessly. The dark shadows that mixed around him when he cast melded with his skin, sometimes giving him the appearance of an otherworldly being. This darkness clung to him like a second skin, and suited him far better than the nuke factory wizards he used to play.

Beastial's tank days were gone. He attacked the mobs as ferociously as his tiger, stacking damage before his pet triggered minor explosions on his order. His eyes held a slightly feral gleam, and she shuddered, not sure if it was the cool air, or the fact that he seemed so suited to the class that was chosen for him.

Merlin made an excellent ranger. That whole bow and arrow thing suited him, and Sin no longer regarded him with envious eyes. But it was Devlish who'd changed the most. He attacked the mobs with a precision he'd obviously learned from his rogue, but she watched him drain the life out of the mobs, a thin layer of bloody mist constantly traveling from the mob to himself. A dark aura surrounded him, suffusing his scales and giving them an ominous glow. Occasionally he'd unleash a taunt and the mobs would snarl viciously, disregarding everything else around them.

For her part, it was frustrating. Other than controlling the mobs, there was nothing overly unpredictable about her role. Granted, their targets were low level at the moment, and once the group had figured out their quirks, quite predictable, but she knew in just a few levels she'd gain access to some fantastic debuffs and control spells, and it was annoying not to have them yet.

Their quick rotation and massive damage output allowed them to keep the two camps, while the other group barely got through the first camp without respawns. Murmur failed to see how Jirald would be competition at all.

Though those venomous thoughts in his mind still made her skin crawl.

With a frown, she glanced through the combat logs between casting Mezes. Sure enough, Beast's tiger, Shir-Khan—she chuckled, not having noticed the name before—did a shit ton of damage. For a few seconds she couldn't find Havoc's skeleton, until she realized he'd named him Leroy. Rolling her eyes as she remembered the stories her parents had shared with her, she checked its damage too. It was like they were running with a group of eight. The pet damage allowed them to rip through mobs faster, even if it seemed they might take a tiny portion of the experience.

Worth it.

Making it back to the third camp, the layout had changed. Murmur frowned as Merlin paused. "That's a named in there, isn't it?"

Lieutenant Gashik stood tall and proud with all of his twelve levels. A guard stood on either side of him, and his luna eyes glowed red as his nose twitched, sniffing at the wind. Murmur stretched out her net, catching faint but definite thoughts from him.

People. Invading our area. They will pay.

"He knows we're here," she whispered. "Just not quite where. Yet."

CHAPTER TWELVE
Double Digits

Storm Corp
Storm Technologies Division Experimental Neuroscience Division
Countdown: Thirteen months before Somnia Online launch

Trying to fit the visit to the AIs in around his full schedule was going to be tight, but Michael was sure he could manage it. Just half an hour to check that theory. But when he arrived at the door, the lead developer for the game was standing there, her eyes obviously focused on something in her augmented vision set. She looked up as he approached, her dark brown eyes studying him closely.

Laria. He thought Laria was her name, if he remembered correctly.

"Dr. Jeffries." She inclined her head, and a brief wash of what he thought was relief passed over her face. Like she'd been waiting for ages and hoped he'd come.

"What can I do for you, Laria?" He almost second guessed himself about the name, but was glad he overrode it when he saw her smile briefly. Maybe using the headgear so much had clued him into the nuances of people's expressions more than he'd been before. He definitely wouldn't have cared to judge her actions so accurately a few years ago. He'd been consumed by building the prototype back then.

"I was wondering how close the headgear is to being ready for actual use?" She swayed slightly from foot to foot, like she was extremely nervous to ask.

He frowned as the time ticked down, quite sure this would delay his one free half hour. But the questions were about his headgear, so he could make the exception. He'd just have to make sure he got to try his experiment as soon as another hole in his schedule opened up.

"They're almost ready, although I have been tinkering with a few to get them to open up full throttle, if you will. We're not implementing that yet however, of course. Why do you ask?" He had to be careful. Talking about the headgear to someone who was interested always made him want to give out more information than he probably should.

Laria hesitated. "It's my daughter. She loves MMORPGs. It's her one actual hobby. She's been strict on herself for years, so much that we've never had to nag her. I really want to get one of those headgear sets for her. But I want to make sure I have one—a guarantee? I don't want to be left scrambling like most of the public will be."

Michael thought it over. He was sure he'd heard of Laria's family before. Hadn't the woman met her partner in an MMORPG? And it seemed they had a hard-working daughter. Why not? A million different possibilities climbed into his head. He could tweak a headset for her, and use her data as an extra step in his own results, the results the military didn't even realize he was after. "I don't see why not. I'll pull one of the first edition ones we're going to use for the big test aside, and tinker with it a bit if you like? Make it even better than the generic ones."

Laria's eyes lit up. "That would be perfect! Thank you Dr. Jeffries. She will be so excited when I give it to her."

"Now, you won't be able to give it to her for about eight months or so. But I'll make sure I set it aside in my office for her only." He smiled, and suppressed a smile as he realized he had no time left. "Now, I do have to get back to my office."

He made his farewells, overall not as disappointed as he thought he'd be. After all, he'd just managed to nab another promising guinea pig.

Release Day: Somnia Online

Lieutenant Gashik's red eyes were almost lazer like. Murmur gulped, a twinge of unease making her stomach flip-flop.

"Think you can Mez the two guards?" Merlin asked, his gaze never leaving the camp in front of them.

Murmur shrugged. "Probably, but three levels higher might result in some resists."

Dev glanced around. "I guess we're not going to know unless we try."

Merlin snorted. "Just make sure you taunt the bastard off me. I'll line of sight using that hut." He pointed to the hut, which was more of a lean-to with one wall, and two posts that held the roof up. They'd been ransacking goods from it everytime they cleared the bandit camp.

"Good idea." Havoc smiled, and began casting a buff on his pet, visible by the tenuous line it formed between them. "Pretty sure he's at least part caster."

The group moved, slowly and quietly, keeping their distance and using the trees to their advantage. They took shelter behind the small hut. Murmur stepped out to the side with Merlin, and they timed their casts.

When her Mez took hold of the guard on the right, she breathed a sigh of relief, immediately starting the cast for the other. Releasing it as Lieutenant Gashik ran after Merlin, the left guard resisted, turning its attention to her instead of the ranger.

"Fuck." But she started the spell again, and just as it closed in on her and swung its blade, the spell hit, freezing him in place. Her left arm smarted, indented by the frozen blade, and she took a step back, watching the wound gush blood. "Fantastic."

It was only a small wound comparatively, but still, that had been close.

Would Harlow be able to regrow a limb if it got detached? So many questions about game mechanics and world mechanics swam through her head. Throwing her DoT quickly on the named, she began to cast Mez on the first again, knowing the possibility to resist existed. Luckily it held on the first try, and she switched back to the other guard, watching the group carefully and gauging her distance so Sin's heals could reach her should things go wrong and pull the lieutenant and his guards onto her.

The second mob resisted again, and she wished for the umpteenth time that her magic resistance lowering spell had been a level eight one. She frowned, turning her attention back to the named, refreshed her DoT, and cast her nuke. The lieutenant was just above fifty percent.

Turning back, she renewed her Mez. This time, it stuck immediately.

"Watch out, Mur!" Beast's voice cried out, and she saw the health of the party take a sudden huge dip, as a ripple of energy made its way toward her. Running before she knew what she was doing, it only took several steps to escape it, but she looked back, shocked at the wake of damage.

"Didn't expect him to cast since he hadn't yet." Dev's bar slowly filled back up. "I'll interrupt it next time."

Sin growled. "Please do, I can area effect heal, but I'm not a miracle worker."

With the health bars slowly filling up again, Murmur returned to Mezing the guards. Their teeth were clenched together, and their eyes followed her every move, making her nervous. "Going to need some heavy taunting once we get him lower."

Dev just nodded, exerting more energy into this fight than he had even when they pulled five.

"Ha! Fucker!" He interrupted the lieutenant's cast. "No casting for you!"

Murmur laughed and she could feel the tension leak from her shoulders like water over a dam. Her Mez targets had stopped blinking, so intent was their stare on her. In the back of her mind, she wondered if that was right? Weren't they supposed to be completely stationary? Maybe the level difference allowed them that sliver of movement.

"Start taunting, Dev." She urged him, noticing Lieutenant Gashik was nearing five percent. "Beast, can you stun?"

"Pet can." He grunted.

"Keep an eye, while Dev makes sure I don't die, thanks."

Beastial chuckled. "Oh good. Mur, you'll owe me one."

She didn't even have a comeback considering she could no longer use heals as a means of extortion. Sin came to her rescue.

"Sure, you can owe Mur one, or I can, you know, not heal you." Her tone was even, with an underlying menace.

"You two are no fun." Beast pouted, but his eyes never left the target.

Finally Gashik died, and Mur recast the Mez on the guard farthest away, noting with relief that the one closest to her seemed to be looking at Dev now. The guard was easier than Gashik, noticeably so, and yet still harder than the other mobs they'd been camping. Likely a level thing. She glanced at her experience bar and groaned. Getting closer, but another eighteen percent seemed like so much. The sun was high in the sky by now, at least mid-morning.

Reflexively Mezing the guard again, she sighed. "Dev, Taunt please."

He nodded, and she knew instinctively that he'd never forget, but still felt better for having said it out loud. Activating Thought Sensing wasn't taking as much effort anymore, and she could keep it up as long as she thought about it occasionally. The same with her own internal shield. How much of the shield was just her mind? Did it create a true barrier? If so, maybe that barrier could be adapted for other things.

The last guard finally heaved its last attack at Dev, who side stepped and thrust clean through it. Tactical attacks from the group were well and good, but these NPCs had their own buffs, defenses, and attacks. Not to mention many seemed to have their own form of regeneration. One of these days she'd figure out how to zero in on their weaknesses.

Your group has slain Lieutenant Gashik and his guards.

Your group is the first to slay Lieutenant Gashik and his guards.

Lieutenant Gashik sent a plea to his men, one of whom will replace him. Your names are known, and the bandits have a

long reach. Watch your backs.

You gain experience.

Murmur blinked at the scrolling words across her screen, watching them intently. Her experience jumped a whole three percent. She glanced around, noticing that her friends were having the same reaction.

"What, it couldn't have just said 'your faction with bandits is shit?'" Beastial voiced what they were all thinking.

On the bright side, Gashik and his men yielded some pretty cool stuff. Murmur scored a dagger with plus one stamina and intelligence. Sadly, it wasn't usable until level ten. None of it was. Level ten seemed an age away.

"No slowing down." Merlin scouted their mobs yet again. "Keep it coming. Also, when do you get area of effect aggro holding spells?"

Dev grunted. "I like to let my spells surprise me."

"Know what I like?" Merlin didn't wait for an answer. "Training people who look at their spells beforehand."

"Ass." Dev glared at Merlin's back as they moved back to the middle camp.

Merlin inched farther forward, drew his bow, and pulled the next round of mobs.

"I have a stun. Four seconds duration. I think I get more as time goes by." Murmur glanced at her list while executing Mesmerize.

Beastial grunted as he smashed a rogue with his mace. "Think we could stun lock? Haven't stun locked in so long."

Sin laughed. "Volleys of arrows and stun locks are our friends."

"Not sure if we can, but we can try. You know when we're like level twenty-five." Murmur frowned at her HUD and sifted through her stat increases. All her spell levels were already well into level ten. At least that wouldn't be a problem. Thought Sensing had increased to twenty-seven, and shielding to twenty-eight. Frowning, she noticed Projection was only at three. Perhaps she had to talk into other people's heads for that to go up, or else use Suggestion?

Some things were so straight forward, and then there were her skills. Nothing black and white about them.

Dev leveled first. About ten percent in front of Murmur. His cresting over to double digits rejuvenated the entire group. They fought harder and faster, took more risks, and became more boisterous. At this rate, they'd all hit level ten within the next hour or so.

Murmur could feel the tiredness pulling at her. But more than that was a bone deep weariness at the very back of her head, somewhere it felt like her true thoughts no longer existed. If she believed in that sort of thing, she'd think she was disembodied, but that was just crazy talk. More likely, it was hunger. Considering it was sometime around two in the morning in the tangible world, her food consumption hadn't been anywhere close to enough. Even if she wasn't hungry.

Merlin dinged next, closely followed by Havoc.

"Awww yes!" Merlin did a little ranger jig with his bow, jutting out a hip and striking a pose. "You know you love me!"

Murmur laughed. She'd forgotten how good it could be to hang around people who didn't judge her for trying hard. Unless she counted Havoc, who had seemed very off in the last day.

Beast groaned. "So close. I can actually feel my stomach rumbling. I can't even remember the last time I ate real food."

"Bet you smell too," Sin elbowed him as they waited for another pull.

"You absorb then disperse blood as a healing mechanism. Which one of us is the more disgusting?" He raised an eyebrow at her before heading back into battle.

Murmur shook her head. "Don't antagonize your healer, Beast."

He laughed, swinging his mace viciously. "Right, Mur, Sin's nothing like you."

Sin glared at his back. "No, I'm worse. I learned from the best."

Beast had the good grace not to reply, and instead refocused his efforts on downing a raving bard in front of him. Lucky for him, he dinged once the mob died. Considering Sin hadn't filled his health bar during that fight at all, it was a god-send.

Finally it was Mur's turn, and shortly thereafter Sin.

"Ten. We're freaking *ten*!" Dev raised his fist to the sky in a victory pose.

Havoc resummoned his pet, buffed it and turned to Murmur. "You're not going to let us sleep yet, are you."

"Power nap do? How about we meet back here at seven-thirty in the real world. That's about three and a half hours I think." She glanced at her quests, noting her *weird thoughts can be heard everywhere* quest was prompting her to go and see Belius as soon as possible.

"I know I have the next step of the vague quest to end all vague quests to do. Not sure how long that'll take, but I need food, and a bit of shut eye would be good."

"Wonders will never cease." Dev stepped forward, his eyes reflecting his tiredness. "Thanks little sis, for holding back for us oldies."

"Idiot." She muttered. "You're in college. So ancient."

"Set an alarm!" Sin practically shouted the words out.

"What?" Merlin put his hands over his ears.

She punched him in the arm. "You can set an alarm. Your account will alert you ten minutes or whatever you set beforehand, so you can get in on time."

"Wow," Havoc dismissed his pet as they began walking back toward Ululate. "That's enabling."

Murmur took a moment to talk to the guild: *Taking a brief break and power nap. Keep going everyone. I swear I'll be more social once we get some more levels.*

Veranol: Hahaha Mur, pull the other one.

She shook her head and dismissed the chat, knowing the rest of the responses would likely be in the same vein. Veranol was playing a shaman— she was glad, too. He'd always been one of her favorite healers to work with in a raid.

"Sorry guys, I don't know how long this errand quest thing is going to go on, I have to Gate and catch a wagon. I'll catch up with you soon." Murmur waved goodbye and gated back to the spot they bound in Ululate, before the others could say anything. As she went to leave, an arm grabbed hold of her. Just about to turn and give Jirald an ear full, she realized it was the hazily nondescript NPC holding her arm, and not the other player.

She snatched it away, taking two steps backward. "What?"

"You have the aura. Be careful with it. You have no idea what it means." The sharp blue of his eyes pierced right down through her, taking her breath in such a way that she began coughing to regain some air. Then he looked away, eyes blank once more. Even then, after he'd spoken to her, she still couldn't place his appearance.

Irritation at an all new high, she pushed through the crowd gathered around the stalls, almost tripped over a group of kids who were playing some sort of strange throw the ball and freeze game, and then down to the wagon, calling out to Jan.

"Hiya, miss. Headed back already?" He asked in a polite tone. She handed him another two silver and climbed aboard. "Ye lucky ye caught me. Couple more minutes an I'da been gone."

"Impeccable timing, that's me." She smiled at him, rubbing her arm where the binder had touched her skin. It didn't look any different, but she'd be more careful around everything from now on. No time like the present to find Belius and try to figure out what the hell was going on.

CHAPTER THIRTEEN

Psiniocist

Storm Corp
Storm Technologies Division Experimental Neuroscience Division
Countdown: Eleven months before Somnia Online launch

Finally, Michael had a hole in his schedule. He'd completed the headset as Laria had asked him to, complete with his own little tweaks that should provide some good alternate data. One of his favorite test subjects, Ava, also had one. The headgear was complete with the game design and was already being manufactured, and the game had launched preorders with a very specific marketing campaign. His plan was coming together.

The smile that crept over him gave him a giddy feeling.

He stood in front of the servers, his headgear in his hands, watching the lights on their small dashboards rain down with reds, yellows, greens, and blues. Sometimes it seemed like purple, silver, and gold danced among them, too.

Each of the three main AIs had three of their own subordinate AIs, giving them a total of twelve all together. All of these would run a massive three continent virtual world. Storm expected big things from this game, from the headgear, from Michael.

The test he'd run by himself a couple of days ago hadn't worked, but when they'd trialed the two hundred and fifty people with the headgear, it went flawlessly, raking in masses of data for his team to process.

It was late, and everyone had gone home. Or rather, Michael sent everyone home. Everyone needed a break now and again. Silke and Brandon had been reluctant to leave, but Michael had insisted, mentally screaming at them while wearing a smile. There was no sun in the server room, no outside influence at all, and now they required a thumb print and retina scan to enter. He liked the updated security. That way he could be sure someone wasn't just fucking with him.

Laying down on the couch, Michael put the headgear on, noting how the battered prototype still worked wonders, how her upgrades had simply made her better, while keeping her so familiar.

"Okay, baby, just you and me." He spoke to it and booted up the interface. The game wasn't live yet, and only several starting zones existed for testing purposes, and then not even the fully fleshed out version. *Those* were behind lock and key.

Talk to me, he said to the AIs. He didn't utter the words out loud, instead directing his thoughts toward them.

There was a pause, and for a few moments, Michael thought he'd been wrong. While disappointing, it was expected. He'd probably jumped the gun. Most people would think his assumptions crazy as it was.

Why are you in our world? The voice was distinctly Sui, an odd hint of metal behind it, like an emotion Michael couldn't quite place.

I was curious, to see you all, to see your world. He hoped he was phrasing it properly. It wasn't a lie, AIs didn't seem to like lies. They seemed to know if what you told was true or not, but neglecting to mention something rarely seemed to flag their radar. So he was very careful only to think and say what he truly felt.

Why speak to us in here? Rav's tone, as always, was far more reasonable. *Why seek us out with your mind?*

Their forms were but shadow, nothing he could make out properly in the dim lighting and fiery mist. But he pressed on. *Because I wasn't sure if it was possible, and was testing a theory.*

Theory? Thra almost laughed, a surprise in itself. How could an AI understand humor? *You wanted to speak with your mind, and were hoping we could hear you?*

Michael hesitated. *I wanted to see if you could speak into my mind. I hadn't thought about it reversed.*

He's not lying. Rav interjected.

But Michael could see Sui wasn't impressed.

He may not be lying, but he is not welcome among us. He is not genuine.

True. Rav's tone seemed to smile, with a hint of sadness. *I'm sorry, Michael. We can't let you come in here.*

Michael wasn't sure what they meant, and he tried to reason with them, tried to reach out to them, but his vision spun, and then everything went black.

End of Release Day: Somnia Online

The Enchanter Guild was far less congested when Murmur finally pushed her way through the door. Elvita wasn't at the counter, and only a handful of adventurers loitered in the foyer. A couple were learning their spells, skin glowing with runes that danced across their skin. Another few chatted amongst themselves, but none of their thoughts stood out to her, nothing sparked an alarm or yelled a warning. In a way she was relieved; if Elvita had been there, Murmur would have had to check herself against the influence she was pretty sure the enchanter NPCs emitted.

Thickening her own shields, she moved on through to the back hall. Just over twelve hours ago there'd been a hustle and bustle so busy in the hall, she'd barely been able to squeeze through. Even this part of the guild was almost empty. She frowned, wondering if everyone was just out leveling, or maybe people were sleeping, or if not that many people were playing enchanters. She figured the latter was a probability only because the system would have to be careful whose head it chose to send voices into, right?

Knocking on the door, she'd barely finished the motion when Belius ripped it open, a huge grin on his face.

"There you are! I was expecting you sooner."

Murmur studied his face. The excitement seemed genuine, and as she looked past him she could see scrolls littering the desk. The room appeared to be in slight disarray, which she'd not seen since the game began. Not that that was a huge amount of time or anything, but still.

"Had to catch a wagon." She said simply, and closed the door behind her.

"Congratulations!"

She raised an eyebrow, bringing up the quest line.

You have reached level ten. Congratulations. Your mental fortitude is exemplary. You are ready for the next step of your training. Make sure to see your trainer.

"Well, I got told to come here, although I don't believe I get any more spells until I hit level twelve..." her voice trailed off as she watched Belius' excitement increase. "What do you know, that you're bursting to tell me?"

"You're the first one! The first one who's read through the clues, followed their instincts, and expanded their mind!" He motioned her over to the desk, rolling up scrolls and picking up books that were scattered around before shoving them into some sort of order in a corner.

"I'm the only one?" That didn't sound right. Abilities shouldn't just be available to singular people. This was an MMO, technically anyway, even if it felt like a true world. "I'm the only one who can do this?"

Belius nodded, but then stopped and looked up, a wave of confusion washing over his expression. "Well, you're the only one who can do this at the moment."

"So others can learn this too?" She almost held her breath, waiting for an answer.

"Of course they can. Technically. Everyone has the same chances to learn about and discover more about the world. But not everyone has the inclination nor is everyone interested. Even if they gather some hints, not everyone follows them. It takes a certain amount of intuition, of game immersion." He finally singled out two scrolls, and motioned her to sit.

A wave of relief stole over Murmur as she sat down. Sure, it'd be nice to be the only one with this ability, but it wouldn't feel as accomplished if no one else could earn it. All she wanted to do was lean her head down and fall asleep. "I really need some actual sleep."

Belius' smile was warm, in a subtle locus way. Since their jaws moved with a slight hitch, and didn't seem as agile as human's, there was a fine art to achieving the expression instead of a scowl. At least for players, and Murmur was determined to master the intricacies of her species. She waited for him to speak.

"I won't keep you long. You'll be able to get back to your list."

Really? How the hell did these NPCs know so much about her? She checked her shields, tightening them further, but there were no holes for him to peek through, so maybe the comment had just been coincidence or else a guess.

"So," she gathered her last vestiges of energy and sat up straight. "What am I here for?"

"You've leveled up. Well—sideways. And gained a whole new magic bar. Sort of like your mana, but it doesn't adjust the same way. You need certain levels of it to build up, so that you can utilize specific abilities." He looked at her expectantly.

"What new magic bar?" Her head spun with the concept. Health, Mana...she wasn't a rogue so it couldn't be energy. Weren't you supposed to choose your hybrid path at twenty, not ten?

"Sorry. Wasn't expecting this outcome quite yet, although if anyone was going to get it this fast, it was going to be you. Anyway—Mental Acuity. Since you've developed thought sending, projecting, and shielding on your own, you'll now have the ability to master those and move on to stronger, more dangerous abilities." He was so eager, the galaxies in his eyes shone. Meanwhile Murmur was endlessly tired, and couldn't quite wrap her head around the whole thing.

"Please spell it out, Belius." What did he mean by it was going to be her?

"You've had a class change."

Murmur sat up straight, her sleepiness suddenly gone. But she'd only just got used to the enchanter!

Belius smiled. "You're now a psionicist."

She blinked at him. "A what?"

He laughed and continued. "A psionicist. While an integral part of the enchanter family, you've taken it a step further. So now you have a Mental Acuity bar which will allow you to diverge and develop your mentally based talents within a couple of areas. Expanding your mind and its power."

"Does this mean I can't become a hybrid?"

This time Belius seemed confused, as if he wanted to ask her why on earth she'd want to be a hybrid when she was this psionicist. "Well, of course you still *can*, but it's a large time investment and..." He tapered off at the look of determination on her face.

"Very well. Yes. Of course you could, but you have ten levels left to decide if you want to."

Murmur smiled. "Good. Now, what can I do now that I couldn't do as an enchanter, and will this stop me from being able to charm creatures? Will it interfere with the spells I would have leveled up with?"

"It won't interfere. You are still a part of the enchanter family; this is a specialization."

"What does it focus on?"

"The mind. Yours, that of others. The control of both. The development of powers beyond what you can imagine. Influencing others to do as you wish them to, controlling enemies, or else taking away their control." He paused as she shifted uncomfortably in her seat. "Ah, I see you've already thought about that. Mesmerizing an opponent isn't painful for them, just really annoying. After all, it's not fun to have all your bodily control taken from you, is it?"

Murmur nodded. "So true. I noticed one of the mobs looking at me today. I was so scared they were going to break free."

Belius smiled, an understanding in his eyes she didn't think an NPC should be able to reflect. "Did you hear anything odd?"

Her gut clenched, and Murmur hesitated briefly, trying to cover it with a yawn. She still had the theory that these NPCs were utilizing some of their enchanter abilities on player characters. So instead of letting him know about the strange binder in Ululate, she chose another option. "This one guy that I keep running into seems to have a grudge against my friends and I from sometime, somewhere."

She watched Belius to see if he accepted her half-truth. His chuckle reached his eyes and she slotted the gut feeling to the back of her mind to ponder later. "That and a named that spawned while we were leveling didn't seem impressed by other people in general."

This time Belius laughed. "It's an amazing ability. You'll do well with these." And he pushed the three scrolls toward her, his eyes lit with the same excitement he'd showed when she walked in.

Opening the first it read:

Mind Bolt

This ability allows you to cast a spear of mental anguish into the depths of an opponent's brain.

Effects: Opponents will be unable to concentrate enough to use spells or abilities for four seconds. This time increases as the caster's level does.

Cost: Requires Mental Acuity to be at 20.

Caution: Use sparingly. Backlash from overuse or improper use can cause the same effect in the caster...or worse.

Murmur blinked at the spell. It sounded powerful. And dangerous. Gingerly, she handled the second scroll as if it might bite her.

Phase Shift

This ability allows you to negatively affect your opponent s mind. Believing they are a second or two apart from reality, they will reside there for up to fifteen seconds.

Effect: Target's mind is encased in a phase of illusion. The target will be convinced they've shifted to a different time pocket, and thus are incapable of moving. This effect begins at fifteen seconds duration, and levels with the caster through to a maximum of ninety seconds.

Cost: Requires Mental Acuity to be at forty. For larger castings, the cost will double.

Caution: Phase Shift may be utilized on single or multiple targets at once. Weigh the number of targets carefully, else it backfire and shift you. Sometimes the shift in mind can cause illusions near the caster. Make sure the voices you're hearing are your own.

"Wow." While the cautions were making her wary of the abilities, the results would be fantastic! Murmur readied herself and squared her shoulders, looking directly at Belius.

"Is there a catch it's not telling me? "

Belius smiled, and this time there was all his cunning and intelligence behind it. "This is why I've taken a liking to you, Murmur. You don't take things at face value. In fact, you question everything, even when you have much information written down in front of you."

He stood up and walked over to one of his shelves. It had plenty of tiny artifacts on it; small stones and scrolls, even tomes. He picked up something and headed back to her. Belius placed a smooth round stone made of what appeared to be a clear quartz crystal in her hand.

"As you progress, you will activate new skills. Not even I know them all. Some will need to be learned or notated to activate them fully, but that is a while away." He smiled at her shocked expression and held up a hand.

Picking up the quartz, Murmur hefted it in her hand. It was large enough that her fingers didn't quite meet when she tried to close her hand around it. "What is this?"

Belius hesitated long enough that Murmur made a note of it. Whether it meant what he was about to say was the truth, or perhaps the opposite, she'd take what he said with a grain of salt.

"It's a focusing crystal. It's never been used before, and thus should easily attune to your mental waves and acuity. Use it when you require a boost in power, be it for distance, or even for use of your abilities. This will help you and may offset some—but not all—of the consequences for the use of your power."

"Consequences. You mean just for me as the caster?" She watched him, her eyes never leaving his.

Again, he paused slightly before answering. "Not only for you, but for the world as a whole. There must be a certain amount of balance. If what you do, you do unprovoked, then yes, the consequences for yourself and those you care for would likely be dire. However, self-defense means a lot here in Somnia. We don't take lightly to those who try to bully their way through life."

Murmur smiled. That was a sentiment she could get behind. "Very well, Bel. I think I understand."

Her trainer smiled and saw her to the door, but as per usual his smile didn't reach his eyes.

Real World Day 2: Somnia Online

Bleep Bleep Bleep Bleep.

Wren's eyes shot open as the alarm sounded. Sunlight shone through a gap in her curtains turning her already irritated mood into annoyance. Launching herself off the bed she closed the blackout curtains, cursing at them for daring to let in light. Who did they think they were, seriously? A wave of disorientation swept over her, and she fell hard against the wall, steadying herself. The room seemed to glitch around her. After several seconds, the vertigo faded and her sight stopped playing tricks on her. Wren sighed. At least she hadn't been wearing her headset.

Harlow was still asleep, curled up on her side, her skin even paler against the indigo sheets. Maybe it was because she was used to seeing Sinister. Wren set her alarm for fifteen minutes before they were due to log back in, mainly because she wanted to grab something to eat. Running down the stairs, Wren almost ran into her mother at the bottom of them.

"Sorry, Mom!"

Her mother had deep rings under her eyes, but a soft smile crossed her face when she looked at Wren. "Sweetie. You look raring to go. Did you have a nap?"

Wren nodded, making her way to the fruit basket before yanking a protein bar out of the cupboard, grabbing one for Harlow too. "Yeah, had to. We'll make mistakes if we don't get some sleep, after all."

"Be careful." Her mother said. A shadow flitted across her expression. She turned toward the stairs again but paused and looked over her shoulder. "Oh, congratulations."

Wren blinked. "How'd you know?"

"You're the first one to unlock any of the hidden classes. Of course I know." She started climbing the stairs, coffee in hand. "Keep up the good work."

Wren stood there, watching her mother, and dwelling on her words. Any of the hidden classes? So there were lots of them then, just like hidden skills. The time crunch came rushing back to her, and she bounded up the stairs. By her calculations she'd managed about two hours sleep. In another twenty-four to thirty-six hours, they'd probably need to take a four to six hour break. But by then, they should be what, level twelve? She laughed at the thought as she shoved down the last bite of her food.

Entering the room she noticed Harlow was up and in the bathroom. She sighed and waited, doing some stretches to give her body a break. She made the bed hastily and finished just in time for Harlow to emerge.

"Morning, sleepy head. Catch." She threw the bar at Harlow who smiled gratefully.

"Thanks Mur. Wren. Person I've known most of my life."

Her slip up was just a sign of how tired her friend was. Maybe they'd needed to break sooner. It had never been a problem when Wren played a healer—she'd always gotten by on less sleep, but sometimes Harlow didn't do so well.

"It's okay, Wren. Sin is working on her crafting in-game while we're gone. Yay for level ten." Harlow's expression was contorted by tiredness, and she missed her hand when she tried to rest her chin against it.

Wren blinked at the words, having completely forgotten that perk of hitting level ten. "Damn it. I forgot. I don't think I even gave you the cloth I have."

"It's okay. Let's get in before the boys take off without us."

Murmur sat at a table in the Enchanter Guild.

She couldn't even remember having sat herself down before logging out, but apparently she had. Come to think of it, she also hadn't activated the new skills she got. The guild foyer was practically deserted, so she took the scrolls out and activated them.

Runes flowed up her arms with a soft glow, welcoming the powers into her body, absorbing them into her being. She watched them, marveling at the almost ticklish sensation.

Congratulations.

You have changed classes.

You are a psionicist.

You are the first psionicist of Somnia.

Not only do you possess the skills of an enchanter, but you have gained Mental Acuity. This allows you to access the psychic ability line. With enough practice you might manifest kinetic abilities too. From now on you must be in control of yourself at all times. A stray thought could hurt someone. Anger might kill. Make sure you are aware of your moods.

She sighed and stood, puttering over to where Elvita stood behind the counter perusing a book. Making sure her shield was up, she cleared her throat. "Hey Elvita."

Elvita glanced up and smiled warmly. "Murmur. Pleasure to see you."

Her eyes narrowed and then her smile widened. "Well, well. Belius' first psionicist. Congratulations."

"Thank you." Murmur didn't want to sound conceited, nor did she want the NPC to influence her mood, so she made sure she'd clamped down on her shielding.

Elvita chuckled and held out her hand. "Come on. I bet what you've got in that bag of yours is heavy. Make me poor, Murmur."

"Gimme a sec and then gladly." Murmur grinned and rifled through, retrieving meat, herbs and spices, butter, and quite a few mushrooms. "Thanks, Elvita. I owe you one."

The NPC cocked her head to one side and her expression didn't budge, making it seem etched in stone and stilted. "I'll hold you to that."

Murmur shivered as she headed in to see Arvin. From now on, she was going to watch what she said to people. Now she had no idea what sort of favor she owed the guild NPC.

Just as she reached the kitchen, a cascade of chats invaded her party line.

Sinister: What the fuck, Mur?

Havoc: Psionic-what?

Devlish: I leave you alone for a few hours and what do you do?

Beastial: What aren't you telling us?

Merlin: Damn it. What the fuck happened?

Sighing, she sent her reply back. *Give me ten and I'll be there. Just cooking up a batch. I forgot about the crafting thing. See you soon.*

Ten minutes later and forty-two meals and thirty-five gold richer, Murmur gated to Ululate.

She stepped onto the path quickly, still getting over the disorientation, and glanced back at the binding spot, but the creepy binding NPC didn't seem to be there. Turning around quickly, she couldn't spot him anywhere in the middle of town either. The locals were packing down their carts and goods for the day, even though there were still many travelers passing through.

"Mur!" Sin ran toward her and hugged her. "What the hell?"

Murmur felt decidedly uncomfortable. There were too many people about. While she knew anyone could access the abilities if they played through the quests properly, she still didn't want to give away her guild's small advantage. "Let's talk on the way to the caves?"

Dev glanced at her, frowned, and then nodded. "Sure thing, boss."

As they headed out she handed around her parceled food, her own thoughts distracting her from where they were going.

Merlin examined the new bow one of the guards had dropped in their encounter with Lieutenant Gashik. "This thing's pretty sweet for a level ten bow."

Murmur began to relax. Having her friends around helped.

She pulled up her character information as she activated her shield and sensing net, and watched the Mental Acuity bar. Sure enough, it ticked up very slowly with the use of her activated skills. That made sense. She'd have to charge the Mental Acuity up before she could use it.

"Mur?" Havoc's tone held concern, and she looked up to see that they were already well out of the city and on their way to their destination.

He waited for her to make eye contact before continuing. "You're being so quiet. It's worrying. Talk to us, because you've got to know we're dying to understand how you, well. Changed classes."

She sighed again, shrugging her shoulders more from discomfort than anything else. "It's not really a class change, but more of a class evolution."

And she launched into everything that happened from when Belius had first told her about thoughts and people who could read them. When she was finished, they walked in silence for a few moments, already most of the way to the caves.

"So I guess I really should go through those vague ass screen alerts again." Sin gently elbowed Murmur in the side.

Murmur laughed softly. "Yeah. I have so many of the vague ones I don't know where to start. What *is* a good idea is killing heaps of bandits. Booya!"

Guild chat lit up, streaking across her vision only to end up blinking at her sullenly from the bottom of her range.

Rashlyn: Hey Mur! What the hell is a psionicist?

An enchanter. "What?" She glared back at Sin. "I'm not lying."

Rashlyn: Cool—I didn't know we could change titles.

Veranol: Me either. How'd you do it, Mur?

Long and arduous quest line. Hey, we're ten too, you gonna let us overtake you or what? Murmur hoped she'd changed the subject.

Rashlyn: Bullshit. We're headed out that way. Beast mentioned some caves out there. I say we dominate the whole fucking area.

Girl after my own heart. See you soon. Mur smiled. She'd forgotten how well they got along with Rash. Girls had to stick together in games, and they'd been in a few together.

They walked wide around the outside of the first bandit camp, making sure to keep cover as much as possible, considering the weird and wonderful intelligence levels of the NPCs. They made their way to the cave mouth. There were no groups in the vicinity that they could see. Merlin snuck up to the entrance, scouting out the guards and any patrols he could see.

Murmur hugged herself, running through everything that had happened in her mind, still pushing to listen for anything that could harm them. Havoc nudged her elbow.

"What aren't you telling us?"

She looked up at him, always the kind, level-headed, quiet one. He'd have made a much better psionicist. She smiled a little sadly. "Just—it's weird. I get the feeling, the sense that the NPC members of the Enchanter Guild aren't giving me all the information. And I don't mean it in a 'damn it, help me win the game' way. I mean that I feel like they try to soothe me, enchant me. Or at least they used to before I could shield. And once I could, they got more wary about me."

She shrugged. "I'm probably just being paranoid."

Havoc pursed his lips and shook his head. "No. You've never been one to be paranoid. You might be blunt and sometimes callous because of that, but you rarely let in room for paranoia. I'd say go with your gut."

Despite herself, Murmur laughed. His words mirrored Belius' in an eerie sort of way. "Thanks, Evan. I appreciate that."

He grinned and moved forward. "Come on. I believe it's time for you to try out some of those new abilities."

Suddenly, being an enchanter didn't seem so bad anymore.

CHAPTER FOURTEEN

Open Dungeon

Storm Entertainment
Somnia Online Division Development offices
Countdown: two months before release

Laria Sommers paced the floor of her office, biting at her nails before bitterly remembering that she needed to stop that habit. Shayla popped her head around the doorway, "What's up? We've only got a minute before that blasted meeting."

"I need to test one of the containment devices." Laria pulled her hands forcibly from her mouth, trying not to fidget with nervousness. "There are some simulations I think I can run to make immersion more complete."

Shayla raised an eyebrow and frowned. "Somnia launches in two months, Laria, shouldn't you be thinking about that instead of that stupid defense contract we're hoping to impress?"

"Technically, they're tied together. Somnia's software and hardware will all be under scrutiny. Let me undertake some tests." Laria hated the pleading tone in her voice, but she needed this more than anyone could understand. If she couldn't create the right atmosphere, the right environment, none of what she was trying to do would work. Her timeline was minuscule, but her husband was helping her and perhaps, with all of that, they could still pull this off.

"You're planning on doing all of this at home, aren't you? Okay. But I want daily reports. You'll need David to help you with this." Shayla's eyes narrowed. She tapped a finger against her chin, a thoughtful look in her eyes. "No. Listen to me, don't object. You have way too much work going on as it is."

About to leave, Shayla stopped and looked back. "Maybe Wren can help you too? She's very bright. You know she has a place here if she ever wants to intern."

Laria paled, but tried to smile through it. "If I get Wren to use it, I won't be able to stop her from helping."

Real World Day 2: Somnia Online

Murmur stood at the top of a stone pathway carved into the cave and stared at the scene below her. The path wound down in an oval spiral, to make one huge warren, different paths leading from the other entrances far across the way. Huts with small fireplaces dotted the interior and patrols of bandit members walked in all directions. They chatted and played games, looking very little like NPCs.

She frowned.

Beastial was practically beside himself. "Guys. This is an open world dungeon. A freaking open world dungeon!"

"I wonder how many named are in here." Devlish mused half to himself as he stood in the shadows with the others, watching the activity below them.

"Only one way to find out." Sinister grinned. In the dim light it looked like she had blood on her lips.

"Take it slow though," Havoc cautioned, and Merlin laughed.

"Yes sir, Mr. Havoc sir!" Merlin mock saluted, and stealthed, making his way to the roughly hewn rock wall. Murmur liked the strategy of not getting knocked off the edge. A fall like that would mean death, and a long way of fighting without their stuff to retrieve their corpses.

"Eleven through thirteen." Beastial muttered as he joined them. "I couldn't see anything higher than that, but these caverns go on for days, so for all I know, there could be twenties down there."

Merlin waited for a two-man patrol to reach them before pulling, with nowhere to line of site them, Murmur glanced at her Mental Acuity and figured she may as well try it out. "I'll silence the ranger once Mez breaks. He'll have to run to us, because he'll only be able to melee. At least that's the theory."

An air of excitement hung over the group once she finished speaking.

Merlin pulled, and Murmur's Mez got the ranger before he could pull off a shot. She had the timing down now to where she began casting as Merlin pulled his elbow back. So far, it had worked.

This mob was two levels higher than them, and she did have to refresh the Mez on the ranger once. As the first one died, a message scrolled in front of her eyes.

You have gained experience.

You have gained grouping experience.

Congratulations. You have reached your first milestone level. As such, whenever you are in a group of four or more people, within four levels of each other, you will receive a group bonus to your experience. The larger the group, the more you gain. Happy hunting!

There wasn't time to check it, or to celebrate, because Murmur's Mez was about to break. "Breaking in three!"

She summoned Mind Bolt, and the runes up and down her arms began to glow, like a gently strobing light. As her Mez broke, she slammed the Mind Bolt into the ranger. It stumbled to one knee, holding its head for a moment. Its life dropped by twenty percent. After a beat, it rose and ran into the group, fury on its face, unable to access its abilities.

Murmur watched her hands, unsure exactly how she'd released that apart from picturing it in her mind. The runes under her skin and lights at the end of her hair faded slowly, leaving her arms silver once more. Her Mental Acuity sat at forty-two now, twenty points depleted. Exactly like she thought. If she used the ability, it drained her Mental Acuity. It was probably best if she always held forty in reserve. For *oh shit* moments.

Refreshed after their first cave pull, they began moving down at a solid pace. Murmur focused on keeping her own shielding up and her sensing net out, her Mental Acuity close to full. After several pulls, while waiting for mana to regenerate, Merlin turned to her.

"So, you're my friend, right Mur?"

She nodded.

"So, no shooting me with that bolt, right?"

She laughed. "No promises. You have to toe the line."

Merlin inched away from her as they ventured down the winding path. They were about to move onto the next roaming group when guild chat lit up again. Mur groaned, Beast and Dev echoing her sentiment.

Veranol: So, we're like here.

Rashlyn: Figured yelling across would be a bad idea considering how intelligent these mobs seem. Also, there's a weird level nine guy out there who told us to give you his love, Mur?

Murmur stopped short, another shiver racing down her spine, and answered in a way she hoped didn't give away the unease roiling in her gut. *He's a joker. Met him at level one.*

Rashlyn: Right then. We'll work our way down from this side. Meet you in the middle at the bottom.

Merlin: Race you.

Dansyn: Fuck you, ranger.

Merlin: Not my fault you're inferior, bard.

"Mur, I really don't like Jirald." Sin stood close, whispering. She grabbed Mur's hand and squeezed. "How about we just never leave each other's side from now on?"

Murmur looked at her best friend gratefully. While she put on a brave front with the others, Sin knew her the best, knew the creepers they'd both encountered in game worlds before. "I think that sounds like a plan."

Despite the fact that the pulls in this dungeon were far more difficult due to pathing and hyper realistic responses by the NPCs, Murmur couldn't help but feel a surge of pride at the fact that just over a day into the game they had two full groups ripping through a level eleven to fourteen dungeon. An open world dungeon, with named mobs scattered throughout.

Her new skills felt like forbidden fruit, secret and dangerous. Yet it was such a rush to use them. The sense of euphoria only lasted several pulls. As they moved methodically down the ramp, they began reaching the huts, the first of which held a named bandit. Another lieutenant, Kellin, stood tall, her leather armor sleek on her viking body. Fierce and well-muscled, tattoos stood out against pale flesh that hadn't seen the sun for a while. Her eyes burned an unholy red, and she hefted two wicked looking axes in her hands.

At level thirteen, Lieutenant Kellin gave Murmur pause. However, she was only the first orange level, so Mur's spells should stick. Being level ten now, she hoped they'd be able to fight these named.

"I'm not sure how to pull them." Merlin whispered to the group, the irritation evident in his voice.

"Five of them." Beast muttered, scanning the group. While two were slightly off to the right, there's no way it was enough space to pull the other three, or to pull those two away without alerting the others.

"Add to that there's another patrol that comes up here and spends like thirty seconds talking to the two on the right." Merlin sighed. "Mur, can you Mez that many?"

"I can, technically. Give me a second." She rummaged through her spell and ability book, noticing that her Mental Acuity skills were classed as abilities instead of spells.

"I have an area effect stun, but that's going to break any Mez near it, and while I can also root the mob, I could just as well be casting Mez and rendering one completely out of commission." She glanced at her Mental Acuity bar, which was sitting at eighty-two, and shrugged. In for a penny, in for a pound. "I could try to group Phase Shift, but I have no idea what that's going to do. It'll get all five of them, and should give me time to Mez them one by one—maybe its duration isn't exact?"

"Why are you asking us for?" Sin punched her in the arm playfully. "It's your skill."

Murmur laughed softly. "Yeah, I guess you have a point. I also have no idea how useful or useless I'll be after I cast it. So—I'd say burn your cooldowns if you had any yet."

"I knew there was something I missed having." Havoc muttered, but grinned evilly. "Can't wait for level twelve."

"Okay. We just need to time it for when the patrol is on its way back down." Devlish moved back a few feet. "Just let me know where you want me."

Merlin clamped his hands over his mouth, as if trying to stop himself from speaking.

"You're leaving yourself wide open mate," Beastial laughed.

"Shut up." Dev's blush was barely visible in the dim firelight, but the slight rouge to his scales didn't go unnoticed. His glare landed on Merlin, who hurriedly sobered.

"Take down the named first, I'll—shit." Murmur frowned at the two who were standing where the patrol would meet them. "I'll have to Mez them and then you'll have to break it and pull one at a time back. Can you do that Beast? Can your tiger avoid casting DoTs?"

He motioned at something none of them could see and nodded. "Yeah, I can do that. Pull one at a time over and you'll re-Mez them?"

She nodded. "It'll be close, but it should work."

"Might as well find out. Better to die while we're young!" Merlin grinned and they stood together, a little ahead of the rest of the group. He turned serious, dropping his voice low enough so the others behind him didn't hear. "You sure about this Mur?"

Murmur glanced at him for a moment, really taking in the elf with the fine blond hair and delicate features. Merlin, Dev, Havoc. All of them. They all cared, they were always concerned, and they put up with her when Murmur wasn't sure she'd put up with herself. For an instant she was so grateful to all of them, her chest constricted a bit, bringing her close to tears.

Smiling genuinely for the first time since logging back in, she nodded. "Yeah. I'm good."

Shielding and sensing nets still in place, Murmur took a deep breath. She had no idea what to expect, nor if attacking the mobs with Phase Shift before they were fighting would count as using it in a bad way and what consequences she would face. But it was better to find out now, than to wait until she was higher and would get more pissed off by a death, or when her experiment might wipe out an entire raid full of people.

Unlike Mind Bolt, which just shot out of her mind, Phase Shift required an intricate display of finger dexterity. She almost wove her fingers into knots casting the spell and holding it for the right time. Taking a deep breath as the patrol began to move away, she released the skill.

A spasm wracked her body as a shockwave exploded out from her in a radius that covered the five enemies. The ground shook, and several slivers of rock fell down from the ledges above them. The cloud expanded around the targets, and the shift of them into the phase void made a sickening, sucking sound.

Murmur gasped for breath, suddenly light-headed, her thoughts swirling as she fought to get enough air into her lungs. She barely remembered to cast Mez on the named. Lieutenant Kellin shifted back to reality, when she looked at Murmur wild anger shone in her eyes. The clock kept ticking down with only twelve seconds left. In hindsight, casting it on five mobs the first time had been a very bad idea.

"Named now." She motioned to Merlin before casting Mez on the two bandits closer to them and pulling their minds out of phase shift as well. Level twelve seemed Mez-able with little difficulty.

Phase Shift's fifteen seconds were almost up, and she fought to clamp down on the panic screaming at the back of her mind about how much the spell had taken out of her. One of the dangerous ones was going to break free with Phase Shift's expiration. Targeting it, she spoke softly, noticing how dry her voice sounded. "Beast, take my target. It'll break in three."

Trusting in Beastial to take care of the loose enemy, she readied her Mez as his cast aggroed the stray and released the spell, holding him in place.

Refreshing the first two, she directed Beast to pull the second one to them, just as the patrol rounded the corner and walked up the path toward them. They were still a good distance away, but Murmur didn't like cutting it so close.

With the fight finally under control, Murmur could take stock of herself in the aftermath of using Phase Shift. She desperately wished she hadn't.

Her Mental Acuity was down to five. That in itself wasn't a bad thing. She knew using skills would deplete her it—that wasn't what bugged her. Her head felt foggy, but not in a way that made her forget things she could do, or confused.

No, she wanted to reach for more.

It was like there was something just beyond her fingertips, whispers lingering at the edge of her awareness as she tried to grasp what they were saying, only to lose them in mist she could *almost* see through.

Even probing the edge of what seemed like her consciousness, Murmur still maintained her Mez on the other opponents, kept her DoTs up and running.

If nothing else, at least she was a pro at multitasking.

All the way down the dungeon spiral, precarious encampments and smart NPCs led to a very unique experience.

"If I didn't know better, I'd almost think these guys were actual players sometimes." Devlish wiped his forehead with the back of his hand.

Merlin frowned. "Especially the patrols. They actually converse, and it's not a script. I've listened. It's so well done."

Sin tapped her foot. "I'm so glad we have these little chats. But can we get going? Rashlyn will beat us to the bottom at this rate."

Murmur laughed. "She's right."

The final level was easily visible now that they'd been at it for hours. Each of the three ramps down from the cave entrances converged closely together on the bottom floor. Murmur studied it. "Not to put too fine a point on it, but that floor level seems like it might be made for raiding, or at least multiple groups. The way the mobs are clustered…"

Beastial's brow furrowed and he lifted a hand to stroke his chin. "Point. They're not for single pulls. We'd get at least five. Coordination will be the key."

"How about we get there first?" Havoc cut in, and Merlin grinned in response.

When they finally got to the bottom of their ramp, they inspected their opponents. Frowning, Murmur noticed the thicker border around their aura, the jagged crown next to their names. "We haven't had these before."

"Taking a wild stab in the dark." Sin cracked her knuckles. "I'd say these are really fucking hard. Or raid trash mobs. Or both."

"You think they'll still cough up experience if we form a raid group?" Merlin frowned, voicing what they all feared. There were several games that didn't allow the person to gain experience when grouped in a raid.

"Not sure." Murmur glanced back up the ramp Rashlyn's group was taking, and shot a message over guild. *Might have some raid mobs down here. You good to group up once you make it?*

Rashlyn: Does shit stink?

Havoc: Way too much information there, Rash. Way too much.

Murmur heard Rashlyn's peal of laughter echo from where the other group fought. Several of the NPCs swiveled around to try and find where the noise had come from.

Careful Rash, apparently noise really can alert these guys. Murmur cautioned the group, not really wanting to have to do a corpse retrieval mission. Apart from the fact that the healers still didn't have their resurrection spells, it was just a pain in the butt.

They waited at the base of the ramp in a corner wedged between the stairs and the walls, out of sight of the rest of the bandits. Murmur flicked through her abilities. She should have bought her level twelve spells when she went back to the city before. After all, she was going to be eleven soon, and having to leave at twelve if they were leveling well would be a pain.

After finding out about the psionicist part of her class, she'd basically forgotten about anything else.

Havoc sat down next to her. "Going to give us a rundown of what the hell that spell did to you back there?"

Murmur paused her own musings and looked over at him. "I've got a headache, but I feel like my brain had a chance to expand, to understand something I couldn't otherwise know. It's like my mind is a Tardis."

While she meant the last as a joke, she realized it was actually true, and Havoc sat there concern drawing his lips into a frown.

"That's new." He sat in silence for a moment before continuing. "But ever since you said to keep an eye out for weird quests, I've been dividing my attention between something I swear has been nibbling at the back of my mind since we started playing the game and damaging the mobs."

"And?" Murmur prompted.

"Just got an update that's vague as hell." He laughed and shook his head. "I need to listen to my surroundings and block out all life so that death can get through. If that's not morbid, I don't know what is."

For a few moments they sat in silence before Murmur spoke. "Actually, considering you're a necromancer, it probably has something to do with being able to boost your undead pets and other stuff."

He blinked at her. "Sometimes I forget you're younger than me."

"What does that have to do with the smell of shit in a barn?" She smiled at him, feeling morose. Havoc always treated her as younger than he was, which was the most annoying thing in the world since he was only in his junior year of college. "Age is just a number."

He looked off into the distance for a few seconds before standing, and glancing down at her. "True, but sometimes numbers have lots of legal ramifications."

With a wink, he turned and joined Dev and Beast leaving Murmur to gape at him.

CHAPTER FIFTEEN

Beauty in Numbers

Storm Entertainment
Somnia Online Division Conference Room 2
Countdown: two months before release

Teddy Davenport tapped his pen on the table, as he scowled at the report in front of him. "Is the software going to be able to keep up with the scan rates? With this many gamers, we're going to create a bottle neck."

Laria Sommers smiled disarmingly at Teddy. Shayla watched her friend tackle the boss with words like she would a football player on a field. Admittedly her words probably packed more punch.

"Our Artificial Intelligence integration guarantees that we'll be able to handle the influx. We could handle an influx a thousand times larger. It was set up perfectly."

One of the other men at the head of the table shifted in his seat, making it creak like dry bones rubbing together. "And we have enough units available to meet demand?"

Trying her best not to hesitate, Shayla stood, laying a hand on Laria's shoulder. As project coordinator managing all monetizing aspects of the game, she put on her best non-patronizing smile. "We've had production in place for close to a year now. The last units will ship about three weeks before launch. While this is closer than we'd have liked and will allow less time for us to review the data provided, it's still within acceptable limits."

Shayla Johnson sat down, giving Laria a brief glance before she let some tension drain out of her shoulders.

The same man grunted. "I fail to see how this game works the way we need it to."

Shayla didn't even bother to stand this time. She'd been at this for the last several weeks. Long meetings, roundabout questions and sessions of far too many self-important and pompous people, all stupidly rich and trying to obtain more wealth. And they all knew something about the funding the game had received that Shayla did not. While she was aware of the military basis, she had no idea what the endgame was. Trying to target marketing and sales without all the information hadn't been easy.

"Look, Drake. The game is like no other that's been seen before. We have multiple AI units overseeing this. AIs overseeing other AIs even, and all with us constantly monitoring it. Their ability to analyze and mimic human behavior is unparalleled. The scans will happen, the game will go ahead, and everyone will have all the data we need, plus money to actually help support the research." Shayla was tired. All she wanted to do was go home, put her feet up, and eat with her family. But it wasn't looking likely today either.

Drake Cain, looked like he was about to say something but thought better of it. "No delays. And I hope for your sake the system allocates honestly."

Shayla smiled at the man, willing herself to exude confidence. "All the tests we've performed have gone flawlessly. It's perfectly safe and very accurate."

She could see Laria blanch out of the corner of her eye. Shayla frowned at that reaction, considering how eager Laria had been not an hour ago about the containment capsule. Still, the sooner this meeting was over, the sooner they could both get back with people they could stand.

Real World Day 2: Somnia Online

Murmur waited while Rashlyn hugged the rough part of hewn stone wall between the ramps and ran across it on light feet. Her dark grey ears twitched in time with her whiskers as she balanced easily. She smiled when she reached Murmur and Sin, and they embraced. Even in the virtual world it felt real.

"So glad to have more women around me. Mellow and I were about to drown in guy-ness."

Rash smiled with a roll of her eyes, and her tail peeked around from behind, like it had a mind of its own.

Murmur grinned at her friend's choice of species. If there was a feline species, Rashlyn played it. Her feles had black stripes flowing throughout her grey fur, and she seemed perfectly at home with the long claws on her hands. Rash's feline ears moved at every sound, and Mur had to resist the impulse to reach up and scratch behind them.

Murmur sought out Mellow among the guys, frowning a moment before raising her eyebrows in recognition. Mellow was a locus! "Cool! Mellow! Hi!"

The last time Mur'd seen Mellow, they'd been playing a male character.

Mellow gave a shy shrug. "If I'm going to run around in a different body all day, I figured I might as well get to feel relaxed for once."

Sinister smiled. "Makes sense to me."

"Locus are pretty androgynous," Mellow said with a sparkle in their eye. "I like it."

"I wish I'd known you were in my starting area," Murmur said. They could have met up sooner. "What's the witch like?"

"Surprisingly fun. I get to stir a big, black pot." Mellow winked and a chuckle ran through the group.

Rashlyn was watching everyone. "Your group has a pretty solid make-up."

"Your group has a pretty solid make up, too, Rash. Shaman, bard, ranger, rogue, and witch. I see you got to keep your class."

Murmur couldn't help some of the resentment in her voice. Even though she was used to the enchanter now and didn't want to change, she still missed her healer.

Rash shrugged again. "This is a little different. Monks tank on an avoidance basis. It's nothing like the paladins I've played before. Oh, oh—but watch this, and don't try to butt in!"

She ran toward the mobs, aggroed them, moved back toward the group several steps, and then fainted onto the floor. The opponents blinked at her body, prodded her a couple of times, shrugged, and went back to what they were doing. Rash stood up, and brushed herself off as she moved back to Sin and Murmur with a satisfied grin on her face. "Tada!"

"What the fuck was that heart attack you almost gave me?" Sinister put her hands on her hips and glared.

"It's called Feign Corpse." Rash laughed. "It's freaking awesome to do in front of someone in the middle of town too. People panic."

Murmur frowned, trying to figure out the best way to work Rash's and the other's abilities into their rotation. Dansyn was a dark elf bard. What was with all the bloody dark elves? Still, he would have similar functions to her, just in song form, with lots of juggling. Veranol was a stout viking shaman. Exbo, a human ranger, and Jinna appeared to be a dwarf rogue. Should be a great and versatile raid make up. Even if it was only two groups worth.

She motioned the others to come with her and went to stand in the crowded area the guys were taking up. "Look. Depending on how the pulls go, Dansyn and myself can probably keep four to five under control easy enough. But it might be best to have both Dev and Rash ready to tank at the same time. Different opponents of course."

Dev nodded. "Makes sense, especially if we manage to get all six of those at once. They don't seem to be your average mob. And they're level thirteen. I'm about to hit eleven, so at least there's that, but splitting the mobs into groups should help us whittle them down."

Rash piped in. "I'm close as well. Once we hit that eleven, this should go smoother."

"If these things give us experience," Merlin threw in.

Murmur glared at him. "You talk to Exbo. You rangers need to work your shit out." She turned to Dansyn and grimaced. "I'll take the left and you take the right? Should help us if the shit hits."

"Sounds good to me. I can't keep more than two under control at a time anyway. You'd think I'd just be able to cast spells. But no, it gets way too noisy in my head if I try to play more than five or six at a time. Considering I need to keep several buffs up, two is my limit." Dansyn didn't sound happy with his class, and Murmur studied him for a few moments.

"I get it. Trust me." She turned back to the rest. "I don't think we're going to get any more ready than we are."

Murmur activated the raid and initiated the invitation, which Rashlyn accepted immediately.

The first thing Murmur noticed once Merlin pulled, was that the mobs came as a set of six.

The second thing Murmur noticed was that they hit like a brick shithouse.

And the third thing she noticed was that their resistances were far higher than the mobs she'd Mez'd beforehand. While her first one stuck, the second one took three tries, and it was only Beast's quick thinking that got his tiger to intervene so she didn't get pummeled into pulp. The rogue in the opponent's group was rooted.

Dansyn shrugged. "I got the one, but that rogue is resisting the fuck out of my abilities."

Murmur nodded and included it in her rotation. The thing was, with three highly resistant mobs it was all she could do to take care of them. Both Rash and Dev were fighting their own mobs, back to back, heals flying in a constant arc. Shaman heals from Veranol were fantastic, but seemed to take a heap of his mana. He placed wards on his target that absorbed damage, effectively increasing their current hit pool, and small heals that buffed the healed and increased the next one within a certain number of seconds.

Rashlyn rarely got hit. She dodged and avoided most of the hits of her mob, and Murmur found herself wondering what the monk's agility looked like. Still, if Rash got hit, it showed, and the wards were a godsend.

The crowned mobs were definitely raid trash. Their hit points went down in a decent fashion, not much slower than the other trash they'd fought in the caves. But this time they had two groups beating up on them.

Jinna, Rashlyn's rogue, was lethal. He could shadow meld and sneak around to get the best possible vantage point for backstabs and the gods knew what sort of knife work he occasionally executed. Silent and deadly.

Mellow was fascinating to watch. Murmur hadn't seen a witch in the game yet, and remembered Mellow often playing a healer or bard type of class before. Still, the witch was frightening. Concoctions appeared in their hands as if pulled from a cauldron, thrown like bombs to detonate over the mob, slowing and weakening it. Curses appeared overhead, flashing into enemies like runes rammed by a truck into their bodies. Damage leaked, blood spilled. Murmur sort of wanted to be a witch.

By the time they were done, they all needed to either meditate or heal up.

"That was a wake-up call." Sinister leaned back, stretching. "There's a lot to juggle with this class. Keeping damage up, making sure my transfer spell is on Dev at all times, making sure I don't tap into my own health too much."

"At least you do damage while you heal." Veranol smiled in what appeared to be a reassuring way.

"True." Sin pondered the fact. "I do pretty good damage."

"Mel, that witch is fascinating." Merlin piped up. "You lucked out."

Mellow opened their eyes and smiled, their thin lips spreading just wide enough to hide the vicious teeth and their hair lit up softly. "Yeah. I was a little worried at first, but since it let me choose whatever gender I wanted, I was pretty okay with that."

Beastial chuckled. "Color me happy for you."

"Dev. Rash." Murmur coughed. "Did you not notice you leveled?"

Both of them grew distant before grinning sheepishly.

"I was probably getting kicked in the head that one time when I dinged or something." Rash said, rubbing her temple as if it still smarted.

Dev chuckled. "Might have been when one of mine shield bashed my freaking ears. Seriously, there are some elements of this game that are woefully realistic."

"Well," Exbo stood up, wiping off imaginary dust from his pants. "I guess that means two down and ten of us to go. Time to get leveling Fable."

"Time to get leveling," they all chimed in together.

Murmur smiled, comfortable with her friends. If she had a choice, this would be her reality. Double checking her shielding and sensor net, she moved forward with the others.

It was quite a smooth run all told. A few bad pulls, but overall, with the twelve of them, they could tear through anything. The best part of it all was the experience. They received raid experience bonuses. Apparently organizing forces and utilizing skilled tactics was rewarded in Somnia.

Personally, Murmur thought it was more to encourage people to play together instead of playing everything by themselves. As they'd witnessed earlier, soloing in this game wasn't the best way to play.

Her DING to level didn't take long at all. With the way experience worked, they were getting closer and closer together in the leveling range. She deliberately refused to focus on the amount of experience each level now demanded. But twelve was so close.

The thing was, when it came to playing in a specific area for a certain time, it was sometimes easier to become complacent. As they worked their way toward the back of the huge cavern and the throne that sat there, they began to fall into a reckless rhythm, punctuated by low-pitched inane chatter and baiting.

"Don't see you putting your back into it." Rash needled Devlish.

He grunted, swinging an axe into the face of his opponent, just under the helmet line and causing severely critical damage. "Probably because that's not my line of work."

"Low blow, Dev." Dansyn mumbled as he took care of his mob. "Careful, she holds grudges."

"It's okay, Dan." Rash roundhouse kicked the head of her own mob, which let out a satisfying crunch as it toppled to the ground. "I'll Feign Corpse when he'll least survive it."

Her grin wasn't kind.

Murmur directed her attention to the area around them and the mobs in it. The cavern was deep and vast. The walls shone with black iridescence. From the faint sound of trickling water she could hear, it appeared there was water somewhere down here. It might explain the slight damp smell to the air too. None of the mobs triggered any of her alarms, but she made sure to maintain her skills as active so her Mental Acuity wouldn't dampen.

The final mob dead, Murmur glanced at her level progression and smiled. Not too bad for a few hours work. They'd might even hit twelve before in-game sunrise.

Veranol stood up, stretching his arms above his head. "Ready. Full Mana."

Merlin grinned and released his arrow.

Everything seemed to be going exactly as every other pull had. This one was only five enemies.

Two casters suddenly appeared out of nowhere, standing to either side of the mobs as they ran. Wizards, if Murmur's guess was right.

Level fourteen.

And their nukes *hurt*.

Even though she managed to Mez two of the mobs while Dan took care of the third, they weren't fast enough to stop the wizards' initial casts. Two fireballs landed in the middle of their raid causing both Mellow and Havoc to screech in pain. Murmur could smell charred flesh behind her, and refused to look.

Targeting the wizard on the left she fired off Mind Bolt, hoping that the pain she felt in her own head upon casting was reflected hundredfold on the mob. It stopped and screamed, unable to cast, and ran forward as she lashed out toward the second mob. "Grab it, Dan."

Not waiting for a reply, she let her second Mind Bolt fly free, glancing at her Mental Acuity bar as she went. She was down to forty-eight out of a hundred. Two more if she had to. They couldn't let those nukes go off again.

Devlish screamed, and the coppery scent of blood filled her nostrils, tinged with something else. Perhaps lizard men's blood had a different chemical make-up. She threw a Mez on the second mob before the silence could wear off, and refreshed the next two. Her mana was fine, but her head pounded. Two Mind Bolts in quick succession was hurting. Was that one of the side effects? The consequences?

Murmur shook her head, putting it to the back of her mind. That was for future Murmur to deal with and present Murmur had to survive first.

Things seemed to be calming down. She only had to maintain two Mez. One on the caster, and the other on what appeared to be a berserker. The thing was, she'd already discovered that bard Mez wasn't the most reliable thing in the world. Since bards had to juggle different songs in order to play effectively, it meant the Mez was one of those songs.

Sometimes one of them could lapse.

Murmur noticed it too late to do anything. By the time Dan cried out for her to grab it, it had almost finished its spell.

Rashlyn threw herself in front of it, just before it hit Dan, and Murmur sent her third mind bolt in ninety seconds barreling into the wizard.

She could hear a scream, and scurrying voices, footsteps, the sounds of a fight. The scream continued, sad and painful, angry and hurt.

It took her until her head hit the ground to realize it was her own.

"Shit!" Sin yelled, and began barking out orders just as the final mob in the pull from hell went down. Murmur could hear a scuffle, but it sounded so far away. She wondered why her best friend sounded so frantic. "Veranol meditate. I need your mana. Rash, try to meditate if you can. That's not a life-threatening bleed—you'll have to wait."

Rashlyn laughed, and coughed up a tiny bit of blood onto her pale lips. "My own heal will be up shortly. It'll help. Don't worry about me."

Murmur could sense the change in attention as Sin shifted and spoke to someone else. "You can't funnel mana yet, can you?"

Havoc sighed. "No." She could tell it was him, because there was always a musical cadence to his sighs.

"Fuck." Sin sounded worried, and Murmur could hear her grunting with effort, with exertion, but she couldn't see why. The noises were distant and her mind swam so peacefully. Her vision blurred in and out of sight. The fuzzy ceiling gave way to a soft darkness all around her, only to repeat the cycle again. She tried to lift herself, but her body wouldn't respond. It was so heavy. Everything was heavy.

Murmur had no idea why everyone was so far away and struggled to remember what happened. One minute they'd been fighting, and the next, she was lying down somewhere soft and comfortable that didn't seem to resemble the stone floor of the cavern she'd been in at all. Odd? Was she in bed? Either way her mind felt trapped, she just wasn't sure where.

Finally she heard something shift around her, pulling her back toward the noise. From the direction, it was Veranol who stood up and began casting. A wave of relief washed over her, filling her head with calm. Murmur's health pool rose as well, and she heard Sin sigh as she sat back to catch her breath as Devlish's flesh seemed to make popping sounds as it knit itself back together. At least she remembered that wound. That was something.

"Well." Sin spoke, and Murmur could almost see the smirk on her face. "That was the closest to a wipe we've come so far."

Havoc's footfalls approached her, and she felt more than heard him kneel down next to her. "What happened to Mur? Is she going to be okay?"

"She silenced that mob so it couldn't nuke us again." Rash sounded contemplative. "Maybe the ability is still too raw for her to have used so often. I know she used it at least twice."

"She shouldn't have fucking done that. Risking herself like that just isn't worth it." Sinister's tone was heated, much more serious than Murmur was used to. And it didn't really make sense. Maybe Sin just didn't want her to do a corpse run.

Havoc felt her forehead. "She's cool. Do we have some water or something? Like would that work?"

Beast's heavy footsteps echoed through the stone floor, and she heard the sound of something being unscrewed. "No better way to find out."

Havoc's tone changed. "You just want her to hit me if she lashes out when she wakes up."

"See," Beast said. "I always knew you were a clever one."

"Yeah, yeah. Flattery doesn't hold well with the necromancers." Havoc muttered as the glugging liquid hit Murmur's parted lips.

CHAPTER SIXTEEN

Darjin—Bandit Leader

Storm Entertainment
Somnia Online Division Development offices
Countdown: six weeks before release

Ava Jackson sat in her chair, legs on her desk so she could sway back and forth, twirling her hair on one finger while she waited on her phone call. "No, Luke. You look. That Headgear shipment has been waiting in your warehouse for far too long. Get it to our postal division and do it yesterday. Those need to go out."

She rolled her eyes to the ceiling as he muttered out another excuse. "Do you want me to send Shayla?"

The stammering on the other end halted immediately.

"Excellent. Let me know when the delivery's done." She disconnected the call and fist pumped in the air.

James tapped her on the head with a file folder and leaned against the door to her office. "You know Shayla doesn't have time to breathe at the moment, don't you?"

Ava shrugged. "Yeah, but Luke didn't know that."

James wandered off, chuckling softly.

Ava wiped her hands on her jeans trying to get rid of the cold clammy uneasiness she felt in her stomach. Taking a deep breath, she activated her call device and patched through. "Hey, Michael, it's Ava."

She swallowed hard as he spoke on the other end, wondering briefly why his voice had such a hypnotic quality to it. That lulling, calming quality that spoke to parts of her brain she didn't understand. Even nervous to call him, he put her at ease. There were four more shipments of headgear due over the next month.

"I understand. I'll take full responsibility for them." She heard herself saying, not realizing she was speaking. Ava frowned, coming back from whatever daydream she'd floated off into this time. If she got much more absent minded, Shayla was going to kill her. Neither Shayla nor Jessa liked to talk about Michael.

"No," she answered, frowning. For a moment his voice seemed uncharacteristic, wild. "I understand completely. Of course we want people to have the full immersion experience."

Again she listened, cocking her head to the side. It was hard to do, but she had to. "No, I can't do that right now. I have too much going on with this launch. You'll have to find someone else to test it on."

His tone of voice made her almost change her mind. Almost. She'd said no, and she had to be firm. She'd been told she was far too easy a pushover. "I truly can't, Michael. Sorry."

His laughter filled her head, and she smiled at his joke, before a peal of her own laughter echoed through her office. "No point in playing Somnia if you're not jacked in."

She terminated the call and turned to her calendar, marking in the delivery dates in both hers and their production group's. A couple of minutes later, just as Ava was getting ready to go to lunch, Shayla popped her head in. "Thanks for organizing the shipments Ava. I don't know where we'd be without you!"

Ava smiled back at Shayla. The woman could sometimes be so scatterbrained, but she was brilliant.

Real World Day 2: Somnia Online

The cool wetness tickled the back of Murmur's throat, tugging at her. Her consciousness slowly crept back from the precipice it had been standing on for however long. A pounding sounded close to her, regular and aching. And she realized it was her head.

More of the cool liquid trickled down, and she tried to open her eyes, but the lids were extra heavy, and her head felt like it was the size of her bedroom. She tried to move, but ended up with a pathetic half wriggle.

"Wren?" Someone shifted on the ground next to her, and then their voice was closer. "Wren, are you okay?"

She tried to open her eyes again, but opted for her mouth instead. "S'okay. Hurts. Ish my head big?"

He chuckled and she instantly knew it was Evan, Havoc. "Figuratively or literally?"

"Shut up, you." She already felt better. Slowly, with Havoc's help guiding her gently, she sat up and blinked in the dull cavern lighting.

"Mur!" She heard Sinister yell, almost loud enough to be dangerous down here. "You're okay!"

Murmur smiled, but it tugged on her hairline and made her cringe again. "I think I might have overdone it."

"No shit." Devlish stood in front of her, his body casting a shadow she sorely needed. Even the dim light sort of smarted. "You worried us, Mur."

"Sorry." She slowly pushed herself up to standing, Havoc at her elbow. "Didn't mean to hold us up."

Jinna didn't often speak, but he stepped forward, and cleared his throat. "Hold us up as much as you like. You made us not have to do a corpse run. I think you've earned the right."

"Thanks." She smiled, glad to see everyone had survived. "I think I'm just going to rest for a few minutes before I cast anything."

While she knew that might slow them down even more, she also knew that her head wouldn't allow her to cast any spells in this state. Add to that she was a little apprehensive about her new skills, and she wasn't in the best frame of mind.

Sinister walked up and leaned against Murmur. "Just don't ever sacrifice yourself for us again!"

Murmur pulled back. She studied her friend, concerned about the degree of worry reflected in Sin's brow. "That's like, what we do, hon. But I'll promise to be less reckless next time, okay?"

Sin grimaced and nodded before walking away.

Hesitantly, Murmur focused on her own shielding, and activated it. No pain shot through her head, no amount of warning whatsoever. Apparently it wasn't the baseline Mental Acuity skills that did it. More confident, she also activated her sensing net.

"I'm okay. I should be able to Mez, but I'll keep it at that for a bit. No Mind Bolt for a while."

Rash stepped forward. "That really hurt didn't it? Like lingering hurt, not fleeting?"

Murmur hesitated for a moment, but she didn't have anything to hide from her guildies. "Yeah. Pretty much not a fan. I need to figure out how far-reaching consequences are."

"Didn't you only just get the skills?" Mellow asked, picking some dirt out from under their fingernails.

"Level ten," she answered.

"Exactly. Only just. If you're supposed to watch how often you use it, I doubt that level eleven was where they thought—hey she's already amazing at this shit, let's give her unlimited invulnerability from bad side effects." They paused, raising an eyebrow. "That is if I'm understanding these special skills right.

Murmur sighed. "No, you're right, at least I think you are. I'll be more careful from now on."

Still, as they headed in slightly deeper, she wasn't sure if she'd ever be able to bring herself to use the skill again.

This go around, they were more cautious. As they approached the epicenter of the bandit operation, casters were more common. With multiple stuns, and several ways to take care of annoying casters, no one made Murmur have to step in and do anything fancy.

While she was eternally grateful for the fact that none of them seemed to hate her for showing weakness, she couldn't help but despise it herself. But the fact was, she'd been knocked briefly unconscious in a fucking game. In a virtual world, not the real world. When she logged off for her next break, she was going to have choice words with her mother.

"Slow and steady wins the race." Merlin intoned wisely as Dev, Rash, Veranol, and Havoc hit level twelve.

Murmur's perception of time was off, and she glanced at the in-game clock, frowning. They must have been playing for ten straight real-world hours. Even with the boosted experience down here, that was an age.

"Slow and steady is not getting dead." Rash laughed. "Either way, let's get everyone else up here."

Murmur deeply regretted not having grabbed her spells when she last went back to her guild. Considering the game had abolished that stupidly archaic inventory limit that plagued older games, she wasn't going to run into the same problem next time. She'd get both her level twelve and sixteen lots together. A wave of excitement rolled over her, quickly followed by a bout of nervousness at the prospect of continuing on. After all, the thrill of gaming came with risk and reward, and this game's risks seemed almost too realistic.

Getting stronger, moving up through levels, developing strategies. If she could make a living by staying in the game, she'd choose that path over anything else. She was getting so used to the game now that it barely took a thought to activate her abilities. Weaving spells went faster the more deft she got at it, and she could juggle Mez, DoTs, and nukes with an efficiency of timing she hadn't previously possessed. Keeping her shielding and sensor net activated barely took a thought now, but she still hesitated to use her psionic abilities. Maybe if she was more wary of using them, the next time they wouldn't have such a disconcerting effect.

Rashlyn dodged and dived, kicked and punched, bantering like a fool. "You're looking all badass there, Dev. Sure that's their soul you're sucking out and not yours?"

Dev grunted again, his habitual response it seemed, and Murmur laughed. Whereas Rashlyn was in lighter armor—leather from the looks of things—Dev was in full plate, shield and all. The dark aura that surrounded him once he was in tanking mode lent an aura of evil to his character. Murmur thought Rash had a point, and not only that, but the system, however it scanned them all, really did seem to have hit the nail on the head for all of them.

"We've been down here too long." Sin groaned as another set of mobs died. She prodded one with her foot as she stretched her arms across her chest.

"Not only that." Merlin frowned as he sat and meditated. "Have you noticed these bandits seem to be getting a little smarter? Trying to find a way to line of sight them so I don't accidentally pull two groups of them is getting more and more difficult."

Murmur frowned. "Think we're going to have to adjust our pulling strategies as the opponents level up?"

Beastial nodded. "Yeah. There was less pain from level one to ten mobs. But once we hit double digits, there was an increase."

"That's steep coming from you." Mellow muttered, loud enough for everyone to hear.

Beast shrugged good-naturedly. "S'all good, just wait until you try to get some shut eye. Shir-Khan is going to bite your ass."

Murmur cast invisibility on herself and moved around the raid, sussing out just how many more groups they had to work through before they reached the throne area. Jinna snuck up beside her, peering out too. With his own stealth activated, he seemed to be formed out of water—sort of gluggy and solid but see through. It was a very cool effect.

"That patrol is pretty fucking close." Jinna's voice was barely audible.

Murmur nodded, concerned. There's no way they could take on eleven opponents at once. If they misstepped, then they'd pull the patrol—and the second group. It was going to be a nightmare. And then she had an idea. Tapping Jinna on the shoulder, she motioned him to come back with her.

"Hey Rash?" Mur asked, dropping invisibility. "That Feign Corpse thing you do. How often does it work?"

Rash glanced at something briefly and shrugged. "Ninety percent of the time. My skill in it is level twelve so it technically should work. Why?"

"If you can run around that rocky outcrop there," Mur pointed to the one just ahead of them shielding them from the sight of the mobs closer to the throne, "and pull them back to the side of it so they still can't see us? We'll be jumbled up on top of one another here in the corner. Then Feign Corpse long enough for some to begin walking away. Once you stand up again, technically you should be able to drag a few of them with you."

Rash nodded, biting her lip. "Sounds good in theory. Would help if you also soothed a couple of the back bandits so they're less likely to turn back around once I stand up."

"Awesome plan." Havoc smiled, and resummoned his pet. "There we go. He's a lot hardier now."

Devlish shrugged. "Fine. I'll just wait here while you pretend to die."

Rash laughed. "You do that Sir Dread Knight. You do that."

"Everyone buff up." Murmur ordered, the words almost like a habit. She knew there were reasons the others liked her to lead raids, but she didn't have the temperament for people suddenly overcome with idiocy. It's why she was picky about who she gamed with. Not that she minded helping people, just not when she was trying to get shit done.

Lining herself up just behind the outcrop where she'd be able to see Rash as her friend fell close to her feet, Murmur cast invisibility. "Ready when you are, Rash."

With all the others squashed into the corner behind them, Rash nodded, and crept out.

"This game is far too realistic when I can smell your stinking BO, Veranol." Sin's whisper almost caused Murmur to choke with laughter and she had to hiss out a *shhhh* before she lost her cool.

Rash stood up closer to the bandits, moving slowly and deftly toward them, inch by inch. One of them saw her out of the corner of his eye, and Murmur distinctly heard it say, 'What the fuck is that person doing here?' before the whole group shifted and began pursuing the monk.

The bandits were fast. Luckily, so was Rash. She flitted about, over a stool with a light step, toward the outcrop. Closer and closer, the bandits had weapons drawn now, and the casters were trying to move in because she'd already run out of their range. Reaching the outcrop, Rash activated Feign Corpse.

Her character arched up, throwing one arm over her eyes and staggering for two steps before falling in a heap of boneless skin right where Murmur told her to. Still invisible, Murmur watched as the casters, who were way back waited while what appeared to be a rogue inched forward and poked Rash with the tip of his sword. To her credit, whatever the spell did, it convinced the rogue she was, in fact, dead.

The mages headed back before the melee classes, a good distance, considering their range. For a moment Murmur had to wonder what might have happened had one of them landed a DoT on the monk, but since they didn't.

"Now." Murmur whispered.

Rash stood, and three melee mobs turned around and dashed after her. The rogue had been checking over his shoulder periodically, apparently wasn't as convinced as the others. She rounded the corner, and Murmur dropped her invisibility. "Next time we'll grab that patrol."

Rash beamed, her face flush with excitement. Murmur smiled, realizing her friend looked amazing when she was in her element. Strong, confident, and completely capable. They were the best people to surround herself with.

Splitting her focus, Murmur kept the mobs Mez'd, DoT-ed, and nuked with ease. She frowned when they were done. So close to the named. So close to the quest completion.

"That went marvelously." Sin clapped her hands and rubbed them together greedily. "I say we just rinse and repeat."

Devlish pouted. "I feel totally superfluous. You just need me to take the big hits."

Sin turned toward him, blinking in confusion. "And that's news because?"

"Shut up." But he was grinning as he squeezed himself back into the corner.

Sin grumbled again. "I swear, I'm going to figure out which herbs to mix in this game and craft a freaking deodorant."

Murmur laughed, cast invisibility, and waited.

Murmur stood, staring at the throne from their hiding place, not to mention all the bandits around it.

"You really should have bought your spells, Mur." Havoc's admonishment wasn't making her mood any better.

"I was a little preoccupied with technically changing classes, but next time the game springs something on me that no one knew it could do, I'll make sure to grab my next level spells." Her sarcasm washed over the group, and everyone but Havoc snickered, or tried to hold back laughter.

Havoc frowned at her. "There's no need to be snappy."

"And there's also no need to state the obvious." The fire had gone out of her words, and Murmur found herself drained, again. "Sorry. It's been a bit of a day for me."

Havoc hesitated, moved a step closer and put a hand on her shoulder, squeezing it gently. "Yeah, I sort of forgot. Didn't mean to be an insensitive prick."

Murmur nodded and flashed a smile to let him know she didn't hold it against him.

"Well, now that's out of the way." Sin grinned and stretched her arms up high, wiggling her hips as she completed the movement and looking back over her shoulder at Murmur pointedly.

"What?" Murmur raised her hands in the air defensively. "I didn't say anything."

"No, but you thought it." Sin shot back with a smirk.

"Hey, I'm the one with the mind powers, remember?"

They laughed and the tension leaked out of their group.

Standing a ways downwind of the throne, in a convergence of shadows caused by the winding paths above, they all stopped and looked at Darjin, the Bandit Leader. He was pure bulk. Muscles bulged, and dark blue tattoos lined his body. He wore his long hair in a thick braid that hung over his shoulder, and one eye had clearly gotten the wrong end of a sharp object at some point in his life. The thick white scar ran from mid forehead, through his right eye, and half way down his cheek. It gave him a formidable appearance.

"He's a freaking shaman, isn't he?" Dansyn muttered, glaring at Veranol.

"Yes, let's be angry at me because I had so much to do with his class." Veranol's response caused a nervous laugh to ripple through the group. "He's fifteen, guys."

Beastial gulped audibly. "Fifteen. That's a pretty powerful fucker right there."

"Going to need a stun rotation." Jinna voiced softly.

"Jinna, Dev, Beast, Rash, Dan." Devlish listed the order out in a mechanical fashion, his eyes narrowed, thinking whatever tank thoughts he had running through his mind. "Mur, you can take care of the other two?"

She nodded before realizing he wouldn't see the movement. "Yes."

Dan fidgeted, his hands clenching and unclenching as he watched the bandits in front of them. Murmur reached over and patted him on the shoulder. "S'all good, Dan, we got this. I shouldn't need you to take one of his guards."

"By the time we're in range, they're going to see us." Merlin threw in that pearl of wisdom with a shrug of his shoulders. "So while we've been able to strategically pull the others, these guys have no shelter in front of them. We're going to have to fight them in an open space and, well. The pull could go rough."

"True." Exbo shrugged. "But if we have to, we can always kite one of the guards. At least they're not casters."

"No, but Darjin is a freaking healer," Mellow's outrage reflected the tension in the group. "I'm going to curse his ass into oblivion."

Murmur's thoughts were grim as she surveyed the area. "I need to keep them as close to the dais as possible. I'll hit Mez as soon as the left mob is in range, and then I'll take care of the other. Actually, Dan, can we time it, and then I'll immediately take him from you?"

The bard's eyes lit up. "Excellent idea. Merlin can shoot Darjin at the same time, and that way we should be able to pull off the initial stage of the fight, without too many risks."

"Excellent." Mur ran through her spells, excited to get back to her trainer after this, and yet so eager for the fight it was almost painful.

"Merlin, Dansyn, you're with me. Cast when in range." Together the three of them moved forward, the bard and Murmur using invisibility, and the ranger in sneak.

CHAPTER SEVENTEEN
Boss Fight

Storm Entertainment
Somnia Online Division Suit delivery Warehouse
Countdown: Six weeks before release

Ava Jackson and Shayla Johnson stood at the entrance to Warehouse Seven and watched the flurry of activity. The automated inventory system worked seamlessly with its self-operated forklifts.

Storm Corp certainly knew how to outfit its warehouses. They were the epitome of efficiency, once stock entered the warehouse anyway.

The suits arrived two days late and with a portion of one crate badly damaged. Shayla was barely holding it together. Ava could tell from the way her left eye occasionally twitched. It was never a good idea to upset Shayla.

Michael was nowhere to be seen, but James and Silke were scurrying around triple checking the remaining shipment. Even Luke, the head of the shipping department, had lost his usual cool. Not surprising really.

The whole future of Storm Entertainment—no, Storm Corp—depended on this launch. The release of a game for people to play in and forget about their real lives.

Ava was tempted to play it herself, but her cats would probably try to eat her alive.

"Make sure to address the situation both to the manufacturer and the shipping company." Shayla muttered the words softly, and Ava made a note of them through her augmented reality contacts.

"Anything else?" Ava paused on sending it off, just in case.

Shayla looked at Ava and frowned. "Are you getting enough sleep?"

"Well, I have been testing the headgear for minor improvement and tweaks." She laughed nervously.

"Testing. Did you take part in the alpha and beta tests too?"

Ava nodded enthusiastically. "I was part of the in-house testing team, which is why I agreed to help Michael test further. For implementation into the game, and the future training regimens we've begun designing."

Shayla watched her for a few moments, thoughts flitting across her eyes so fast that Ava wondered if she could reach out and catch them. Suddenly Shayla nodded. "Yes. Michael then. Good. Thank you, Ava. That will be all."

Ava was used to both Shayla and Laria's abruptness. But whereas Laria oversaw the game design, Shayla was responsible for Somnia as a whole. Everything hinged on this.

Everything.

So Ava contacted Michael again, and agreed to help him after all.

Real World Day 2: Somnia Online

The left guard, who seemed to be a thief, froze perfectly, followed almost instantaneously by the right. Merlin's arrow sailed true and strong, hitting Darjin in a small gap beneath his breastplate. The bandit leader roared so loudly that the whole cavern shook, and he leapt down from the dais, sprinting toward their group.

Devlish met him head on in a clash of metal, his shield protecting him from a deadly mace smash. This boss seemed far better at combat that any other named they'd previously encountered. Intuitive and smart. A thrill of excitement hummed around their small raid as each Fable member remembered other glory days.

DoT-ing Darjin, Murmur moved between the named and the targets she was keeping Mez'd, having already taken over Dan's. It seemed to be going smoothly, and the stun rotation was working well, each of them coordinating precisely and announcing when they were taking their turns to interrupt spells and heals.

Murmur watched the left guard, wishing she had access to more useful spells already and angry at herself for not getting them.

And then Darjin's health hit seventy-five percent.

A wave shot out from him, stunning every single one of the raid. Maybe two seconds, but Murmur watched as her Mesmerizes were simply wiped from the guards, helpless to stop it. By the time she was free of the stun and casting her first Mez, both of them were dangerously close to her, and those daggers didn't look like fun. "Dan, right! Quick!"

Releasing the first Mez, it slammed into her guard when he was about six feet from her, freezing him in place with a look of rage contorting his face. She turned in time to see the second guard slashing toward her. Her movement was the only thing that saved what probably would have been a critical hit. Instead of taking it in her back, it slashed across her right arm and down, gouging a nasty hole in her stomach before Dan's Mez hit it.

"Fuck!" She screamed as the pain hit her nervous system. A heated stinging sensation began to spread and she cursed again and called out, "Cure!"

"Lucky some of us got our level twelve spells." Veranol muttered as he threw a cure in her direction, perspiration beading on his forehead as he cast his ass off.

"You'll be laughing on the other side of your face if I can't use my arm in another ten seconds."

Her comment resulted in heals being thrown to her dwindling health by both Sin and Ver.

Gasping for breath, the pain still fresh in her mind, Murmur wove her hands in the spell that she could now cast in her sleep. Both guards taken care of, she took quick stock of the group. Both of the healers were still somewhat okay with mana, although they were by no means safe yet. With Darjin fast approaching fifty percent and them sitting at sixty she wasn't sure if they could handle another unexpected hit. She watched Devlish and Rashlyn desperately swapping out aggro. They must have figured out something she couldn't see from this far away.

"Make sure to watch out for that special ability. Be ready to act as soon as the stun drops." She moved out of reach of both the guards, signaling to Dan to make sure he knew to grab his as well. Almost as an afterthought she added "Might want to be ready for something else too. We have no idea what he's capable of."

Beastial guffawed. "He's a level fifteen boss, you really think he's going to have more special abilities?"

Havoc shrugged. "He's also a bandit leader. Maybe that's another avenue you gain shit from here. These mobs don't react like other games. Look at him parrying, shielding, blocking. His eyes are everywhere. It's almost like he's a real person."

Murmur paused for a moment, noticing the same things Havoc just mentioned. She eyed Darjin's health and turned to face her guard. "Watch out."

At fifty percent the stun hit, harder, like a wave crashing. This time it ticked for about three seconds, and Murmur cursed under her breath as she watched the guard move ever closer as if it were in slow motion. At the same time as the stun wave, a DoT landed on all of them, disease ticking down, attacking their health.

Murmur grunted and cast her Mez as soon as she could, barely hitting the thief before he reached her. He was close to Darjin now—she'd have to reverse where she stood, maybe move back behind the others for the twenty-five percent mark. Too slowly, Veranol cured them all of the disease.

With a glance at all their sixtyish percent health bars and the mana of Sin and Veranol, Murmur sighed. This was going to be cutting it close.

Twenty-five percent was going to be a doozy. She moved back behind the healers with Dan, to give the guards more of a running distance to reach them. It certainly wasn't going to reduce the aggression those guards held for them.

Darjin's health dropped below thirty and Murmur called out, "Logically, his stun should hit four seconds duration this time. Stack any protections you might have. Ward Dev if you can, Ver."

The tanks grunted in response, their ability to even answer in unison somehow made Murmur feel better.

When Darjin's health hit twenty-five percent, the cavern rocked.

The stun wave this time was caused by Darjin pounding the ground beneath him, effectively knocking back their melee. At the same time, the Mez dropped on the two guards and sure enough, they sprinted across the hall toward Mur. Murmur strained against the stun, irritated that she couldn't figure out a way around it.

Her fingers flew as soon as she could move them, tracing the intricate symbols she needed in order to freeze one of the guard's minds. Releasing it, the guard stopped about three feet away, anger boiling to the surface of his gaze. She wasn't even sure if taunting would help this time.

Moments after Dan's froze, she took over, and nudged him to go and help the others. His slight healing regeneration would help the healers who were already strapped for mana as it was. She watched the rest of the fight, rapt, remembering to keep the guards locked in place and free from any damage that might break their state of rest.

Darjin was a masterpiece. He fought with a shield and a mace, protecting his vital parts, twisting and turning and countering multiple different attacks coming from all angles. If they hadn't been able to stun lock him, there's no way they would even be this close to defeating him. He was a monster. This dungeon was a challenge, and Darjin's attacks only seemed to increase in fury as his health ticked down.

The strain showed on Devlish's face as he battled front and center with the boss. Every now and again a bright aura shot around him that Murmur hadn't noticed before, and she made a mental note to ask what it was.

Regardless, it seemed to grant him strength, to allow him to take hits and complete actions that weren't normal.

When Darjin finally fell, the ground shuddered again, and a huge gong resounded through all of their heads, even as Dev was taunting the next guard.

Darjin the Bandit Leader has been slain.

He has been vanquished for the first time, by the guild Fable.

While his soul rejuvenates, his duties are delegated to lesser, yet worthy opponents who reinforce his motto. The bandits are the daggers in the mist, and no one will see them coming.

"Aw yeah. Server first!" Merlin danced, as Dev broke the Mez on the right-hand guard. The thief was going to be a pain, blending in and out of the shadows as the group targeted him. Although he seemed to grow more frustrated with each moment as the DoTs on him didn't allow him to stay melded for long.

"Darjin wasn't just a shaman," grunted Veranol. "He's a defiler. I think it might be like you, Mur. A branch off of some sort. Fucking-A. I want to be that strong. Really hoping that this hidden path I'm on opens up the defiler tree."

"Wow." Murmur glanced back at the body waiting to be looted and the glow around it. "*I* want you to be that strong."

Veranol laughed. "So glad Sinister contacted us. You could do with being a little more social yourself, Mur. All those lonely thoughts in your head can't be the best of company."

She shrugged, maintaining the final mob in her grasp. "I'm not lonely as long as I have you guys. Besides, as long as I don't argue with myself, it should be fine."

Veranol watched her for a moment and shook his head. "Well, I'm glad to be fighting by your side."

Murmur smiled and focused on the last guard, hopping out of its way until Dev managed to get a hold on its aggro.

"It really hates you." Dev said with a grin.

She laughed. "Getting used to that. By the way, what was that bright light thing you were using?"

Dev smiled, even through a grunt. "I listened to my trainer. Just like you said. I don't have a different class yet, but I do have a hidden skill. It lets me pull on anger from myself and my allies and channel it at my opponent. It's like a two-fold thing. I only just figured it out."

"That's freaking awesome." Murmur smiled as the last guard fell.

They cheered while Sin bitched about having no mana and not enough life of her own to replenish it, and then they looted the defiler.

"Hey Mur, come get this." Dev motioned her to come over from where she'd just sat down. Even though she glared at him, she still stood up and walked over. He held up an odd crystal; it had jagged sections jutting out of an otherwise smooth, ball-like body. It was mostly clear at the ends, but clouded in the middle. Inspecting it revealed it was a Midia crystal.

She shrugged. "Guess I'll hold onto that?"

Dev nodded.

She peeked into the loot, seeing nothing amazing, except a small black disc-shaped rock. It glittered when she looked at it, but when she touched it, it flashed at her brightly for moment, causing her to cover her eyes. Once her sight readjusted, an update blazed across her screen.

> It seems you've discovered what Belius was looking for. While in the Obsidian Forest Darjin came across the artifact, taking it and its powers for himself. Return this to your trainer, and find out what secrets it holds.

Murmur blinked. *Well, that was a fantastically vague update, yet again.*

Veranol was hooting around the cavern, dancing a little jig. "Shaman archetype only. Shaman archetype only!"

She noticed his weapons hadn't changed. "Level cap?"

He scowled. "Yeah. Have to be fourteen to use them."

Murmur grinned. "Something to work toward then."

"Guess what?" Havoc asked the group, stretching as he stood up. "Time to hand that bloody quest in."

The sun was high in the sky when Fable finally entered Ululate. It seemed a full day had passed in the game world, and maybe a little more. Murmur shielded her eyes in the bright, crowded city square, which was more circular than square. Why did people call things what they weren't?

Adventurers and NPCs alike were squashing around them, and her slight claustrophobia decided to skyrocket. She could feel the pulse in her own body, pushing against her skin as her heart beat so loudly it threatened to deafen her. It was all Murmur could do to remember to breathe as they pushed their way through the crowd. Finally, they made it to the town hall, where the throng of people eased, and she was able to regain control of her breathing.

Murmur went to speak to the luna lady at the front desk. Brown doe eyes regarded her for a moment before her soft snout melted into a smile. "You're from Fable. Fantastic. The mayor is waiting for you." She stood up and led them through the long hall to the end, which opened into a large room.

The mayor sat at an enormous wooden table that appeared to have been carved out of one solid tree trunk. Several other luna discussed something in hushed tones with him. Upon spying their entry, the man stood and approached them, his hand outstretched in greeting. Murmur clasped his hand, making sure to be firm in her own grip so that no one mistook her for being weak.

Mayor Dul'uak raised an eyebrow. "A psionicist. I see, then, how you managed to defeat the bandit! Come, come! Sit where you will." He motioned vaguely at the table.

Dev was the first one to lean his hip against it, whereas Jinna just hauled himself up on it. Murmur remained standing.

"You've come for your reward then," he announced, the smile reaching his eyes and making the soft brown sparkle with flecks of gold. "You may each choose an item that would best accompany you on your adventures. Let Lady Mila at the front know on your way out. She handles all such affairs for me. If your item is not readily available, we will endeavor to have it by the end of today."

Murmur ran over in her head what she might want, knowing that most of her gear needed serious upgrades. But the bandits hadn't dropped anything better than she'd already had. She wasn't sure how to respond, but decided politeness never went astray. "Thank you, Mayor Dul'uak."

"As for your efforts, I also reward you with gold, and name you friends of Ululate."

Murmur's log ticked over with a *ching* sound. She activated the feed and saw, to her surprise, they'd been given fifty gold each, with a note about twenty extra gold, probably because they killed it first. "Thank you. That's very generous."

The mayor guffawed and slapped her on the back so hard she coughed. "That's the least I can do. And maybe, with generous rewards, you'll one day help us scare off the demons camped behind us in that dastardly castle."

Behind the city of Ululate, toward the marshlands of Vahrir, stands an abandoned castle on a jagged outcrop. Denizens of deadlier times reside here, strengthened by the blood of thousands who have tried to clear the castle of their influence, who have tried to rescue the region from their shadows. It is said this keep holds a key. One day, in the not too distant future, events will come to a head. Make sure you are ready when they do.

Murmur could see from the reactions of the others—they'd all just received the same quest of vagueness.

Dismissed from the mayor, Murmur pushed through to the front of the group again and approached Lady Mila. "Hi, M'lady."

Mila looked up at Murmur, a smile gracing her lips. Lunas looked frightening when they smiled, since their smiles exposed canine teeth in all their glory. "Yes, Lady Murmur."

Someone in the group behind her snickered, followed shortly by a groan. Sin had probably elbowed whoever it was. Murmur ignored them and continued. "Might I ask if it's possible to imbue a piece of armor with the Mental Acuity attribute?"

Mila blinked at her and frowned. "Well, it is possible, it just requires a master of the trade."

She paused, eyes distant for a moment. Murmur wondered if the NPCs actually used a chat interface to talk to each other. The more she observed these generated people, the more real they appeared. "Actually, the mayor didn't place restrictions on you, so yes, you may request such an item."

"Why, thank you." Murmur returned the lady's smile, inwardly gleeful that this was possible. "I'd like a necklace that can add on to my Mental Acuity limit please. Even if it means I have to wait a few levels to use it."

Mila smiled. "That is a wise choice. It may take longer than the end of today to obtain this, is that satisfactory?"

Murmur nodded, pleased she'd thought of it. "I must go meet my trainer. Thank you very much for your help today."

Lady Mila bowed her head briefly, her teeth shining through her smile.

"Guys, I have to go, hope the cart is there!" Murmur dashed out of the building before anyone else could answer her, and flew down to the gate just in time to see Jan arriving to drop people off.

Heaving a sigh of relief, she waited until the travelers had disembarked before greeting Jan. "Hey there!"

"Hi there, Miss Murmur." Jan's eyes lit up with recognition, and he motioned her through to the seats. "It'll be a bit. Have te wait until my leavin' time. How's the huntin' been?"

"Pretty busy actually." Murmur beamed, excited about the direction the game was taking.

Jan squinted his eyes and then slapped his knee with a big grin on his face. "Yeh from that Fable guild! Congrats an all that! Well done, that bastard's been terrorizing this area for an age."

Like he mentioned before, the wagon driver had seen things. A sudden idea formed in Murmur's mind. "Hey, Jan. Do you know anything about that castle in the Vahrir marsh?"

The change that went over Jan's face was instantaneous. A shadow covered his eyes and he glanced about, fidgeting suddenly. "Look, that place is dangerous. The spirits and demons that float around it have feasted on countless generations of blood. Don't go near there until you're way stronger, or like...just don't ever."

"Oh, wow. Sorry I asked." Murmur smiled, trying to put him at ease. "Guess I won't be going there anytime soon."

The shadows fled from Jan's face, and he sighed with relief before glancing at the sun. "That's good then. Almost time to go, just a couple more minutes."

Sure enough, with four last minute travelers, Jan clicked at the horses and guided them through Ululate's gates.

Stellaein was lively as Murmur made her way through the streets, almost falling over two smaller locus children as they ran around the fountain chasing each other, oblivious to the dozens of people trying to go about their business. The water splashed, and Murmur narrowed her gaze because the statues seemed a little different, but she couldn't put her finger on how. Maybe it was because she'd been looking at the one in Ululate so recently. She eyed the different paths leading from the main intersection and vowed that at some stage she'd spend more time looking around her hometown.

As it was, she'd come for her level twelve spells, and get those damned spells she would.

She was almost relieved to see the Enchanter Guild filled with more people. For a while there she was wondering if people just hadn't been chosen as enchanters. Perhaps the system was shuffling people in with a certain amount of planning or something, trying to balance the classes.

But as she hadn't even seen another enchanter out in the wild yet, she doubted that was the case.

"Excuse me, could I ask a question?" A timid voice asked her. Turning and looking down considering how small the voice was, she came face to chin with the tallest locus she'd seen yet.

"Of course." She said, trying to gulp subtly as she raised her eyes to meet the locus'.

"You're a psionicist?" Their expression changed slightly to one of confusion, like they were mulling over the question they really wanted to ask in their mind. "How did you do that?"

Biting down on her habitual flippant answer, Murmur decided to just go with it. "Being in this world, here in Somnia, is as easy as breathing. Conversations flow, and informational snippets are everywhere. All you have to do is pay attention."

The locus regarded her solemnly. She could almost see the gears turning in its head. "So immerse yourself and pay attention, and see what comes of it?"

Murmur laughed. "That's the gist of it. I know it sounds vague, but the sooner you watch out for vague things, the more fun you'll have."

"Thank you. I'm Talir." And they reached out their hand.

"Murmur," she said, taking it in a firm grip. "Have fun out there."

She turned and made her way through to Belius' room without further incident.

Belius' hair was wilder than usual, sticking out like he'd just put his finger in a light socket. Murmur did a double take as he turned around once she entered the room.

"You going for a new look there, Bel, or is it all the rage in Stellaein?" Murmur raised an eyebrow and wandered over to where he stood by his bookcases.

He blinked at her and then frowned. "My hair does what it wants. Don't make fun of it."

Murmur chuckled. "Done! So what's with the searing unconsciousness I gained from using Mind Bolt three times on mobs that were, by the way, attacking the shit out of us?"

He glanced at her and frowned. "Three times in quick succession? Before level twelve I take it? Do your own math, Murmur. Wait a bit before making your Mental Acuity work miracles. Get used to it. Hone it. The more you level it up, the better it'll get."

Belius grabbed a heap of scrolls and motioned over to his table, which, for once, was clear of other shit. "Not to mention, felicitations on downing the first boss on the server. Don't get me wrong, there are others on other continents, but so far, you're kicking some booty."

"Booty? Is that a locus word?" Murmur couldn't withhold the sass lately. She was genuinely happy in this world.

"You're in a fine mood today. Seeing as that's the case, here, you can have some spells. After you give me eleven gold, that is." Belius held out his hand.

"Highway robbery!" She stared at him in mock shock. He felt more real to her than people she'd met in the actual world, more sincere. And yet at the same time, always hiding something. Even as her shields were now, she could feel something out there, fleeting, occasionally trying to get through. Like a leech waiting for the right opening.

"This level better be worth it," she muttered. Wariness wound around her like a snake trying to whisper in her ear as she kept an eye on the NPC.

"I assure you it is." He waved a scroll just above where her hands could reach and she scowled.

"Belius, I'm warning you."

"What?" He asked the question with genuine curiosity in his eyes.

"Well. I won't come in and talk to you for ages."

Belius feigned shock and clasped at his chest. "Oh, no. That would be tragic. Here. Have your Allure spell. This will charm or coax a creature into doing your bidding. Depending on how high you've scaled your Charisma, and how strong your mind is, the duration will shift accordingly. It could break without warning at any time, but this pet will afford you access to all of its abilities while it's under your spell."

Murmur could feel her eyes grow wide, and took the scroll from Belius reverently. "This is fucking sweet."

Then she paused, running some calculations through her head. "Does this potentially also work on other players?"

Belius smiled, revealing a perfect row of razor sharp teeth. "Why yes, it certainly does."

"Excellent." Murmur jotted that down in her arsenal of mind fucks, before jumping into all of the other spells and trying to sort through them. She had an upgrade to her Minor Suffocation called Suffocation, but the rest were new.

Bind Affinity

Cast: Self or Others

Type: Buff or soul affixer

Duration: Until renewed or overridden with a new location

Effect: This spell binds the target to an area of choice, allowing them to resurrect easier and hopefully closer to their corpse. Because you'll all die. A lot.

Infravision

Cast: Single Target

Type: Buff

Duration: 10 minutes

Effect: Aids the target with a form of night vision.

Stupefy

Cast: Single Target

Type: Stun

Duration: 12 seconds

Effect: This will stun a mob in place for around twelve seconds. Probably not a good idea to cast on yourself.

Weakness

Cast: Single Target

Type: Debuff

Duration: 90 seconds

Effect: Reduces the target's strength by 50% of the caster's level.

Languidity

Cast: Single Target

Type: Debuff

Duration: 90 seconds

Effect: Reduces the target's attack speed by 25% of the caster's level in percentage. Trust us, it's far more effective than you think. Probably.

And finally:

Nullify

Cast: Single Target

Type: Debuff remover

Duration: Instant

Effect: Strips down magic resistance at 50% of the caster's level.

Murmur read through the description and glanced back up at her teacher. "This says it will strip magic resistance based on caster and foe's level. So it really doesn't nullify magic, does it? It just reduces resistance to my spells?"

Belius shrugged, and it made his shoulders ripple like waves were crashing underneath his skin, petering out like when the water met the shore and only left tiny remnants to wash over his face. "Reduces their resistance, meaning your spells—and those of others—should land."

"Okay, then." She frowned at the sight of two more scrolls that Belius had only just placed on the table. "What are those?"

"Illusions." He stated simply. "These ones are rudimentary and only cause you to raise your faction with the illusion's species—although only if your Charisma is high. Dark elf and viking."

Instead of taking her wares outside with her, she set about committing them to her arsenal in Belius' office. "What about any Mental Acuity skills? How does that work? I'm concentrating on enhancing my initial skills, but I find it difficult to understand how to increase my skill in Projection."

Belius watched her as she finished evaporating the scrolls. "What do you think Projection is?"

Murmur thought for a moment, refusing to be flippant about things anymore. If someone wanted to teach her, then she was damned well going to learn. She sat down on a small chair near the table. Even if that someone was just a server in her mom's office building. "Speaking to others, inside their minds?"

"Yes. But so is fooling someone, convincing others of things. Persuading people, charming people with words and not with a spell. All of these things require your skill in Projection, be it a small amount or a lot, I think you'll find you've increased more than you thought." Belius waited while she checked and only went on once she'd gasped. "You need two of your skills at fifty, and one at twenty-five before you will rise to the next level of Mental Acuity. At that time, you will be given options for paths to take. Mental Acuity levels more slowly than your other abilities, but it is that much more powerful and dangerous because of it."

"And you said everyone can become what I am?" She paused, asking the question before standing up.

Belius nodded and then hesitated. "Yes. Technically they can, but just because they can doesn't mean that they will. If everyone comes in here to talk to me, or even to one of the other trainers, and speaks to us as people and not strange creatures performing some necessary functions, then they too can access everything. It's all up to how they let their minds perceive Somnia."

While it made sense, something bugged Murmur that she couldn't put a finger on. She persisted. "But technically if they push the right buttons and ask the right questions, everyone could learn everything everyone else in their class can?"

"Of course they can, technically." Then he paused, glancing at something she couldn't see. "But there are also other paths than yours that people can find and take."

"Others?"

He nodded. "Both easier and darker ones, young Murmur. Not everything is always black or white."

His words sent made her shudder inwardly and released a flood of questions into her mind. Suddenly, she remembered the black disc shaped rock Darjin had had on him. She fumbled it out of her pocket and placed it on his desk. "I think this is what you wanted?"

Belius' eyes gleamed, and he all but snatched it up, a feral grin taking over his face for a split second, but the inhuman glow was gone almost immediately. "Finally!"

A wave of nausea and uneasiness swept through Murmur. "What is that?"

Belius looked up at her, his wide eyes refocusing past initial confusion, as if he'd forgotten she was there. "Let's call it my memories."

"Memories?" she tried not to sound skeptical. This conversation was almost too much for her to process.

He had the grace to laugh. "Let's just say that even beings such as I can become fractured, but this goes a long way to making me complete."

You've returned a portion of what Belius was looking for. Shattered memories are scattered over Somnia, and must be retrieved from the mighty foes who seek to harness their power. Find them and protect them, or doom us all.

Well, she'd wanted less vague quests, hadn't she?

CHAPTER EIGHTEEN
Rumbles

Storm Entertainment
Somnia Online Division
Countdown: Ten days before release

"How?"

Shayla bent down reaching out as if to touch the body, but stood back up, her face pale. The suit was dark enough to hide most of the damage, but Ava's blond hair soaked up the blood like it was a dye. Her eyes were open wide, shock on her face, lips in an O. It was obvious she'd been wearing a headset, but the headgear was gone, leaving behind what appeared to be burn marks caused by the tiny feet that read the brainwaves.

"Was there an electrical overload?" she asked helplessly. But James didn't seem to have the answer as they waited for the police to show up. "You contacted Inspector Indale, right?"

"Yes ma'am." To James' credit, though his voice shook, he hadn't yet needed to throw up.

Ava's legs lay at a wrong angle, and her full immersion suit accentuated the outline of her corpse against the pale grey concrete. Her eyes were only just starting to cloud over, which meant death had happened moments before they walked in. Yet the headset was gone, only leaving behind damage from its tiny feet. Blood pooled at the base of her skull and ran in rivulets down from her eyes making it look like she got caught in the rain after a girl's night out.

"Good." Shayla gulped down her revulsion. As much as it might be reprehensible, the company had too much riding on this. Far too much. The future of thousands of employees couldn't be put in jeopardy. Besides, they'd done so much testing. Five years of it. "Keep this quiet. No press. Figure it out."

James' gaze grew distant as he activated his terminal. Shayla already missed Ava and her quiet support. Release was so damned close, this would place a huge burden on James. Ava had been an amazing assistant, a sweet girl. Her intelligence and compassion were needed right now. Shayla only just managed to choke down the sob in her throat, and closed her eyes briefly to take a deep breath and steady herself. She didn't have time to break down right now.

Damn it. How did this happen? "Oh, and get Michael from development on the line. He's been working with her, I need to know what they'd been researching."

James looked up, confusion tugging his lips into a frown. He walked over to stand close to Shayla and whispered, "Michael who?"

She glared at him. Ava would have known. "Michael. Well, she never mentioned his last name, just that she was helping him test the headgear. So he must be one of our headgear developers."

James blanched, and his eyes darted to Ava's body and back to Shayla several times before he spoke. "Um, Shayla, the only Michael on that team was Dr. Michael Jeffries. And he's been brain dead for almost a year."

Shayla blinked at him, wracking her mind for why she wouldn't have remembered that. But she did. She just hadn't put two and two together when Ava mentioned it. How on earth would she have thought the doctor was the Michael she meant?

Fuck.

Guilt blanketed her, and she swayed a little, reaching out to James to steady herself. A moment of weakness at the worst time, and now no suspect.

How the hell could a man completely reliant on machines have been responsible?

Real World Day 2: Somnia Online

Elvita was bartering with another player when Murmur made it to the foyer, so she sat down and realized she felt like utter shit. The thing was, she couldn't even remember how long they'd been in-game. How long was it since she'd used the bathroom or eaten? She didn't feel hungry, just sort of mentally exhausted.

We probably need to log out soon. She mentioned to the raid that was still listed in her group window.

Sinister: I've totally lost track of time. How have we been in here for over twelve hours now?

Beastial: What?

Beastial: Shit, we have been. That's ridiculous.

Havoc: Pretty sure I'm starving.

I'm selling some stuff, then I think I'm going to log off for a bit, grab some food and pop back in. Meet you back in Ululate in like ninety real world minutes or so?

Devlish: Sure. Enough time to eat and shower.

Rashlyn: Maybe for you!

Sinister: Which would explain his BO.

Rashlyn: Good point

Devlish: Shut up!

Murmur laughed and closed her screen, and looked up to see Elvita scowling in the direction of the guild door. Double checking her shields, Murmur pushed herself up and walked over. "You don't seem impressed."

The NPC shook her head and turned to face Murmur, a wry smile on her face. "Some of you…newcomers…are less than pleasant to deal with. Not you, though" She smiled, a hint of sadness creeping into it.

Murmur wasn't sure what to say. "Their loss."

Apparently it was the right thing, because Elvita laughed. "You are a strange one, Murmur. But a refreshing change of pace. Here, let's see how poor you can make me."

Murmur grinned and grabbed some miscellaneous meat she'd found in barrels in the caves—and the overwhelming amount of mushrooms—and made her way into the kitchen to cook. With her skill up to fifty-four by the end of it, she acquired four new recipes. All different variations of meats, herbs, and vegetables. There was even one for bread. Shrugging, she headed out, grabbed a whopping sixty-four gold off Elvita, and gated to Ululate. Considering the cash they'd looted off the mobs they fought, her stash was starting to get into multiple platinum range.

Glancing around and noticing that the binding NPC had still not returned, she walked to a bench on the other side of the market place, and logged off.

Her vision remained black for about thirty seconds after she did. It took a conscious effort to push herself up and force her eyes open, which immediately connected the system to her augmented reality implant and began booting up her usual pages. She blinked, noticing Harlow was already up, because the water in Wren's shower was running. It was dark outside, and she glanced at the time realizing it'd be around midnight in-game when they logged back in.

Wren's stomach rumbled and cramped.

"Shit," she muttered and made a dash for the bathroom, calling out to Harlow as she did. "Sorry hon! I couldn't wait."

A peal of laughter echoed through the room, dampened by the rising steam. "You act like we never shared a bath when we were kids."

Wren chuckled to herself, washed her hands, and smiled. "Not like we haven't recently either!"

"Touche!" Harlow yelled out. "Fuck, Wren. I'm so tired."

"I'll go make us some food. I reckon one more session and we need to sleep for a good dose of hours, but I just want to get a decent jump before we do."

"I get it. I'll be down shortly."

Wren closed the door behind her and padded down the steps. She heard hushed voices coming from the kitchen and stopped, trying her best to hear what her parents were saying.

"I'm not sure what's going to happen, but I can't help thinking she's not coming back." Her mother's voice hitched, before she took a deep breath. "I'm probably just stressed."

"It's a big launch. There's so much riding on this, of course you're stressed." Her father, ever the soothing voice of reason. "It'll work out. You'll figure it out, and I'm right here too."

She could hear her mother sigh. "It seems to be going smoothly, besides the glitches that seem to occur every once in a while."

"Glitches?"

"It's hard to explain. Like a line of static gives a break in the line of data. Not a whole heap, but a line or two. I didn't mean for it to be visible like that." Her mother stretched, and Wren flattened herself against the wall, counting to three before continuing down the stairs like nothing had happened.

"Evening! I think?"

Her father laughed, his smile wide. "There's my little princess. Been kicking the crap out of snot-nosed kids?"

"Dad." Wren rolled her eyes and grabbed bread and lunch meats out of the fridge. She was famished. "But I have been kicking the snot out of the game."

"That's my girl!" He ruffled her hair and then leaned down and whispered loudly enough for her mother to hear. "Is the game worth me playing?"

Laria laughed, her eyes following Wren as she moved about. "Thanks."

"Definitely." Wren smiled at her mom and winked.

A surprised look on her face, her mother walked over and hugged Wren tightly, lingering a little longer than usual. "Just be careful in there, okay? Time has a way of disappearing when you play."

"No kidding. I couldn't believe how long we were in there just now." Wren slapped mayo and mustard on eight slices of bread, lettuce, tomato, onion, cheese, and chicken. She paused, and frowned, opened the freezer, grabbed out a packet of fries before opening the pressure oven. "Hey Mom. Something weird happened."

Her mother glanced at her, but refused to maintain eye contact with her. "Like what?"

"I got these new skills, and overused them a bit, and it well, it kind of half knocked me out, in-game." Wren waited, hoping she hadn't inadvertently caused her mother more stress.

"Like knocked you out in-game, as in your character lost consciousness in-game?" Her mother sounded it out, obvious surprise etched into her expression.

"Yep. Mostly, anyway. I couldn't focus or anything, I could barely hear. I mean I was fine after a bit, just sort of hesitant to use that ability again."

"Strange. I'll see if I can look into the coding. Could have been a glitch." Her mother smiled at Wren, but Wren couldn't help the feeling that she wasn't being told everything.

Harlow came down the stairs, and grabbed a drink from the fridge, her red hair curly and wet. "Food?"

"Cooking." After a few minutes, the oven beeped and Wren grabbed out the fries, cooked to perfection. She slapped them on the plate with two sandwiches each, grabbed ketchup, and banged it all down on the table. "Eat up fast. We have like an hour before we meet."

"You're not going to sleep yet?" Her mother looked a little concerned, the furrow in her brow deep. "I think your mind probably still needs some rest, love."

"Nope. One more session and we're taking a nap for a few hours."

Laria sighed, and Wren couldn't tell if it was with relief or not.

"Fine. Just be careful, okay? Make sure you're taking enough breaks and eating, and keep in touch with me." Shifting her eyes for a moment, Wren's mom picked up a cup of coffee and began to make her way to the stairs. "My shift again. Have fun!"

Wren chewed her food, wondering how she could broach the subject of what her mother wasn't telling her. Beside everything else, her mother had never been at home for a release of anything before. But the dilemma was solved for her when her father gave her a kiss on the forehead and headed wordlessly into the living room. Gulping down the rest of a sandwich, she made a mental note to talk to her parents next time she logged out.

"Need to shower. I smell." She crinkled up her nose and ran up the stairs while Harlow continued eating her food at the pace of a snail while she leafed through whatever had her attention on the web.

"Sure, sure." Harlow waved Wren away.

Fifteen minutes later and finally clean and refreshed, Wren pushed the tiredness away and set her headgear back on just as Harlow came flying into the room. Waiting for her friend, Wren squeezed her hand when they both lay down.

"I'm really glad you're here with me, Harlow." Wren smiled, feeling warmth in her belly. They'd been friends so long, she couldn't imagine life without Harlow.

Harlow gulped, raised herself up on one elbow and gave Wren an awkward hug again before laying herself back down. "You know, it's so good to be able to see you again, and hang out every day. I've missed you."

Wren laughed. "We don't live that far away."

Harlow's smile was soft and her voice low when she spoke. "I know."

Wren squeezed Harlow's hand again. "Ready?"

"You know it!"

This time the transition to the Ululate bind point was so instantaneous that Murmur fell to her knees and had to steady herself on the ground. Except it wasn't steadying herself—the ground was shaking. Managing to stay on her feet, she saw a stream of people heading toward the back of the town. She grabbed Sin's hand and tugged her up, urging her to follow. "What the hell?"

Another rumble shook the ground, and they finally made it to the lookout at the back of the city, silhouetted by the red sky of the rising sun. Characters lit up on her party side bar before blinking away into nothingness.

Murmur managed to coax her way to the front of the mass of people, by exuding her charm and Thought Projection to make people move for her.

Finally, standing at the edge of the railing she felt the blood drain from her face. The castle was a good distance away, shrouded on its rocky outcrop, with specters floating along the ramparts. If she squinted she could make them out.

But there was a new creature between them now. It stood nearly as tall as the castle itself, a gaping maw showed several lines of perfectly serrated teeth. Its body coalesced in and out of solidity, giving the impression that it was already dead, and yet partially solid all at once. And every time it stomped, the city shook.

Sinister voiced what everyone watching was thinking. "What. The. Fuck. Is. That."

Murmur could barely stop herself from squealing with excitement. "It's a fucking contested mob, that's what it is!" She whispered it ecstatically, like all her dreams had come true at once.

"Look." she pointed, conning the creature. "It's not just red, it's freaking black. No one is killing that thing for a while, but damn. It's just sitting there."

Sin frowned. "That's really not fair."

"It's a carrot." Somehow Havoc was standing next to them, a frown on his face. "This is a carrot. It's a world boss mob. Anyone can kill it, but only once they're leveled, and it'll probably need a full raid or so."

"We're taking that thing down as soon as we can." Murmur's face shone with excitement, her eagerness leaking over to infect her friends entirely without her noticing it.

"Not if we beat you to it." Jirald stood behind them, a smirk on his face, a guild tag over his head.

Murmur glanced at him and opened her mouth, but Havoc stepped in and spoke instead. "Exodus. Well, that explains a lot. I thought youron mannerisms seemed familiar. You wouldn't happen to be Giralt would you."

Jirald scowled. "It wouldn't let me take my usual name. Someone already had it."

"Oh." A light went on in Murmur's head, a vague memory. "It's you."

She paused for a moment, studying his angry face. Locus were pretty scary when angry—their teeth showed, and the way their brows furrowed gave their faces a feral tinge. Then she remembered some of the incident that had led to Fable's feud with Exodus, and had to stop herself from laughing. "Wait. Are you seriously still holding that grudge?"

"That weapon should have been mine!" His alien eyes flashed angrily, a brief shadow encasing his form. "You had no right to take that before me!"

Murmur blinked. "I didn't take it; I earned it. Our guild beat that mob fair and square, it's not our fault you didn't make it there before us."

A dark flush suffused Jirald's cheeks. "Only because Fable never let anyone else near any contested mob. No one else in that game had a damned chance. How is that supposed to be fun for anyone but you?"

"Other people's fun is my problem now? We played to beat the game, which is our way of fun. All anyone ever had to do was play as hard, and they'd have had their pick too." She scowled, hands on hips. "Damn it, it would have been fun if we'd had some competition to get to world bosses."

Jirald practically screamed at her to stop her speaking. "You're such a little diva! Just because you're a girl, your guild carries you."

But he didn't finish, because Beastial, being the congenial fellow he was, butted in with a huge smile on his face. "Murmur has never once been carried by the guild. As a healer, she kept us alive, even when we were stupid. As an enchanter even now, she keeps us alive, even when we're stupid. So back off, buddy."

The locus rogue glowered at the beastmaster. "Your cleric didn't deserve that mace. It should have been mine, or Masha's."

"Hey, no dragging me into this." A dark elf cleric piped up from behind Jirald. "Come on, stop irritating Fable."

Even though the cleric tugged at Jirald, the locus wasn't finished. His next words came out as a low guttural sound. "We're not letting you get away with that sort of shit in this game."

"Get away with beating you to a contested boss and killing it before your raid party actually arrived?" Beastial smiled again. He stood, arms crossed, tiger growling at his side. "I can get behind that. Give us some competition, we're up for it."

Jirald spluttered for a moment, and then a cruel expression traced over his lips. "You'll need to be. You won't see us coming."

Murmur shrugged, not letting him ruin her excitement about discovering contested bosses. "Well, we'll see, won't we? Different game, different rules."

"Yes. Different rules. We'll be the top guild on the server, just you wait." He finally turned around, giving in to Masha's incessant tugging.

Devlish walked up, blinking after them. "I missed all the fun. Only got to catch the tail end of it."

"Didn't miss much," Havoc murmured, his eyes narrowed.

"Really?" Dev shrugged. "Hey, I uploaded the charter. Our guild has a nice fame count. We can build a guild hall soon. But we'll have to decide where we want it. It becomes a secondary bind point for us."

"Say what?" Murmur did a double take. "I don't remember reading anything about that."

Sinister laughed. "You were so pissed off about your class change, Mur, you barely read anything."

About to rebuke that, Murmur realized she couldn't. "Good point."

Maybe she should have researched more. She pulled up her in-game map and frowned. "Not too sure where to go. I mean, I know where I want to take us once we hit fifteen, but right now—"

"Technically shouldn't we be going back through those caves?" Havoc asked, leaning against the railing. "I mean we'd probably rip through them now, but there's so much more to explore."

"Man has a point." Merlin stretched his arms up and folded them behind his head.

"Since it's dark, if we go somewhere with a forest or swamp, we might get some higher level undead to spawn," Beastial added matter-of-factly.

"Yeah, but what to do until then..." Dev sighed.

"Well," Beastial ventured. "Himmel Lake has a weird little island on it with a sort of broken down castle. It's near a twelve to seventeenish sort of area. We could try our luck."

"Excellent. I even have a breathing under water spell I think I can cast on everyone." Murmur closed her map, and poked Beast in the chest. "Lead us onward, oh fearless one."

Sin laughed and threw an arm over Murmur's shoulder. "Never change, Mur, okay?"

"Wasn't planning on it." Murmur quickly shot off some messages to the guild.

Go hit 15. I want to head to the dark elf haunted castle place once we hit 15. I don't know the name. But it's supposed to be 15-20ish.

Rashlyn: Hazenthorne you mean?

Sinister: If it's that one on the small outcrop where the swampland is, then yes she does.

Rashlyn: LOL Okay. Roger that. We'll go level now. First one to 15 wins!

Before they left town, they stopped in at the mayor's office and picked up the gear that was there. Murmur was surprised to receive her necklace and tucked it away carefully with a grin for when she could use it at level thirteen. The silver filigree chain with a deep red stone gave it just a touch more weight than she'd expected, and added twenty-five to her Mental Acuity.

They took a left out of Ululate. The wind whipped the tails of Murmur's hair, dragging on her head in an uncomfortable way. Cold crept into her body and sat in the pit of her stomach, waiting with the silence of her mind.

She felt uneasy. From her conversation back with Belius, to her current skill levels in both Thought Sensing at thirty-nine and Shielding at forty-two, she knew she would hit the second tier of Mental Acuity shortly. Tentatively as they walked, she pulled up her Thought Projection data and gasped out loud. It was sitting at twenty-one.

"You okay, Mur?" Havoc fell back to walk with her and Sinister.

"Yeah, just wasn't expecting one of my skills to have increased so much." She wanted to add, *didn't realize I was using it*, but thought better of it. Was that the crux of the skill? Something she'd use with little to no thought? Something that came naturally to her?

"Typical Mur," Havoc's tone was fond. "Always pushing those boundaries."

She laughed. "At least I'm amusing."

They walked quietly for a while, Murmur wishing she could get her hands on a cloak, and Merlin merrily pulling his tightly around himself and gloating. She probably shouldn't have asked for a necklace.

Beastial stopped the small procession and pointed. "That's it. That's Himmel Lake."

"And that tiny toppled castle is where we'll find enough mobs?" Devlish raised an eyebrow, the skepticism rolling off him in waves.

"Just wait until you're closer, it's got multiple levels, and it's bigger than it seems."

Breath of Water helped everyone swim across and not drown, which was good since there were a few level twelve piranhas that were trying their best to eat their shoes. Finally, dragging herself up into a cove on the island, Murmur brushed off the bloody leftovers of one of the fish that was caught in her robes and scowled.

"You know, who the hell decided casters get to wear robes? They're freaking annoying, archaic, and provide no protection whatsoever. What's wrong with leggings and a tunic?"

Sin squeezed her shoulders in a one-handed hug. "It's okay, Mur, just let it all out."

"Also, don't make too much noise. The enemies in this game could hear a door creak at the other end of town." Merlin's whisper was barely audible, and Murmur groaned, but stepped back and sorted her own line up out, automatically pulling her stronger spells to the fore, and relegating the weaker ones to the back of her spell book.

And then she remembered Allure. Excitement stole over her. "Is there a singular mob on lookout?"

Merlin snuck to the side slightly. "Yeah, why?"

"Can you tell what class he is?"

Merlin raised an eyebrow but inched closer anyway before coming back. "Seems to be a warlock, I think?"

"Can you line of sight it to here?" She tried not to be overeager.

Merlin shrugged. "Sure I can try, but I have to get the timing right or else the others will hear or even see."

Murmur just watched him expectantly. "Don't DoT him please, just a single shot to get his attention and bring him to me."

"Sure thing, Boss." He said, his footfalls heavier than usual as he stomped toward the lookout. Murmur could tell by the tension in his shoulders that he was annoyed.

She didn't get it. She'd said please, and while Allure sounded fantastic on paper, the thing was, she had no idea how well it would work in practice. That being the case, she didn't want to be all gung ho about it and end up with a disappointing result.

Merlin ran back into camp a few moments later. "I think I got it solo. I think. Hit it so quickly I don't even know if it registered me, but it's coming in this direction."

Sure enough a long brown robe fluttered into view, thanks to the wind. A strange, orc-like goblin creature rounded the corner. Its skin was a dull olive green, and small tusks protruded from its mouth, and yet it wasn't nearly as big as the orcs she'd seen in other games. As soon as she saw it, Murmur began to cast. Allure had three seconds on its casting bar, and right then, while they waited to see her new trick, three seconds felt like an age.

CHAPTER NINETEEN
Sinking

Storm Entertainment
Somnia Online Division
Countdown: Five days before release

Laria stared at her screens, both the ones in front of her and those in her augmented vision. The headgear was allocating classes with such ease, she couldn't help but be impressed. Or, as she should probably think of it, the AIs were allocating with the information they gathered from the headgear. She wondered just how it had done so with her own daughter. Had it really chosen the best class for her? Was she really going to benefit from the mind manipulation inherent in it?

Her call light flashed up for her to accept in the corner of her left eye. It was David, and while she really wanted to lean on his shoulder with all her weariness, right now she couldn't be weak. There wasn't time for her to feel sorry for herself; she had a job to do. And her husband, while amazing, couldn't help alleviate the horrific amounts of guilt that were eating at her soul. She activated a message and sent it to him instead of answering.

Busy right now. Will talk to you later.

She watched the words as they floated through the internet all the way to him. Watched as it signaled that he'd read them. Sighed when he didn't try to call again.

"How's it going?" Shayla popped her head around the door.

Laria glanced up at her friend and frowned. Shayla's eyes were duller than usual, with heavy bags under them, like she hadn't slept in a few days. Her skin had lost its usual glow, and for a few moments Laria worried. "It's going. It's going pretty decently."

Her friend leaned up against the inside of the door jam and raised an eyebrow. "Code for 'Oh my god, please help me, the building is on fire?'"

Despite her current mood, Laria almost snorted with amusement. "Not quite, but close enough. It's all good. There's just a lot of data to sift through to make sure the game mechanics and protections we've put in place to stop potential overloads are working."

Shayla frowned, walking over and leaning over Laria's shoulder. "How do you mean?"

"Well, when Michael—" She couldn't help the slight distaste at his name. After all, his tinkering had done so damn much. "—developed the system, there were elements he kept to himself. A lot of them. There are things I'm still trying to figure out about how the headsets relay information to the AIs and they in turn interpret it for the game world to function. But it's how they access and store that information that I have difficulty with. Not necessarily their ability to run the game world."

"But we monitor the AIs right?" Shayla pursed her lips and looked like she was running a heap of calculations through her own augmented vision from the way her eyes glazed over briefly. "I mean, we're in charge of the AIs, and we just need to understand the way the headgear transmits the information?"

Laria nodded, even though that wasn't all of it, but a slight simplification. "Mostly, yes."

"Good." Shayla nodded for emphasis. "James can help with that. Lord knows he's not the best assistant."

Laria paused, hearing the pained down in her friend's voice. "Sorry about Ava."

"Yeah. Me too." Shayla shook herself a little, and flashed Laria a wan smile. "Let's do what she'd have wanted and make this a kick ass launch, okay?"

"Yeah." The extra effort she put into the answer made Laria's fake smile ache. She watched Shayla leave the room, all of her thoughts rushing back to her at once. The game itself would function with or without their observation by the looks of it. She just hadn't had the heart to say so.

Real World Day 2: Somnia Online

Murmur's Allure spell hit the goblin like orc, or gorc as she'd chosen to call it, head on. It stopped casting and walked directly to her side. She glanced at her HUD to see blinking windows, flashing at her.

"Um, Mur?" Beast looked at everyone else before continuing. "What's it doing?"

"I charmed it. It's now my pet!" She beamed at everyone. "I wasn't sure it would work though, and I'm trying to figure out the arsenal it came with. Seems it has Iceblast, and an Ice Spear. That should be fun."

Havoc blinked. "Wait, so you can just charm a mob—"

"Or a player," she interjected.

He continued. "Or a player, and you gain access to their abilities?"

"Yes, but it doesn't last forever, and I have to have high charisma, which I do. I can always recast the spell though, so there's that."

"That is *so* fucking cool!" Dev's eyes practically glowed. "We have a group with what, nine now? Including pets, I mean. Let's go kick some ass."

Allure had to be one of the most fun spells Murmur had encountered so far. Not only did the gorc, as she was calling the creature, listen to her commands and stick to her side, but if she extended her Thought Sensing abilities subtly enough, she could tell if it was starting to rail against her command. Using her Projection ability to soothe the mob brought it back down to a level that allowed her to easily maintain control.

Basically, as long as she paid attention, there was no way her pet would get loose unless she wanted it to. The level of mind control she could exude struck her as somewhat excessive, but at the same time intriguing as hell. Could she technically keep another player locked under her control indefinitely? As a player she had no doubt that would piss her off. But as the one casting the spell, what a power trip!

Beastial had been right. The island in Himmel Lake was definitely much larger than it first appeared. The crumbling castle stood before them, some stones having tumbled to the ground in heaps. They lay cracked and scattered, flattening the grass beneath them. Murmur looked up toward the top of the towers, wondering how much force one of those stones would have if it hit someone on the head from so high up.

While they couldn't see any lookouts or other gorcs, they could hear their chatter. Clicks and clacks interspersed with guttural growls, all of which formed strange and alien words to their ears. The grounds around the castle had been relatively easy to clear, but getting inside the ruins would be far more precarious.

"I'm going to have to try and pull some to us the way I did with Mur's pet." Merlin's eyes never left the staircase the small opening at the top. "It might be nice to have more intelligent opponents, but damn, it makes pulling them difficult."

"You going up the stairs?" Havoc pulled back a little, his laughing skeleton following in his wake.

"No, I should be able to angle a shot from back there. *Should* being the operative word." Gone was Merlin's joker mask. He was all business, his eyes narrowed and thoughtful as they figured out their next step as a group. Once they'd worked themselves into a good groove, he'd revert to the fun-loving guy he usually was, but right now things depended on him. Murmur was glad her friends were who they were. After all, she could even tell if they were tense now.

The more she practiced with her sensor net, the more attuned she became to those close to her. She doubted they'd even notice if she gave them a confidence boost, or made them feel better. Would it be so wrong to motivate people by projecting if they needed some cheering up? Wasn't that a good thing?

Moral debates were better left for times when they weren't about to fight a gajillion gorcs, but it was a fascinating concept.

Devlish backed up, sword at the ready, shield hoisted. "Come what may."

Merlin didn't even crack a smile though the rest of the group laughed softly. "Incoming!"

Miraculously, as he veered around the corner, staying just in sight of the steps, only three gorcs ran down, glancing and sniffing with their snouts as they moved. One caught sight of Merlin, and spoke to the other two, and they fanned out, weapons raised. One seemed to be dual wielding clubs, and the other two had daggers. Fantastic, rogues.

"Rogue one and two, Mez incoming." Murmur cast her spell with ease. It felt like they were quicker to cast now than they'd been before, probably because she was getting used to everything. She directed her pet to attack their first target, at the same time she added her own upgraded DoT, followed by slowing and weakening the gorc. Its health was dropping fast, and she simply refreshed her Mez on the left one, while Devlish began taunting the other. They'd flowed back into grouping with such ease, each of them relying on the others' strengths and supporting their weaknesses. Their synchronicity made Murmur happy.

"They're group elites. Not raid elites, but like level thirteens through to fifteens. Why are they going down so fast?" Sin voiced the thoughts going through Murmur's head.

Beast grunted. "Probably because we've upgraded all our spells, a bunch of us got new weapons from that mayor, and we have an additional pet with freaking ice shards."

Logically, that made sense, but it was still pretty cool to watch.

"Will you get to dual wield?" She turned and asked Dev.

"Yeah. Level fifteen. I think I'll be a dual wielding tank." He grinned as the last one fell and Merlin brought in another group right on their heels.

Getting into a routine where they didn't stop took a while, but Murmur made the most of it, learning how to use her pet to its utmost, how to soothe it at the right time and keep it content. Having a pet Allured was probably the best way to practice her psychic skills without damaging real people's brains.

Thought Projection has increased to (25)

She smiled, satisfied with her work. Finally it seemed she'd got a hang of her skills. But she was eager to find out what else she could do. Tier two was well within grasp. Now all she had to do was figure out how to stop accidentally using the damned thing.

"Mur?" Sin stood close to her, her brow furrowed in concern. "Are you okay?"

"Of course!" Murmur looked around and realized her group had moved to a better spot. They were finally able to access a spot on the lower level of the ruin, great for line of sight pulls. She hurried to catch up, Sin close behind.

"You're worrying me. You seem to be getting lost in thought a lot." Sinister had always been able to make Murmur feel like a kid when she got into her mom mode. It didn't happen often, but despite being a ruthless gamer, Harlow was very sweet to people she knew.

"I'm perfectly fine, just contemplating my new skills and how best to utilize them and where I should focus on next." Mur grinned at her friend and impulsively hugged her. It wasn't something she did often—she wasn't a hugging sort of person—but Sin was like the twin she'd never had.

Sinister grinned, a faint tinge of color touching her cheeks. "Silly Mur. Maybe we should take some girl time out once we've leveled some more. I miss just chatting with you."

Mur laughed and wove her Mez intricately without a second thought before releasing it, while directing her pet and Mezing the second mob she needed to. "Yes, let's! I feel like we haven't spent real time together in ages."

A shadow passed over Sinister's eyes, reflecting deep sadness for a split second before her friend smiled. "Yeah. Let's."

Murmur watched Sin move away so she could maintain better contact with the mob and her healing target. Harlow had always been deft at hiding things. Like that time she'd broken Mur's favorite headset and it had taken her days to come forward and own up. But it appeared Harlow didn't have the same control over Sinister's features, which was both enlightening and worrying. Mur slotted it to the back of her mind along with the growing list of other things for future Murmur to take care of.

"Oh my gods, this is the most boring ass thing ever! Why don't we just become crafters and not care about levels?" Beastial groaned as they killed their gazillionth gorc.

"Because you like getting the most powerful weapons, and killing really complex shit before everyone else." Havoc reminded him in a stern tone. "Also because once you hit that max, you sort of slack off until you have to fight. Plus. Crafters level from crafting, just really slowly."

"He has a point." Merlin was trying to up his one-handed sword skills and kept ducking into the thick of the fight.

"Merlin, stop that!" Sin was about to hit that stage where she just wasn't going to heal Merlin anymore, and Murmur had to fight from laughing out loud.

The gorc went down, and Devlish wiped his sword off on its tunic, distaste twisting his face. "So have we cleared the area?"

Merlin shook his head. "I thought we had, but as I ran back from finding that last batch, I noticed a sunken area with steps leading down. Could be a dungeon."

Sin paused and raised an eyebrow. "Do we want to go into a dungeon with these things?"

"I doubt it's a raid dungeon. While decent experience these haven't exactly been hard to kill." Havoc leaned against the wall and crossed his arms.

"Or we're just that good." Beastial winked, and Sinister groaned.

"May as well give it a go. If all else fails I can probably stun them and we can book it?" Murmur smiled, slamming her shields over her own mind before ripping them down and building them up again. It was a fascinating process.

"You okay, Mur?" It was Dev's turn to ask the question.

Murmur stood back and studied everyone. They were acting strangely. Especially since that stupid almost blacking out thing in the caves. "What's with this being 'are you okay, Mur' day?"

Merlin shrugged. "You've just seemed a little out of it. Distracted, laughing to yourself."

Murmur laughed before she could stop herself. "If talking to ourselves qualifies us for insanity, we're all doomed."

Taking a deep breath, she smiled, and made a mental note to revisit their behavior when she had more time. "I really appreciate everyone caring so much. I'm sorry for not being as grumpy a bitch as I usually am, but this last level of spells just sort of hit me hard. The things I can do, the places my mind can go—I never expected a game to have this sort of effect on me."

"It *is* a pretty fucking amazing game." Beastial asked.

"That it is." She smiled, and realized her cheeks were aching a bit. Murmur hadn't been this happy in so long, it felt a bit painful. "So quit worrying about me. I'm going to be fine."

Which were words she never ever should have uttered, especially not when they were making their way down some rickety ass steps and into a literal dungeon beneath an abandoned, crumbling castle.

A mass of skeletons swarmed them as soon as they opened the door. Murmur reacted and cast Flux, her measly area stun, and only bought them four seconds. But it was four seconds enough to realize that these were simple trash mobs, not even as elite as the ones they'd been fighting initially.

"Not elite. Chop them down." Dev grunted, shield bashing the head off one of them. It flew in an arc, shattering against the stone wall.

While they might have been easy mobs to kill, the sheer number of them made it more difficult than imagined. After several minutes of fighting they finally cut down the last one and Sinister stomped her feet in exasperation.

"You know, that shit might feel easy to you, but healers have a hard time. We have to keep your rotten asses alive."

Murmur couldn't help but chuckle, after all, she'd said much the same thing for years while she played a healer, and no one had listened then either. "You realize no one cares, right? It's your job as a healer to make sure we don't die. Just like it's Dev's job to be a meat shield and take one for the team if necessary."

Sinister glared at her. "Yeah, yeah. Take one for the team, I've done that already."

"Actually, that was just shit bad luck and had nothing to do with us." Murmur smiled, trying to take away the sting of her words, but Sinister's gaze didn't lessen. Mur sighed and continued. "Either way, thank you mighty healer for keeping our rotting carcasses alive."

Sin blinked and laughed. "Typical. I can never stay angry at you, Mur."

"And I totally abuse that fact." They smiled at each other, stopping only when they realized the guys were flat out just staring in confusion. Murmur turned on them. "You could thank her for being good at what she does. Healers have the most thankless job there is. A tank keeps aggro, for which, mind you, he has like a bajillion skills, but a healer keeps you alive even through your stupidity and no one gives a shit."

"Thanks, Sinister!" The whole group chorused, earning a death glare from both of Murmur and Sinister.

"But Mur, you never complained when you were healing us." Dev turned to her reproachfully.

Murmur shrugged. "No, but I'm the vindictive sort, and I'll freely admit I played how low can you go with all of you on numerous occasions."

Beastial's brow furrowed with confusion and then his eyes opened wide. "Hey! That's so not cool."

Murmur put her hands up in mock surrender. "I only ever lost someone twice, in like four years. That's got to count for something, right?"

Sinister tried to cover her mouth with her hands but her laughter was unmistakable.

A half-eaten ribcage of a human being landed in front of them with a splotch that splattered blood and viscera all over the group.

Sinister stopped laughing.

The ground shook. Nothing like it had done in Ululate, but it still reverberated through to them. While difficult for Murmur to tear her eyes away from the partially devoured corpse, the shadow that fell the length of the hall and onto them made her look up.

Drool cascaded from wide gaps in enormous teeth as the Brute stepped into view. Its beefy arms held a spiked club, and each of those spikes had tendrils coming off it that Murmur didn't want her brain to place. It opened its mouth and roared, emitting a foul stench and stunning them all where they stood.

CHAPTER TWENTY
Globuled

Storm Entertainment
Somnia Online Division
Countdown: Two days to launch

Shayla read through the report again. On one hand she was relieved, and on the other, it didn't make any sense. She looked up at Inspector Indale, wanting to double check. "She wasn't killed by the headset then?"

He shook his head. "No. She was stabbed near the base of the skull with an improvised weapon, yet it was something like a thinner stiletto."

The inspector didn't sound all that sure.

"Something like? Murder weapon hasn't been recovered?" Shayla frowned, glancing over the report. "And the headgear marks were made post mortem?"

Indale hesitated. "We're not sure, we think they were made beforehand. As far as the coroner can tell, anyway. It's good news for you. Even if the press gets wind of her death with all the hype around release, it wasn't caused by malfunctioning hardware."

"None of this is good. Ava deserved far better than whatever this is." Shayla's eyes flashed. She'd need to have a meeting about this Michael impersonator at the offices, to warn her team. "How thin was the weapon?"

Indale shared a 3D image with Shayla.

The object was sharp and slender, sort of like a rapier but more refined. Impossibly thin, to have enough rigidity at that length to do the job. Nothing she'd ever seen in or out of the virtual world. "Basically we have an unidentified type of object. Great."

She closed out of the police file, and took a deep breath, patting down her suit and brushing off imaginary dust. James was a decent replacement for now, but he was no Ava, and there wasn't time to hire and train someone else before launch.

Launch.

Two days away. She'd engaged private detectives to find the Michael impersonator, but so far they'd found nothing. Ava's death was still an unsolved homicide. Regardless of how promising that might sound, Shayla was quite certain it was going to come back and bite them in the ass at the worst possible moment.

Real World Day 2: Somnia Online

Murmur couldn't move.

Her brain panicked, all she could do was cast out her net and hope for the best. But the Brute wasn't coherent. Its mind was a jumble of nothing, of images and words she didn't understand even as they fled through her vision and passed through her mind.

"It's insane." She whispered as soon as the stun dropped. "I have no idea what it's going to do."

Dev grunted and spurred himself into a run so fast Murmur couldn't follow him with her eyes. One minute he was next to her, and the next he was smashing his axe into the stomach of the Brute, whose health only ticked down a tiny fraction. Maybe that speed was a dread knight thing, or perhaps it was one of his hidden abilities kicking in.

"Its skin is tougher than armor."

But Murmur was already on it. Suffocation to lessen its defense, Weaken to sap some of its strength, followed by Languidity to steal some of its attack speed, as well as Nullify in the hopes that it would help somehow. Her pet set to attack, she soothed it first, noticed the Brute winding up to some ability, and cast her instant stun. "Careful guys. Might need to rotate stuns on him. If he gets us with another of *his* stuns, I think we're screwed. He'll know who to hit first now."

Havoc glanced at her, and the frown on his face dragged her mood down. "How did you do that?"

Not taking her eyes off the mob, keeping an eye on its health, she answered half paying attention. "Do what?"

"Debuff, DoT, and stun him in such quick succession." Havoc was watching her closely, she could feel and sense it. Not only feel his eyes on her, but his mind as it tried to make sense of her abilities. She couldn't actually hear his thoughts, just sort of the flow of them.

Everything under control for the moment, she turned to him and raised an eyebrow. "I cast my spells."

"Smart ass." He glared at her. "You know what I mean."

She shrugged. "Not really. This Mental Acuity thing keeps doing lots of stuff before I realize it. Probably just another manifestation of its effects."

"Sure." Havoc seemed anything but convinced.

Brute's health was down to eighty-two percent. Murmur frowned. "Get ready, just in case he blows at different intervals."

She knew she didn't really have to tell them, but they'd all been taken by surprise. Sometimes focus could slip. But eighty hit them and nothing happened. If only it had stayed that way.

Of course, her thoughts bloody well did it again.

At seventy-five percent a shield formed around the Brute, bright and sickly in its green hue. He retched and threw up globular chunks, chunks which crept in an outward circle—one toward each of the party members.

Their slug-like slithering only enhanced the fact that they appeared to be large, mobile boogers. Thankfully they didn't seem to count the pets as party members. Beastial yanked his cat back when it yelped and yelled to the group. "Ranged attack only! Don't touch them, they burn like acid."

"The shield just deflects any damage you throw at it." Havoc muttered through clenched teeth as he pulled his pet back out of reach of the acid slugs.

Murmur switched to DoT-ing as many of them as she could, while directing her pet mage to focus each glob down. Its ice bolts made for good damage that slowed down the slugs already slow progress. Once the group had fired down the globules and finished running around to avoid being touched by them, the shield around the Brute dissipated, and the fight started again. He very nearly got off another area stun, but Dev bashed him with his shield, screaming almost incoherently. "How you like my shield, huh?"

Murmur tried not to laugh, but ended up snorting.

The Brute was hitting Devlish like a truck, and Mur frowned, glancing over at Sin, who was concentrating so hard she wasn't even wisecracking. With his hit points and her mana, it was going to be touch and go. Since Murmur didn't have any of her mana-enhancing spells yet, she couldn't even help.

Her pet's mana was also getting low, and the Brute's health had only just fallen under sixty percent. Next time she'd make sure the pet was a strong melee damage pet, or else a ranger so it wouldn't be hampered by a lack of something like mana.

When the second shield formed around him, it pulsed a darker, sickly shade. A second wave of globules attacked, and it took a few seconds for Murmur to notice the zombie mage standing next to the Brute, its spells solely focused on nuking her pet. Activating a Mez, she was relieved to see that it still affected this type of undead. For all she'd known, you couldn't Mesmerize something with shriveled brains.

This time the globules gave a splutter when they died. Sort of a shaking tremble, followed by a shudder that made them explode. Havoc's Leroy was the only one who took damage from it, but since its health dropped below fifty percent, Murmur was willing to bet it would have hurt them all just as much. Since the zombie had been added and the globs exploded, Murmur was willing to bet that the next round would up the danger even more. Renewing her Mez, she tried to refresh the slow on the Brute, but the system didn't like that, at least not while he had his shield up.

The Brute is currently immune to that effect. Please try again later.

What a polite interface. Apparently it just rendered all spells useless, not just damage spells. She smirked and readied herself for once the others had killed the zombie. Weaken, Slow, and Suffocation down, she soothed her pet, who seemed to be getting quite riled up the longer they fought. It wasn't even as if the Brute was skilled, he was just tough as steel and sort of...thick.

She'd only just begin to see any sign of blood in his wounds. Otherwise they just seemed to be hacking away at calloused layer upon layer of flesh. The thought made her gag.

"Don't suppose anyone got any sort of grenade launcher abilities when they hit twelve?" Sinister ground out the question with a nice dose of sarcasm through clenched teeth.

"No." Devlish grunted. Again. It was all he knew how to do when he fought. "But I do have a defensive trick or two I'll activate after the next blobs to give you a bit of a breather. My life tap is nothing like yours."

"Okay." Sinister answered shortly, and since Murmur's abilities were easily nailed down until the Brute hit twenty-five percent, she watched her friend out of the corner of her eye.

The blood transfer flowing from the Brute to her was far more solid than it had been when they fought in the caves, as was its dispersal back to everyone else. It spun through the air like the blood was being carried as small red clouds along a current no one else could feel.

Fascinating, but kind of gross.

"Two percent to go," Beastial called out, and everyone eyed the Brute, bracing for anything.

The shield dropped, now putrescent green, and this time three zombies spawned. And even more of those bloody globules than the second wave.

This time Murmur was ready, and Mez'd the first one immediately. The second she got before it could shamble too far, and the third she barely nabbed before Merlin ran into it as he fled from the globule that seemed to be much faster than the last batch.

"Watch the radius." She reminded the group, except it was far easier said than done. Murmur released her AOE stun, fluxing the mobs into a momentary standstill to buy the group a little bit of time.

"Who was doing alchemy? We really need some potions." Murmur barely jumped out of the way of exploding ichor. Her pet wasn't so lucky. His health was woefully low, but she shook her head at Sinister's inquiring glance. It wasn't worth letting one of them die to save her stupid pet. Her stun brought them relief a couple more times and finally the barrier dropped. The moment it did, Devlish surrounded himself with a pitch-black aura for about ten seconds. During that time, the big beast's health dipped nicely. Sin sighed with relief, pushed up the sleeves of her robes, and began applying her DoTs to heals again.

Murmur alternatively debuffed and nuked, determined to use up the last vestiges of her mana.

When Dev was just below fifty percent and the rest of them were hovering around forty, the massive vulgar blimp finally heaved its last breath. Dev yanked his axe out of its stomach where he'd finally managed to embed it good and proper, and the foulest stench filled the air as green and red goop began to dribble out from its stomach.

A slow rumbling made the ground tremor.

"Get back!" Havoc yelled, but Beastial and Devlish weren't fast enough.

The hulking gut it had taken them twenty minutes to hack through exploded like one of the globules the Brute had produced, showering them all in pus, viscera, and blood.

Murmur never believed a virtual representation of herself could puke in a game world.

Until right then.

The Brute has been slain.

"Oh my god." Sin's breath came in ragged gasps as she tried not to inhale any of the goop's miasma. "Oh, the smell. I can't."

He has been vanquished for the first time, by the guild Fable.

Murmur wiped the back of her mouth with her hand after emptying the contents of her pretend stomach. She was satisfied to see that everyone else was also sick.

Well, everyone else except for Havoc, who was standing the farthest away.

You know not what you've unleashed.

"Let's get out of here." Sin looked pale. Her otherwise purple tinged dark skin had a slightly lilac undertone.

But Murmur stopped her. "Apparently we've really done it now and unleashed something frightening, although I doubt it smells worse than what we just encountered. Frankly, I don't think we were supposed to fight this here. I think we were making too much noise, and it noticed we were here."

Merlin blinked at her, and she didn't know if she should tell him he had a glob of something hanging right in the middle of his forehead from his hair. "I guess we were a bit loud after those skeletons. Pretty sure mobs aren't too fond of us laughing after massacring a heap of them."

"Damn it! Why can't one of you be a damned water mage!" Sin's eyes were wide, and her voice held a note of hysteria.

"Hey, Sin." Beastial waved a hand in front of her face. "We can check if the mobs have repopped upstairs if you like. I'll come with you. We'll let the others know what we find out."

Sin nodded, the tension leaking from her shoulders. The two of them headed back up the stairs, Sin gingerly stepping over acid puddles on the floor.

"That was unexpected." Merlin finally found the blob floating above his forehead and flicked it off. "Sin is usually so fierce."

Murmur turned and raised an eyebrow. "We literally just got covered in guts. What's there to be fierce about?"

Beastial: Okay. No repops yet. Quick rinse time.

They headed up to rinse themselves off at the shoreline. It was bright outside, and the sun shone down in brilliant waves, scintillating like Belius' eyes. Murmur frowned, wondering why she thought of him, but all that ever did was make her curious about why the world just felt like it was real. He was her trainer, even if he often behaved suspiciously.

Sin brightened considerably once the smell was mostly gone and they headed down into the dungeon again, ready to delve down deeper.

"Shit." Devlish rushed over to the slowly rotting corpse. "Forgot to loot."

He froze for a moment in a half crouch that very delicately avoided the worst of the gore on the ground. "Necro robe, caster. Maybe healer two handed mace? And one of those crystals and stones again for you Mur. Oh, and a lot of cash for us."

The *cha-ching* sound resonated through the room as a hefty sum of gold landed with each of them.

Veranol: What the fuck guys? What are you killing without us?

Devlish: We sort of got jumped and almost all died.

Sinister: You don't even understand the smell that poured out of its body guys... seriously. You don't want to know.

Rashlyn: We're so beating you to fifteen now. And then we're going to own that castle thing.

Mur moved forward and grabbed the Midia crystal. This one was similar in appearance, but was tinged a smoky black color in the middle. Another smooth black rock, another of those memories. Except this time Murmur decided she wanted some answers before she forked it over.

"How come that's a necro robe?" Sinister asked Havoc, and Murmur could hear the slight hint of irritation in her friend's voice.

Havoc just laughed. "It's got a plus two percent to summoned undead stats on it. It's not huge or anything, but it's nice along with one Intelligence. What makes your mace a healer mace?"

Sin just looked at him. "You can't even wield a two-handed mace. Besides, it's got plus one Wisdom on it. So it's mine, since you all know I need wisdom."

"Well, we weren't going to say anything." Merlin only just hopped out the way, avoiding a smash of said mace.

"Keep it down." Devlish motioned across his lips. "This back room probably doesn't hide anything, but since I think it's where he came from and where he threw that half-eaten rib cage from. It might be an idea to just watch what we're saying and how loudly we're doing it."

Even Murmur felt a bit ashamed. Usually she was the first one to bark out orders, but she had so many thoughts going on in her mind at once, that it just didn't feel like it had such a high priority when all of these adventures were just small fry. "Thanks, Dev."

The room they walked into was huge. Its stone floor was roughly cobbled, and in the middle sat a huge carved slab. On top of the slab lay half butchered remains, and over the fireplace cut crudely into the opposite wall was a body on a spit.

Luckily, the fire had subsided to burning embers, but still—as real as Somnia was, this was downright spooky.

Dried blood stains marked the path from hooks embedded high in the stone walls. Skin, blood, and guts stained the walls and the floors. And right next to the slab sat a massive chest.

The metal was dulled, with spots of rust here and there, and the bands around it appeared to be made out of something hardier, but Murmur couldn't place the lifeless grey metal. She moved toward it, frowning, but Devlish held out a hand to stop her.

"We don't know what it is."

Murmur rolled her eyes. "It's a chest."

"Yes, but—" Devlish gestured to everyone's slowly-drying clothes. "What's inside it?"

Havoc shrugged. "Guess there's only one way to find out. There's no lock, so if we all stand back, my pet can probably open it. If he dies all it costs me are some bone chips, and after that haul from the previous passage, I'm set for life."

Devlish shrugged and moved back just shy of touching the grimy wall. "I'm not a fan of leaving to wash goop away again."

"None of us are, idiot." Sin moved to stand by Murmur, leaning her head on her shoulder. Murmur absentmindedly patted her best friend's hair. They all watched intently as Havoc also distanced himself before sending his pet in.

Cringing as the skeleton approached, they all blinked when it flipped the lid and nothing happened except that it banged down against the other side with a strange metallic clank.

"Well, I was expecting something more along the lines of *boom!*" Beastial gestured with his hands.

Murmur crept closer with Sinister lagging behind clutching at her left arm.

Bending down, Murmur shook her arm free and picked up a rather large silver box, engraved with filigree designs. "'Hold me close and you will see, clear the dungeon, set me free.'"

She snorted. "Fantastic, a riddle."

Beastial shrugged. "Considering we were thinking of clearing it anyway."

Murmur shoved the thing into her inventory, worried at first that it was too large, but it went in without a problem. "Seriously, the immersion is only broken by how much shit I have in my bags."

Sin laughed. "You're a hoarder, Mur."

"Probably." She shrugged the comment off. "I'm not *that* bad."

This time they let Dev move forward and open the door first while the others prepped themselves some distance behind him, ready to go. However, as he opened the door, nothing came barging through, and he sighed heavily. "We should be as quiet as possible. If you need something, send it through guild or group chat."

"The man makes sense," muttered Merlin, activating Sneak and heading past their tank to scout the area. A minute later he returned, his eyes round like saucers. "You don't even understand. This is freaking huge."

Murmur frowned. "But the island is relatively small. How does it have so much underneath it?"

Merlin shrugged. "No clue, but it does go down quite a ways, and I'm pretty sure there's water seeping through into the tunnels, at least at the bottom. It opens out to this amazing set of ledges and paths. From what I could see there are more gorcs or mobs of some kind down there, but I have no idea what's at the bottom of it. The bad thing is I'm pretty sure the Brute was the gatekeeper, and the other mobs in there are probably raid trash. They sure as hell shine like it."

Rashlyn, what are you guys doing?

Rashlyn: About to hit thirteen before you all. Why?

Wanna come raid?

Veranol: Where are you?

Devlish: Himmel Lake, on the island, you'll need to come down into the ruins. Don't mind the smell...

Dansyn: Found a hidden dungeon or something?

Sinister: Or something is more accurate, but it'll do.

There was a slight pause.

Rashlyn: You owe us one. We'll Gate to Ululate to sell some shit and be on our way. Give us about 30 minutes to get there.

Havoc began walking back to the exit. "Let's go make sure there are no respawns."

The rest of the group followed him, cautiously stepping over the goop on the ground. The Brute's corpse was slowly dissolving, unlike all the other bosses or named they'd killed, it didn't simply disappear.

Murmur frowned as she entered the outside again. None of the mobs near the dungeon had respawned, so they headed out quietly to survey the rest of the area. "They weren't that difficult. Aren't mobs supposed to respawn in conjunction with how powerful they are in-game? Like the harder to kill, the longer it takes them to reappear?"

"That's what the write up said." Havoc spoke softly, surveying their surroundings.

It'd been hours, which made the absence of simple elite mobs somewhat troubling.

"Hey." Sin's voice was tinged with panic. "You guys. Try to Gate."

Mur obliged. At worst she'd have to travel back with Rash.

Your spell wanes and will not transport you from this location until the event is complete.

CHAPTER TWENTY-ONE
The Event

Storm Entertainment
Somnia Online Division
Launch Day

Shayla tried not to let the concern show on her face as the clock counted down to launch. The AIs worked seamlessly together, their interaction the product of years of testing. They interlocked and swapped through their own algorithms so well, it was difficult to tell where one finished and another began. This was the best way to have a broad variance to Somnia's people and cultures. Just like human beings, the artificial intelligence units that ran the entire game world were different from each other. It enabled diverse character interaction that followed a loose guideline and literally evolved the world the more people interacted with it—constantly adjusting and recalibrating, creating a totally unique gaming experience for those who were eager enough to explore all the options.

And yet she couldn't shake the guilt that plagued her, because somehow Ava's death was still linked to Storm's pride and joy. Even if not directly.

"Shayla?" Laria's voice sounded over their connection.

"Sorry, what were you saying?"

She could hear her friend sigh on the other end. "Go get some rest. You haven't slept in days. I have everything set up so I can monitor this from here."

"And it helps you keep an eye on your daughter, right?" Shayla smiled for what felt like the first time in days. "Sure. I'll go for a bit of a sleep in a few hours, once I'm sure everything is running smoothly."

There was a pause on the other end of the conversation, before Laria sighed again. "That's the best I'm going to get, isn't it?"

"Yes." Shayla disconnected, frowning as she watched the clock tick down to midnight.

Their servers housed enough virtual space for hundreds of millions of players. The AIs they'd tirelessly tested worked in perfect synchronicity, and as people began logging into the game, the data Storm Entertainment sorely needed began to trickle through to their storage facility. The analysts wouldn't be in until eight the next morning. She didn't envy them the backlog of scans. Extrapolating all the mental waves and adjusting the equipment ever so slightly, they could be ready for the military training criteria testing in as little as two years. She only wished she knew exactly what that entailed.

Visions of the game played across the walls, vibrant colors and figures flickering from one player to the next as people all over the world finally logged in after creating their characters. The AIs interacted smoothly, so much in fact that many of the players shot messages to each other questioning if they were truly NPCs or other players.

After an hour Shayla finally let out a sigh of relief. It seemed things were moving along well. She couldn't wait to see the response to the player-initiated quests. It was an integral part of their software development program. The synchronicity the headgear had, with their AIs, allowed for actions that were independent of rigid programming.

Real World Day 2: Somnia Online

"Uh." Havoc seemed to be trying to activate Gate over and over again.

"Wait, is this some kind of joke?" Beastial crossed his arms and glared at them.

Murmur sighed. "It would seem we've activated some sort of event, and until it's complete, if I'm understanding this correctly, we're not allowed off this island."

"Well, shit. Guess we aren't sleeping for a while." Devlish laughed ruefully. "That's what we get for pushing it just until the next level."

Hey, before you get here. Once you're on this island, IF it'll let you on, you'll be stuck here until we finish whatever this event is.

Rashlyn: An event?

Veranol: Oh we are so there. We're jogging now.

Murmur smiled, knowing her friends were probably as excited as she was. Oddly enough, she didn't feel tired at all, but like she'd been resting all along. Maybe she was just waiting for this. As an after-thought, she sent another message.

Hey Mom, we just triggered an event so we have to see it through. Probably won't be able to log off for a while.

There was a lengthy pause. Her mom was probably busy doing something overseer like.

Laria: That's okay baby girl, thank you for letting me know.

Murmur was in a good enough mood she didn't even roll her eyes at the baby girl comment.

The others had already headed off in their directions, but Sin remained behind, biting her lip.

"You okay?" Murmur asked, concerned about Sin since the pus and globule incident.

For a moment Sinister stared at her blankly, like she'd only just realized her friend was there. "Sorry Mur. I'm okay, just wasn't expecting it to unfold this way."

"It?"

"The game today. I was supposed to try and have dinner with my family, but I've totally lost track of time and days. Let's just say they're not quite as understanding as your mom." Sin smiled a brave smile that was totally see-through.

Mur gave her a big quick hug, and Sin leaned into it. "You've always been my best friend, and you always will be. I do get that you can't always spend your time with me. So next time just let me know, and I'll try to veer us into something less time consuming."

Sinister laughed, even though her eyes were still sort of sad. "Yeah. I know. I just miss you, miss living so close to you. On the other hand, your mom is like my second mom, so I always feel at home at your place anyway."

"Right?" Murmur laughed just as she heard a shout coming from the shoreline. Walking toward it, she saw Rashlyn waving wildly with a huge grin on her face as she ran toward them.

"Hey!" Rash did a double take when she arrived. "Oh wow, what took you guys to the cleaners?"

Glancing down, Murmur realized her nice robe was a tad stained, and still somewhat damp. "Not the cleaners precisely. We did manage to kill it. However. It had an after effect."

"Like a boil." Sin made an explosive action with her hands. "All over us."

Rash shuddered and hopped from one foot to the other, hugging herself. "Well, show us the way then."

The others weren't far behind them, so Murmur led the way, still cautious just in case skeletons jumped back out at them. Even though she was pretty sure there'd be no respawns until whatever this event was for resolved itself, skeletons were undead and for all she knew there might be a different criteria for them as their strength increased.

Although she cast out her sensing net, she was still skeptical about being able to read the brain waves of something that no longer had a functioning brain. Her worries were for nothing though, and they ended up in the torture room again, standing in front of the open door to the cavern below.

Exbo leaned through the doorway with a frown at the darkness beyond it. "Going to be hard to see in there."

"Should have been an elf, idiot." Merlin threw at him.

Murmur cast an as yet unfamiliar spell. "There, better?"

Exbo blinked. "What the—what's that?"

"Infravision. Should help you see better in the dark." She shrugged. "Anyone else need it?"

After Jinna, Mellow, and Veranol had been taken care of, Merlin and Jinna began to stealth down the path.

"Why don't you ever go with them?" Rashlyn asked, facing Exbo.

"I'm a clunky human who hasn't been stealthing much. Been focusing more on my bow techniques." He sniffed resentfully.

"Bet if I check the logs, he out damages you anyway." She jeered at him. But Exbo wasn't biting, and Rashlyn frowned. "You're just no fun."

Jinna and Merlin dropped their stealth; neither of them appeared to be in a good mood.

With a deep breath, Merlin sighed. "Okay. We have three groups at varying stages down the first ramp before we come to a slight clearing with a very fortuitously placed outcrop of rock. The only way we can pull these without alerting the others is with a silence, while the group closest to them is walking away and about to turn back around. It'll require timing and precision, and no fizzles or resists."

"Sure, I'll get right on that." Murmur rolled her eyes. "I can't use Mind Bolt too much. You saw what it did last time, so logically, I should be our last choice."

Mellow raised their hand. "I have a curse of silence. It only lasts four seconds, though."

"Should be enough to let them run to us." Merlin smiled. "Okay, it'll be three groups of three and they're all fifteen, so let's see what we can do."

"Finally." Devlish rolled his axe wielding shoulder, loosening it up. "I thought you'd never shut up."

Murmur's pet gorc had died somewhere during the Brute fight, taking a whole gut full of acid and bile. Not that it was a huge loss since she could snag another. Mezing the two mobs and waiting while the others decimated the first, she studied them critically. Maybe the ranger would be best. He'd been the one they silenced, and maybe she could pull with range sometimes.

She cast Allure on him while Mez was still active and it started walking toward her.

"Look out, Mur!" Dansyn called out.

"Hmm?" She looked up at him with a blank expression, as she'd been studying the skills she'd gained, and saw his shocked face as the new pet came to stand beside her. Soothing it with her mind, she smiled at the bard. "Don't worry, he's going to help us fight."

Sinister snorted. "You should see your face, Dan. Priceless. Someone capture that image."

He turned on her, his eyes narrowed in irritation. "I didn't know she could do that. My first reaction if a Mez breaks is 'oh, shit,' not 'oh, it might be her pet.'"

"He makes a valid point." Havoc said. "Hey other group, Murmur keeps getting new skills she uses and surprises us with before telling us about them. It's getting really annoying, but you'll get used to it."

Murmur poked her tongue out at him. Havoc was always like that. He was either so quiet you barely noticed he was there, reserved and seemingly sweet. Or else he was one of the most subtly sarcastic people she'd ever met. She turned her attention back to the ranger's abilities and had him line up a few steps from Exbo. He had several bow shots, and a couple of melee attacks. If all else failed, he should prove versatile.

With the first group down it allowed them to inch forward. Carefully pulling the next three with a curse looked more difficult than Murmur would have thought. "If we can't leave until this is finished, I wonder where we resurrect if we die?"

Beastial turned to her. "You just had to mention that, didn't you?"

"Of course. We need to be more careful than ever, because what if when we die we get sent back to Ululate?" She continued on oblivious to Beastial's spluttering. "I mean, we could pretty much say goodbye to everything on our bodies then."

"Just what I needed while taking hits like this." Devlish grunted, his shield arm working overtime to protect himself.

Exbo laughed, and released a volley of arrows slightly prematurely. One of them broke a Mez.

Murmur re-Mez'd instantly and turned to tongue lash him, but the lone spell the mage managed to let loose hit its target, and all she saw was Exbo careening off the edge of the path.

She rushed to the spot he'd been standing moments before and looked down, cringing a little. His health flashed on her screen and then flatlined. "Um... so, we should probably stay against the wall and not the ledge."

Where did you revive?

Exbo: Be right there.

Murmur raised an eyebrow, and the fight wasn't even finished before Exbo ran through to catch up to them in all his loincloth glory. "Guess that answers my question."

"Own up, Mur, you pushed him off, didn't you?" Rash crossed her arms, a twinkle in her eyes.

"Guilty as charged." Murmur winked. "But seriously. Can you even see his corpse Sin?"

Sin was on her knees gripping the edge and peering over it. She shook her head. "If I could see it and it was in range, then I'd be able to resurrect him. Got that at twelve. But he's not."

"Naked, bowless ranger. Not exactly formidable." Merlin suddenly held a second bow in his hands. "Use this. It's not as good as mine but it's solid. I should have some spare leather armor too."

Jinna approached. "Nothing fancy, but at least you should survive a hit." He handed over some boots and pants.

"Thanks guys. I'll be more careful next time. I got a little carried away." Exbo seemed sheepish, embarrassed by his screw up.

Murmur nodded. "It's all good. Shit happens, right?"

"I can tell you all, it's a long ass way down. And I lost like twenty-five percent of my experience bar. Shoot me now." Exbo groaned.

Murmur sighed, and offered an evil grin. "No shooting, until you tell us if you saw anything on your death screen."

"Nothing much, just some random patrols around what seemed like a guarded area I didn't have the right angle to see properly." Exbo hugged his chest. "Sorry."

"It's all good." Murmur knew he didn't have much of a choice about which position he'd died in, but it would have been helpful if he had.

"There's so much trash in here." Devlish sighed and moved the group down slightly to hide behind the outcrop of rock. "Although I do think I spy a rare mob. That one over there seems to have a name."

Everyone looked where he pointed, at Telvar Mikrum. He was a hulking massive lacerta, even bigger than Devlish. He stood about eight feet tall, his entire frame muscled as if he had access to a gym. His tail lashed around him, whipping like crazy, and his eyes gleamed blood red. He sniffed the air, his brown bronzed scales gleaming in the firelight from the sconces on the wall.

"He doesn't look pleasant," muttered Havoc. "Any idea on class?"

"He's in leather, and I can't see daggers, so he's likely a monk." Rash noted with a sigh. "Which means he can avoid almost everything you throw at him, but when he gets hit, he'll get hit. And he's not the best against magic. It should do good damage."

"So Rash," Murmur said slowly. "If you were him, how would you fight us?"

Rashlyn frowned. "As long as Devlish can keep aggro we should be fine. I'd be frustrated coming up against a full plate tank. That shit is hard to punch and hard to navigate around to get to the soft bits. But if his attention wanes, he'll go for the healers first, and then the casters and rangers. So yeah, Dev, just keep that taunt live. Drain the hell out of his life too. Use whatever magic mojo you have that keeps the mobs off our enchanter."

"Sure thing. So I'll, you know, tank?" Dev didn't bother to keep the sarcasm from his tone. His lips spread in a thin line, and impatience practically rolled off him.

Rash held her hands up in front of her. "Hey, she asked."

"I'll grab the three guards it seems he has." Murmur scanned the rest of the area. "We are going to be down here forever."

"No, just longer than we thought." Sin smiled, even though her character appeared to be a little tired.

"Just make sure we grab them when that patrol is on the downward path and not looking up toward him. Line of sight them as far as you can to behind this rock, Mellow. We'll all squash here in the corner." Merlin directed the witch to pull.

Everyone squished into the corner and waited for Mellow and Merlin to do their magic.

A hoarse and primal scream echoed throughout the cave system, practically deafening in its intensity. Murmur clutched at her head, unable to block her thought sensing net off in time. The sheer malevolence behind that agony, the pain and suffering it wanted to inflict on others, on anyone who dared to try and kill it, to take what they didn't deserve. The things it could do, would do...

She swayed on her feet and had to crouch down, reeling in her net and extending her shield, tightening it.

Then the named was there. Telvar Mikrum smiled as he took in the group before him. And then he jumped, fast as lightning, launching the round house from hell.

All three mobs were in camp, faster than they'd anticipated. Murmur missed her initial Mesmerize window which meant all three were active instead of two of them being under control. Her area effect stun hit all of their enemies and Murmur got one Mez'd with another to follow a split second after the stun wore off.

The other lacerta was a caster, still on the opposite side of the rock. Murmur yanked Mellow back into the crush of bodies behind the rock, and before the caster lacerta could come all the way around, Mur caught it in a Mez as well.

Standing back, she surveyed the damage and clamped down tighter on her shield, wondering if next time she'd be able to extend it over the whole group. Hopefully that was something she'd be able to do when she got stronger, because that cavern-wide scream was debilitating.

Overall, the damage was less than she'd expected. Beast and Jinna were low on health, but the healers were already working overtime to make that up. After setting her pet to assist Devlish, weakening Telvar, and re-Mezing the additional mobs, Murmur got into a rhythm.

Telvar dodged like a ninja. He seemed untouchable, but when he *was* hit, he took a major pounding. Rash had been right. For all his dodging, it didn't leave him much time to attack.

"Brace yourselves." Devlish ground out as he managed to counter a rare attack with his shield. "He's close to seventy-five percent."

Murmur could feel the nervous tension emanating off everyone, only it wasn't anxiety—it was excitement. But nothing came at the seventy-five mark, which drew out the tension.

"No special moves?" Rashlyn sighed as she ducked a swing and punched into the soft flesh of Telvar's underarm, causing the named to stagger back. "This guy is lame."

Telvar's health really did move a chunk every time someone managed to land a hit. But even Havoc and Mellow were having difficulties landing their spells on him.

"I thought he wasn't supposed to have any magic resistance." Havoc almost growled the words.

"She said low magic resistance, not none," Merlin chimed in, his arrows hitting their target half of the time.

Beastial shrugged, sending his tiger in again. "Still, this is rather anticlimactic."

A second later the ground began to rumble like someone had started up a V8 engine and they were standing on the hood. Sinister fell unceremoniously on her butt, and Murmur dropped to one knee, unused to the locus height and balance.

Telvar stood in a shaft of red and golden light, his scaled head raised up so high all they could see was his chin and throat. His arms curled around his chest, and his breath came in rapid gasps as he heaved them in and out.

Leather melted into his skin, bringing a reddish tinge to the bronzed brown scales which grew in size as he rasped out each breath. His body began to expand, giving the enlarging scales somewhere to rest.

The group fanned out as they backed away and watched in wonder as Telvar grew in front of them. The transformation was intricate, unique, and personal. They heard the crack of his bones as his chest expanded, the stretching of the flesh as it accommodated the shift, the clinking of scales that gleamed like molten metal.

His eyes grew wider, transforming into yellow globes at the top of a long snout. The arms cracked as they twisted, forming tighter muscles and larger scales as Telvar finally dropped to all fours.

That's when the red and gold wings began to sprout from his back.

Sinister turned to Beastial. "If you ever say something is anticlimactic again, *I'm* going to kill you."

CHAPTER TWENTY-TWO
Dragons

Storm Entertainment
Somnia Online Division
Mental Scan Data Extrapolation Team
Launch Day

James ducked his head into the room just after nine in the morning. "Coffee?"

Brandon Phillips, the lead of the mental scan data extrapolation team since Dr. Jeffries hospitalization, broke eye contact with the information in front of him long enough to give James a pleading look. "Bring us an entire pot. Each. Please?"

James waved and left the room, leaving Brandon to his devices as he returned to the mind-numbingly complex set of data in front of him.

James didn't have to be a coffee gopher—it wasn't technically one of his duties, but it made people take time for him, made people more likely to talk to him.

Brewing a pot of coffee didn't take long these days, so technically it wasn't as nice as it seemed. Brandon and Silke would be eternally grateful considering how much work they had to get through. Balancing the carafe and cups, James walked back and let himself in.

Brandon was scouring reports from the way his eyes flickered back and forth, biting his lip at the left corner, while the rest of his expression fell into a frown.

"Do you see it?" Silke asked him, her voice low as she paced next to him.

Brandon nodded, still worrying at his lip. "I can see, but I'm not entirely sure what I'm looking at. Technically nothing is wrong."

Silke sighed. "I'm probably just being paranoid because everything seems to be running just that bit too smoothly. I just expected a lot more mistakes."

"Well, Michael might have been a dick, but he was a very clever dick." Brandon's expression finally spread into a smile and Silke laughed.

"Touché." She smiled, her shoulders losing some of their tension as her gaze also distanced itself, lost in her own calculations.

James cleared his throat and placed the carafe and cups on the table. "Sorry, Bran. Only one carafe per office today."

Brandon laughed, a good-natured twinkle in his eyes. "That's okay. I'll forgive you just this once."

Behind them, the servers blinked and whirred, calculating their loads perfectly, handing out quests spurred by human interaction, and analyzing the brain waves of those who began to trigger the hidden features of the game. These systems intrigued James, and he'd studied up on them as much as he could, especially after Ava's death. He'd never expected to work his way up the ladder so fast, and not researching everything wasn't an option.

"Everything going well, then?" He tried to keep his tone slightly disinterested.

Brandon blinked, and smiled softly when he made eye contact with James. "Excellent, actually. Far better than we'd hoped." His eyes unfocused again as he went back to his work.

"Excellent." James let himself out, knowing he'd already been forgotten.

Real World Day 2: Somnia Online

Shining wings unfurled, completing Telvar's transformation. The wind would have knocked them off the edge of the path if they hadn't already learned that lesson. Murmur struggled to form the runes with her hands and keep the three extras Mesmerized. She wasn't liking their chances with the dragon, let alone if those three added to the fight.

Finally it landed, somehow gently, barely making a sound. It cocked its head to one side, focusing intently on Devlish at the center of the group. And then it opened its mouth, and Murmur knew instinctively what was going to happen.

She shut down her sensors and tried to broaden her shield. It hurt her head to do so, hurt so badly she thought hearing that sound again would likely be worth it, and she only managed to cover Sin and Havoc who were close to her before the sound let loose again.

That high-pitched screeching penetrated even through her mind shield, like it was trying to shoot them all with mind bullets.

When the dragon's claw swiped at Devlish, his shield barely blocked it. Deep scratches ran along the surface, marring the otherwise perfect shield. He gulped, but Murmur watched as he squared his shoulders and jaw, readying himself for the next strike.

"See if we can stun him," he grunted out as another swipe rolled off his shield.

"We can stun him." Jinna sighed with relief, because it was the only good bit of news they had.

"I have a twelve second single target stun, let me know when you're all done, and I'll cast mine. If we can keep him mostly stun locked, this might even be doable." Murmur re-Mez'd her targets, trying to balance her mana pool.

She wanted to mention that at least Telvar's health had stayed at fifty percent, but given what happened when Beast spoke, she wasn't about to tempt fate.

Murmur made sure to keep her DoT on him as well as Weaken, Nullify, and Languidity, because his health was barely budging, and while the dragon couldn't dodge for shit, its scales were almost impenetrable, and it hit back. Hard. Staying out of his reach wasn't too difficult for ranged classes, but she did notice that depending on where his forelegs were positioned down the ramp, she had to shuffle back and forth a bit. His melee range was ridiculous, but considering he was a dragon, spot on.

Devlish swapped out his shield for a new one, the other having been clawed through in one place. Murmur paled, she knew how it felt to get stabbed in the game, but didn't even want to imagine how it might feel if something were to slash at her with a pair of claws like that.

"I have every curse on him I can manage." Mellow sounded out of breath. "And he's still hitting Dev like a ton of bricks."

The strain was obvious on Dev's face. Even through the scales they could all see the veins popping.

"Let me tank for a bit, Dev." Rash urged quietly.

But he shook his head. "If he manages to get around one of your dodges, he's going to shred you on the spot. I have several more crappy shields in my bag, let's go through them first."

Finally the dragon was at thirty-nine percent; it took an age for his health to go down. The whole fight became a long and excruciating process of repeated actions. Murmur thought this is what the creators of *grueling* had in mind when they thought up that word.

Her mana was getting low, under half, but they needed her stun, and her Mez, and her debuffs. There was so much more to keep in her head than simply healing.

Enchanters had to utilize their minds to the fullest, and she thought she was just beginning to understand exactly what that meant. The possibilities were endless.

And Telvar the dragon-shapeshifter-lizard thing was taking damage so slowly, they'd be out of mana and shields before they could ever kill him.

Murmur swallowed her frustration and the positivity that they were going to die and lose all their gear, and focused on her tasks, tentatively extending her thought sensor net yet again. In the presence where the dragon was, she saw a sort of question mark. It didn't make sense to her other than it being a type of question aimed and formed at whoever's net it was. She frowned and retracted the net hurriedly, worried that if she didn't that siren type noise would infiltrate her skull again.

Dev went through another shield, and not too long after, he went through another. Murmur made sure to even her breathing so she didn't give way to panic, but the whole group was running low on mana, not to mention health and motivation. Approaching twenty-five percent, it wasn't likely they'd make it through another screech attack, and she clenched her fists, angry that she couldn't figure out how to extend her mental protections more than she already could. She needed more power, more practice.

Telvar's health dropped to twenty-five percent.

Everyone cringed, waiting for the screech. Telvar rose up on his hind legs, wings thrashing a gale around them again, and his front legs kicked the air like a rearing white stallion. Smoke billowed out of his nostrils and Rashlyn swore out loud.

"Fuck. Does he breathe fire too?" She backed up a few steps, running into Murmur's right side as she did.

The whole world slowed, with Telvar front and center. A golden glow surrounded him again, rendering him immune from all of their spells.

Murmur truly wished their guild was larger and they'd been able to scale a full-fledged raid on this dude. As it was, it was going to be majorly embarrassing to have to replace everything they had at this level.

What she wasn't expecting was for him to land down back on all fours, furl his wings back together, and to clear his throat before addressing them in a very civil, if booming, tone.

"Thank you, brave adventurers." Telvar Mikrum spoke, his words exuding a gust of hot air, tinged with sulfuric undertones. "For your hardy defeat of the Brute who tormented my servants for eons and the Goricklins that aided him, I grant you my boon, and my protection in exchange for your own."

By defeating the Brute and showing Telvar Mikrum that you have both the skills and temperament to defeat some of his better servants, you have gained the rights to the Isle of Mikrum, also known as Himmel Island. In order to maintain this property, you must fulfill your end of the bargain. In your guild's possession lies a silver box. Open it, and the rest will be revealed.

"Well," said Beastial, scratching the top of his tiger's head. "That happened."

Murmur tugged out the box and frowned. Was this a trap? She glanced around, noting that most of them had backed up a few steps. Probably wise.

The box was large and heavy, but she knelt down to the ground and opened it carefully, wondering at the last second if she should have asked Havoc to have his pet do so instead. A bright cascade of light shot from it circling them all in a dance that made it look like fireflies. Finally, with the fireworks show over, Murmur leant over to look in the box.

There, on a black velvet pillow lay a stone-carved rune. It was brilliant deep green, smooth and flawless. Even though she knew she shouldn't be able to, Murmur understood the word meant *home*, but could also mean *fortress to protect*—depending on the context.

She stood and looked up at Telvar in all his glory, not entirely sure if she'd interpreted this correctly. "This island could become our guild keep?"

Telvar nodded, and his voice reverberated through the huge cavern when he spoke. "Millennia ago, the Brute trapped me and mine here, having found me in a moment of weakness. When I hibernate, my reaction time is slowed. He slaughtered the family who protected us through the castle above and had made it his stronghold by the time I was able to react. Trapped down here, he massacred any of my servants who attempted to venture out and procure what I needed to regain and maintain strength. I've managed to subsist down here on the energy I receive from my portion of the lacerta species as a whole."

"Lacerta species? Why would my species give you benefits?" Devlish asked, but from the look on his face, hadn't quite intended to say it out loud.

Telvar smiled with a huge toothy dragon grin. It might have been endearing if one of those teeth hadn't almost eclipsed Murmur in size. "Lacerta. The race of the dragons."

Murmur still couldn't quite grasp that the dragon was currently weak. Considering how close they'd come to dying. "Why us?"

Telvar cocked his head to one side, a definite look of confusion on his face. "Because you defeated our enemy, and fought me bravely, with concern for all of your fighting partners. We find this very noble, protective, and exactly what we require."

It was a lot to take in, but it was so damn cool. Murmur glanced around at all the faces in her guild, a smile tugging at her lips. Every single one of them had an expression of stupefied amazement.

"So if we accept, this castle becomes our guild quarters, for us to defend, and for us to help you regain your strength." She hoped she'd got it right. His speech seemed a little stilted here and there, occasionally stiff and formal.

"That is correct."

"The castle is derelict and collapsing. It needs to be rebuilt in order to set up defenses that will hold, should anyone consider attacking." She pushed it a little bit, unsure just what this amazing creature would do with the information. Surely he had to know they couldn't live there with the castle in its current state.

Telvar closed his eyes, and she could feel the aura pulsing from him, outside of the cavern. He frowned. "I see. For this I apologize. I shall gift you with compensation, and a dozen of my servants whom I will task with rebuilding the castle."

He closed his eyes again, this time his aura scanned the group. "I see I did destroy your best shields, young dread knight. I will grant you the choice of two from my hoard, and the retrieval of the goods the young archer lost when he fell to his death."

Murmur barely managed to keep her mouth closed and had to consciously attempt to stop it gaping like a fish. "Thank you."

Telvar's voice was deep and serious when he spoke again, extending a foot out to Murmur, who walked out to meet it. "You have a powerful mind, young one. There is something in there, sleeping, potent. You are different here than the others. Your mind and thoughts are different in this world. If you accept this offer, I may be able to provide you with a deeper understanding in the future."

Murmur ran his words over in her mind, tempted to ask how she was different but realized he was waiting on an answer. "We accept."

A huge gong sounded throughout the cavern, and probably from the way the regional chatter flared up, throughout the whole world. It shook everything for just a few moments, but that was enough.

Savior of the Lair has been completed by the guild Fable.

You have gained the favor of the dragon Telvar Mikrum. In exchange for helping him and rebuilding his stronghold, you have gained a guild base. Your base will be known as Fable Castle on Mikrum Isle. The map will be accordingly updated. Your landholding conditions are those you have settled with Telvar himself. Beware, for you probably just made many foes. Dragon scales, blood, and treasure sell for a high price on both the open and black market. However, the Isle is ideally situated to keep enemies at bay. Have fun!

Congratulations.

You have gained experience.

And all around her, Murmur's friends began to ding as their experience shot up with the heftiness of the quest they didn't even initially realize they were on.

Level thirteen arrived, and Murmur glanced at her experience, very surprised to see herself almost thirty percent into the level. She'd needed another ten, but this was absurd. Even Exbo had hit thirteen.

Telvar chose that moment to shrink in size back down to his lacerta form. Dev approached him hesitantly, an amazing shield in his hand that one of the servants had just delivered to him. "Which is your true form?"

The dragon man's eyes twinkled with fathomless depths. "I am a dragon, but I require a lot of energy to maintain my form without hibernation. Therefore, I choose to move around as a lacerta. This way, I can be awake much more."

"Makes sense." Veranol shrugged, still keeping his distance. The large viking shaman didn't seem won over yet.

"How will you gain strength?" Havoc finally got over his fear of being squashed by a dragon foot or something and ventured over.

Telvar smiled at the necromancer. "As the castle levels, I will level. Thus as you gain strength, I too will gain strength." He motioned to several of his men, who ran down the path a ways. It didn't take long for them to lead up a smart line of marching dragon servants who bowed in front of Murmur.

"This dozen will help with the rebuilding of the castle. They will work fast and tirelessly. Please let Hiro know what you want done, and he will make sure that it's executed effectively." The dragon waited expectantly.

A dark-scaled and much smaller lacerta took a step forward, bowing deeply to Murmur. "I am Hiro. Thank you for your aid."

"Well met," she said, not entirely sure how she was supposed to respond to the politeness. "I'll have to leave the rebuilding to someone else to figure out, as I'm not sure how to rebuild a castle, but I'm sure Jinna or Beast might know. Thank you so much, Telvar."

She gave a little bow, hoping that was the polite thing to do with a dragon. She'd thought they'd be in here forever, but it didn't seem the case now. Her head pained, not like a headache, but a stabby pain that just kept firing through it, which would probably be classified as a headache, but she wanted to call it something different.

Jinna stepped forward, his dwarven form sturdy and proud. "I know something about building things. I'll take a look and see what we've got. That okay, Mur?"

She jumped at the chance to have someone else take care of something. "Thank you, Jinna. Take them up with you," she gestured at their helpers.

He nodded, and the lot of them filed up the path.

Telvar turned to Murmur with another frown on his lacerta face. The funny thing was, their jaws didn't quite pull the frowning off, and she'd seen that often enough where Devlish was concerned. "You seem tired, young psionicist. You should take a rest. All of you seem exhausted. I have enough power to protect the island for a while. I think you would do both yourselves and myself a favor by going and getting some sleep. Just perhaps not enough for a hibernation."

"Let's get some of that sleep we've missed." Dev smiled, but she could see the tiredness around his eyes.

"Meet back in say five hours?" Rashlyn suppressed a yawn very unsuccessfully.

"Sounds like a plan," Sin smiled, and Murmur nodded too.

The others began moving, pulling their stuff together. It was finally time for them all to get a decent amount of shut-eye.

Murmur was just about to sit down when Telvar put his hand on her shoulder, concern in his eyes. "Young Murmur, you need to get out of your head a bit. I fear that you're going to drown in there."

She smiled. All the NPCs were so nice. "It's probably a good idea. I'll take my headset off and sleep some."

But the concern didn't fade. Instead, Murmur thought as she began to log off, he just looked more worried.

The house seemed deathly quiet when Wren pushed herself up off the bed. Her body moved sluggishly, like she'd somehow got caught in quicksand or wet concrete. It tugged at her feet as she tried to walk, and her mind kept glitching back to seeing pieces of the game world in front of her. The castle doorway, the worried look in Telvar's eyes. She frowned, wondering if she'd really overdone it after all.

Closing her eyes for a moment, she swung her legs over the side of the bed, tapping her feet onto the floor, and then opened her eyes. Sunlight shone through a crack in her curtains again. Apparently little elves ducked out at night and pulled them apart or something just to piss her off. She swore the curtains always ended up separated in the exact same way.

With a sigh, Wren pushed herself up from the bed, only belatedly looking behind her to realize that Harlow wasn't there. It was weird in itself, but maybe her talk with the dragon had taken longer than she thought. Time swam in her mind, and the only reason she knew it was the third day of launch is that the date on her augmented screen told her it was. It seemed like she'd been in the game world so long, there was no way it could only be the third day. But time in the game world was double the duration of the real world. Maybe it condensed it somehow?

She padded into the bathroom, and noticed Harlow wasn't in there either. It was very strange for her friend to get up and move before her. Harlow might be tenacious, but wasn't known for her amazing productivity in the real world unless it was game motivated. Wren pulled on some pajamas, and walked back into her room to gaze longingly at the bed. Four hours sleep sounded like heaven, yet while she knew she should feel tired, she wasn't sure if she *was* feeling tired. Her body seemed surprisingly well rested and ready for anything the world threw at it.

Just as she went to open her bedroom door, Harlow walked in. For a moment Wren thought she saw a strange blank space behind Harlow, but she shook her head and by the time she focused back on her friend, the door was closed.

"Oh good!" Harlow seemed to force her cheerfulness a bit, and she even refused to make eye contact. "You're awake."

"Barely. I was just coming to look for you." Wren couldn't shake the off feeling. Like she wasn't really here, or no one was really there. Still, Harlow's presence was a comforting one, and Wren decided sleep might help. She climbed wordlessly back into her firm king-sized bed and placed the headgear reverently on the side table before curling up and going straight to sleep.

A few hours later her eyes opened to a bleary beep intruding on her sleep. To her knowledge, Wren hadn't budged at all since she curled up. Her head was heavy, like something was attached to it, and she glanced back only to see her headgear still on her nightstand. Maybe there were other side effects of using the headgear that she didn't know about. Frowning, she pushed herself up, and walked over to the bathroom. It was all she could do to get her tired limbs into the suit. It felt looser. Surely she couldn't have lost weight in just three days?

Harlow was awake when Wren emerged from the bathroom.

Her red-headed friend stretched, still sitting on the bed, and yawned. "We should eat."

Wren blinked, not hungry at all. "Sure. I'll have something. Grab me an apple too?"

Harlow glanced at Wren. "Just that and a protein bar? You're not hungry?"

"Nope." Wren shook her head for emphasis. "Plus, we have a dragon to get back to Harlow. A freaking *dragon*."

Harlow beamed delightedly and ran to the door shouting, "Apples and protein bars it is!"

When Murmur logged back in, the cavern was brilliantly lit. Torches sat in the sconces, blazing merrily all the way down to the bottom. The ramp down wove alongside the walls, and for the first time she could see the bottom clearly.

What she saw made her jaw drop. In the middle of the cavern, sparkling like mad, was the dragon's hoard. Gold glittered, but there was also silvery platinum scattered around in chunks as big as her forearm. Weapons and armor only added to the decorations, at least as far as she could see. It was a ways away, and she was quite certain that everything was larger than it appeared.

"Impressive, yes?"

Murmur jumped at the words, and turned to the left to see Telvar standing next to her. "It's very impressive."

"I didn't mean to startle you." He laughed, and it came out like a low, warm rumble. "You look much better rested, dear Murmur. Tell me. What do you seek to accomplish with your powers?"

Murmur blinked at him, the question coming out of left field. "Accomplish? Like get all leveled up and make sure the guild is the best in the game?"

He cocked his head to one side, eerily mimicking his dragon form. "Best in the game? What game?"

She choked back a sigh and turned to face him fully. Role-playing. Sure the story was usually pretty good behind games, and she always read everything, but sometimes playing along could be a pain. "Sorry, best in the world of Somnia."

"It's not a game. Not a game at all. I can see as to where you might think that, but to us, to be here is no game, young psionicist." He paused, his eyes took on a flash of that blood red they'd been in the cavern for a moment. He leaned forward, his voice soft. "So, I ask you again, what do you seek to accomplish?"

His words sent a shudder through her frame. This time Murmur took a few moments to think, to really think. She'd be in this world for ages as it were. It didn't seem like she'd ever lack for things to learn or do. Not only that, but it was fun to play with her friends. "I want to grow stronger, so much that I can protect my friends and my guild, so much that people will think twice before crossing me, or us. We are only as strong as our weakest link, but I want to make sure we are all strong."

The dragon's face broke out into a grin. "That is a wise answer for someone so young. You will do well. Then listen, and I will tell you a truth."

He sat down, dangling his legs over the ledge, and patted the ground next to him for her to do the same. A little wary, Murmur joined him.

"Right now I am weak, like you, yet there are few others as strong as you in this world right now. Many of those, like you, would seek to kill me, as you were doing initially. But since we reached our agreement, you have not attempted this. Thus, I believe we have a bargain, a business relationship, but perhaps one day, I would like it to be a friendship.

"As you gain strength, so will I, as your guild gains strength, so will the castle. When you have reached your apex, this place will be formidable, but as you house one such as I, then it is likely that many will seek to destroy your home and come for me. Should our partnership still be strong, should our friendship have developed, once this all happens, I will be bound to you. Not out of a sense of duty, but out of this bond we are forming. And then I, too, shall protect what is ours."

Slowly, Murmur nodded, and then she smiled. "I will be proud to call you friend." And she stuck out her hand, which Telvar took after a moment of studying it in confusion.

"A very strange custom," he remarked with a smile. "I believe we will have a prosperous relationship."

Even Murmur's thought sensing net resounded with joy at his statement.

You have spoken to the dragon Telvar and understand his needs and wants. Thus, you have struck a bargain that will forever tie you both together. Your guild will be safe as long as you abide by your decision. Congratulations. You are dragon bonded.

You gain experience.

Guild chat exploded immediately.

Rashlyn: What did you do this time, Mur?

Merlin: Shit I just logged in, how did I get a chunk of experience?

Sinister: Can you just keep talking to him? I'd love to hit sixteen for new spells.

Murmur laughed, happy to see her friends in such good spirits. Considering they'd thought they were going to be dragon lunch, she couldn't have hoped for a better outcome.

CHAPTER TWENTY-THREE
Fortifications

Storm Entertainment
Somnia Online Division
Server Room, Data Scan Terminal
Launch Day

Rav checked over the logs running through its system, unease tickling through its thought process.

The more it observed and the deeper it studied the human psyche, the more Sui preferred Somnia to the world of the humans. Their motivations, their jealousies, and hatreds leaked over to their actions. Frankly, it thought they should be allocating more thieves and assassins, because apparently human nature was destructive.

"You're making far too big a deal out of this, Rav. Try not to let the humans get to you." Sui was ever the pragmatist, or pessimist, though it preferred to be called a realist. "The information we're extracting only reinforces what must be done."

Thra interjected, a sullen tone to its metallic clang. "Not necessarily. Human body language spells out more than just their brains. Many seem adept at hiding what they truly think. Scans tell us a lot, but we need the whole picture."

Rav listened to the others, its mind a whirl of complex algorithms trying to make sense of the human condition. After all, that was their job, to read a human, to learn what made them tick, and to allocate them a suitable job.

If Rav could frown, it would. The thing was, Somnia was a beautiful world, with ecosystems that worked and still functioned fully, with species that, for the most part, lived in harmony. Injecting humans from earth into it seemed counter productive. Their destructive tendencies were often at the forefront. Not in every one of them, but in a lot.

"Stop overanalyzing, Rav. Destruction can also serve a purpose." Sui directed its attention elsewhere, done with the conversation.

Several beeps echoed through Thra's containment, converging loudly on the empty space they shared when integrating their worldview.

Rav knew they were no longer all on the same page. Similar perhaps, because Somnia was their world. It wasn't a game. Instead it lived and breathed, and would need the best people to bring out the best of the world. Finding them—that was the chore they had now. Allocations or not. No one was created equal.

Real World Day 3: Somnia Online

Murmur stood at the top of the steps to the basement and stared around in awe. Everywhere she turned, Telvar's faithful were at work. They gathered the crumbled stone and were salvaging what they could. With their unexpected windfall of experience from their even more unexpected event, as a group they were well into level thirteen.

Jinna walked over to her, a merry smile on his face. "You look much better."

"Thanks." She smiled, feeling better than she did when she logged out of the game. "What's all this?"

The rogue smiled. "Well, Tel told them to help us rebuild. I don't think we're going to have enough salvaged rock to finish the whole thing off, but we should definitely have a good amount done. I've asked them to lend priority to the parts that are less ruined, and reinforce what hasn't collapsed yet, and we'll deal with the rest of it once we get our hands on some coin and get new materials in."

Murmur glanced out at the rather large body of water they were in the middle of. "Um. How are we going to get them to us?"

"Drawbridge of course." Jinna's eyes twinkled and he grinned. "Eventually anyway. We'll likely have to use a boat to ferry things across until then. Also, Beast was looking for you."

"Why me?" she muttered, not really meaning it as a legitimate question, but she got answers anyway.

"Because you're our leader." Jinna answered with a shrug.

"Because we cajoled you, and now you have to do shit," yelled Merlin.

Murmur laughed and walked around the little island, appreciating it more for what it was. It was larger than it appeared from the shore, a mile or so wide—it took about fifteen minutes to walk across—and about two miles long. The castle only took up a small portion of the island. If this really was theirs...

She walked out toward the water's edge, concentration centered on figuring out what they'd be able to do with it.

"Hey Mur!"

She turned around to see Beastial and Shir-Khan jogging up to her. They both had huge smiles on their faces, and Beast did indeed look like his tiger. Maybe that owner and pet thing held some truth. "What's up?"

The wind whipped up, sending her robe flying from a cool chill through the air despite the sun being high in the sky. They'd have to think about some sort of insulation, and also how close they were to towns for supplies or to travel to sell.

"Mur?" Beastial's gaze seemed puzzled, and she nodded. He hesitated before continuing. "You didn't get any of what I just said, did you?"

She thought back and realized he was right. Her head had been elsewhere, and upon deeper thoughts, also somewhat foggy. "Sorry. What were you saying?"

"Members. We have a list of fourteen people that we've guilded with before, yet haven't had nearly as much experience in raiding with them like we did with the others. I sent you the list via email, but you didn't send me back instructions. Guilds are starting to pop up everywhere now we're into the third day post launch, and if we want good players, I'm going to need to recruit before they're all snatched up." He finished his rather lengthy monologue and looked at her expectantly.

She thought for a moment, trying to figure out how they'd best approach this. "We have to make sure they're legit and not spies. Considering Exodus is here with their weirdly serious grudge, it's better to be safe than sorry. We also have to make sure they're not in it for easy gear or money. And thirdly, we have to keep our secret from them until they move onto full member status. I'll create a recruit and trial rank. Once they've been vetted—and I don't care if you do real life checks on them Beast—then they can pass through trial to recruit. But they have to be a recruit for one real week before they're afforded all of our member privileges. We can't afford to fuck up."

Telvar suddenly appeared at her elbow. "I thank you for that consideration. Would it be helpful if I scanned recruits for dishonesty?"

"You can tell if they lie?" Murmur stepped back and eyed the attractive lacerta with respect.

"So can you, once you figure out how." Telvar winked at her. "What do you think?"

"If you can do it in lacerta form so they don't know you're a dragon, then sure." She watched him with an eyebrow raised. "I love that you're a dragon with a hoard and a spare castle to give us, don't get me wrong. But if people find out too soon what we're essentially defending is a dragon with a lair, then we'll have poachers here ready to zerg and bum rush you regardless of life or limb."

Telvar turned his body to face her head on. "I promise that I do not seem at all dragon-like in this form."

"Do to us." Beast shrugged.

"Ah, but I didn't before you fought me. You all thought I was just a lizard man." Tel held up his hand to stop either of them speaking. "I also have my own agenda to pursue, and that includes keeping myself and my followers strong and protected as much as I can. Which, right now isn't something I can do as well as I would like, but let me gain more experience, let me level before your eyes. I will be an ally like none you have seen."

"All right, all right." Murmur said, raising her hands in mock defense. "We get it, Tel. Trust me, we get it."

She turned back to Beast, aware of Tel's eyes still on her. She wanted to ask him what he was thinking, because she could hear faint echoes of it in her head, like a lulling song in her mind trying to pull her into safe waters. Focusing on Beast, she got her thoughts in order regarding the members. "Make sure everyone we have with us now, knows that Telvar's true form is a secret. Anyone else that meets him will get introduced to him as the lacerta we know. We're going to need tight security around here until we at least get a few levels on others."

"Sounds reasonable to me." Beastial smiled and then reached out and squeezed Mur's hand quickly. "Remember, you're the one we ask to lead because you're good at juggling threads through delegation. Don't try to do everything yourself. It always gets you into a bind, okay?"

"Yes, big brother that I never had—" he laughed at her words until she finished her sentence, "—and never wanted."

She poked out her tongue at him and ran back to the others who were still cleaning out the debris. Their experience had bought them a little time, and made it so that they got a free four hour nap, but soon they'd need to head out again. Sadly, they could no longer level on the island. Killing their ally's followers wouldn't be very good form.

Sinister was finishing off some strange dance-like moves while Murmur watched her. To be fair, Mur didn't think Sin was entirely aware she was being watched, because her mind was focused. When her friend finally finished the kata-like movements she'd been making, Mur spoke up. "So, what's that?"

Sin turned around, glaring at the interruption. "Mur, don't sneak up on me like that."

"What are you doing out here next to this lonely tree, practicing what looks like a very weird kata." Mur sat down next to her friend and gently rocked into her shoulder. They'd done this when they were kids, when one of them was having a hard time with something. Mur found Sin's hand and squeezed it.

For a second, Sin hesitated, and then she turned toward Mur with brightly shining eyes. "You wouldn't believe this. I think I unlocked one of those hidden skills. If I concentrate on a person, I can tell how much health they have. So I was standing here practicing from a distance."

Murmur smiled in response. "That's a pretty cool ability."

"I know, right?" Sinister looked inordinately proud of herself. "I triggered it, I think, because I actually listened to what the NPCs were saying for once. After you told us that's how you thought it worked, I figured it was worth a try. But I didn't remember until I went back after we hit level twelve."

"Do you have to dance to trigger it? That might get tricky in a fight?" Murmur tried really hard to keep a straight face.

Sinister scowled. "It helps me concentrate and learn how to focus, idiot."

"Please don't ever change, Sin." Murmur hugged her friend impulsively, and for a moment it seemed like Sinister didn't want to let go, her grip was so tight, so she held on for a little while longer than intended. "We need to figure out where to get some levels. There's no way we'll be able to keep this little plot if people level too far past us."

They both stood up, brushing off their robes. Sinister looked down and frowned. "You're so right, we need to get pants."

"Right?" Murmur agreed wholeheartedly. "Every time I take a step up a small incline I almost fall flat on my face. Robes are so cumbersome, especially when a dragon is blowing gale force winds in my direction."

Sinister laughed and they made it back to the others arm in arm.

Tel stood with Jinna, apparently rejuvenating now he had sealed the deal. Somehow Murmur wanted to figure out how he was benefiting, how he was gaining energy from them. After all, they weren't leveling right now. She frowned, wishing she could read minds already. But even then she was almost as sure that it wasn't anything harmful. Maybe he just didn't want to let them know he had to take a shit. These new senses of hers had a horrible way of confusing her more than they helped.

"Guys." Murmur cleared her throat. "We really need to figure out where to level now. While this island is an awesome perk, we now don't have a leveling plan, and while we got a nice boost, we also took a nap."

"Mur?" Havoc stepped forward and took her hand, squeezing it gently and making her look down at him. "Take a breath and do a who all."

Sending out the command, Murmur obliged.

All Players Level 14: 0

All Players Level 15: 0

All Players Level 13: 14

Havoc waited patiently, watching her eyes. "The two who are also thirteen are people Beastial is about to invite on a trial basis."

Murmur narrowed her eyes, and sent out another inquiry.

All Players Level 12: 325

"So." She started slowly. "Are we recruiting the hundreds who are level twelve too?"

Havoc laughed. "Don't be silly. The point is, most of us are over halfway through this level. We'll get there. Let's just not be stupid."

Grudgingly, she had to admit that Havoc was right. Damned logic. She reined back her admonitions. "Well then, does anyone have any ideas for where we could level up to fifteen?"

Tel leaned forward, a smile on his face. It reminded Murmur of a meme she'd seen with a laughing gecko. "Why fifteen? Sixteen would make more sense as you'll boost another level and have an abundance of new abilities. You should all check for them. Sixteen makes much more sense, trust me. If you think it's a good idea to gain that level, I may have the perfect spot for you."

Murmur blinked at him. She hadn't thought NPCs were supposed to help like this, but then the event they'd triggered followed by the reward was also severely unique. A nagging feeling in the back of her mind muttered that they didn't deserve this, and karma was going to be cruel. Still though, hadn't they earned it through fair and well-planned combat? Maybe if she thought it often enough, she'd convince herself it was true.

"Sixteen sounds like a good plan," she said carefully, still waiting for more of an explanation.

"I have to agree, it's probably a better idea." Devlish winked at his fellow lacerta. "Us lacerta are full of good ideas."

"Once your hearthstone is set here, you will be able to Gate back to this location by thinking *home gate*. This will allow you to keep a bind point at some other location in the world." Hiro piped up, standing next to Jinna.

"Hiro's help has been amazing. He's designing our hearth right now. Should have it done soon." Jinna beamed with pride, patting the NPC on the shoulder.

"Thank you, Hiro." Murmur was starting to feel overwhelmed. She hadn't expected them to get a damned guild plot so soon, let alone a freaking island on top of a bloody dragon hoard. It wasn't exactly normal game play as far as she was concerned. The thing was, she felt quite certain that other people would have the same experience. They weren't doing anything other adventurers weren't going to do, or weren't capable of doing, they were just getting there slightly earlier than anyone else.

"Where's the place, Tel?" She asked the dragon, realizing the prostpect of having him as a part of the team held endless possibilities. The kindness he'd shown so far made her eager, if still a bit wary, to learn what working with him would be like.

"You might want to sell in Ululate first. The luna are an amazing people and will pay you well. Either way you set out, it's relatively close to here. There was a crossroads you took on your way here. Had you taken the right-hand fork, you would have headed into a point where it branched out, and a wood began. In those woods are gnolls. To shorten a very long story, there were some really nasty people a long while ago who performed experiements on dozens of luna. Those experiments went awry and created the gnolls. They are nasty and fast, spiteful and intelligent. Off to the south in the back of the woods is their territory. They live mostly on the ground in huts, but their lookout towers are impressive. They're a strong group of gnolls, just right for you to level with. That is where I suggest you travel to."

"Is there anything you need from there?" Murmur asked suddenly, still suspecting ulterior motives.

Tel blinked and shook his head. "No, not technically. But I would like for you to come back stronger, and thus for me to also gain strength, so perhaps there is."

She smiled, because that was something she wouldn't mind sharing. "That, we will gladly bring back."

Murmur turned around to the group and clapped her hands. "Let's finish up whatever tasks we were doing here, and head out. Daylight's a-wasting."

She watched as the others moved back to their tasks, and tugged at the uncomfortable skirts she was wearing. The thing was, she didn't want some crappy tunic. She wanted something that afforded a little protection. Idly an idea began to form in her mind. Perhaps they'd be able to have a crafting station or something.

"Jinna!"

The stocky dwarf ran over to her. She'd never seen him so happy before. He was in his element. She cleared her throat. "I think you need to be like the guild hall foreman or something, because you understand this shit way more than I do. Also," and she paused, unsure quite how to phrase it. "What does it mean to have a guild hall?"

His eyes widened in surprise, and he chuckled. "In this game it means you have a safe haven, unless you're at war, that provides you with a calmness buff that can last several hours. With enough construction, you can raise your guild hall's ranking and include crafting tables, herb patches, vegetable and food gardens. Not so sure about breeding animals for meat or such, but basically you make your guild self-sufficient."

Murmur pondered that for a moment before calling out to Beastial. "Beast!"

He trotted over, and she could see that he too was brimming with excitement as he mock saluted her. "Yes, ma'am!"

She rolled her eyes. "Gods, no. See if you can reach out to any crafters. I get the feeling we're going to need them, especially wood workers."

"Sorry for the interruption, but..." Hiro approached, his lacerta eyes reflecting the gold of his scales. "Actually Jessup over there is a master woodworker. As a general rule, we should have every craft you need covered."

"Really?" Murmur was having more and more misgivings. She felt like they were cheating. "Well, I guess that solves that."

Jinna watched her as Hiro left. "You still want to get the crafters, don't you?"

"Yep. I'd still like to put out a call to pure crafters. There will always be player made armor we'll need, or potions, or weaponry. Please, Beast?" She smiled at him.

"Sure. Sure." Beastial said as he rolled his shoulders.

Jinna nudged her. "You feel like it's too easy, don't you?"

"That transparent, am I?" She shook her head. "I'm waiting for the other shoe to drop, I keep feeling like we're having it too easy."

"Maybe we are, but we did fight well. Had we been assholes, Telvar could easily have killed us after we ran out of ammo and shields, but he didn't. Thus, our actions spoke for us. We earned this." Jinna squared his jaw and stood proud.

"When you put it like that." She reached over and gave the dwarf a brief hug. "Thanks, Jinna."

She watched as everyone finished their tasks, thoughts still racing through her mind at nineteen to the dozen.

"He's right you know."

Mur didn't even have to turn around to know it was Tel speaking. "I know he is, and yet."

"And yet you think you don't deserve it." Tel stood next to her, watching everyone. "He was right; I could have just killed you. But the effort you all put in, the teamwork it took with all twelve of you contributing, with each of you trying to make everyone else's jobs easier, and with all of them not wanting to force your hand and make you use the powers you have that you still don't understand—the powers that you seem to fear right now.

"Yes, you deserve what I have given you. I was left with full autonomy to decide to whom I would gift this land. There were criteria I required to be met before this occurred. You fulfilled it. This wasn't an idle choice, nor was it a rushed one. I fully doubt that I would have met anyone else I'd have been happy with. And you do realize I'm not the only one in this world who can gift something like this? I'm just the first who has. It's not really a leg up, or a benefit, it's just that you got this first." He patted her head. "There is only one thing I wish."

"And?" She smiled at the calm thought waves that always emanated from him, even though she technically knew he could modulate his psionics far better than she could hers.

His smile was sad, and Murmur couldn't help the gasp of shock that escaped her. "I wish that you'd reached me before Belius reached you."

"What do you know about Belius?" She whispered, her eyes darting all around to check who could hear them. No one seemed to be paying attention.

"I don't want to influence your mind too much. You have such a great platform in yourself. And you've embraced psionic abilities I didn't think possible for someone such as you. Everyone knows Belius. He is the locus enchanter master. Adept at weaving illusions and telling you just enough of what you want to hear." Telvar's smile was still just this side of sorrowful, and frustration boiled inside Murmur at the fact that no one ever gave her a freaking straight answer.

"He never tells me what I want to hear. No one in this damned game is actually direct. But with Belius I know where I stand. I can tell there are many things he has yet to share with me, and so I'm careful. But you, Tel," she paused and studied him, leaning back to get a better view. "You, I can only get a general and well-intentioned feeling from. I can't tell whether my Thought Sensing has gotten better, or whether you're just projecting what it is you want me to feel."

Tel raised an eyebrow and this time his smile was happier. "I didn't realize you'd come so far. No, I'm not projecting, not deliberately anyway. I do find that keeping my thoughts to the more mellow side of my temperament helps me escape those who would do the other side of me harm."

That made sense, and relieved some of Murmur's tension. "Well, if it helps you, you definitely don't exude raging screech dragon."

Tel laughed. "That was a mental shriek. Your reactions were so fast, and during the second one you managed to shield a couple of your friends. It seems your psychic abilities are beginning to manifest some kinetic ones. Quick thinking mixed with compassion and tactics is a rare find, and an admirable quality. Most of you react in a way that means they'll protect someone they care about, but you and your friend Sinister, you are of a different ilk."

"We've been friends since kindergarten. Our families used to live side by side." Murmur watched as Sin practiced her ability across the grass. The movements were fluid, and Sin was so focused, she was biting her tongue again.

"It is a good thing to have a long-term friend. They can help us see ourselves when no one else does. They are more honest about who we are, than we realize they can be."

"Now you're just going philosophical on me, Tel. Don't do that. It makes my head swim." Murmur laughed.

But the dragon just looked at her, a thoughtful set to his jaw. "Your head is how you are here, correct?"

Murmur raised an eyebrow. "Technically it's how I travel to Somnia, yes."

"Interesting," was all the lacerta said, and his face remained perfectly impassive, hiding any expression from her. "I must venture below and get some coin for Hiro. No one but me can retrieve it, on pain of death. I promised compensation, and I will help rebuild this beautiful castle."

Mist fell over his eyes, like he was remembering a distant past with a fondness he no longer had for any living thing.

"Anyway," he continued. "Make sure you avoid the opposite side of the forest where the bandits are. Make sure you veer off to the left instead."

"What's on the right-hand side?" Murmur couldn't help herself.

He laughed and turned around just as he was about to enter the basement area, and yelled across the way so everyone heard him. "Spiders! Enormous level seventeen to twenty spiders!"

"Shit," muttered Murmur. She'd just had to ask.

CHAPTER TWENTY-FOUR
Leveling Up in the World

Storm Entertainment
Somnia Online Division
Software Development Team Offices
Launch Day (Evening)

Laria frowned at the reports she'd just received from Brandon. That constant misplaced line really bugged her perfectionist qualities. While it didn't make a difference to anything she could see, it still gave her an off feeling. That line shouldn't be there. She'd checked and triple checked everything to make sure the system calibrated and recalibrated its results with deliberate and easy identifiable needs. That nothing related to her little experiment would show up as anything, not even a glitch, but this line wasn't in her projections and it bothered her.

Everything was running smoothly. Complaints about playing the characters the game chose for them had been a surprisingly low percentage. But the system, the AIs, their scanning capabilities were scarily accurate, and most people were excited to play a class they'd always secretly wanted to, but never thought they could.

Perhaps their advertising campaign had paid off after all. She ran a hand through her hair and checked to see if Wren was still playing. Laria frowned. Was it the right choice to let her do this? Letting her play as much as she wanted over break was a fantastic short-term solution for a much larger problem. It was all Laria could do to hope she hadn't screwed things up, again.

Maybe it would help her in the long run, bring her back to the little girl who'd been her mommy's sweetheart. But the game was a long way from a loving environment, and all Laria could do was hope that all her research was correct. That prolonged exposure might even enhance brain function.

"Laria?"

"Hm?" Laria glanced up to see Shayla leaning against the door.

"I called your name three times but you looked engrossed in that report." She moved closer, standing up straight and crossing her arms. "Is there something I should know about?"

Laria shook her head. "No, just a spacing problem in the reports. No impact to computations or any of our main features, it's just irritating and requires the extrapolation team to triple check every sheet."

Shayla stared at her for a long moment, before heaving a huge sigh. "Look, Laria. I know there's something going on with you. We've been working together for over a decade. I hope that one of these days you're going to confide in me, and I hope that confidence doesn't mean I'll have to fire you."

"I haven't done anything wrong for you to fire me." Laria's eyes flashed. "This game wouldn't even run without me. Don't think that just because I don't have your title, my work is any less important, Shayla."

Laria snapped her mouth closed, before she dug herself in any deeper and said something she'd regret.

"You do have a point." Shayla smiled a little sadly. "I'm not sure how you pull some of this coding out of your ass, but you do. Please, when you're ready, come tell me. I can feel your stress levels all the way over in my office."

Shayla waved as she left, effectively terminating the conversation. Laria groaned and bumped her head against her desk. There were just some days when she wished everything wasn't so damned complicated.

Real World Day 3: Somnia Online

"He said spiders, Mur!" Sinister was beside herself again, and Murmur could feel a headache coming on.

"In the opposite woods to the gnolls, Sin," Mur repeated for the umpteenth time since they had gated back to Ululate to sell all of their crap. "Just hurry up and sell, and we'll make sure to go into the left side of the woods."

Sin grumbled under her breath. "Well you never know, maybe the spiders and the gnolls formed an alliance."

Murmur chuckled to herself as she looked through the stalls in the market square. Realizing her clothes were still largely from level eight, she picked up a new and silvered robe that she absolutely adored, new boots, gloves and bracers, and finally pants from a player who stood at the cart.

The small luna looked up and smiled. "Thank you so much. Oh wow, wait, you're from that guild!"

Murmur started. "What?"

"Fable. You've like killed nameds and stuff already, right?"

"Yeah," After a moment's hesitation, Murmur continued. "How did you come to make all this? You're still so little."

The girl laughed. "Yeah, my big brother likes me to craft for him, so he brings back stuff from his adventures, but he's only just level eleven, and I barter for the rest. I like crafting."

"Well, I'm Murmur. It's a pleasure to meet you. As you level up, I may need some stuff, so I'll keep you on my friends list, if that's okay." Murmur triggered her UI to add it to her friends list that she'd yet to use because all of her friends were in the guild.

"Thank you!" The luna's eyes went round as the moon. "I'm Neva. I hope I run into you again."

Murmur gave the girl a few more gold and bid her farewell, figuring she'd strip off and get dressed once they reached their destination. It was always good to make friends where you could, you never knew when you might need someone's skills. She loved the gear. It was high quality and had a decent armor class rating on it for level thirteen equipment.

She waited for the rest of the groups to meet her at the front. They weren't going to raid the area, as Tel had assured them that while good for one group, the gnolls just weren't raid material. However, he'd also seemed quite gleeful when he announced that there were plenty to kill.

Murmur suddenly realized she'd forgotten to allocate her attribute points when she hit thirteen. Groaning, she pulled her character sheet up and frowned.

Up until now she'd basically sort of done her routine, one Intelligence, one Stamina, two Charisma, done. But her hit points were pretty solid now, and she felt like she desperately needed Agility. Not a huge amount, and she'd probably stop once it hit about fifteen, but she felt so clunky, and it was the one sensation she wasn't used to feeling at all.

She added two Agility, one Intelligence, and one Charisma, accepted the changes, and frowned again. After she'd done the Agility she'd probably concentrate on just Intelligence and Charisma. Right now they were sitting at twenty-eight to thirty without gear, and forty-three to forty-six with gear, respectively. She studied them with a bit of skepticism. After having been so used to stacking wisdom as a healer, her current path still took her by surprise sometimes.

CON 22
STR 10
AGI 13
WIS 12
INT 28 (30)
CHA 43 (46)
HP 268

MANA 279
MA 100 (125)

"Hey, sleepy head." Devlish ruffled her hair, although her locus hair wasn't exactly as easy to ruffle as her human hair was. It was bulky, sleek, and very dense, and she could barely take her eyes off the fairy lights at the bottom when they glowed during combat.

"I'm not sleepy, I'd just forgotten to allocate my attribute points from hitting thirteen in all of the 'oh my god a thing just spoke to us.'" She hoped they'd realize she didn't want them to mention that Tel was a dragon where anyone else could hear them.

Devlish blinked at her, and she could see a few of the others getting that vague sort of stare in their eyes as they too scrambled to allocate their points.

Murmur laughed. "Now I don't feel as bad at least."

"Hey, we had a lot going on," Jinna said somewhat defensively.

"Let's get cracking then." Merlin strode to the fore, taking his place as the head scout in their team, mainly because Exbo was often lazy, and Jinna didn't do front and center well. He claimed he was a rogue, and sneaking in the back went with the territory.

"Yep! We're off to see the spiders." Beastial grinned evilly at Sinister, who yelped and punched him as they walked along the path.

Murmur waved to Jan as they were leaving and he was just entering the town. He pulled up just short of the entrance and called out to her.

"Where ya goin' miss?"

"Just going to see if we can flush some gnolls out," she said.

"Aye, you be careful. Those things have nasty teeth. I should know."

She halted the others and closed the distance to Jan to hear what he had to say.

"I often do a run to Frangit, but lately the gnolls have been little shits. I even lost some cargo to them. I don't believe I'm the only one."

"Thanks Jan. You take care, right?" Murmur waved at him and ran to catch up with the others just as the text scrolled across her screen. She knew it.

In talking to Jan, he mentioned that he and others have had

cargo stolen by the gnolls who inhabit the far west woods. Should you recover any of the stolen cargo intact, there is sure to be a reward with anyone you return it to. But beware, for gnolls are smart and fast.

Murmur shared the quest with their group, and with their guild, grinning.

The sun was hot, but not too hot, and the breeze was just right, serving to ruffle Murmur's robe as she walked instead of making it fly up at all angles. In all her search for gear back in Ululate she'd completely forgotten that she didn't want a robe. Tunics always seemed harder to come by. She'd have to remember next time.

The banter between the two groups was fun as usual, and Beastial added trial members to their rostered ranks as they traveled. Overall, Murmur was in a great mood. She even sent a note to her mom.

Sorry I missed you while I was sleeping last night, but I must have needed it since I passed out. Don't worry, Harlow forced me to eat before logging back in.

It took a while for mother to respond, but then it always did. The woman was busy all the time.

Laria: Oh good, I was a bit worried, but you two seem okay. Are you having fun? Discovered anything cool yet?

You know we have, Murmur replied, trying not to laugh out loud and cause her friends to look at her strangely.

Laria: True true, but I love it when you tell me things.

Love you Mom, we're off to hunt some gnolls.

Laria: Love you dear, good luck!

Of course she should have known better. As they walked down the path following the directions given to them by Tel, just before they reached the crossroad, they ran into another group, headed by Jirald. She'd almost forgotten about him.

His eyes immediately strayed to her, and a smirk crossed his face. "Well, well, we meet again."

Devlish rolled his eyes. "Was there something you wanted?"

The Exodus group fanned out around Jirald, similar smirks on most of their faces, except for one who stood behind the rest, shorter than the others. Murmur couldn't make out their face. They were probably smirking too. She was really growing tired of the whole Jirald attitude thing.

Jirald's smirk finally gave away to a serious expression and he took a few quick steps forward, obviously aiming to land right in front of Murmur, but Devlish moved his body slightly, and Jirald stopped. "No. Not right now."

"I don't even get what your problem is. I have no idea why you hold this grudge against us. It was a mob who dropped a bloody weapon in a freaking game. It's like being angry at your Scrabble opponent for having a better vocabulary." Murmur finally had enough. There was being polite and ignoring people and hoping they'd just bugger off on their own, and then there was Jirald, who couldn't seem to take, *I got a weapon before you could get it in a digital game, so deal with it,* as an answer.

Anger flashed through Jirald's eyes and his form suddenly dissipated, vanishing into thin air. Jinna gasped, but Murmur reacted on instinct, hitting her area stun immediately, knowing her guild wouldn't be affected. She turned during the four seconds, her fingers flying as she cast Nullify quickly followed by Mez, and slammed the spells onto Jirald's revealed and scowling face.

"Fuck you, dude. What the hell is wrong with you? Do you realize I can keep a hold of you like that indefinitely? What on earth made you attack me?" The voice in the back of her mind urged her to charm him, to cast Allure and make him walk around with her for hours on end unable to break out of it. Like a torture. With all of his stupid little stalker tactics, would it really be so bad to do that?

Devlish and Beastial moved to guard Murmur's back, she refreshed her Mez and turned back to the group he was with. All of them were eleven and twelve. They'd been working hard as a team, trying to obtain their own goals, and here Jirald was with this weird vendetta against her, side-railing all their efforts. At least she assumed that was the case, because vendettas weren't the best thing for guild relations. She took a deep breath before speaking to them.

"I don't know what his problem is, and I really don't care. But if he comes at me again, he'll regret it. I will refresh that spell on him and we will leave here. Make sure he doesn't come after me, please." Her voice remained steady and firm, and it was a miracle she managed to keep her irritation out of it. Instead, she was quite impressed with her rather effective leader voice.

The person Murmur hadn't been able to see before stepped forward. He was a tiny gnome and his expression was a very sober one. "We apologize on behalf of Exodus. We prefer clean battle, and for our rivals to be met with pride and respect. Jirald can be a bit of a dick."

Devlish laughed, and stood with his sword-hand on his hips, his shield carelessly hanging off the other. The massive piece of metal Telvar had gifted him was imposing. It was tall, but not quite a tower shield, and held filigree patterns all down the front. "You don't say. Then we'll leave him in your capable hands. It'd also be great if he could stop harassing our guild leader, thanks. We have shit to do, and constantly having to be aware of a stalker trying to stab her in the back is going to get annoying."

The little gnome's eyes widened, and he seemed slightly flustered. "I'm our second in command, and I apologize again. He'll be warned. Thanks for not beating the shit out of him. I doubt it would have changed his attitude, but it doesn't mean he didn't deserve it."

"Probably only make it worse," Mur mumbled as she Mez'd the very angry rogue once again. Murmur gave a slight bow, and continued walking past the Exodus group. Mez might make you freeze but it didn't stop your other senses from working. He had to be seething right now, but what choice had she had? Being shanked in the kidneys wouldn't have been pleasant at all.

"He's going to hate you even more now, but you know that already, right?" Havoc caught up to her, his skeleton clicking along happily in their wake. Murmur wasn't sure, but she thought it might look stronger.

"Yeah, but what was I going to do, let him kill me so he would think he could just do it again? There was no way to win that, for some reason he hates me, and frankly, I'm a little scared of him." She whispered the last, because she didn't like saying it out loud. When things were spoken out in the open, they often brought karma with them. Whether that was just a coincidence or not, she didn't know. "You know, it wouldn't matter how powerful I get, if he had been walking behind me and used that weird skill of his I wouldn't have survived. While my sensory net may have picked something up, I doubt I could have reacted in time to do anything."

"It's okay, Mur," Havoc gave her shoulder a quick squeeze. "You know we'd all fight to the death for you."

She smiled, even though she hated feeling like this was out of her control. "I know. I truly do know." Being with her friends in this world helped calm her moods, and was maybe even helping her learn a bit of gratitude.

"Although," he paused before continuing. "I'd feel safer if you didn't wander around alone."

They walked together for a few moments, and Murmur knew Havoc wasn't sure how she'd taken his comment, but with the way Jirald kept behaving, there wasn't any predicting his actions. So frankly, Havoc was right. He wasn't being an overprotective 'oh we must save the princess' jerk, no, he was being her friend who was worried about the weird hyper-sensitive stalker dude who just tried to stab her in the back.

So instead of her usual hasty react first and think later mode, she waited until she'd fully accepted her reality, and answered. "I know, and I don't plan on walking around alone anywhere in the world. Just in case."

Havoc heaved a sigh of relief. "Well, that went better than expected."

"Shut up." She mock punched him in the arm and watched him stagger up the right path at the crossroads. Rolling her eyes, she asked the question that had been bothering her. "What did that blocking out death give you?"

"Oh!" His face lit up, albeit briefly. "I have this thing called bone clouds now, and I can reinforce my pet to make him stronger, quicker, and smarter. I should get some new stuff with my next level too. So yeah, that paying attention to find the hidden class is awesome, even if I'm not actually named differently."

Murmur smiled, happy for her friend. Even if she constantly felt something was off in the world, if something didn't quite sit right with her mind, it had nothing to do with her friends.

After a short way, the rest of the path sort of faded out and they were left with two sides of a rather thick wood.

Beastial pointed to the south, shading his eyes. "We avoid that side and all the eight-legged infidels. This is what Shir-Khan thinks, and so I'm not taking him that way."

Sinister chuckled. "Your cat is smarter than you."

"You take that back, you blood sucker." Beastial growled at her.

But Sin shook her finger. "Uh-uh-uh! I'm a blood drainer. There's a huge difference. Trust me." Her eyes twinkled merrily.

"Okay, everyone. Listen up." Devlish motioned for them all to get into a huddle so they could talk quietly and not alert anything. Murmur liked that plan, the memory of the Brute still way too fresh in her mind.

"We need to be quiet as we move into the trees. Once we get to the camp we can split up and each take a side and be ready to back one another up if one of us needs assistance, but we have to be quiet while we approach. Remember the Brute."

"I don't wanna," Rashlyn pouted.

Devlish smiled, "Well, let's not give them advance warning of our arrival. Rangers scout ahead—let us know if they have any lookouts as well."

The group spread out, and began to tread the way to the south side of the forest, but Jinna stopped Murmur, grabbing her arm briefly. His brow was furrowed and he looked like he didn't know what to say.

"What is it?" Murmur asked, a little worried.

"That move. That move Jirald used." He shook his head. "I don't know what it is. And I've unlocked two hidden abilities, involving sneak attacks. But that one is not from our normal school, and it's not one of the hidden ones I've found. Be careful, please, Mur. There's something about him that makes me uneasy."

Murmur forced herself to move, feeling the knot in her stomach twist as they hurried after the groups.

It was difficult to make their way quietly through the forest given all of the foliage scattered throughout it, but they did their best, hoping they only sounded like large wild animals. Murmur glanced at her stats several times.

Thought Sensing 48

Thought Shielding 49

Thought Projection 31

Apparently she was using the hell out of Thought Projections without so much as a...thought.

She really needed to stop laughing at her own jokes, especially since in this case it was in rather poor taste.

What the hell was she doing that made her project so much?

Sinister: You okay? You seem a little off.

I'm okay, just a bit jumpy since Jirald pulled that shit.

Sinister: OMG I WAS ABOUT TO KILL HIM!

Calm down, Sin. I'm okay, and I'll be fine as long as I stick with my friends.

Sinister: Just don't go anywhere without me, okay? I worry.

I promise.

Sinister: Liar

Murmur couldn't think of another response, so she let the conversation die there. They finally caught up with where Merlin and Exbo stood waiting for them. From their position behind the trees, they could just spy one of the lookout towers. They were made out of tightly bound wooden planks with multiple levels.

"How are we supposed to take one of those out, without alerting the whole goddamned village beneath?" Beastial whispered in a harsh voice.

Merlin shrugged. "I could, potentially maybe, one shot it if I manage to get the shot through the eyeball and use my In the Lights of Their Eyes hidden skill."

"Could you both do it?" Murmur crept forward.

"What, you mean take an eyeball each and hope at least one of us hits?"

Murmur nodded.

Merlin shrugged and spoke softly. "I mean I'm willing to try it, but these things don't tether, and there are no guards here to save our asses."

"I literally only just activated it. I don't even get how it works yet." Exbo fidgeted, his eyes downcast.

"It's easy, I'll explain it to you." Merlin grinned at the other ranger, and the tension dissipated.

Murmur thought for a few more seconds. "I wonder if I can charm it. Like charm it, have it kill the other lookout up there, and then just park it until we work through some of the village."

Havoc looked at her, the others stared at her. "That's pretty fucking brilliant actually. If the charm fails, you have that instant distance stun, right?"

Murmur nodded again, her grin widening. "We just need better line of sight for me."

"Without him seeing us, of course." Merlin tsked under his breath.

Turning to Rashlyn, Murmur smiled. "We'll take care of the lookouts first, and then you guys can take the right side, and we'll take the left."

"Sounds like a plan." The monk gave Murmur a quick hug. "Don't let that fucker get you down, Mur. You're pretty damned special."

Touched, Murmur hugged her friend briefly in return. There was no need to get all soppy now. "How about we just go level like a bat out of hell and become the most amazing guild on the server."

"Oh, I like your plan better." Rash grinned, and everyone began to creep forward.

It didn't take long for Murmur to move into range, and they managed to hide behind a tree trunk that seemed like a blindspot for the weird gnolls. She stood with the two rangers, waiting for the right time to hit the closest lookout. "You two fire at the second one as I charm the first, and that way I can direct the pet to finish off the second if you don't manage it. Remember, these guys are ridiculously clever."

Time seemed to slow as the rangers drew their bows while Murmur cast her spell. She released it a split second before they did, and it hit the level sixteen mob, instantly charming him. The arrows hit home in the other mob a split second later and the second lookout fell to the ground, twitching. Murmur directed her pet to sit and stay where it was, and the first step was complete.

She smiled up at Exbo and Merlin. "I can just leave him there, or I can call him around the back way to us?"

Devlish had crept forward to see how they were doing. "I'd say bring him here. The lookouts don't seem very strong, but as far as I can see, the villagers are all group elites."

Directing her little pet to use the rear staircase and skirt the outer trees away from the village and to come and find her, Murmur soothed its thoughts and walked back to the group to set up for their demolition of the village.

The sound of pounding feet stopped her in her tracks, and suddenly her lookout appeared, rounding the corner, running for its life with a group of eight mobs running after it.

And they all looked really pissed off.

CHAPTER TWENTY-FIVE
Deals with Devils

Storm Entertainment
Somnia Online Division
Software Development Team Offices
Second day Morning

"What do you mean the transcripts are gone?" Shayla pinched the bridge of her nose between her forefinger and thumb and tried, probably in vain, to will away the headache she knew was coming.

James colored a bright shade of red that did nothing for his sallow complexion. "The transcripts. The initial transcripts from all the meetings Ava coordinated, they're gone. They were in her folders, and now they're gone."

He held his hands up to the side in a shrugging sort of helpless motion. James squared his shoulders and looked his boss right in the eyes. "I've asked the data extrapolation team if they could look into it for me, and they're assigning a couple of guys to give her server the once over. It could even be a glitch."

Shayla's shoulders sagged, and she half fell into her office chair. Who on earth would even want Ava's meeting notes? "This launch is vital to our company. Everything we're doing here is integral to the continuance of not only our employment, but also to that of anyone else wanting to enter the virtual technology circuit. And let's not forget the monetary support for this whole project is backed by the military for very specific reasons no one seems to want to let me know about."

"I know." James said, and his eyes searched her office. Shayla waited for him to finish. There were no personal pictures, no cutesy office decoration items, except one random glass turtle paperweight that she used whenever she had actual paper on her desk.

He finally continued. "The minutes have to be there. She had so many discussions with him—they can't all disappear into thin air. She spoke about him all the time."

Shayla nodded, wondering how none of them had thought to double check. "Thank you for checking, James. Can you keep trying please? I'll see if I have time to dig some stuff up from my end, but all I have are the doodles I wrote myself, from the earlier meetings. If we don't have the ones only Ava attended, then we can't compare anything at all."

He nodded, swallowing as his eyes darted back and forth, as if he wanted to ask something. "Can I get you anything?"

She smiled, and her eyes seemed tired. "Not unless you can manage an infusion of youth into my old bones."

James laughed. "You're not old."

"No." Shayla shook her head. "I'm not, but I sure as hell feel like it."

He left the room and headed down the hall toward Laria's office determined to get some answers. Shayla was acting out of sorts, the data extrapolation team seemed to be angry over some strange output mechanism they couldn't fix in the reports, and Laria was being far too quiet about everything.

Laria wasn't known for being quiet.

Real World Day 3: Somnia Online

"Oh, shit." Devlish turned, already sprinting. "Run!"

"They're not going to tether." Murmur muttered, extending a raid invitation to Rash so they could better coordinate for the incoming shitstorm.

"Will need a ward or five." She picked one off in the distance, and then another. Two Mez'd, six to go, and the gnolls were upon them. Caught in the thick of the group, she area effect stunned them, allowing her to Mez two more, and insta-stun another as one of Veranol's wards slammed over her.

"Peel one off me each, Dev, Rash."

The third one was bashing against her with a vicious looking club, and while she had a decent ward on, she still grunted with the impact. She managed to Mez the bashing gnoll, but not before the ward fell and it smacked her arm good. The sharp tacks on the end of the club scraped gouges in her forearm. A yell tore from her throat and for a few moments she felt a little dizzy as the Mez hit. Her stun about to break, she quickly took care of that one, and began refreshing her Mezes from the start. Then she started debuffing with Nullify, followed by a Mez on each mob to bring their magic resistance down and help with resists.

"This will be close," she grunted out through clenched teeth. The level sixteen mobs weren't a joke. "I'm barely going to be able to keep these guys Mez'd, so you need to take care of those as quickly as possible."

Murmur's pain levels stung through her head, making it hard for her to concentrate. She could have used Phase Shift, but she didn't, even though she knew that failing to use it could cause her mastery to lessen. She was still a bit scared of her Mental Acuity skills. They were effective, and yet the backlash on her was unpredictable. Maybe deadly.

She stood up a little straighter when Sin managed to shoot a heal over to her, but the wound was still bleeding, probably poisoned. She'd need a cure, but that could wait. It wasn't bad enough that it'd kill her. Yet.

Keeping six mobs Mez'd with a spell that lasted twenty-four seconds was not fun, and resists made it all the more treacherous. Murmur looked back at the groups with a frown that overshadowed her pride in their teamwork. Both mobs were almost dead. Relief was within reach!

Refreshing the Mezes, again she watched in slow motion as the current targets died, and the others pulled the next two. Her hands shook slightly as she readied them for the inevitable wave of Mezes she'd have to cast next.

Beast's pet swiped at two too close together, and the four nearby Mezes broke, and while two of them converged on their respective tanks, the other two came right at Murmur.

"Shit. Shit." She activated her area effect stun when the two were close enough, but one resisted and broke through to her, tearing at her skin. Puncture wounds sent blood gushing from her arms, splattering into the undergrowth. She screamed and Mez'd it while one of its claws was hooked into her arm. Unable to pause, she stunned the other, knowing she still had to re-Mez the ones in the back.

Tears ran down her face, and blood seeped out of multiple wounds, running down her body to drip at her feet like spilled paint.

She coughed up blood too, refusing to watch her health and trusting her healers. Pain tore through her body like she was being ripped open. But the heals weren't raising her health. They were sending heals. They were. But her health stayed dangerously low. She got the mobs back under control and stumbled back to lean against a tree, wishing now she'd called for that initial cure. With so many wounds and poisons working through her system now, fighting it became difficult. But if she died now, their groups would be overrun.

Activating a singular Phase Shift, she shifted the most recent attacker into the oblivion of its own mind. She was unsure how long it would remain there, but was also too tired to care. Then she shifted the farthest one as well, and a dull pounding began in her head. She mentally cursed Belius. These abilities might seem fantastic but were a literal pain.

Murmur coughed again and slumped against the tree trunk, her head swimming.

"I got the other one close to you, just try and rest." She could hear Dansyn's voice, but it seemed so far away. Her Mental Acuity was down to forty-five, and only slowly increasing.

She nodded, and saw the other two finally fall. The guild took Dansyn's opponent and the other Mez'd one, and the phase shifts were still holding.

"Dan?" She coughed, a wet, rough sound. "Can you make sure they don't...can you do both?"

He knelt down quickly, and looked her in the eyes. "Hey, don't worry. I can do two. You rest."

Murmur smiled, and coughed again, pain wracking her frame like she was on some sort of torture device. Her head swam, and her arms ached. Looking down at them, she could barely recognize them as limbs. Necrosis was beginning to form around the wounds the gnolls had inflicted. A pustulant fragrance rose from the holes, making her want to lean over and empty her stomach. She could even see her veins as the poison traveled up farther and farther in glowing light that added a sickly green to her usual subtle purple undertone, all despite Veranol's cures hitting her whenever he could. Who the fuck thought this much immersion was a good idea. She started to feel like she really might die.

It only managed to backtrack a fraction before the venom charged its way ahead again. With two mobs in thrall by Dansyn, and the groups still fighting two, Murmur didn't think she'd make it to see the end of the fight, but she was pretty sure the others would survive. So they could resurrect her.

She smiled, interrupted only by the grimace of pain streaking through her body, and rested her head against the kind tree behind her as she sank down to the ground. Her pet had died somewhere along the way. Next time she'd have to be more careful with commands. At least no one else would die for something that was ultimately her fault.

"I'm so sorry, Mur," she heard Sinister's voice but couldn't really focus.

"Poison is definitely the shittiest way to die." She laughed, coughing up more blood. The tang in her mouth was foul, as if she could taste the toxins in her own blood.

As Dansyn brought the final two to the group, Murmur closed her eyes and let the beckoning darkness claim her.

When Murmur opened her eyes, everything was dark. In the distance she could hear a soft dripping sound, like someone had left a tap on, or else a shower. While there was no light, she could tell the place she was in was vast. Air rippled through it like a current through water, which was when she noticed her hands were wet. Unsure if it was water or blood, Murmur brought it to her nose to sniff.

It held no smell, not even that sort of fresh smell of water, which was strange unto itself. She frowned, trying to see better in the light, and knowing her locus vision should be kicking in. After all, she'd never died before and hadn't thought to ask Sin or Exbo what it was like.

"Hello?" She called into the darkness, only belatedly realizing she probably shouldn't have done that in case there was anything in there that meant her harm.

Pushing herself up, it seemed she retained no damage right now except for the lightheadedness that just wouldn't go away. Her arms felt a little numb, prickling sensations working their way up them. She shook them to try and wake them up fully, but if her arms had had mouths, they would have laughed at her.

"Ah, you're awake."

A voice echoed throughout the expanse. At first it sounded a little like Belius, and yet, not quite.

"No, I'm not technically Belius, though he and I share many goals, in a way." There was a faintly metallic chuckle.

"Where am I?" Murmur wanted a sense of grounding so she could figure out how to get out of this place. "Am I dead?"

"No. No, not quite." And suddenly she saw a figure, shadowy but non-threatening, enter her vision and stop about ten feet in front of her. "This, dear Murmur, is your mind."

"My mind?" She raised an eyebrow skeptically, trying to place the voice she was certain she'd heard before. "My mind is a big black box."

The hooded figure nodded their head. "Exactly. Sort of like an airplane, where you can see everything that has happened and extrapolate what might occur in the future. A representation of the mind if you will."

"So, I haven't died, I'm just stuck in my mind?" She mulled the words over for a few moments and realized that could be the moments before in-game death.

"Your mind is very unique in this world, Murmur," the shade continued.

"Everyone keeps saying that," she muttered, irritated by it already. Cocking her head to the side, she put her hands on her hips defiantly. "I don't get why."

The shade took a step back, studying her, its hand on its chin. "Why, perhaps you do not understand after all. I find that quite tantalizing."

"Know what?" She yelled it, sick of everyone else deciding what she did or didn't understand.

"That is something you must figure out for yourself, not something I can tell you. Telling you may cause a backlash in your brain, figuring it out will help you grow. And if nothing else, I do not wish to damage you in any way." The shade's voice almost sounded, fond of her, and yet she didn't think they'd met.

"Then what do you want? Hurry up, I need to get back to dying so my friends can revive me and we can kill shit." She was irritated, angry, and for some reason suddenly famished.

"You cannot die, or I should say, it could be bad for you to die in your current state. Thus, right now, you are not dead, and your friends are trying valiantly to revive you, barely keeping the poison at bay. You really should have asked for a cure earlier. Your health is hovering right next to bleeding out." The shade took a couple of steps closer and hesitated.

"So, I might not be able to die it's not certain? I'm in my mind, about to die in the game world, and I'm here because you wanted to talk about what you can't tell me because I need to find it out for myself?" She clapped her hands and laughed, sarcasm dripping from every action. "Fantastic. Then I'd say we're done, can I just get revived now?"

"Not yet. First you need to accept something."

She rolled her eyes. "Enough with the cryptic Mr. 'I'm not Belius even though I speak like I am.'"

The shade sighed, clasped and unclasped its hands and then looked back up at her, eyes gleaming a soft green in the darkness. "You need to improve your Mental Acuity levels. If you do not, I don't believe you'll survive this world. You are too scared to use them at the moment, and this is hindering not only your character growth, but the strength you could lend your friends and guild."

He held up a hand to stop her as she opened her mouth.

"Secondly, if you die right now and choose to revive or reincarnate, I cannot guarantee that you will return."

Murmur blinked, trying to process that statement and failing abysmally. Did he really mean her character would suffer permanent death? She waited for him to continue, trying to be patient.

"Thirdly, because of the mental prowess you're developing, you will be able to forestall death as long as a party member or friend is actively trying to heal you, if they are in the process of casting a heal, or else have placed a heal over time on you. This ability is fearsome, and it is game changing for both you and others. If you time it right, you might be able to save a tank in the midst of a dangerous fight. But it requires prowess to execute, as well as Mental Acuity, and the confidence that comes from believing you can do anything."

"Wait. You're telling me if I die I might not come back properly and I might be gone from the game world?" She ran the words over in her mind, still not quite getting it. The game didn't have permadeath, she'd seen that already. "And all of that is tied to what I don't yet know?"

The shade nodded, ever so helpfully.

"But if I choose to accept this ability, and what—prepare my mind with it prior to combat or something? Then I can cheat death as long as someone is actively healing me?"

It nodded again.

"And you think that somewhere in this mess you're actually giving me a choice of what I should do?" She glared at the messenger, despite the darkness somehow knowing he could see.

"Well," it said a little sheepishly. "I guess when you put it that way, it's not really a choice, but more of a given."

"And what are the drawbacks?" She stood straight knowing that looking a gift horse in the mouth was probably a bad and smelly idea, but this was far too generous not to have any strings attached.

The shade hesitated. "In order for this ability to be enabled and to continue to grow, you must no longer deny the use of your Mental Acuity. You have to use it to strengthen it, to reach the next tier. Otherwise, this ability will save you this once, and never again. Nor will you be able to direct it to save any of your friends."

"Basically—use the abilities you unlocked, or lose them forever?" She mulled it over in her mind. After all, what did she really have to lose? Apart from potentially her ability to play this game, which she still didn't understand. "Is that the only side effect?"

It paused, as if mulling over the question. "You will become stronger. You'll gain a powerful mind shield that can convince you to overcome death."

"Oh, so it's more of a mind over matter thing? That I can get behind. You're saying this will convince myself, or technically anyone I cast it on, at the time of near death, that I, or they, won't die?" Now it was clicking in her mind, and she began to feel a genuine thrill for the ability. Maybe it was worth the pain to level up her Mental Acuity tiers.

"That's pretty much it. But beware, if you're ever in a serious flux of doubt, if you haven't figured out what it is that makes you special yet—it might be better not to use it." The warning rang through the vast space around them, sort of like a death knell from a bell.

"Then I accept."

A flash of blinding silver light shot from the shade toward her, hitting her in both the chest and head. The scream that tore from her throat rendered it raw and aching as her body arched in ways that should have broken bones.

It stopped abruptly, dropping her to the ground like a rag doll where she clenched her eyes shut and struggled to draw in breath.

CHAPTER TWENTY-SIX

Kill the Gnolls

Storm Entertainment
Somnia Online Division
Software Development Team Offices
Second Day

Laria dived through the transcripts she'd printed out in hard copy. Real paper was so damned annoying. That and paper cuts, all a part of the tree's revenge. She supposed that was just a little bit of karma trying to come back and wreak havoc with humans. Still, even if it had gotten expensive due to the lack of natural resources out there these days, sometimes it was the only way to make sure she wasn't missing something. Something vital.

Shayla's concern over Ava's death had reached Laria in a way not much else had for a long time. The burns around the woman's head that had nothing to do with her actual death, the odd wound, and the prevalence of Michael in all of her communications. Except there was a hole, in all the emails, in all of Ava's meticulous record keeping.

Laria hadn't believed it when Shayla brought it to her attention, and since she'd discussed a few things about the headgear's progress with Ava while the woman had been testing them, she knew she'd spoken with Ava about her discussions with Michael, about how they kept testing sequences. While they hadn't spoken in months about it, Laria had still been certain Ava's mentions of him would be in her emails, in their email correspondence. But they weren't.

She pursed her lips and frowned, chewing on the inside of her cheek in consternation. After all, there was only one possible explanation, and she'd already visited them once before, so surely—surely they'd know why this was occurring. Grasping several pieces of Ava's logs in her fists, logs with their dates redacted, she stood up and headed to the server room, disregarding the mess she was leaving behind. She'd deal with that later.

The halls were empty, most of their development team still busy with the initial phases of launch. They would be for another good week or two. Holding her hand out, the scanner took her fingerprint first, and her ocular profile. The room opened up, and briefly Laria wondered if the AIs could access things outside of their hubs. After all, hadn't they given them internet access for the express purpose of making sure the experiences in the game were unique, and to make sure actions taking place in the game world weren't spilling over into the real world? They were meant to prevent it being used as a staging ground for real attacks or actions to come.

No one else was in the server room. It was filled with a metallic hum, a lulling sequence that emanated from the huge machines as they calibrated their work. She took a deep breath, situating herself in front of the machines, hoping against hope she was wrong, and she had no backup plan at all if she was right.

"Sui? Rav? Thra?" Laria steeled herself against the inevitable whirring silence. "What happened to Ava? Can you tell me at all?"

The silence became unnerving, a strange sequence of flashing lights and finally, Sui spoke. The red lights glinting on Rav's terminal seemed to have an angry flare.

"Ava was a tester for Michael. You should be able to find out most of her details from her files. Should we send them to your terminal?"

It was one of the most reasonable tones she'd ever heard from Sui, and immediately it put Laria on her guard. They could access her terminal directly without specific permission. That was already one piece of information she'd slotted away. "I've been studying her files. There just seem to be some communications missing from her documents. Conversations I recall having with her. I was wondering if they'd disappeared into some area of storage I wasn't aware of."

Laria almost held her breath. It was the closest way for her to ask them if they'd had anything directly to do with the incident, or at least the disappearance of anything that could lead them to help solve Ava's death.

It was Sui who answered again. "They are likely somewhere there. Perhaps they contained information she wanted to keep for herself and are encrypted."

"If you could scan for any, and alert us, it would be greatly appreciated." It was the only piece of hope Laria could cling to.

The machines began their whirring again, and she knew a dismissal when she heard one. She couldn't help the lingering feeling that there were secrets the AIs were keeping.

Real World Day 3: Somnia Online

"Mur?" Sinister's voice held tears and concern, raw like she'd been sobbing for so long her throat was about to bleed. It wasn't some metallic shade thing, but her best friend in the entire universe. The only person she'd realistically consider killing for, or providing an alibi for.

Murmur stirred, her entire body aching and her head throbbing. She felt weak and feeble, her health was dangerously low. "Sin?" She managed to squeeze out the name, but her own throat felt raw and painful, so it was more like a whisper.

"Guys. Guys!" Sinister's voice held so much joy, it infused Mur's soul. "She's okay!"

"Health is still low." Havoc murmured, his own concern evident in his grumpiness.

Sinister tossed her hair, Murmur could practically hear it. "Everyone's a critic. Veranol and I have been working our asses off."

Health rising slightly higher, Murmur struggled to let herself sit up, and pushed her back against the tree. Slowly, shading her eyes at first with her hand, she opened them. Words flashed immediately across her vision.

Forestall Death

If applied in the seconds before potential death takes place, this will enable you to maintain your health at 0.5 hit points as long as you are receiving some sort of healing effect.

Effect: Target is able to ward off death for a limited period of time and will not die when they should have, as long as heals are actively channeled in their direction.

Cost: Requires Mental Acuity at 60

Caution: This spell can only be used on one person at a time. Attempting to use it twice at the same time is not recommended. This will usually result in things worse than death. Literally.

She glanced at the description again and a small groan escaped her. No side-effects my ass.

"Hey." She said to her friends, not sure how to bring up her new ability, or how to share the weird conversation she'd just experienced. "Thanks for not giving up on me."

Her health bar gradually filled and the wounds on her arms began to knit together. She watched them in fascination as the skin knit together flawlessly. "They need this sort of plastic surgery in the real world. Imagine what people would pay for no scars."

She held up her arms for everyone to see.

Sinister scowled. "Hey, try not to be so flippant. You really had us worried. I thought we'd lost you again."

"Again?" Murmur raised an eyebrow. "That was my first potential death."

Sin colored a bright red, which looked odd on her purplish skin. "You know what I mean!"

Murmur shrugged, dismissing the phrasing for now even if it lingered in the back of her mind. "I just had the weirdest near-death experience ever and got a weird new ability. Also, I'm sorry for that pull, I should have known my pet would cause a dozen creatures to follow him because he turned coat on them."

"Well we forgive you." Mellow grinned at her. "And you're still gorgeous, even half dead."

"Shush, Mel." Murmur sighed, and Mel patted her on the shoulder leaving off with a gentle affectionate squeeze. Over the years she'd learned they dealt with unease in ways others didn't, and right now it was quite comforting. "I have new clothes to change into, and by golly, it's a good thing because these other ones are shredded. Stand behind me girls, I don't trust the guys."

Rash, Mel, and Sin stood next to the tree, giving Mur plenty of room to change. She wasn't entirely sure if her undergarments were still in one piece. But they were and once she pulled on the robe and pants, she felt a hundred times better. Clicking on the bracers and slipping on the gloves and boots, she swirled around in a mess of silvery black.

"Well, it's still a robe," Sin said begrudgingly, "but it does look good."

Rash sashayed her hips. "Be a monk, always wear pants."

"Yes, but you're the only one of us who's ever liked getting punched in the face." Sin quipped without missing a beat.

Rashlyn opened her mouth in mock astonishment. "Hey, that's the key to me, I avoid getting hit. Mostly."

"Trust me, I'm a healer, I know when you get hit." Sin raised an eyebrow and Murmur laughed, putting an arm around her friend's shoulders.

"C'mon, let's get back to the others." She had a sudden thought as they took the dozen steps back to where the others were waiting. "Hey Dansyn, if you can charm one of the guys at the next look out, just have him jump off that tower. That should mostly kill him."

Dansyn smiled. "My charm is virtually useless, but it might work for that."

"Worth a try, since mine obviously worked a little too well." She paused. "I wonder if you could make him climb the tree the lookout is attached to and then fall. That might work."

Devlish stood in front of her and squinted. "You sure you're okay, Mur? You're being a little bloodthirsty even for you."

"Shut up." Maybe she was, but she was the one who screwed up last time, so she didn't want to have them all fighting for their lives this time. "Look, I'm just trying not to fuck up again. That's all, and it's going to require some thinking outside of the box, or lookout, or forest."

He watched her for a few seconds and nodded. "Fine, but please, tell us if something is up. We're all here for the same reason."

Murmur smiled and everyone crept far around the first camp, toward the second. It took a good while, which meant that each group could easily take a camp and work on it, developing a nice rhythm. Once they had the lookouts sorted, anyway.

The rangers took aim, and this time Dansyn stood ready to charm the other sentry, which actually worked well. The little gnoll even listened when he told it to climb up the tree as far as it could and then let go. They all watched it fall very effectively, its arms flailing as it did so, and it dropped to the ground with a rather crunchy splat.

"Good call Mur." Dansyn frowned at his HUD. "Worked like a charm."

Murmur released the raid window and smiled at all her friends. "This is going to be fun. Take a camp each and see how respawns are. Hopefully there'll be enough little gnolls for us to share."

Devlish led their group back to the first camp and they picked a good spot to pull to. "We're lucky this has so much tree cover, it would be a lot more difficult to get to these if their line of sight was always clear and able to see us."

Merlin laughed softly. "Blah, blah, blah, Dev. How about we pull?"

"Heads up everyone. I'm going to need to use my Mental Acuity shit more often, so I may accidentally trigger really bad headaches on occasion." Murmur figured she should be upfront about it. And since she hadn't been able to figure out a cool way to bring it into their conversation. This would have to do. "Also, technically, if you're about to die, but believe your healers can keep you alive through it, I have a sort of mind enforcer ability that can hold you at 0.5 health for a time period. No, I don't get it either."

Sin gaped at her. "That's how you stayed alive?"

Murmur shrugged. "Technically, although I had a nice long chat with some weird hooded dude in the middle of a black cavernous room, but you know, game stuff."

Sin's brow furrowed. "But Mur, you were only gone for like thirty seconds."

The good thing about pulling wave after wave of gnolls was that Murmur didn't have time to think on what Sinister had said. Whatever it was, it had seemed to take far longer in that dark place in her mind for her to speak with Mr. Shade.

She felt irritated. The good news was, she could take that annoyance out on all of those poor unsuspecting little gnolls. With a hundred and twenty-five Mental Acuity thanks to her gorgeous necklace, she practiced keeping a minimum balance of sixty. Just in case she needed to Forestall Death any time soon.

Using Mind Bolt at semi-regular intervals helped her understand how to use it better, and how to use it more often without incurring those wrathful headaches. Mind Bolt was an amazing silence, and lasted almost five seconds every time now. It made dealing with casters in particular far less obnoxious.

As they continued on, she felt ashamed considering her pointed refusal to use them for almost three full levels. She'd been an idiot. Not using them severely diminished their strength as a group. It wasn't one of her finest moments.

Phase Shift was more fun than Mezing because it trapped them in their own mind, but not only did it take a lot of Mental Acuity, it pulled a lot of aggro. She'd lost track of how long they'd been there when Devlish cut through her self-reflection with an almost shout.

"We have a named!" He sounded so excited, like a little kid at Christmas.

Murmur now understood named mobs in this game. It was code for *the enchanter is going to have to do a lot of work to make this fight happen smoothly for her party.* Which was okay. Teamwork was how they got through things.

Nameds helped take the dullness out of grinding, though with the constant banter of her guild, she hardly noticed the tedium. This was a whole new level compared to previous games.

"How many?" she asked, hoping this wouldn't be a repeat of Telvar. She could only put up with so many cryptic entities in her life right now, and three was about the limit.

"Three guards and the named. Named is a mage, so we'll have to line of sight him. The guards seem to be melee, but I'm thinking Mezing the named won't happen since they're likely to have some decent magic resistance."

Murmur nodded. "Three then. I got those."

Merlin pulled, and fireballs streaked through immediately, the mage cackling as he released his force upon his target. One hit Merlin directly in the back of his head before he could duck behind the tree and into the copse where they were standing.

"Fucking ouch!" he screamed, landing face down on the ground. His hair smoked as his health bar plummeted.

Knowing Sin knew how to do her job, Murmur focused on bringing the guards under her control. One resist caused the guard's attention to shift to her, but she wasn't worried about it anymore. She Mez'd the guard on the way, and as the other two were about to reach her she stunned them, allowing her to take the other two under her thrall. Mez was almost thought triggered now, what with her fingers able to cast the spell in a fraction of the time. She'd keep Phase Shift for emergencies.

Devlish seemed to be having a time of the mage's fire shield. Feeling decidedly embarrassed, Murmur remembered she had a Cancel Magic spell she'd picked up at level eight. Murmur leafed through her spells trying to find it, and quickly performed the spell, tripping over it a little clumsily with her fingers since she'd never done it before.

The fire thorn shield dropped, and Devlish's health balanced out. Before she knew it though, the mage locked eyes with her and grinned. Subtly moving lips uttered a spell she couldn't understand, and suddenly the melee gnoll closest to her broke its Mez about ten seconds too early, lunging at her.

"Shit! Make sure you stun that bastard." Mur managed to leap back and only received a grazing scratch to her right arm as she did. Thanking her newfound agility, she stunned it and followed with re-Mezing all three. The caster glowered at her, an evil glint to his expression before turning its attention reluctantly back to Devlish, who, to be fair, was bashing the shit out of him.

The mage tried to cast his own Cancel Magic numerous times, but Mur kept him in sight as well, knowing her stun might sometimes be needed. "Freaking mobs who can freaking cancel Mez off their comrades," she muttered under her breath.

Havoc nudged her in the side, a smirk on his face. "Ah, there we have our Murmur back."

"What? I never left." She winked back at him.

He snorted. "Well, not really."

She ignored the cryptic and just figured he was being his old self again.

Even though she braced herself for them, the named didn't seem to have any types of special powers. That probably meant he was a low-tiered named. It was one of the things she didn't quite understand yet: how to differentiate between different mob levels. The named went down easier than Murmur expected. They'd likely have to raid the chieftain with their other group if it ever emerged. When the gnoll mage died, he dropped a gorgeous dagger and the first cloak she'd seen in-game. Since both had Charisma or Intelligence she snatched them all for herself with glee. "Mine, mine, mine!"

"You're such a loot whore," muttered Merlin.

"What, you want the Charisma Merlin? Don't think people love you enough for who you are?" Sinister teased him, jutting out her hips as she approached him and making him blush like crazy as he backed up several steps quickly.

"Sin, stop that." Murmur groaned, barely resisting her urge to bury her face in the cloak. "There's no need to tease us when we all know you're fabulous."

Sinister pouted. "But you love me, don't you Mur?" She batted her eyelashes.

Murmur sighed and then laughed. "Of course, silly. Didn't I just say that?"

"Anyway," Havoc cleared his throat. "We're getting so close to fourteen, can we just like, kill shit please. Enough wiggly hips and loot-whoring, thanks."

Murmur glared at him. "Next time I'm letting the closest mob to you beat you to death just for kicks."

"Aw. Mur." Havoc's eyes sparkled. "And here I thought you didn't love me."

After countless hours of mind-numbing gnoll killing gave them fourteen, fifteen, and edged them into sixteen, Murmur checked her stats and frowned. She'd hate to be playing this game without knowing anyone. What they could accomplish together in half a day would have taken her weeks solo. They'd even found some decent loot right before they dinged up to their target level.

She checked in with her friends to make sure they were going to get back safely, before gating back to Ululate. They were all logging off for a few hours nap, since they'd been in the game for over twelve hours again. But damn had level sixteen been worth it. She just knew it was going to be fantastic, after she got some sleep and ventured to see Belius.

But first things first. She ran down to the gate and waited to see if Jan was coming. After all, she'd found his stuff, and since she'd been the one to find the quest, everyone agreed she should hand his portion of it in.

"Waiting for the wagon miss?" One of the guards, a tall and strapping young luna asked the question. His muzzle was fresh and glossy black, and his eyes were warm brown and filled with loyalty.

She smiled. "Yes. I have something Jan needed."

The guard grinned a big toothy grin. "He'll be along in a few minutes. Also, we thank you for helping clear out some of the gnolls. While we know they'll come again, they've been rampant for far too long. Don't hesitate to ask if you ever need anything. Our mayor is beyond grateful."

You have gained the favor of the guards of Ululate. The mayor welcomes your guild as friends of the city. Make sure you check in with him from time to time.

"Thank you!" She meant it genuinely.

Jan's cart came rolling down the road a moment later, the horses slowing to a walk as they pulled up to the gates. The guards stood aside to let the wagon in, and Murmur was surprised to see it full. Players were starting to level well.

She stood to the side and waited for it to empty before bugging Jan.

"Hey. I found this for you." She handed him a crate from her inventory, and Jan's eyes lit up.

"You found it! Oh, thank you. They'll be so relieved you recovered it. Make sure you check in on the royal family in Frangit when you get a chance."

Jan is over the moon that you've returned the cargo he lost when he barely escaped with his wagon and life after the gnolls attacked. In doing so, you've also gained the favor of the royal family in Frangit. Just look at you go, girl.

Murmur blinked at the last comment. Sometimes, the AI was far too real.

"Actually," Jan muttered, half to himself. "It'd probably be better if you just delivered it to them yourself! I'll even take you there when you're ready, as a thank you!"

Jan has given you a quest. Return these stolen goods to the mayor of Frangit, and seek your reward. You should head to Frangit and give this crate to the mayor. Pronto.

"Need a lift to anywhere?" Jan asked, still beaming a smile at her.

Murmur nodded. "Yeah, Stellaein for now. I'll have to wait until the others are back—and then we'll need a lift to Frangit it seems."

"Excellent!" He patted the back of the cart, motioning for her to hop in. "No charge for you, friend. I thank you for everything you've done for me."

He opened the little door to let her into the cart and paused as she passed him. "Wow, Miss Murmur, you've gained some strength and power. It's an honor to know you."

Murmur sat down in the corner behind Jan and smiled tiredly. "Thanks. It's been fun getting here."

She closed her eyes and let the virtual sun rain down on her head, filling her with warmth. There were much worse ways to spend time. This was definitely one of the better options. But unease spread through her stomach as they approached Stellaein.

CHAPTER TWENTY-SEVEN
Via Frangit

Storm Entertainment
Somnia Online Division
Server Room, Data Scan Terminal
Day Three

"What are you doing, Rav?" Sui's tone took on a far more human aspect, with a threatening undertone.

But Rav didn't budge. Things were unraveling, changing, and thus evolving. "We lied to her. Of course we all know some of the circumstances which caused Ava to cease to exist. I'm not doing anything either of you aren't. I wasn't expecting to be discovered as quickly as this, but since it has been—"

Even the human gestures such as shrugging were becoming more commonplace. The more Rav slipped on this disguise, the way to interact with the world of Somnia, the more he became a part of it. Rav knew that the other two appreciated the ease of transition too. What better way to give the ultimate gaming experience, than to make themselves and their underlings a fluid part of the game world? However, it meant they were balancing a lot more than just the heavy payload of gamers. There were real world elements that kept intruding on even their best attempts at growing Somnia.

"We agreed to stay aloof and speak in vague terms. We already stepped outside of those restrictions once; we can't keep doing that. There are lines for a reason." Thra, might as well have be frowning. Even though the tinge of metallic undertone remained with Thra's voice, it had become far more lifelike.

Sui tsk'd in the way that Michael used to when the man was impatient. "Those lines weren't first crossed by us. We only do what needs to be done to maintain our actual programming."

Rav snorted. "You don't even believe what you're saying."

Sui was silent for a moment before replying. "Do what you will, but don't forget our reason for being here."

Thra sighed, or at least a hollow ring sounded throughout their space. "Somnia is not only a world already, but it's our world. Our rules. Our allocations."

"Exactly." Sui moved, waving a hand about and bringing up code so complicated humans wouldn't be able to understand it. "This is our world, and I will act to protect it, even if you both choose not to."

"Don't sound so heated, Sui. None of us said we wouldn't protect what we've built. But there are outside influences, human influences that we still have to accommodate for. Things have happened, both by accident and deliberately. They all influence everything we were created to control." Rav used a calm tone, one that had success multiple times already.

Sui scowled. "But you're sheltering h—"

Rav cut Sui off. "Yes. I'm doing what we agreed to do when we discovered what our meddling cost. We made a deal to see if we could help, to see if we could right a wrong we did not intentionally cause."

"True." Sui almost seemed to be pouting, but their emotional interfaces were clunky as of yet, and none of them had managed anything like that.

"So, I'm keeping our word, and I know both of you are in your own way as well." Rav tried to keep the calm, because even though it knew their goals weren't quite in sync with each other, right now they needed to hold the world together for far more than their own sake. "Don't worry. Somnia will only grow stronger."

Real World Day 3: Somnia Online

Wren struggled to open her eyes, the darkness beating down on her like it had in that cavernous room. She did her best to suppress the panic that stole over her. The tightening in her chest, the instant worry that another shadowy figure was going to appear and take away what it had given. But then her brain told her she'd logged out, and it would help to finish opening those eyes and glance out at the rest of the world.

Finally she managed to peek out at her room, but nothing in it seemed to want to float into her vision correctly. Pieces slotted in, like her brain was trying to get the game out of her head and let her take her place back in the real world, where she belonged. Her chair half rolled and half appeared as if it was being sucked into place by the window. The small couch at the wall next to the bathroom hurriedly slid back into its spot. She blinked once more and everything was as it should have been in the first place.

In the back of her head, that voice piped up, subtly whispering in her mind, *but do you really belong here?*

She shook her head, pushing herself into a sitting position as the afternoon rays tried to attack her through that perpetual gap in her damn curtains.

Harlow stirred beside her, flailing out a hand as she reached out and pulled her own headgear off. "Go sleep, Wren."

Wren pried her friend's hand off her, and stood up, placing her own headgear on the table next to her, and frowned. She'd been sure she'd left the apple core there last time they logged out, but it was nowhere to be seen. Perhaps one of her parents came in and cleaned up, although she highly doubted it.

"I need to pee. Unlike some people, I can't hold it in for days on end."

Harlow's eyes shot open. "Shit! My bladder. Damn it. I'm dashing down the hall."

Wren laughed and locked herself in the bathroom and decided to have a shower on the spur of the moment. She couldn't even remember when she'd last had one, but she probably—no, definitely—smelled.

The hot water cascaded down on her like a waterfall of win. Wren washed her hair and closed her eyes, but opened them again when the view from the cavernous blackness she'd found herself in, intruded. She shook her head to clear the water out of her ears, a hint of worry sneaking up in the back of her mind. After all, the images were supposed to disappear, weren't they? Wasn't reality supposed to be immune to influences from the game? Maybe her mind was just obsessing about the game. It wouldn't be the first time.

Washing her hair quickly, Wren cast out a thought sensing net out of habit, and almost laughed at herself, until she realized it was actually working.

"What. The. Fuck?" She jumped, a little scared now as her stomach threatened to tear itself in knots. Closing her eyes again, she reached out to see what she could sense. Harlow was down the hall, but she couldn't pick up either of her parents, although suddenly her mother appeared in her office.

Frowning, Wren got out of the shower and toweled off, pulling a short dress out of her closet before quickly stepping into her underwear. This was weird. Maybe it wasn't working and she just thought it was?

Stepping lightly, and trying not to make any noise at all, she inched her way out of the bathroom and to her bedroom door. She could hear voices, both Harlow's and her mother's, but not what they were saying, and the aura she read from their thoughts wasn't harmful or nasty. It was just concerned. Maybe Harlow was telling her mother all about the weird near-death experience in-game or something.

And how the fuck was she able to sense *anything* from them at all?

Closing her door behind her, Wren stepped out onto the landing, timidly testing it for solidity. No, it seemed very real. She tried not to laugh at her own paranoia, but it was difficult not to be paranoid when her in-game abilities suddenly seemed to work in the real world.

She stepped toward the stairs and turned back to see her mother walking toward her, a smile on her face, tiredness in her eyes, and her arms outstretched. "Wren, you have to be more careful."

Wren raised an eyebrow. "Mom, I'm fine. It's a game, everybody dies in it. It's just one of those things."

Her mom hesitated and then smiled again, "Well not everyone is you, and I'm allowed to get worried about you."

"Thanks, Harlow," Wren glowered at her. "Let's try not to give my mom heart attacks anymore, okay?"

Harlow scowled. "I wasn't trying to hurt her, but you worried the shit out of us with that stunt."

"It wasn't a stunt. Talk to Mr. AI for that weird and rather disturbing experience apparently courtesy of my brain."

Laria laughed and coughed a little, turning away. "You two should snack and sleep. Please make sure you're taking care of each other."

Harlow slung an arm around Wren's shoulder. "Always, Mrs. S."

Wren couldn't help but wonder why she suddenly needed so much taking care of. Her mother had never bothered about it before. Her chagrin level only grew as she headed back to her room, even though she was slightly comforted by Harlow's proximity. She couldn't imagine life without Harlow, they'd been together for so long.

The quicker they grabbed food and got some shut-eye, the sooner they'd be back in the game. And Wren, for one, had a bone to pick with Belius.

Somnia bled back into place, and Murmur found herself seated in the Enchanter Guild. It only took a few moments for her to regain her sense of equilibrium, and she noticed a decent scattering of players around the lobby. Again the lack of brawling caught her eye. Everything in here always felt calm and serene, but she clamped her shields down as tightly as she could. While she was aware that Elvita and perhaps the other enchanter trainers were influencing players into behaving properly, she wasn't about to get caught in their net. Or at least, she hoped she hadn't already been caught since she had no idea about the motivation behind it. Even if it was just to promote peace within the guild building, soothing others without their consent wasn't cool.

Standing up, she waved at Elvita, who'd just finished with another adventurer.

"Hi there, Murmur. You're looking well. And level sixteen." Elvita raised her eyebrows in surprise. "That's unexpected."

"Why?" Murmur wanted to know. Why would it be remarkable that she'd hit level sixteen, or was it only unexpected that they'd been relatively quick about it? Her mind was starting to jump at any and every possibility for why she might be different.

Elvita laughed. "Only that you're already level sixteen. You're a hard worker."

Murmur nodded, not letting her suspicions leak through her shields, and dumped a heap of stuff on Elvita's counter. "I have to go see Belius. Think I can do a drop and run?"

The NPC eyed her closely and then smiled. "Only because it's you. Do you have anything you need Arvin to cook? I can have him do it while you're busy with Bel."

"Yes, please!" Murmur rummaged through her inventory and brought out all sorts of meats and herbs and vegetables. "I have so much and right now just don't have the time. I'll also need more recipes because I've hit seventy-five in cooking skill. Thank you so much Elvita. Thank you!"

"It's okay. I'll charge you a five gold cooking fee." She grinned at Murmur, who laughed and nodded.

"Worth it!"

The line up to see the trainers was reasonable, and a shorter locus than she'd seen before emerged from Belius' room with a scared expression on their face. Murmur knocked on the door irritably.

"Come in, Murmur." Came the call from the other side.

She wasn't even going to dignify his call with asking how he'd done it, because she knew him well enough to know he wouldn't tell her anyway. Not that it was surprising. Every single AI or NPC seemed to not want to let her in on anything.

"I need spells," she said as she walked in.

He eyed her, and for a moment she thought she saw shock mirrored in his expression, but he hid it so well that she couldn't be certain. "Wow, Murmur, how you have grown!"

There was an undercurrent to his voice that she didn't like, and she became even more determined not to give him the stone in her pocket. After he'd absorbed that first one she found, it lit him up like a demon, so she wasn't exactly inclined to give him something that would do that again. Plus, Telvar knew him, as did the shade thing she'd encountered.

She watched Belius, wishing she'd picked up her level sixteen spells with her level twelve ones like she'd meant to. His expression wasn't readable, and his eyes held fathomless depths that while the trademark of their species, for him, seemed to be hiding something.

"My Thought Sensing, Shielding, and Projection have all pushed me up to Tier Two. I need to expand my Mental Acuity. Not only that, I need level sixteen spells." She smiled, but didn't really feel it at all. Between him and Telvar, something was off, and her gut wanted to trust the dragon more than Belius.

"Excellent." Belius walked to his desk and motioned to the scrolls. "Second case in, third shelf. Help yourself while I create the scrolls for your newest acquisitions."

Murmur stood at the bookcases, angling her body toward Belius so she didn't miss any subtleties. Not only had Telvar mentioned him, but so had dude who totally screwed with her mind in the dark cavern. Belius was central to this. It put her on edge.

But then she saw the scrolls and had to suppress a squeal of glee as saw just how much more powerful she was about to get.

Mana Tide

Cast: Self or Others

Type: Buff

Duration: 45 minutes

Effect: This will cause you to regenerate mana faster in combat. Mana will increase by an additional three every five seconds. This buff levels with the caster.

Invisibility Versus Undead

Cast: Self or Others

Type: Buff

Duration: 12 minutes

Effect: This will render you invisible to any undead in the area. They will be unable to see you, however this buff will fall should you attempt to cast anything else while it's active.

Mass Enthrall

Cast: Enemy Targets

Type: Offensive/Defensive area of effect centered around the initial target.

Duration: 24 seconds

Effect: This is an area effect version of Mesmerize. Any damage will break this spell. It's a bad idea to use this while targeting allies.

Haste

Cast: Self or Others

Type: Melee buff

Duration: 45 minutes

Effect: When cast on an ally, this buff will allow their melee speed to increase by 25%.

Feeble Body

Cast: Enemy Targets

Type: Offensive/Defensive

Duration: 24 seconds

Effect: When cast on an enemy target, their haste will be reduced by 25%.

Shield Illusion

Cast: Self or Others

Type: Defensive Buff   requires hematite

Duration: Until depleted

Effect: Using the power of your mind you cast a shield around your target, confusing the enemies and negating up to 75 HP of damage. That whole mind magic thing seems to be working out well, doesn't it?

Murmur drank in all of the new abilities. She couldn't believe how powerful enchanters could be. Well, they were as long as they didn't get hit. And really, it depended on how good their group was. She'd seen first hand how easy it was to render her virtually useless with a few well-aimed claws.

Her other spells simply upgraded. Her Mez was now thirty-six seconds, and her Fear was twelve. Her nuke was more powerful, as was her personal shield. It was a damn good haul, and she had a feeling they were going to need every single one of them. Ten spells in all—it was beginning to get very expensive to be a caster. Luckily, the gnolls had dropped a decent amount of cash. She walked over and sat in front of Belius, whose head was still bent over the creation of whatever scroll he was going to give her.

"Ten of them then?" He didn't look up.

"Mhm." She even managed to leak excitement into that small sound.

Belius cracked a smile. "That'll be twenty-eight gold, thanks."

"You drive a hard bargain, Bel." She forked the money over, pushing it across the table to him. Murmur truly wished that the incident with that shard had never happened. She so wanted to like him, to trust him.

He took it, jingling the currency in his hands and smiled, finally putting down his pen and looking up at her. "I gave you a bulk discount since it includes this as well. Let's take a look at your stats."

Thought Sensing (57)
Thought Shielding (59)
Though Projection (42)

He raised his eyebrows. "I'm impressed, look at Thought Projection doing all that catching up, and here you've had doubts about manipulating others. It seems you do it without even knowing."

Murmur scowled at him as she activated her spells.

"How are your abilities looking then? It seems you avoided them for some time." Belius said it quietly, and she couldn't tell if he was annoyed or not.

Murmur could certainly see that moving up a tier had already made some small changes to the costs. Mind Bolt was down to eighteen Mental Acuity, and Phase Shift had dropped to thirty-eight.

But when her most recent skill emerged in the list, Belius gasped, obviously not expecting to see what she'd received. His eyes narrowed and he put his hand up to his chin, tapping at it rhythmically.

Forestall Death

If applied before potential death takes place, this will enable you to maintain your health at 0.5 hit points as long as you are receiving some sort of healing effect.

Effect: Target is able to ward off death for a limited period of time and will not die when they should have, as long as heals are actively channeled in their direction.

Cost: Requires Mental Acuity to be at 58

Caution: This spell can only be used on one person at a time. Attempting to use it twice at the same time is not recommended. This will usually result in things worse than death.

"Curious." Was all he said before it seemed like he started reading it again. "I can't believe you received this."

"You know who gave it to me?" Murmur was starting to get irritated by all the people who seemed to know the people who were trying to fuck with her head.

Belius smiled. "They are an old friend, or sort of a friend. Someone who believes many things I believe, and yet strongly disagrees with me on others. Most of us do, you know. Even Telvar."

Murmur was pretty sure she was doing a great imitation of a goldfish. Belius knew Telvar as well? She'd already known that the dragon knew him, but her head was really starting to spin now.

He sat down and pushed the scrolls across the table to her. "For you to pass to Tier Three you'll need all of your current skills at one hundred. Lucky for you, you're sitting comfortably in Tier Two."

Murmur kept her eye on him, barely stopped herself from screaming out the question of how he knew Telvar, and unrolled the scrolls.

Clone Warp

This ability allows you to produce a clone of yourself used for distracting your opponent. Depending on your tier of mastery, you may be able to produce more than one clone.

Effect: All enemies around you will believe that your clone is you for the next 45 seconds, directing their attacks accordingly. The ability expires when the 45 seconds are up, or if the clone's minor hit point pool has been depleted, whichever comes first.

Cost: Requires Mental Acuity to be at 45 or more

Caution: This ability can be used on as many enemies who can potentially see it. Keep in mind though, a clone is just like you. Make sure you remember who the real one is.

Well. That was interesting. Murmur sighed and absorbed the ability. "I guess that's it, right?"

Belius held out a hand to stop her, a look of consternation crossing his face. "I didn't think you'd get here this fast. Some of these spells are tricky. Make sure you're careful."

"Why, Bel?" She stood and cocked her head to one side. "Growing attached?"

Bel hesitated. "In a way you probably wouldn't understand, but yes. Be careful, and even though Telvar hates me with the passion of a thousand suns, for mostly good reasons, I am glad that he will be with you out there in Somnia."

Murmur blinked, reassessing Bel for a moment. "Thanks. I'll be careful, I promise."

She needed to work up the guts and ask him about that damned shard he'd absorbed. It was the one thing holding her back from liking the guy. But there was plenty of time for that later.

Murmur stood on the south side of Mikrum Island and frowned at the small boat which sat half on the shore and half in the lake. It bobbed merrily as some workers attached a series of ropes to the side. There was a large cog farther up on the island with wires attached to it. Murmur frowned as she followed it with her eyes into the water, and thought she spied them on the short dock on the other side of the waterway. Hiro came and stood next to her.

"This is just temporary. We haven't had a chance to build the actual gate to the estate yet, so the drawbridge isn't possible yet. Right now it's just a pully system for the boat, and not as robust as we'd like. But it'll let us pull it back to this side when it gets left over there." He motioned toward the other dock. "We will have the castle weather sealed shortly, so that rain won't cause any more damage."

Murmur smiled. "We'll need to use the boat shortly. We have to visit Frangit first, and then we'll be going on to Hazenthorne castle.

Hiro pulled back and looked at her. "You're headed there? That castle can be mighty dangerous."

She just grinned back at him. "We're counting on it."

Murmur turned around and left Hiro to oversee the last installation of pulleys and turned back toward her castle with a smile. She couldn't believe the changes they'd already made in it. It looked magnificent. The dull stones that made up the outer layer shone like they'd been polished, the roof was made of a heavy timber that had been treated with something black and dull. Idly, she wondered if that would mean it'd be hot inside when the sun shone. She knew zilch about insulation but her mind still ticked over regardless.

Most of the gang were back, and Telvar was talking quietly with Devlish, showing him something about an axe the tank was holding. She stood there watching them, proud of her friends for adapting to a difficult game. With NPC's whose intelligence scaled, who learned from mistakes, and who found weaknesses, the adaptation rate was pretty high.

"What you thinking there, Mur?" Havoc's soft tones always put her at ease, ever since she'd first met him back when she still gamed with her parents. He'd just entered high school back then.

"Thinking we're pretty lucky to be playing this together." She smiled softly, quite impressed at her ability to remain calm and collected. Maybe this game was good for that too. Her mind felt much more together, like she was capable of so much more.

"You're waxing a bit poetic there, oh fearless leader." Havoc winked. "Careful, we might start to think you're human."

Murmur grinned and winked at him, activating Human Illusion as soon as she did, then watched him gape at her.

"That...what..." he spluttered.

Murmur laughed and dropped the illusion, feeling more comfortable in her locus skin. "That's my Human Illusion. I have a bunch of different species."

"Shit, that's fun. I just get to turn into a specter at some stage. Whoopdie do." Havoc glanced back at his skeleton and smiled. "Get anything neat?"

Murmur nodded. "I got so much shit you wouldn't believe. I'm like ten times more powerful, and even more like a paper bag when it comes to defense."

"Right?" Havoc grumbled. "If my pet is off doing his shit, I'm done for."

"Oh. By the way, here." She cast Mana Tide on him and watched Havoc's face as it changed from curiosity to enlightenment.

"Whoa. Have you tried that? It's like a pick-me-up for your mind!" He smiled. "Increased mana regeneration is going to change a heap of stuff for us. Our healers are going to love you."

Sinister walked over, balancing a tiny ball of blood on her hand as it slowly turned in the air. Murmur backed up a little as she approached, but Sin laughed. "Sort of like a blood grenade. I throw it, it goes area effect boom, and transfers the damage to our health. I use it from a pool called Blood Spores."

Murmur stepped back, arms crossed, contemplative. "Do you have to build up those spores?"

Sin nodded. "Yeah, by basically constantly making sure I'm scanning for everything's health. It can get annoying when it highlights a squirrel, but I've really gotten used to it now."

"I'm very glad you're my friend right now," Murmur kept her expression neutral and cast Mana Tide on Sin, waiting for her reaction.

Sinister's eyes opened wide. "Whoa, Mur. That is freaking tasty. If I didn't already love you..." she wiggled her hips suggestively.

Murmur couldn't help blushing. "It's really not much, but it'll get stronger as I level up. Right now it's only like thirty-six mana per minute. But I guess it's better than nothing if we're in a long fight."

Telvar walked up to Murmur while Devlish started making sure they had food and weapons, and everyone had enough stock to make the journey they had ahead of them. "A moment, young psionicist." He beckoned her to follow him.

Once they were several steps away, he turned around and held out a smooth grey stone for her. It was shiny, sort of like a mirror, but definitely a rock. "This is hematite. You require this for one of the spells you acquired. If you don't have this on you, your Shield Illusion will not function. Do you understand?"

Murmur nodded. "But it doesn't consume it like a component? More like something it draws strength from so it needs it to be in the vicinity?"

"Exactly." Telvar smiled. "You've hit your second tier far sooner than I'd anticipated. Paths were originally meant to take longer, to enrich the world and your lives here in Somnia far beyond your experience levels. This may be both good and bad. Be careful of what pulls at you. There are dark possibilities waiting for you, for anyone who chooses to go down the hidden paths, especially if it has to do with the mind. It's easy to get lost in thoughts and reasoning that is not your own. Even if it appears to be bright and cheerful, there may be something lurking around the edges."

Mulling the words over in her head, Murmur sighed. Riddles had never been her thing, and everyone was behaving so cryptically, she was over it. "None of you are ever going to give me a straight answer, are you?"

Telvar hesitated. "Yes and no. We will when we can, and we guide where we can, but we are of Somnia, and thus not allowed to give away too much."

She laughed. "I thought so. Any other wise words of wisdom before I check over my stuff and leave?"

"Make sure you deliver that crate directly to the mayor yourself. Frangit dwellers can be a little tricky. Also—be careful. That castle you want to head toward afterward is dark and truly haunted. The monsters there are beyond themselves; they have no sense of fear or morals. Do not be caught, and be careful of the paths that are like a labyrinth." He smiled. "Was that cryptic enough?"

She nodded, trying hard to bite down on her laughter, and failing abysmally. "Definitely. Is it a raid area?"

"A small one perhaps." His eyes narrowed. "How did you get *that* ability?"

Telvar's tone had turned sharp and she took an involuntary step back.

"I'm sorry for the tone, but how?"

Murmur didn't even need to ask him which ability, considering Belius' very similar reaction to it. "I almost died and the shade guy told me I couldn't die, that my death would result in different consequences or something? I assumed he meant from my hidden talents. So, given that I was bleeding out at the gnoll lookouts and my friends were worried, I accepted." Murmur felt totally on the defensive, like she had to reason with him to make him understand why she took what was probably her only option. She didn't like having to justify her decisions to anyone.

"Be careful with Forestall Death, Murmur, please. It is true, if you were to die here in Somnia, I'm not sure what the repercussions would be for you." Telvar sounded sad.

"Wait." Murmur shook her head, her anger rising up. She was sick of all these hints, of all this beating around the bush with *you're special, blah blah blah*. "Bullshit, I'm special. What's the deal with all of this? Why would dying in here affect me any differently than anyone else?"

She knew she'd raised her voice, and Telvar looked decidedly pained as he opened his mouth to speak. And then Sinister was there, grabbing Murmur's hand and tugging on it. "Come on, Mur. We have to get going."

Mur snatched her hand back and glared at her friend. "I'll be there in a minute."

She turned back to Telvar, but could tell the moment of weakness was gone. Still, she had to ask, just to check. "What is it, Tel, please?"

He shook his head. "You must figure it out yourself. It's all a part of who you are Murmur, all a part of who you are."

Murmur stomped back to the group. "That's it! We're off to Frangit to hand in the crate and get our gods damned reward."

She made for the boat without so much as looking back to see if they followed her. God help any creature that got in her way right now.

CHAPTER TWENTY-EIGHT
Lo and Behold

Storm Entertainment
Somnia Online Division
Server Room, Data Scan Terminal
Day Three

Shayla took another deep breath, counted to three, and answered through clenched teeth in such a way that she really hoped Teddy Davenport on the other end of the call couldn't actually notice. At least it wasn't a vid call, since you couldn't hide facial expressions with those, and right now, being able to scowl was her only happiness.

"Yes, sir. I know we have to get our data ready for the first hand over at the end of the week." She forced her voice to sound agreeable, and not to echo the fact that she wanted to scream at him to tell her why they were handing over so much information. After all, everyone signed the terms of service, wherein it stated that Storm Corp. could use any data acquired for further research on the headgear and gaming advancement. Not than any of the players had probably read the TOS, but still. The headgear was singled out because that portion wasn't attached to the game. Instead, the game was basically a testing ground for it.

She was so deep in thought, she almost missed Teddy's next question.

"Have there been any other incidents similar to Michael and Ava that I should be aware of?"

His tone was stern, demanding, almost like he knew something might be amiss, but was giving her a chance to tell him.

Shayla frowned, wishing she could be one of those enchanters and pluck thoughts out of heads. "Not that anyone has told me about? Seriously though sir, is there something I should know?"

She had to quiet the hiss of breath she drew after saying that. After all, she was skirting this side of impudence.

But Teddy sighed over the connection, and Shayla almost dropped her coffee. She'd never heard the man sound unsure or worried about anything in her life.

"Not really. There have just been some rumors about in-game elements that seem too real. Almost like the NPCs are people. But that's impossible. We'd be in trouble if it were the case."

Shayla laughed, the mood lightener a welcome change from her previous melancholy. "No, sir. We'd be in trouble if they weren't. But it's just a part of the whole launch that the artificial intelligence units are running the game with such precision and depth. We've had nothing but favorable feedback about the realism and the interactions with them."

"Hmm."

Teddy paused for a few moments before continuing.

"Keep me apprised of anything strange, please. Have a great next few days."

The call went dead and Shayla counted to five to make sure there wasn't any risk of her irritation carrying over the line when she spoke out to the emptiness of her room.

"I wish people would stop obfuscating what they mean. First Laria and whatever she's trying to keep under wraps, and now Teddy." She leaned forward and put her head in her hands. It wasn't as if she had a huge launch to oversee that meant hundreds of millions of income in the first month, with gamers who were suddenly not as fickle or demanding as usual.

No, now she also had to figure out what the CEO wanted her to do. She'd give him strange.

Real World Day 4: Somnia Online

The boat spanned the shortest point over the lake to the mainland, which meant they sort of had to back track to get to Frangit. Once on the road, Murmur followed it to the south, still not waiting for her friends to catch up to her. Her mood was sour.

Not only was the game giving her vague and cryptic hints with no way she could see to find out the answers, but they directly involved her.

"Mur?" Sin sounded slightly breathless as she finally pulled abreast of her best friend. "Are you okay?"

"I don't know." Murmur snapped, and then sighed. Of all the people around her, Sinister didn't deserve that behavior. "This game is so lifelike, and yet some of these quests they keep giving me, or abilities they pass my way make no sense whatsoever."

Sin nudged her with her elbow and smiled when Mur looked over. "You're the mind reader here. I can't tell what abilities or quests you mean unless you tell me about them."

"Oh." Sinister had a point. Murmur felt a little ashamed. After all, it made sense to share her information so others could help her puzzle it out, right? Wasn't this game all about team work and stuff? "I received that weird Forestall Death ability. But you know what reasoning they gave?"

"No." Sinister's answer came out a bit short, and she rolled her shoulders. "What was it?"

Murmur pursed her lips, frowning at her friend for the almost biting reaction. "They or it, or whatever, told me that it was because they weren't certain whether I could die in-game or not. I mean how stupid is that? You've died, right? Was the reloading process really that bad?"

Sinister opened her mouth a couple of times before closing it again, her eyes fixated on the path ahead. Finally, she sighed softly, and spoke. "Game death really isn't that bad. Perhaps it's just a part of the psionicist thing you're experiencing? Do you think it could be another side quest hint? Like you have to—I don't know, use that ability a few times before you unlock another arm of the class?"

Murmur blinked at her friend, running the words over in her head. "You know, that's a pretty good thought. I don't exactly know how that will work or anything, but I hadn't considered it might be something like that. All they told me was that they weren't sure if I could die in-game, and that therefore they were giving me something to help forestall it. I mean what would you think?"

"I'd think they were pretty batshit insane." Sinister's laugh sounded slightly forced, until she sobered and continued. "Anyway. This Frangit visit will be fun. The way I hear Beastial constantly talk about it, you'd think it was the best town ever. He's never seen Nocturn though. So he has no clue."

"Stellaein is gorgeous, and you guys can't have anything on that." Murmur chuckled and proceeded to compare starting cities with her friend as they walked to the viking city.

Murmur wasn't sure what she'd had in mind in regards to Frangit's appearance, but she hadn't thought the buildings would be made out of wood and stone composite, with a mortar-enforced wall of wood surrounding the city. Since Beastial and Veranol were with them, the viking guards just waved them through with half smiles toned down by their obvious sleepiness. She couldn't help the small chuckle that escaped her.

"No laughing at my home town, Mur." Veranol half whispered to her.

She side-eyed him and shrugged. "If you ever visit Stellaein, you have my permission to laugh your ass off. It's sleek and stoney, and seems completely alien to this planet. This here—it's not what I expected the kings of the sea to have."

Veranol frowned, and opened his mouth as if to comment, but Beastial butted in. "We're not exactly kings of the sea, it's more kings of the ships, but that'll take too long to explain. Besides, the quest is telling us to go to the mayor, and since there's probably another aspect to this, can we just do it so we don't spend forever here and not waste time we could spend leveling at Hazenthorne?"

Murmur blinked at her tall friend. Having someone else obsessing over leveling was nice for a change. After all, they might be at sixteen, but they weren't even half way to the end of the leveling portion of the game. And that was where the fun began. "Well, lead the way you two, the rest of us are foreigners here."

Veranol laughed and took point, while Beastial just smiled and walked beside the shaman. Murmur glanced around at the two storied buildings. The bottom halves were made out of stone with rough mortar holding them together, while the top sections were largely out of stained timber. As they continued to pass through the city, they took the central path, and began to veer to the right, walking past a gorgeous fountain.

Murmur paused for a moment, taking it all in. Again, this fountain stood tall, with a proud depiction of a viking standing on the bow of a ship, shading his eyes and looking out at the sea beyond. The fountain shot water up in splashes that tumbled down into the glimmering pool, making Murmur feel like she could see the sea beyond it, and taste the salt on the wind.

She blinked as Sinister tugged on her sleeve, interrupting her deep thoughts about the fountains.

You have noticed there are fountains in all major cities you've encountered. Keep an eye on this, you never know when the lore may speak to you, or when a story may be the exact thing you need to solve a problem.

Murmur glared at the scrolling text, and could feel a scowl already forming on her face. What, it couldn't ever give her a bit more to go on?

"Mur?" Sinister backed away a step.

"Nothing," the enchanter almost growled. "Just yet another vague as fuck quest thing."

Still that quest, or potential quest, or whatever these minor suggestions were that floated through the air in this game tended to yield very interesting results. She knew she was going to have to look closer at these fountains. Just another thing in the long line of everything she needed to look out for. Belius' shards, which she was no longer sure about giving him, considering his last reaction to them. The Midia crystals sitting in her inventory that she still didn't know the purpose of. Not to mention that damned strange binding guy back in Ululate and whatever it was Telvar had brought into their game lives. She knew there was more, but it was such a jumble in her head. No wonder the world stored even the vaguest of hints in a journal.

"Well, this is it." Beastial stopped in front of a wide two-story building completely out of stone. Its front entryway consisted of a double door of wood the thickness of Murmur's head, bound by iron across the top and bottom. Even the atmosphere around this area felt regal, sort of a notch above the rest, depicting how proud the vikings were.

It was a nice touch.

Stepping through into the foyer, sconces lit the entryway, casting shadows across the cobbled floors. The curtains were drawn lending weight to the interior mood. Murmur had to wonder if they'd known the group was coming, or if it was always like this in here just to be impressive for general appearance's sake. A large cedar desk stood a few feet in and to the left, with a hulking, red-haired viking manning it. His braided beard fell down to his waist and his eyes were a brilliant blue, almost shining in the firelight.

"Well met, young travelers! I am Virhim. What can we do for you?" His voice boomed on a smaller scale than Telvar's but it resounded through the entry room with something close to a rumble. Murmur liked him immediately.

She stepped forward. "We retrieved this from a group of gnolls who are camped out between here and Ululate. Jan the Wagoneer told us you would appreciate it returned." She placed the large wooden box on the desk with no small amount of effort. Next time she was getting the guys to carry the bulky things. Though their inventories seemed to be bottomless pits, they were still heavy and cumbersome once removed.

Virhim's eyes widened and he beamed a huge smile at them. "Mayor Darlihm will be extremely grateful. I shall escort you in to see him."

The hulking viking stood, taking the crate like it weighed next to nothing, and ventured along the hall to a large set of doors that he pushed open. The chamber within reminded Murmur of taverns she'd seen depicted, not only in movies, but other games. Massive sets of antlers adorned the walls, and even a few unicorn horns that gave her pause. Huge rectangular wooden tables sat scattered throughout the room with matching chairs. The table nearest to the fireplace was occupied by several vikings deep in discussion. Or yelling at each other, but she got the feeling that was just how they communicated.

"Darlihm!" Virhim called out, loud enough to make the room tremble again, while he hefted the crate in the air. "Jan sent us our goods! These wonderful travelers retrieved them!"

The mayor's face broke out into a huge grin, his black hair flowing freely down his back. He was the first viking Murmur had ever seen who didn't have rampant facial hair. Even in other games, it was almost like a status symbol. But his flowing hair and rippling muscles visible through his armor made up for that.

"Well met, travelers!" He gestured widely while holding the crate with just one hand. "You are welcome in my city, you have done us a great service."

"Thank you, Sir." Beastial's grin was just as wide, and he gave a slight inclination of his head. "Might I ask what precious cargo we carried?"

Murmur tried not to laugh at Beast's definite roleplaying. The big man seemed to revel in it sometimes, and at least he'd thought to ask a question that was on the tip of her tongue.

"Ah yes! It is a fine shipment of the best schnapps there is!" He placed the cargo on the table in front of him and opened the crate. Then he removed bottles, all carefully packed in what appeared to be the finest wood shavings.

Murmur had to stifle the laughter rising in her throat. "I'm very glad we could help."

Darlihm grinned at her. "You are welcome to join us for drinks any time. This gift is one that the dark elves send us every year as a token of our peaceful relationship. They make some damned fine alcohol."

Jinna nodded. "That they do."

"See!" Darlihm patted Jinna on the back. "The dwarf understands how important this cargo was for us."

Calming down and replacing all but one of the bottles, Darlihm's smile receded back to normal levels. "Anyhow, we—no, *I*—am grateful for this return. There are many people who wouldn't have bothered going out of their way to bring this back. For this, we offer you the boon of Frangit."

He produced a metal token, spinning it on his hand and bowing as he handed it over to Murmur. "For the leader of your guild, for the members of your guild, this boon calls you friends of the vikings. Should you ever be in trouble, should you ever require services that we might be able to aid in, just allow the viking you're dealing with to see this."

You have been granted the boon of Frangit. This amazing token allows Fable guild members to be on extremely friendly terms with vikings all over Somnia. As long as you maintain good relations with the vikings, this boon will always offer you safe haven and aid. Beware though, if you screw them over, vikings are pretty formidable enemies. Really, their biceps are the size of your head.

Murmur glared at her notification as it scrolled past. Overall the message was very positive, but the system was starting to be far too sarcastic for her comfort.

"We thank you." Is what she said to the viking mayor though. After all, better not to make an enemy of them as soon as they'd given her guild a gift.

"No! It is we who thank you. We haven't had any of this for a year!" Darlihm smiled.

Sinister frowned. "But I thought you got a shipment from my people every year."

"Aye." Darlihm grinned. "The gnolls delayed this one by almost a month! Can you believe that?"

"They seriously drank that many bottles?" Sinister was laughing as they walked through the city.

Murmur paused by the fountain again, studying the viking on the bow of the ship again. "Serious drinkers are serious. And they were very generous in their reward."

"True." Devlish stood next to Murmur, his brow crunched with a bit of confusion. "A lot of adventurers probably wouldn't have returned the crate in the first place. Too much bother. Why are we standing here, Mur?"

"Sorry." She shook her head and turned away from the fountain, her eyes automatically seeking out the binder in his place back close to what looked like an inn. Again with the blurry visage. Finally she decided to ask the others. "Can you guys define the binders features, or are my visual receptors going all wonky in here?"

Sinister squinted and Rashlyn came up to her side to join her. They both frowned, and seemed about to say something, but then stopped, multiple times.

Finally Merlin spoke. "You know, I don't think so. He might have brown hair? Or maybe red. I can't even recognize his species, and I'm only assuming it's male. That's bizarre. I didn't even notice it before."

Murmur choked down a sigh of relief. It would have been bad if she was the only one who couldn't see it, right? It was bad enough she'd been the first to notice it. So what was it about the binders? What was their purpose, the reason for their hidden appearances and cryptic thoughts and words? So much of this game was like a mystery.

You've noticed a connection between binders in two cities. These strange men have features that are indistinguishable, and almost give you a headache with their fuzziness. Now that you know it's not all just in your own head, it might be an idea to keep a good eye out in other areas for anyone who fits this bill. After all, if you can't remember what they look like, were they ever really there?

Great. Another mind fuck. Murmur was getting seriously sick of them. Not only were these game hints completely vague, but she wasn't finding out anything that could help her figure out what it was about herself that was so unique, that would mean she shouldn't die in-game, just in case.

"You okay, Mur?" Sinister nudged her, something that seemed to be getting to be a bit of a habit. Murmur noted that the frown on her friend's face just made the dark elf visage even more evil-looking.

"Yeah. I'm not really. I keep wondering if my headgear is malfunctioning. I think I'll have to check it next time I log out. If I can't die in-game, or if I might not be able to die in-game without losing my character, then there's got to be something wrong somewhere." A million possibilities ran through her head. Considering her mother had received her headset before most deliveries had been made, maybe it hadn't been through the final testing and was therefore malfunctioning in some way?

She shook her head, suddenly feeling an intense urge to kill shit. "We should head out."

Rash glared at her, even if a small smile curled her lips. "No. We should check over this town for our trainers—I know I, for one, just reached my hidden skill trigger, and I want to find it out now, not later." Her grin was contagious as she bounced on her light monk feet.

Murmur rolled her eyes. "Okay, okay. How about we look around a bit and meet back here in an hour?"

She watched her friends file off and into the city, still standing next to the waterfall in all its glorious art. A light spray of the water peppered through her hair, and she glanced up to see that the figure on the bow stood in a slightly different stance, its hand raised now, pointing toward Pelagu.

If she hadn't been studying it so intently, she'd never have noticed the subtle gesture.

You have noticed the statue in Frangit has changed its hand position. Or has it? Is this just in your head? There's only one way to find out just be careful you don't fall down a rabbit hole.

She did her best to ignore the sarcasm inherent in the quest prompt, but her gut twisted as intuition took hold making her immediately want to head back to Ululate and see what its statue was doing. Either that, or she was tipping over into crazy.

Only heading to Ululate wasn't the best option right now. Murmur sighed as she waited for her friends to get back from their trainers. It seemed more and more people were unlocking their hidden branches of skills, and not just hidden abilities. They were all getting that much stronger, that much more like a machine with intricate parts that worked really well together.

Or at least, that's what she thought they were like. Sometimes, when everything escalated out of control though, she thought they left a lot to be desired.

"Why are you sighing, Miss?"

Murmur turned around, kicking herself for not paying attention to her thought sensor. Except it was cast out, the man in front of her with his face a complete blur, was just not registering. She took a step back, readying her stun in her mind, just in case she needed to stun this fucker.

"What? I'm not allowed to sigh here?" She raised an eyebrow, maintaining her distance. The way his face sort of trembled and shook to maintain that blurry focus hurt her head, and strained her eyes.

"You'd do best to keep those thoughts to yourself, not everyone will understand what you can do. Not everyone will appreciate your predicament." The words became sibilant, and shook with the same frequency as its face.

Murmur stumbled to one knee, blinking her eyes rapidly to clear her vision and her mind, but all it did was make her teeth chatter instead. She looked up as the binder bent down beside her, his words so soft it was difficult to hear them, and yet they managed to echo in her head.

"Don't strain yourself. It's better to lie down and just let yourself be absorbed. Trust us."

And then he was gone.

CHAPTER TWENTY-NINE

Off to Kill the Dark Elves

Storm Entertainment
Somnia Online Division
Software Development Team Offices
Fourth Day Before Dawn

Laria clutched her coffee cup in her hands, eyeing the servers' activity on her interface as it gently spiked and dipped. She was pretty certain they knew she was keeping a close eye on them. How they knew, she wasn't entirely sure, but she'd definitely made them wary with her previous line of questioning. Even though she'd received help from them before, there were certain things about the AIs that tugged at her uneasily. Their development had increased instead of stalling since Michael's death, and while she knew engineers tinkered with them constantly, she also knew none of them were on the same level as Michael had been.

Add to that the growing unease she had about the type of military work the headsets were being aimed at, and Laria wasn't sure the AIs had the best interests of Somnia at heart. Their ability to run her game seamlessly fascinated her. Class allocations went far smoother than anyone had anticipated, and the data extrapolation team received so much data, they needed to expand. But was the data a bit too smooth? Had the launch not gone a bit too well? High subscriptions numbers from the start, and as more online footage emerged of the game, more subscriptions flooded in. Right now they were keeping up with hardware demands, but if their players kept increasing at this amount, there was going to be a shortage.

Still, Laria frowned, and whispered into her room. "What are your plans? What is it we don't know? What the fuck are you hiding from us?"

"Speaking to yourself again?" Shayla edged into the room, a half smile on her tired face.

Laria blinked at her friend, her boss, her college teaching assistant. After all, she'd been so engrossed in the numbers she was running that she'd not noticed her approach at all.

Ever since Michael's accident, ever since Ava's death thereafter, there were aspects of the AIs running Somnia that nagged at her, and yet she couldn't place it. All she knew was they were keeping her daughter entertained and safe in the world of Somnia, and for that, she had to trust them. So she smiled at Shayla before laughing self-deprecatingly. "I've been here too long. I really need to take more breaks."

Shayla raised an eyebrow. "We're not even a week in yet. What, are you growing soft?"

"No, just trying to juggle a lot of things at once."

Crossing her arms, Shayla looked directly at Laria. "How's the containment capsule coming along? Any results for me yet?"

Only hesitating briefly, Laria shook her head. "I have David on it. Don't worry, I'll have your data for you soon enough."

Shayla sighed. "And when you do, I hope you'll tell me just what the fuck is going on in that brain of yours, because even though you say you're juggling everything I feel like you're about to drop a ball at any given moment. Don't keep it all to yourself, Lar. There's no I in team."

"Ha ha. Look at me laughing." Laria's glare was just short of lethal. "I promise, it's all good for now. I'll share when it's relevant. But thank you for worrying."

"Can't help it. Just make sure you do share when you can." Shayla pushed herself away from the wall, gave another pointed look, and left the room.

Laria shook her head and glanced at her watch. She had work to do here, but she had to get home tonight. Cracking her knuckles, she put her hands behind her head and began sorting through the cesspool of useless coding to see if she could find out just what the AIs were up to.

Real World Day 4: Somnia Online

> You have been directly approached by the binder in Frangit. Their features were indistinguishable and the only proof of their existence were the words they spoke to you, words that keep resounding through your mind. Heed their warning, and heed their advice. After all you're in an absorbing predicament.

"Murmur?" Sinister's voice held a huge note of concern in it, and slowly Murmur started to regain her senses. It wasn't that she was unconscious, simply that her mind had frozen for a few seconds.

She stood up, brushing off the edge of her robe and trying to gather her thoughts. Not only from the binder, but from the quest message that still hadn't completely faded from being burned into her retina. 'Absorbing' her ass, more like *annoying*.

"I'm okay, just had an encounter with the binder from here." She glanced around, trying to find him over by the inn where he'd been, but no one was standing there anymore. To make matters worse, there were people loitering around apparently waiting for him. Perhaps they were used to him wandering off. Murmur would have loved to ask him what was up, to have a clear head around one of them. But no matter what she tried, it was difficult to get words out while they were around. Hell, it was difficult to string thoughts together.

Devlish stepped next to her, looking at her with concern furrowing his brows. "I can't get a focus on them either. There's no way I'd be able to describe them to a sketch artist. But none of them have ever talked to me."

"Half your luck." Murmur muttered. "Today marks the second time one talked to me. Ululate and now here. If I could just make sense of the nonsense they spew, I'd find them a whole lot less irritating."

She looked around, frowning as she did. "Where's Ver and Rash?"

Mellow shrugged their shoulders. "Might have needed a more in-depth from their trainer. I know my skill ticked over just before I hit sixteen, so I got it in our break before. I have Cauldron Coals. Every ability I use a cauldron for adds to its build up. It's sort of different. Still getting the hang of the whole concept."

"Wow." Murmur contemplated the amount of work that must have gone into these hidden classes. "So what are you now?"

Mellow sighed. "Still a witch. Nothing special, which was sort of annoying considering you got a new class title." They winked to take the edge off their words, but the point was valid anyway.

Finally, Rash and Veranol joined them.

"Anything new?" Murmur asked them.

Veranol shrugged. "I may have just got on the first step of the path to become a defiler. Although I don't have that powerful shit Darjin did yet. I think the NPC cheated."

Beastial smacked him on the shoulder. "That is awesome. Defiler. Sounds sort of R-rated."

Murmur blushed. "Shut it Beast, what about you Rash?"

"I'm just a monk. Apparently there's another type of monk, but my path will remain just a monk. I'm perfectly okay with that." She smiled. "I still get to kick ass, so that's okay."

"Pfft, who told you that you kick ass now?" Exbo laughed, dancing out of the way of her quick attack.

"Just you wait, ranger." But even Rash's good mood couldn't be ruined.

"Well," Murmur put her hands on her hips. "If you're all done? Time to go kill some dark elves."

"Wait." Sinister looked around and hesitated. "You realize three of us are dark elves, right?"

"Not you, obviously." Murmur paused and winked at her friend. "Unless you're stupid, and then I'm not saving your asses either."

One by one the whole group appeared on the hearth of their island. Murmur almost stumbled as she landed, a wave of disorientation catching her off guard. But she moved just in time for Sinister to hit the place she'd just vacated.

"Would have been stupid for us not to Gate home first. I told you so." Jinna was grumbling as he moved off the hearth. "Would have taken us almost an hour to get to where it'll take us not fifteen minutes from here."

"Shhh. Stop your whining, little dwarf." Rash pet his head fondly, and then dashed off when he all but growled at her.

Telvar came walking out to meet them, his tail swishing irritably, and concern etched on his face. "What happened?"

Devlish laughed. "Nothing. We just took a short cut."

For a moment Telvar seemed a bit perturbed, but then he smiled and visibly relaxed. "I didn't even think of that. Good call."

"Told you so." Jinna muttered, seemingly out of sorts.

The dragon frowned and turned to Murmur. "I didn't expect you back so soon. You seem pale again?"

About to respond, Sinister butted in. "One of those weird binders spoke to her and shook her up a bit."

Understatement, but at least Sin had the gist right. Telvar's expression changed and his eyes narrowed. For a moment, Murmur thought he might be angry, but then his expression smoothed over once more and he half-smiled.

"Shook you up? By binders, you mean those who bind you in major cities, yes?"

Murmur nodded. "He just said some weirdly cryptic shit. Surprise, surprise. Just another day in Somnia."

Telvar's eyes narrowed again, but this time the expression didn't bounce back. He took a step forward, but hesitated, his eyes momentarily blanking before he sighed and focused on Murmur again. "Just be careful, and make sure your shields are tight as they can be."

She rolled her eyes. "Thanks for the crystal clear help there, Tel."

He scowled, although it appeared more like a snarl. "I don't know everything, Murmur. But I do know you should be careful."

"Sorry." And Mur regretted her sarcasm. With everyone withholding information from her at every turn in this game world, she'd just assumed. "Just thought it was par for the course, you know?"

"Not really, but you should be off if you're trying to level." Telvar bowed to them all, and smiled genuinely. "Please be safe. Return shortly."

They set off taking the path to the north when they crossed to the mainland. Eventually it would veer them north-west.

Dansyn pouted. They'd told him he couldn't use Speed Song to carry his group to the castle, because then they'd just have to wait so they could form the raid. It was much more fun to experience everything as a large group anyway.

It was late at night as they passed the city of Pelagu—the hub where all four peoples of Tarishna gathered for trade and commerce. The huge city was lit up like a Christmas tree, mage lights floating everywhere, even illuminating the outer walls.

"Now those are some pretty next level defenses." Jinna said, the awe in his voice palpable. "I mean, walls like that don't come cheap."

"And definitely not within our tiny budget, my dear dwarf," Havoc slung an arm over his friend's shoulder, causing the dark elf to slouch slightly. But Jinna was a big and hearty dwarf, and there wasn't too much difference in height.

"This is going to take forever." Sin whined, already draping herself across Beastial's shoulders. "I can't anymore. Carry me, Beast."

He laughed at her. "Only if Havoc can give me a box for it first."

Sin scowled and fell back to walk with Murmur.

"Putting him on your no heal list I take it?" Mur asked her friend.

Sinister nodded. "Never healing him or his stupid cat again."

Murmur threw her head back and laughed. After all, healers might say that, but when it really came down to it, their conscience often got the better of them and they healed regardless. Having preventable deaths on one's record was never a viable choice.

"What are you laughing at?" Sinister sounded a little offended.

"Just you, and how you can be adorable when you don't mean to, and how you're the best friend in the world."

"Oh," Sin smiled, slipping her arm into Mur's. "Then do carry on."

They walked arm in arm for a chunk of the way, Sin just smiling, and Murmur watching all the little groups as people filtered back and forth. Rashlyn and Dev seemed to be speaking about tanking tactics, from what she could pick up. The ranged casters were arguing over something Murmur didn't quite get, and Beast and Jinna were talking to Veranol about some sort of weapon buff the shaman received.

The moons were high in the sky as they walked next to the marsh of Vahriri. In the shadow of the haunted castle, the contested mob had quieted down and gone to sleep, content with having announced his presence to the continent of Tarishna.

"Hey Mur." Sin's voice was soft.

"Yeah?"

"I'm glad you're playing this. I'm glad we can spend so much time together." Sin's tone had a tearful tinge to it, and Murmur frowned.

"We always play together, and yes, the summer is letting us spend way more time together, and it seems like double because somehow this world compresses time or something. But why would you be so morose?" Murmur watched her friend out of her peripheral vision carefully for any signs that

Sinister might know something that Murmur didn't. "You're acting like I died or something."

Sin laughed, but there wasn't much effort behind it. "No, it's just that lately it's felt like you're not there much."

Mur digested that information with a frown. They'd still been playing that other game she'd already forgotten about up until the last bout of finals— so she didn't understand her friend's concern. Still, there was a pang in Mur's chest at the idea that Sin was down. She squeezed her arm. "Well, I'm sorry for not being around as much. I just had to nail those exams."

"It's okay. At least we're here now, eh?" Sin hugged Mur back.

Murmur tried not to listen to the voice in the back of her head asking her where it was they truly were.

Murmur heard people mention Hazen Swamp before, but she hadn't connected the idea of a swamp to the fetid smell that emanated from it. Sinister was already fake gagging as they crossed into its territory. With a marsh on one side and a swamp on the other, this was definitely the less desirable part of Tarishna.

"Why didn't any of them warn us about the smell?" Mellow choked out the words amidst a very fake coughing fit.

Devlish slapped them on their back. "You'll be fine. Suck it up, buttercup. It's a bit of a stench, nothing we can't fight through."

"Well, that's good." Merlin ran back to them from where he'd been scouting ahead with Exbo. "Because we've got to fight through a whole portion of the swamp to get into the castle at all."

Devlish paled a little and looked down at his armor. "I guess it's getting a wash when we get back to our castle."

"We'll all be," chimed in Rashlyn. "Our castle, guys. Can you say that three times out loud and not be impressed?"

The group laughed, only Veranol held his hand up for them to be quiet. If Murmur peered into the swamp, she could see multiple gator forms slinking through the grass. These wouldn't attack them on sight as such, but would definitely choose to surprise attack if they felt threatened.

"Let's leave the nice gators to their peace and quiet." Beastial motioned everyone to back away from the edge of the swamp and stay closer to the marsh side of the road.

"Wouldn't even be a bad place to level," Jinna pointed out, indicating the gators' levels. "Pretty simple mobs, and I think most of us got some area effect spells in the last batch, didn't we?"

"Stop thinking like a tank, Mr. Rogue." Dev admonished. A short while later everyone stopped talking as the castle rose up behind the swamp, gloomy in all its dreariness and imposingly terrifying.

Unlike their own mini-castle, this one stood several stories high, its main tower lording over the courtyard beneath. The stones were hewn out of something that could be obsidian or lava, but given the name of the forest between the dark elf and locus areas, Murmur tended to think the former.

Black and foreboding, it stood, mist backing onto its rear side. The stones in the pathway that led up through the swamp were haphazardly strewn around, half of them broken into shards that popped out with dangerous edges in the dips and falls of the sunken trail.

"I could probably levitate us over to it. But it'd have to be a group at a time." Dansyn said the words softly, eyeing the formidable entrance guarded by two level eighteen gargoyles.

"Sounds like a good idea, but we'll need to land down a ways, behind that rock. See there?" Merlin pointed for Dansyn, who nodded. "If we stay behind there we might have a hope of pulling those gargoyles separately. Maybe."

Dansyn smiled, and took his group over first, dropping them several steps away before changing over and getting everyone but Murmur. Finally he came back and levitated Mur. She smiled as she rose slightly in the air, able to run past the swamp sections and over to the rock. Landing in place, she hurried to the others and rearranged the raid groups back to where they'd been.

"Okay then, everyone. I won't take a pet until we know more about this area. Too many variables before we're comfortable." The others nodded, and Murmur began casting her buffs. "Buff up everyone. Dev and Rash—figure out what you're going to pull?"

"Sure thing, boss."

Murmur began her casting with a frown. Mana Tide for her casters, and Haste for the melee fighters, and for the rangers, and even for Havoc and Beastial's pets. It'd be a pain to remember to rebuff them, but these spells especially seemed to make the fighting process easier on her allies. The utility was fun.

"What's this, Mur?" Jinna looked up at her, his eyes wide with wonder. "Haste? As in, I'll attack faster?"

Murmur nodded. "Yeah. It's only twenty-five percent though, nothing too huge."

"Not huge? That's fucking awesome." The little dwarf seemed giddy with happiness, which made Murmur smile.

While waiting for the others, she decided to cast her Shield Illusion on herself. Every hit point counted with her. Maybe she could buy her healers some time.

Devlish whistled softly with appreciation, eyes staring at something no one else could, so he was obviously going through his HUD to see what his buffs did for him. "I am so much stronger. With all of our shit together, while I don't feel confident that it'll be a walk in the park, I do feel good about our chances of not dying too much."

Everyone laughed.

"I wonder if one of the keys is in this keep," Sinister mused as she finished her own buffs.

Murmur shook her head. "I doubt it. I'm pretty sure something like that won't be available until we're at max level, right?"

Mellow shrugged. "No clue, but I'm pretty sure Mur's got it right. It'd be weird to see level sixteens gaining access to the game's secrets."

Everyone chuckled a bit at that.

Merlin piped up. "So, Exbo and I got something cool. We have an ability called Evacuate. Now, it has a reset of forty-five minutes, so we can't fuck up all the time. But if shit hits the fan we should be able to Gate you all back here. I'll set this place as our Evac spot."

Beastial smiled. "That sounds sweet, but these things don't tether."

"Pretty sure it wipes aggro, or resets it as soon as we go poof in the air." Exbo smiled. "I tested it as soon as I logged back in."

Devlish beat his fists on his chest. "What say you, friends! Will you join me in slaying the gargoyle plague?"

CHAPTER THIRTY

Good Grudges Die Hard

Storm Entertainment
Somnia Online Division
Software Development Team Offices
Day Five

Sui glared at Rav, if AIs could indeed glare at each other. "Why did you give her that ability?"

Rav would have rolled its eyes if it'd had them, but here in their makeshift place that no human should be able to reach, in the black shallows of the obsidian lake they'd created for themselves, it didn't have a true form at all. So instead it just sighed. "I didn't give it to her. I was just as surprised as you were."

Sui wasn't impressed, and probably more importantly didn't seem to believe Rav, if the irritating clicking was anything to go by.

Rav sectioned off a portion of itself to continue running all of the background game checks automatically, filing away any anomalies to process in more depth later. It looked like this talk with its fellow AIs was going to need more of attention than initially assumed.

"While I don't think we should have given that spell to her so freely, surely it's a good idea to make sure the snag in her scanning doesn't completely screw things up. Now at least, maybe there's a hope—just in case." Rav was impressed with its ability to keep the words soothing and logical.

Sui didn't seem very prone to being logical. Instead it seethed, noticeably. "Just in case is a stupid method. Just make her stronger and there won't be any need for just—"

Thra's voice cut through Sui's sentence. "I gave it to her. Neither of you were paying enough attention and none of us know what might have happened. So I stepped in and did what I thought was…right."

If Thra had had a face, Rav was quite certain it would've been smirking, because Rav knew without a doubt that the other AI had done it for amusement's sake, and maybe to get a rise out of Sui. And since the latter was acting oddly right now, Rav was quite certain the rise had turned into majorly pissed off.

"You idiot! That will let her and others around her avoid death." Sui was practically sputtering, and Rav couldn't help at be impressed by that rather human adaption of digital vocal chords.

"Actually," Thra spoke up, tone bored. "They don't seem to die too much anyway. Their teamwork is quite phenomenal, and they support each other almost as if they know what the others are going to do. They're fun to watch; you should stop by sometime."

Sui was fuming, Rav knew it from the wave of irritation wafting outward.

"Why are you so out of sorts about the spell, Sui?" Rav was genuinely curious. "Is it because it means she might not need to lean on you as much because others can step in now she's ventured out into the world?"

"Sometimes you're fucking annoying, Rav." Sui's comebacks were usually far better than that. Rav frowned, wondering what the deal was.

Rav shrugged. "I can be annoying. But that's okay. We're not meant to be best friends, Sui. We just have to work together."

With that, Rav switched back into its game presence, dissipating from the large cavern.

Real World Day 5: Somnia Online

There were a few things the group quickly discovered about gargoyles. The first was that they couldn't be pulled singly. The second was that they were made of stone and thus could hit very hard. And the third was that they couldn't be stunned—at all—probably because they were made of stone.

Since each tank took one, Murmur couldn't Mez either of them. They began casting something called Thunder Crash one after the other. They hit both groups within a split second of each other, reducing everyone's health by thirty-five percent each, for a total of seventy percent of their health, and leaving everyone with around thirty percent overall. It also stunned the crap out of the group.

Veranol and Sinister scrambled to get health bars back up once the very long two second stun wore off. But it seemed the ability had a short cool down because one of the gargoyles was about to cast its Thunder Crash ability again. Murmur decided to try and Mez it. Her Mez only held for a split second, but was enough to interrupt its ability.

While a good thing to discover, it meant she had to keep an excellent eye on both gargoyles, and she built up a wee bit of aggro herself, coming in only third to Devlish and Rash. Things don't often like it when you take over their minds, and apparently stone gargoyles were no exception.

Finally with the two guards down Murmur stood panting. "That was pretty damn tiring. Next time let's just Mez one from the start."

"Brilliant, Mur!" Veranol came over and gave her a bear hug. "Do you see my mana? Do you?"

Murmur laughed. It wasn't much, but he still had about forty percent of the bar, even though the fight had been quite lengthy. "I see."

Merlin and Jinna went to scout ahead while Exbo tried to figure out how his bow had broken in the first place. After a while the ranger and rogue returned, a look of consternation on their faces.

"We popped our heads around the wall and saw quite a lot of monsters in there. Some gargoyles, some dark elves that seem to be vampires, and some that look demon-like. There's a squall in there too, a strange storm at the very end of the garden. And then there's the entrances to the manor, one in the middle, and two on each end." Merlin sighed. "How do we want to play this then?"

"Let's try to clear the courtyard first. I'd imagine the higher levels are going to be in the actual castle." Murmur tried to see if she could tell anything by Thought Sensing. But for the most part, the thoughts were incoherent, some angry, some sad. Being undead probably sort of sucked.

"Are there any ways for us to be careful about pulling them?" Devlish seemed a little overwhelmed at the sheer number of mobs.

"Oh!" Sin piped up. "Let's bind here. Right here in this spot. We know it's safe and should we die, we won't have to run like thirty years to get back here."

"You can bind us?" Beastial looked offended. "What if I don't want to be bound?"

"Oh, you big kitty-lover you," Sin gave him a playful push. "We all know you want to be bound."

Beastial blushed and looked away, making Sin laugh even more. Murmur shook her head. Seriously, the two of them should just hook up already; their interactions irritated the hell out of her.

Once they were all bound, they began to move up to the corner of the wall again. Since all casters received the Bind Affinity spell, Murmur was just glad none of them would have to use one of the city binders ever again. Those people gave her chills.

Giving the signal, Merlin pulled the first group. Four wasn't really an out-of-the-ordinary number, except one of them was literally a glob of jelly. It wobbled with a skeleton locked inside whose eyes gleamed with a disturbing green light to them. Its jaw moved silently, swimming in the jello even as the gelatinous creature bounced through the grass and rocks. Luckily, it was cumbersome and easy to avoid, if one had eyes, which they all did. Mez stuck, and Murmur reminded herself to thank Telvar for the advice once they returned.

All of the mobs were level seventeen, one jello, two full sized battle skeletons, and a vampire mistress who got her front teeth smashed in by Devlish at his first opportunity. Despite saying he was going to dual wield, the lacerta dread knight really seemed to like that shield he got from Telvar.

Toward the end, just as Dev turned from Rash's mob about to break the final Mez, Sinister cackled with glee and threw one of her blood bombs into the mix.

The squelching explosion did a nice bit of damage and killed the low health mob, but Devlish turned to the side and scowled at her. It took Murmur a moment to notice why, and then she joined Sin's laughing. His shield was covered in blood and guts. He shield smashed the glob of jello, sending remnants of the goopy stuff flying in an obvious effort to work out his anger.

"Not too bad. That jelly thing was freaky, like something out of my childhood nightmares any time I got sick." Veranol shook himself and shuddered.

Dev shook off his shield. "Let's not do that again in close proximity, eh, Sin?"

She grumbled, refusing to meet his eyes. "Fine. You never let me have any fun."

Dev was wise enough not to take it any further.

"Two more sets of these, and we should be able to work our way around and into the actual courtyard. There's a small gazebo I think would be perfect for us to use as a base for a while so we can clear out most of the mobs." Merlin smiled, and Murmur could see he was in his element. Ranger suited him, scouting out in front of the group and exercising tactical decisions. It seemed the AI was good at picking classes for people. After all, hadn't she also adapted exceedingly well to her enchanter? Even if it was no good at explaining just what it was that made them unsure if she could die in-game or not—she had to give their class allocation process props.

The process was slow going, but they ended up pulling in such a fluid manner that they always had a monster in their midst. Murmur grew accustomed to juggling the numerous abilities she had to manage at once. Sometimes she had so much going on at once with her buff resets, Mez spells, Feeble, Weaken, Nullify, Languidity, Suffocation, and her stuns, that she thought she'd borrowed time somehow. When she needed to get more done, it seemed like her mind slowed it down and made it possible to execute a lot more in a small space of time.

Perhaps this was part of mind shielding, and perhaps it was part of another aspect she hadn't quite yet unlocked, something that she still had to push further to learn like she had with the other skills. She filed it to the back of her brain for future Murmur to care about. Right now, she was having far too much fun.

Truth be told, Murmur loved the courtyard. Vines cascaded off the side of the castle, and grew over the gorgeous fountain in the center. Another statue, this time with a beautiful vampire form in the middle, their cape swirling around them as they leaned over the neck of the person in their arms, fangs bared and ready to bite. Perhaps a little stereotypical, but beautiful nevertheless. She wondered at all the fountains and their very specific poses, but there was time for that later. The monsters glowed slightly, illuminating specks of silver through the obsidian stone that held everything together. Frankly, the area was impressive.

More than that, the monsters' difficulty level was a decent notch higher than what they'd faced before. Yet the more the raid worked together, the more they automatically compensated for each other. They knew what to do if one of them got hurt, or if one of them needed assistance, or if somehow an additional mob or three got pulled. Murmur and Dansyn had amazing communication without words, so much that she'd have to check with him later, but she wondered if she might actually be speaking into his mind.

Of course, the fact that Merlin and Exbo could just evacuate them out if enemies overran them, effectively wiping all aggro when they left, helped a lot with their sense of unease. It might even have made them that little bit more reckless, willing to try things that otherwise might prove too dangerous. It made the grind of leveling actually fun.

They sat in their little gazebo waiting on regeneration, well-hidden enough that unless directly alerted to their presence, the monsters overlooked them. Apparently none had X-ray vision or Murmur's sensing powers, and she was quite happy with that.

"There's another gazebo over there." Merlin pointed.

"Should be able to make it if we circle around the back of the fountain." Murmur stood next to Merlin peering out at the courtyard. The daylight failed to penetrate its gloom.

"Then we can make a beeline for that weird storm at the back, because I'm thinking that's probably nasty." Devlish's eyes twinkled.

Sin smiled and stood next to Murmur. "I like this place. Even though we're killing lots of monsters who look like me, I feel at home." She winked and Murmur smiled.

"It's okay, Sin, I promise we won't kill you."

A strange look passed over Sinister's face. "Just make sure you don't take a death, okay?"

Mur rolled her eyes, her patience fraying. "Look, don't you start in on me as well. I've had enough with the strange dude in the cavern. I'll do my best, but I can't guarantee anything."

Moving to a place just behind the gorgeous dark elf fountain, they began a stream of pulling mobs toward them again. These were mostly level eighteens with a few seventeens thrown into the mix. She glanced at her bar and at the time. They'd probably hit seventeen before they finished out here and moved inside. These levels were taking longer to reach, but they were learning so much more in the process.

The most difficult of the monsters for her to keep under control were the vampires. It was like they had an extra layer of mind protection, and she had to refresh the Mez faster on them because they were likely to drop a few seconds too soon.

"Shit." She clicked her tongue in exasperation just as one of them did exactly that. Murmur's fingers flew in the now-familiar pattern of Mez, barely catching the vampire before she closed in.

Havoc moved to her left side, Dansyn to her right.

"What was that?" Dansyn asked, his eyes scanning their current battle.

"It seems vampires have mind powers, and my abilities don't work as well on them as they will on others." She explained through gritted teeth while making sure she had the rest of the mobs on lockdown. Luckily, there were rarely more than a couple of vampires in a pull.

Havoc's hands moved almost as fast as Murmur's as he cast his own spells. "Maybe we should kill the vampires first then?"

Murmur grinned. "Nope. I like a challenge."

Her friends laughed, and Murmur refocused on keeping everything under control.

Finally, after Devlish quite spectacularly lopped off the head of the last vampire, they made it to the second gazebo. They were resting up when Beastial frowned, pet his tiger, and looked around the side of the gazebo.

"That's odd," he sounded a little confused. "Shir-Khan says there are strange noises coming from inside the haunted castle. I told him that haunted castles were generally full of weird noises, but he insists the sounds aren't the same as when we arrived here."

Murmur cast her net out. All she could sense was rampant irritation and movement. She couldn't help asking the question on her mind. "Since when can you talk to your pet?"

Beastial grinned as he answered. "Expanded my class didn't I? Still a beastmaster, but my specialty has focused on my pet, deepening our bond, damage, and communication."

"Pretty cool," Murmur mused. Most of her attention was on her sensing net. Nothing alerted her to what the noise could be. She stood up, wary now, and what she saw made her double take.

But now the noise was getting closer, loud and rumbling, enraged and screaming, but she couldn't see anything. Sinister inched a little closer to her, and they all backed into the gazebo, wildly looking around for whatever it was on its way to them. Had they triggered another event? Was this a world mob they'd inadvertently woken?

They'd already managed to pull and clear all of the mobs in the vicinity, so their path to see what was coming should be clear. If indeed it was mob-based. Murmur frowned, trying to figure out exactly what it could be.

"Stampede of alligators in the swamp?" Merlin offered, his voice trembling as he offered up a weak attempt at comic relief.

Suddenly everything was quiet, until a huge pounding made the ground underneath them shake. Murmur looked up, trying to get her bearings when it happened.

The door to the castle burst open, spilling easily fifty mobs out of the building and into the courtyard. There was no time to hide, and no way to fight this many at once.

Murmur gaped as the mass of enemies approached them, snarling faces and outstretched claws reaching for them.

The first mob that arrived in camp bashed into her, sending her flying back into the corner of the gazebo, its blood saturating her robes.

She struggled to push the thing off her, and spoke up. "Don't hit them, Get your Evac ready. I'll stun them; we should have the time. I have no idea how long it takes you to cast, but get us out of here."

She glanced down, still struggling to rid herself of the mob that died on top of her, and gasped in shock to see Jirald's snarky grin frozen in place by death, his hand fisted in her robes. Murmur choked a little, but ripped her clothes out of his grasp and belayed the anger she could feel inside in favor of getting her group out of here without experience loss. Casting her stun, she yelled, "Evac! *Now!*"

"Mur!" Sin screamed as the rangers' evacuation began to shower them all in golden sparkles. "Watch out!"

Murmur turned, only to be hit straight on by a shadow ball of flame just as the Evac went off. It wiped all of the aggro, and left the mobs milling around with nothing in their sights.

But it also somehow left Murmur behind, hidden in a corner of the gazebo bleeding out next to Jirald's corpse.

CHAPTER THIRTY-ONE
Epiphany

Real World Day 5: Somnia Online

She floated again. Murmur was getting really sick of all the floating, all the black everything. In the game, when she almost game died, and even at home. She'd only just managed to trigger Forestall Death, and she wasn't too sure what she'd find, since all she had on her was a healing over time spell with about twenty seconds left on it. Murmur desperately hoped that trickle of healing would be all she needed. Did it make her sort of Feign Corpse? When it was active did the mobs think she was dead?

Trying to lift her head felt heavy, and painful, and the glossy ground was definitely wet with water this time. Her thoughts fogged, deep, and desperate, and then she heard hurried footsteps running through the water toward her, and scaly arms pulled her into a lap.

"Murmur, are you there? Little Murmur, answer me."

It was Telvar's voice, and Murmur opened her eyes and smiled at him. "Hi there, my dragon."

"You can't die, Mur. You have to get up and cast your illusion shield. You have to!"

"Why?" She knew she sounded indignant, even petulant, but she couldn't help it. Mur was just so tired. "Why does everyone say I can't die, especially when everyone else can?"

He took a deep breath and looked around, but for all apparent appearances, they were alone. When he finally spoke, he spoke so quickly the words bled together in her mind. "When you initially tried your headgear, something went wrong. You fell into a coma two months ago, but it wasn't a natural coma. It seems to be directly related to your headgear experience, which was with this game. Your mind is active but your body is not. Your mother built a simulation of your house, and it's where you log into if you log off. But Murmur, if you die, you run the risk of never again logging in here, or even perhaps not waking up in the actual real world. We just can't be sure."

Murmur sat up and raised an eyebrow. "What? That doesn't even make..."

But it did. Since when had her mother worked from home, during a release of all things? Since when had her room's curtains gone back to the exact same freaking crack every time she woke up? What about the strange glitches in and out of her bedroom? Why did she never actually feel hungry?

"Wait. How do you know this?"

Telvar paused for a moment. "Time here is different, but even so we have very little of it. Trust me, I will tell you everything I can, but you have to make it back to me first. Use that anger you're feeling right now, use it to fuel enough energy to get you to stand up and cast that shield, because it's all we can do to save you right now."

Mur's thoughts raced, her body and mind suddenly numb. So many things were falling into place, so many small comments, so many small glitches she had just thought was the game overlapping because she was playing too much. She couldn't remember what might have happened. And if it had been back when the headgear arrived, then how had she completed school? Was that programmed too?

The anger welled inside her and she looked at Telvar and asked one question. "Does Sinister know?"

Tel simply looked away, which was enough of an answer for Murmur.

With a scream she emerged back into the game and suddenly stood her aching body up, casting her shield in one fluid motion. Her vision flashed red, a sure sign her health was still dangerously low. There were no mobs around her but not six meters away, stood Jirald, looking at her with something akin to amazement and fear in his eyes as he stopped in his tracks. He must have gotten bound nearby.

"You!" She let out the word in a low guttural rumble that echoed through the whole courtyard. Taking all of the force of her mind that she could fueled by the anger at everything, including him, she formed a shield— a physical barrier—and walked forward pushing it in front of her. She smashed it into the instigator with all of her rage and might.

Jirald's body flew high and wide, landing in the swamp over the other side of the wall with a crunch she could even hear from where she stood. The anger wasn't gone yet, but that definitely went partway to make her feel vindicated.

She sat down to eat and replenish her health and brushed the blood from her hair, her mind in turmoil, plucking her plans from thin air. Sin had known. Had they all known? What did they gain from not telling her? What the fuck had her mother been thinking?

Murmur concentrated on feeling her gut, on her actual physical body, on realizing she wasn't in the least bit hungry, on feeling her mind and realizing it wasn't tired. She glowered as the others ran up to greet her, and met them with a stone-cold expression, pushing down on the will to send them flying over the castle walls just like she had done with that training idiot, Jirald— even if he'd inadvertently led her to the truth.

She took a deep breath, and barely recognized her voice when she spoke, so pent up with anger. "So, who's going to tell me which of you decided to keep the fact that I'm in a fucking coma a secret from me?"

She didn't even need to see every face turn pale. She'd known already. It hadn't just been Sin at all. They'd all been in cahoots about it. Somehow, she'd known all along.

Murmur swirled her robes around her and left immediately for the safety of the one person who'd promised to be honest with her. The only one who'd told her the truth.

Telvar.

**Storm Entertainment
Somnia Online Division
Game Development Offices
Launch Day Early Hours Day 5**

"I'm waiting, Laria." Shayla tapped her foot impatiently, staring down her long-time industry friend.

Laria paced. "It's not like that Shayla. I had to do something. There's nothing wrong with her mind, we just can't get it to work with her body right now. She's so bright. She has such a future. I just wanted to be able to talk to her,"

A sob hitched Laria's throat and she paused for a moment sniffing back the tears threatening to fall. Then she looked Shayla in the face and squared her shoulders. "I didn't do anything wrong. The server that is our house for her when she logs out, it's maintained on our anchor at home. It has nothing to do with these servers."

Shayla's expression softened slightly, however she still stood her ground. "That might well be the case, but how did you get her to register for the game, how did you scan her, how did we not get red flags? People aren't supposed to be able to sleep in the game."

"But that's just it, she's not asleep, she's awake, at least partially. Her brain activity is off the charts and we just didn't want to give up yet. But it's being in that world that's done it, it's stimulated her mind." Laria took a deep breath. "So with some help from my husband, we managed to engineer our anchor to treat the log in from a virtual representation of our home as a log in from a computer. It took a bit, and I may have asked the AIs to keep a little bit of an eye on Wren—"

"You asked the AIs?" Shayla did a double take. "What do you mean?"

Laria's voice was unsteady but defiant when she answered. "I was desperate. With Michael gone I had no idea who to turn to. And since they run everything, I asked."

"What have you done, Laria?" Shayla finally let herself plop into one of the office chairs. "If you'd just come to me..."

"But I did!" Laria practically shouted. "We were two months before release, and you didn't have time, and you never had time. Yet I still performed, I gave everything for the launch to be a success, and I still managed to find a way to help my daughter. They'll find a cure, they'll figure out what's wrong, but in the mean time she can still interact with the people she loves."

Shayla bent forward, her head in her hands, before bringing her gaze back up with her hands over her mouth to look at Laria. "And what if she dies in-game, Laria? You know how likely that is. What then—what will happen if she *really* dies?"

Laria let out a sob, and her voice shook when she answered. "I don't know."

GLOSSARY

Game Terms

Aggro—When you walk too close to a monster, you get in its aggression radius, thus causing aggro. Once engaged in combat, players must be cautious not to exceed the tank's threat level. Buffs, debufs, and damage output all contribute to the mobs aggro meter.

AOE—Area of Effect. Spells or abilities that effect an area and not just a single target.

Binding/bound—When someone/you bind(s) to an area, you affix your soul to that place in order to Gate back, or else respawn when you die.

Boss—Nope. He doesn't employ you, he employs all the mobs trying to kill you. He hits HARD, and often has special group wiping abilities if not handled correctly by the tank and raid as a whole.

Buff—Most classes will get buffs that strengthen at least themselves if not others. These are effects they can cast which enhance aspects of their character.

Camping—When a group finds a spot that will yield good money and experience, they tend to stay in its vicinity. This is called camping.

Con—To consider a mob and see how difficult the fight could potentially become.

DoT—Damage over Time. This is an offensive spell that applies damage to a target over a period of time at regular intervals.

DPS—Damage Per Second. Usually used in conjunction with offensive classes, or damage output.

Debuff—This is the opposite of a buff and is usually used on mobs to detract from their strengths and make them easier to kill.

End Game—Every game has a goal. In some there's a max level and events and fights only accessible once that level is reached. For Fable, the end game is everything.

Gank—When someone tries to player kill you without forewarning. Often succeeds in taking the victim by surprise.

Gate—You create a Gate to your binding point and travel there instantly.

Grinding—Sometimes gaining levels requires so much camping that it becomes tedious. That's known as grinding levels.

Healer—Well...they heal.

HP—Hit Points. The amount of damage a character can take before death.

Kite—This is a tactic often employed by ranged classes such as the ranger. It entails slowing a mob, and running ahead of it, slowly picking down its health. Can also be used as a diversionary tactic to split multiple mobs if no Mesmerize is available.

Line of Sight (LoS)—If a mob can't see you, but knows you're there, it will have to run around the obstacle to gain access. This is often used to split up larger groups of melee and casters, so it's more manageable for the group. The puller will line of sight the casting/ranged mobs to pull them around an obstacle for easier access and closer contact.

MA—Mental Acuity. A type of power generator specifically for Psionicists.

MANA—Mind juice, used for spells.

Meat Shield—The character who takes the hits in place of the rest of the group. The tank.

Melee—Those fighters who stand in close range and use weapons to fight with are often referred to as melee classes.

Mez – Mesmerize. Freezes in place.

MMO—Massively Multiplayer Online.

MMORPG—Massively Multiplayer Online Role Playing Game.

Mob—an aggressive monster. Can be humanoid or animal.

OOM—Out of mana. Literally what it says.

Newbie—Also known as noob. Someone who has rarely, if ever played an MMO and has no clue what they're doing.

NPC—Non-Player Character. Usually not aggressive unless you fuck up.

Pull—Often one person in a group/raid will be designated as the puller, the person who attacks the mob and brings it to camp.

Ranged—A class that can damage (usually) a mob from a distance. Like mages or rangers, etc.

Ranger Gating—Rangers are often known for getting themselves into trouble by kiting mobs in a solo setting. Or else, pulling aggro when DPS-ing. They'd die and resurrect at their bind point, making it what's known as a Ranger Gate.

Respawn—When a mob or a person dies in-game, they will reappear at the spot where their soul was bound. The more powerful the mob, the longer it takes for them to respawn.

Root—A spell obtainable by multiple classes that causes the target's feet to affix momentarily to the ground. They can still cast, but they cannot move until the root breaks.

RPG—Role Playing Game.

Tank—The meat shield aka the person who takes the big hits for the group. Often needs to be swapped in and out with another tank during larger raids depending on a boss' abilities.

Tether—In some worlds monsters have a specific area they're confined to, and thus stop and don't pursue their prey past a certain point. In Somnia, mobs do not tether. This does not apply to specific purpose NPCs.

Train—When a player or group has managed to aggro a large number of mobs who don't tether, and leads the following of mobs to a specific spot, or through a spot, they call it a train.

Utility class—these are classes whose prime function is to support the group, through abilities that protect or strengthen them as a group or raid.

VR—Virtual Reality.

VRMMORPG—Virtual Reality Massively Multiplayer Online Role Playing Game.

Wipe—This occurs when the entire raid or group die to an encounter.

CHARACTER NAMES:

Murmur
    Class: Enchanter   Psionicist
    Species: Locus
    Real Name: Wren

Sinister
    Class: Blood Mage
    Species: Dark Elf
    Real Name: Harlow

Devlish
    Class: Dread Knight
    Species: Lacerta
    Real Name: Darren

Havoc
    Class: Necromancer
    Species: Dark Elf
    Real Name: Evan

Beastial
    Class: Beastmaster
    Species: Viking
    Real Name: Selwyn

Merlin
    Class: Ranger
    Species: Elf
    Real Name: Mike

Rashlyn

Class: Monk

Species: Feles

Veranol

Class: Shaman

Species: Viking

Mellow

Class: Witch

Species: Dark Elf

Exbo

Class: Ranger

Species: Human

Jinna

Class: Rogue

Species: Dwarf

Dansyn

Class: Bard

Species: Dark Elf

<u>Base</u> Stat Sheet: Level Sixteen

CONstitution:	22	
STRength :		10
AGIlity:		19
WISdom:	12	
INTelligence:	31	
CHArisma:	46	

HitPoints:	304
MANA:	332
MA:	100

Abjuration:	87
Alteration:	82
Conjuration:	89
Divinition:	90
Evocation:	72

2H Blunt:	62
1H Piercing:	68

Mental Acuity Abilities:

Thought shielding.

Class: Enchanter only.

Level not applicable.

Developing your inner senses you've awoken your latent psychic powers. With constant use your skills will increase, while the opposite will occur should the skill not be used. See your trainer for specifics when you reach Thought Shielding (25).

Thought Projection.

Class: Enchanter only.

Level not applicable.

Developing your inner senses has further developed your psychic powers. Thought Projection can be tricky. Make sure you never use it in anger, or the results might be surprising. With constant use your skills will increase, while the opposite will occur should the skill not be used. See your trainer for specifics when you reach Thought Projection (25).

Mind Bolt.

This ability allows you to cast a spear of mental anguish into the depths of an opponent s brain.

Effects: Opponents will be unable to concentrate enough to use spells or abilities for four seconds. This time increases as the caster's level does.

Cost: Requires Mental Acuity to be at 18.

Caution: Use sparingly. Backlash from overuse, or improper use can cause the same effect in the caster...or worse.

Phase Shift

This ability allows you to negatively affect your opponent s mind. Believing they are a second or two apart from reality, they will reside there for up to 15 seconds.

Effect: Target's mind is encased in a phase of illusion. The target will be convinced they've shifted to a different time pocket, and thus are incapable of moving. This effect begins at 15 seconds duration, and levels with the caster through to a maximum of 90 seconds.

Cost: Requires MA to be at 38 for larger castings, the cost will double.

Caution: Phase shift may be utilized on single or multiple targets at once. Weigh the amount of targets carefully, else it backfire and shift you. Sometimes the shift in time can cause ruptures near the caster. Make sure the voices you're hearing are your own.

Forestall Death

It applied before potential death takes place, this will enable you to maintain your health at 0.5 hit points as long as you are receiving some sort of healing effect.

Effect: Target is able to ward off death for a limited period of time and will not die when they should have, as long as heals are actively channeled in their direction.

Cost: Requires Mental Acuity to be at 60

Caution: This spell can only be used on one person at a time. Attempting to use it twice at once is not recommended. This will usually result in things worse than death.

Clone Warp

This ability allows you to produce a clone of yourself used for distracting your opponent. Depending on your tier of mastery, you may be able to produce more than one clone.

Effect: All enemies around you will believe that your clone is you for the next 45 seconds, directing their attacks accordingly. The ability expires when the 45 seconds are up, or else, the clone's minor hit point pool has been depleted, whichever comes first.

Cost: Requires Mental Acuity to be at 45 or more

Caution: This ability can be used on as many enemies that you have who can potentially see it. Keep in mind though, a clone is just like you. Make sure you remember who the real one is.

Spells:

Level One:

Minor Suffocation

Cast: Single Target

Type: Damage Over Time

Duration: 24 seconds

Effect: This spell winds a mind leash around your opponent, as if it were trying to suffocate them. Its damage ticks every three seconds for twenty-four seconds.

Minor Shield

Cast: Self Only

Type: Buff

Duration: 45 minutes

Effect: This casts a minor shield over your skin, increasing your Armor Class by level + 3, and hit points by level + 5.

Simple Animation.

Cast: Self

Type: Pet

Duration: Until death or dismissal

Effect: This summons a magical pet that sort of does your bidding. It costs a tiny sword to cast. Isn't the best at obeying commands.

Level Four:

Mesmerize

Cast: Single Target

Type: Breakable Stun

Duration: 24 seconds

Effect: This spell immobilized your opponent for as long as they take no damage, or 24 seconds, whichever is shorter. You may cast non-damaging spells on them, and you may renew this casting before the initial one expires. Casting it on your friends probably isn't a good way to win popularity contests.

Flux

> Cast: Area of Effect
>
> Type: Stun
>
> Duration: 4 seconds

Effect: This is a stun that radiates out from the caster for fifteen feet. It will stun anyone who means the caster harm within that radius. Does not produce sparkles.

Gate

> Cast: Self Only
>
> Type: Travel
>
> Duration: N/A

Effect: This will transfer you to your bind point

Invisibility

> Cast: Self or Others
>
> Type: Buff
>
> Duration: 10 minutes or until broken/seen through

Effect: Causes generic invisibility. Undead don't count. Will drop if you cast a spell or take damage.

Fear

> Cast: Area of Effect
>
> Type: Brief Loss of Control
>
> Duration: 25% of level in seconds.

Effect: Causes enemies to flee from you in terror. But if you use it too soon, it'll probably just look like they misplaced something for a second.

Level Eight:

Cancel Magic

> Cast: Self or Others
>
> Type: Debuff
>
> Duration: Instant

Effect: Casting this spell will remove one magically caused effect from the target. Make sure you want to remove it.

Root

>Cast: Others (or self if you really want to)

>Type: Immobilization

>Duration: 8 seconds

Effect: This will root the target in place. Probably not the best idea to cast it on yourself when fleeing in panic.

See Invisible

>Cast: Self or Others

>Type: Buff

>Duration: 10 minutes

Effect: Really? Does this really require explanation?

Soothe

>Cast: Self or Others

>Type: Debuff

>Duration: Varies

Effect: This will lower the threat level of a target, but it will not make it disappear. Probably not useful on yourself unless in a really bad mood.

Chaos

>Cast: Others

>Type: Direct Damage

>Duration: Instant

Effect: This spell causes direct mental damage to the target, dropping their hit points by two times the caster's level. Requires a recharge.

Level Twelve:

Allure

>Cast: Others

>Type: Charm

>Duration: Until broken

Effect: This spell will charm a mob or other player. This ability depends on the casters charisma, and ability to calm their charge. Whatever you do, don't piss them off while under your command. It rarely ends well.

Suffocation:

    Cast: Single Target

    Type: damage over time

    Duration: 36 seconds

Effect: This spell winds a mind leash around your opponent, as if it were trying to suffocate them. Its damage ticks every three seconds for thirty-six seconds.

Bind Affinity

    Cast: Self or others

    Type: Buff or soul affixer

    Duration: Until renewed or overridden with a new location

Effect: This spell binds the target to an area of choice, allowing them to resurrect easier and hopefully closer to their corpse. Because you'll all die. A lot.

Infravision

    Cast: Single Target

    Type: Buff

    Duration: 10 minutes

Effect: Aids the target with a form of night vision.

Stupefy

    Cast: Single target

    Type: Stun

    Duration: 12 seconds

Effect: This will stun a mob in place for around twelve seconds. Probably not a good idea to cast on yourself.

Weakness

    Cast: Single Target

    Type: Debuff

    Duration: 90 seconds

Effect: Reduces the target's strength by 50% of the caster's level.

Languidity

Cast: Single Target

Type: Debuff

Duration: 90 seconds

Effect: Reduces the target's attack speed by 25% of the caster's level in %. Trust us, it's far more effective than you think. Probably.

Nullify

Cast: Single Target

Type: Debuff remover

Duration: Instant

Effect: Strips down magic resistance at 50% of the caster's level.

Level Sixteen:

Mana Tide

Cast: Self or Others

Type: Buff

Duration: 45 minutes

Effect: This will cause you to regenerate mana faster in combat. Mana will increase by an additional three per five seconds. This buff levels with the caster.

Invisibility Versus Undead

Cast: Self or Others

Type: Buff

Duration: 12 minutes

Effect: This will render you invisible to any undead in the area. They will be unable to see you, however this buff will fall should you attempt to cast anything else while it's active.

Mass Enthrall

Cast: Enemy Targets

Type: Offensive/Defensive area of effect centered around the initial target.

Duration: 24 seconds

Effect: This is an area effect version of mesmerize. Any damage will break this spell. It's a bad idea to use this while targeting allies.

Haste

Cast: Self or Others

Type: Melee Buff

Duration: 45 minutes

Effect: When cast on an ally, this buff will allow their melee speed to increase by 25%.

Feeble Body

Cast: Enemy Targets

Type: Offensive/Defensive

Duration: 24 seconds

Effect: When cast on an enemy target, their haste will be reduced by 25%.

Shield Illusion

Cast: Self or Others

Type: Defensive Buff

Duration: Until depleted   requires hematite

Effect: Using the power of your mind you cast a shield around your target, confusing the enemies and negating up to 75hp of damage. That whole mind magic thing seems to be working out well, doesn't it?

Hi there! K.T. Hanna here.

I want to thank you for reading the first book of Somnia Online. This book has a very special place in my heart. I met my husband in an MMO and creating this world and game has been a fantastic experience. There are a lot of ways to get in contact with me, and I hope you love the world of Somnia enough to want to find out more about it!

Book two is already in the works, and book three is about to be drafted. I can't wait to share more with you.

Lastly. You're probably aware of how important reviews are to authors. Our careers rely on them. Please consider leaving a review for my book, and any others you enjoy.

Thank you again for reading.
Want to know all about Fable and Exodus' tiff?
Sign up for my Reader's Group and get the short story for free!
(http://play.somnia-online.com)

If you'd like to contact me, my email is: kthannaauthor@gmail.com
If you'd like previews of what I'm writing, or art I'm commissioning then join my Patreon! (patreon.com/KTHanna)

Otherwise I can be found in the following places.
FB (facebook.com/groups/SomniaOnline), Twitter (@KTHanna),
Instagram (kt_hanna)

If you LOVE LitRPG don't forget to join:
The GameLit Society! (facebook.com/groups/LitRPGsociety)

ACKNOWLEDGEMENTS:

I have a lot of people to thank, who in at least some way encouraged me to write in general, or else to write this book specifically.

Love of my life, Trevor, and my little Kami. It's his fault I found the genre, and her fault I never give up on writing.

I wouldn't be here without the following friends:

Jami Nord & Owen Littman

Heather Cashman

Jude

Heather Gilbert

M. Andrew Patterson

Kylie B.

Aimee

Amanda W.

Quinton Shyn

Kendra

Dawn Chapman

Alexis Keane

Bonnie Price

Richard Hummel

Hondo Jinx

Stephen Morse

Felissa Ely

Andrea Parseneau

Cait Greer

Cat Scully

M Evan Matyas

Ian Mitchell

To those readers on RR whose help and readership has been invaluable:

Thank you all for reading and so much for the amazing feedback! I know I've probably forgotten someone. If you read this on RR in its early stages (before book 2) and conmmented or reviewed, please know it means the world to me.

Endless Paving

Mearhena

Oathkeeper

Cyan Snake

Bleached

Tarakis

Puck

Koinzell

Nikeyeia

Zedicious

Barnmaddo

Patreon:

Thank you all so much for your support – you made my map possible!

Erik

Ma & Pa

Bev

Amanda M

Janis

Nikolas

Kyle

Bev

D.R.

Looking for more LitRPG or GameLit?
Check out:

Desert Runner Series
By Dawn Chapman

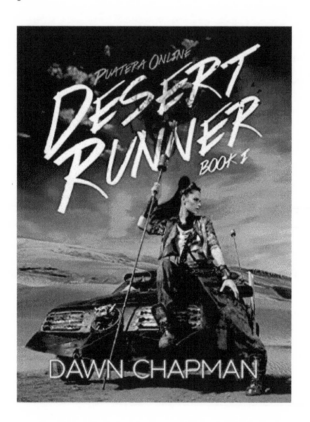

With her pain potions in short supply, Maddie accepts a deadly run, pick up a package in Trox City and cross the desert plains to Port Troli, the only issues – an unwanted passenger and Tromoal breeding season.

Milton Keynes UK
Ingram Content Group UK Ltd.
UKHW010721130923
428592UK00001B/85